PRAISE F

"Djuna's stories are a rebirth, an unnerving resurrection of classic science fiction and horror concepts, given quivering new life by another cultural perspective. Unendingly involving, their stories turn us upside down; they require us to right ourselves, and we come out of the process changed. A powerful voice in SF and dark fiction!"
— JOHN SHIRLEY, author of *Demons and Black Butterflies*

"In South Korea, Djuna is a pop-cultural savant, a public intellectual, and a literary mystery all wrapped into one. Djuna's identity is known to no one, as the author has been writing under a pseudonym ever since their debut in the mid-1990s. Wonderfully rendered here by Adrian Thieret, Djuna's stories are an engrossing hymn to diversity and to the hybridization of genres, teeming as they are with transgender cyborgs, vampire girls, space-faring teddy bears, and other scary-but-endearing figures of the post-human. Glinting beneath their aesthetic of the horrific, the grotesque, and the absurd is this writer's poignant insights into South Korean society."
— SUNYOUNG PARK, University of Southern California, editor of *Readymade Boddhisattva: The Kaya Anthology of South Korean Science Fiction*

"Filled with bold and grim humor, Djuna's fiction creates dream-like worlds where hardly anything looks familiar or predictable. It inspires readers to stretch their imagination and to take a fresh look at a number of the basic premises that set the boundaries of contemporary society—including those concerning gender, sexuality, individuality, humanity, race, or ethnicity. Here is a work of a profoundly inquisitive, erudite, and creative mind. Adrian Thieret's highly readable translation will make this anthology a gratifying read for Anglophone enthusiasts of speculative fiction and Asian literature."
— YOON SUN YANG, Boston University, editor of *Routledge Handbook of Modern Korean Literature*

EVERYTHING GOOD DIES HERE

DJUNA

EVERYTHING GOOD DIES HERE

by DJUNA

Foreword by Kyu Hyun Kim
Translated by Adrian Thieret

KAYA PRESS

The Rabbit Hole, originally published as 토끼굴 in 대리전 (2006, Igaseo). *Through the Mirror*, originally published as 거울 너머로 건너가다 in 용의 이 (2007, Booksfear). *Memoir of a Joseon Bride*, originally published as 구부전 in 미스테리아 (2015, Misteria) and 구부전 (2019, Alma). *Pentagon*, originally published as 펜타곤 in 나비전쟁 (1997, Oneulyegam) and again in 면세구역 (2000, Kukminseokwan; republished in 2013, Bookstory). *Under the Sphinx*, originally published as 스핑크스 아래서 in 면세구역 (2000, Kukminseokwan; republished in 2013, Bookstory). "The Battle of Broccoli Plain" and "Sea of Fog," originally published as 브로콜리 평원의 혈투 and 안개바다 in 브로콜리 평원의 혈투 (2011, Jaeum & Moeum). And *Jezebel*, originally published as 제저벨 (2012, Jaeum & Moeum; republished in 2023, Itta).

27 26 25 24 4 3 2 1
Published by Kaya Press / kaya.com
Distributed by D.A.P. / Distributed Art Publishers / artbook.com / (800) 388-BOOK
Design by Chanshin Park / Illustration by Yeni Kim

Library of Congress Cataloging-in-Publication Data
Names: Djuna, author. | Kim, Kyu Hyun, 1963- , writer of foreword. | Thieret, Adrian, translator. | Djuna. Chejŏbel. English.
Title: Everything good dies here / Djuna ; foreword by Kyu Hyun Kim ; translated by Adrian Thieret.
Identifiers: LCCN 2023028849 | ISBN 9781885030764 (paperback)
Subjects: LCSH: Djuna--Translations into English. | LCGFT: Short stories. | Novels.
Classification: LCC PL994.235 E94 2023 | DDC 895.73/5--dc23/eng/20230703
LC record available at https://lccn.loc.gov/2023028849

This publication is made possible by support from the USC Dana and David Dornsife College of Arts, Letters, and Sciences; and the USC Department of American Studies and Ethnicity. Special thanks to Stephen CuUnjieng and the Choi Chang Soo Foundation for their support of this work.

Additional funding was provided by generous contributions from: Tanzila Ahmed, Chitra Aiyar, Chantal Rei Alberto, Sasha Ali, Hari Alluri, Heidi Amin-Hong, Stine An, Akhila Ananth, Tiffany Babb, Manibha Banerjee, Neelanjana Banerjee, Terry Bequette, Hung Bui, Cari Campbell, Emiliana Chan, Susan Chan, Sam Chanse, Alexander Chee, Anelise Chen, Anita Chen, Dehua Chen, Jean Chen, Lisa Chen, Floyd Cheung, Jayne Cho, Jennifer Chou, Yvonne Chow, Caroline Chow, Elizabeth Clemants, Tuyet Cong Ton Nu, Herna Cruz, Timothy Daley, Lawrence-Minh Bui Davis, Glenda Denniston, Susannah Donahue, Taiyo Ebato, Irving Eng, Matthew Fargo, Peter Feng, Sia Figiel, Sesshu Foster, Sylvana Freyberg, Diane Fujii, Joseph Goetz, K A Hashimoto, Jean Ho, Ann Holler, Huy Hong, Jacqueline Hoyt, Lisa Hsia, Jonathan Hugo, Adria Imada, Susan Ito, Ashaki Jackson, Carren Jao, Mia Kang, Andrew Kebo, Vandana Khanna, Nidhi Khurana, Seema Khurana, Swati Khurana, Joonie Kim, Seonglim Kim, Gwendolyn Knight, Sabrina Ko, Timothy Ko, Robin Koda, Juliana Koo, Sun Hee Koo, Rika Koreeda, Emily Kuhlmann, Eileen Kurahashi, Paul Lai, Jenny Lam, Iris Law, Samantha Le, Catherine Lee, Helen Kim Lee, Hyunjung Lee, Marie Myung-Ok Lee, Stacy Lee, Whakyung Lee in memory of Sonya Choi Lee, KC Lehman, Edward Lin, Carleen Liu, Veronica Liu, Mimi Lok, Andrea Louie, Pauline Lu, Haline Ly, Abir Majumdar, Jason McCall, Sally McWilliams, Sean Miura, Faisal Mohyuddin, Greg Monaco, Russell Morse, Adam Muto, Wendy Lou Nakao, Jean Young Naylor, Kim Nguyen, Kathy Nguyen, Viet Thanh Nguyen, Vinh Nguyen, erin ninh, Dawn Oh, Julia Oh, Eric Ong, Tiffany Ong, Camille Patrao, Thuy Phan, Cheryline Prestolino, James Pumarada, Jhani Randhawa, Amarnath Ravva, Maria L Sandoval, Nitasha Sawhney, Carol Say, Andrew Shih, Brandon Shimoda, Luisa Smith, Roch Smith, Jungmi Son, daniela sow, Nancy Starbuck, Karen Su, Rachana Sukhadia, Robin Sukhadia, Rajen Sukhadia, Kelly Sutherland, Willie Tan, Zhen Teng, Wendy Tokuda, Frederick Tran, Monique Truong, Patricia Wakida, Dan S. Wang, Aviva Weiner, Duncan Williams, William Wong, Amelia Wu and Sachin Adarkar, Anita Wu and James Spicer, Stan Yogi, Kyung Yoon, Shinae Yoon, Mikoto Yoshida, Patricia Yun, and many others.

Kaya Press is also supported, in part, by the National Endowment for the Arts; the Los Angeles County Board of Supervisors through the Los Angeles County Arts Commission; the Community of Literary Magazines and Presses and the Literary Arts Emergency Fund; and the City of Los Angeles Department of Cultural Affairs.

Finally, special thanks to Kaitlin Hsu, Paul Liu, Austin Nguyen, and Ruby Yassen for their work on this book, and to Wah-Ming Chang and Chez Bryan Ong for their design help.

CONTENTS

FOREWORD

Flights of Imagination on Wings Made of Leaves

by Kyu Hyun Kim

Anthony Burgess once wrote that diligent readers of a novelist end up developing an image of what that person looks and sounds like in real life. A considerable gap typically exists between what we imagine about an author based on their fiction and what they are actually like. Djuna—whose representative science fiction stories are collected for here in English, thanks to Adrian Thieret's fantastic translations—poses an extra tough challenge in this regard.

Ever since they first appeared on the scene as a film critic and then a science fiction writer, Djuna's "real-life" identity has remained a mystery even as they successfully pursued a highly productive professional writing career. Given the cavalier ways in which privacy tends to be treated in South Korea (though things are slowly getting better according to my younger friends and colleagues living there), this is no mean feat. Djuna's "profile" picture on Twitter (now X) is a photograph of a cute rabbit. And when some years ago, *Cine21* solicited comments from Djuna about Korean cinema, the accompanying illustration represented Djuna as a human-shaped being whose single, thoughtful eye stared out from a boxy computer screen. Impressed by that image, I used it as inspiration for my own attempt to illustrate what I imagined Djuna to look like—though my version, outfitted in slacks and a super-smooth unisex Mao jacket, looks like a futuristic version of Ernst Stavro Blofeld from a 1960s James Bond film.

But Djuna's ability to maintain this remarkable level of privacy is not the only reason it is so difficult to conjure up an image of the author. I am, for instance, familiar with what the novelist Kim Young Ha looks like. I have seen his public lectures, his television appearances, and have read quite a few of his novels and stories. And the image of the "real" Kim Young Ha—a bespectacled Korean man of indeterminate age, cleanly shaven and neatly dressed with, as A. A. Attanasio might put it, "long, intelligent fingers"—is not that far removed from what I would imagine the novelist to look like based on his writings.

Such a proximate relationship between perception and image is however unlikely to be the case between Djuna's writings and their physical appearance. Their wildly inventive yet off-kilter stories might lead one to envision them as a cluster of slim, white-clad, androgynous humanoids endowed with the graceful physique of a ballet dancer; or perhaps clones who share a collective consciousness like the altruistic alien Nestor in the charming Star Wars rip-off *Battle Beyond the Stars*. Or maybe actual monozygotic siblings. The Djuna dreamt up by their most dedicated readers might very well possess a female body—a possibility not that far-fetched given the pronounced empathy Djuna has for the I-deeply-despise-this-situation-I-am-stuck-in-but-I-gotta-do-my-best attitude that characterizes the many teenage girls and professional women who appear in Djuna's fiction. Yet, try as I might, I have found it impossible to come up with a face that could do justice to the clear, scintillating brilliance of the imagination on display in Djuna's work: somehow their face(s) keep(s) shifting, or is/are always obscured by some naturally but perfectly placed object before it/them, much like a painting by René Magritte.

Full disclosure: I first came to know Djuna not through their science fiction but through their film criticism and cultural commentary. Even though they have been prolifically producing science fiction within the HiTEL internet community since 1994, I only became aware of them some years later. South Korea's somewhat awkward transition into a prosperous industrial democracy in the early '90s was heralded by the erosion of state censorship (demonstrated by, for instance, the theatrical release of a completely uncensored version of Neil Jordan's *The Crying Game*), as well as the gradual dissipation of prejudices against certain forms of popular culture such as cinema and comics. This in turn led to a vibrant cinephilic subculture, which found fertile ground in the new ecosystem of the internet. Djuna gained a substantial following within the HiTEL internet community that encouraged this flourishing discourse on film criticism and appreciation. Even so, their voice has always remained wholly distinct and unique. Djuna was almost entirely alone in their defense of genre films and their critique of the elitist, chauvinistic ideas about cinema that underlay the cinephilic drive of late '90s and early '00s in Korea. Writing about that period now, I find it difficult to convey just how refreshing and exhilarating it was for me to read a fellow Korean defending the merits of Dario Argento's or Mario Bava's horror films, or propounding in rational, persuasive, yet witty prose (as far removed from fanboy rantings as one could possibly imagine) the great acting skills of Peter Cushing or Christopher Lee in Hammer Gothic horrors, instead of pontificating about Andrei Tarkovsky or Jean-Luc Godard.

By the mid-2000s, I too had discovered Djuna's science fiction writings, beginning with *The Trans-Pacific Express* (Taepyeongyang hoengdan teukgeup, 2002) up to and including *The Proxy War* (Daerijeon, 2006). Once again, I was as blown away by the scale of their imagination and mesmerized by their nonchalantly but never self-consciously "cool" prose. Simply put, I had never before read anything like Djuna's stories in the Korean language. Take, for example, "Square Dance" (Seukwe-eo daenseu, originally written in 1997 and collected in *The Trans-Pacific Express*). Still to this day one of my favorites among Djuna's output, it reads like a previously unknown short story that has been written by an Anglophone writer—one positioned somewhere in the gnarled family tree of science fiction scribes stretching from Leigh Brackett to James Tiptree Jr. and on through Nina Kiriki Hoffman—and translated into beautiful Korean. The title novella in *The Proxy War*, on the other hand, is unmistakably grounded in the Korea of early 2000s, specifically the city of Bucheon, renowned these days for its annual International Fantastic Film Festival. Until then I had never before read a Korean-language novel that incorporated so many life-like details about contemporary Korean culture and society into a galaxy-spanning fictional universe reminiscent of Douglas Adams's *The Hitchhiker's Guide to the Galaxy* and the film *Men in Black*, and yet completely sui generis in the end. "Rabbit Hole," from that same collection, invokes *Alice's Adventures in Wonderland* only to spin off into a terrifying vision of an apocalyptic future that somehow also functions as a reminder of the surrealistic oppressiveness of a contemporary South Korean childhood. Needless to say, by the time I read these stories, I had become a certified Djuna fan and a regular unpaid contributor of film reviews to their website.

It would require a book-length study to properly analyze and explicate the reasons why Djuna's fiction is so enticing and challenging, so classically SF in its stimulation of our "sense of wonder" yet at the same time so ahead of the curve in terms of what we expect from "Korean literature." To be sure, Djuna's stories have evolved over the last twenty-six years. Their fictional universe has steadily expanded, their characters assuming ever more colorful and diverse guises—human and non-human, organic and machine-based, somewhere in between, a little bit of both and beyond all such categories entirely. Sometimes Djuna's stories seem abstract—radically streamlined like a mechanoid-hybrid being that's shed its cumbersome organic bits so it can better approximate its ideal of pure intelligence. At other times, their stories can be so hardboiled it feels as if they could be used as a nutcracker. Djuna has experimented with worldbuilding in stories that span a variety of distinctive tones, flavors, and agendas—through the collections *Not Yet Gods* (Ajigeun sin-i aniya, 2013) and *The World of Mint* (Minteu ui segye, 2018), or in the Linker Universe stories first unveiled in the "The Bloody Battle of Broccoli Plain" (Beurokolli pyeongwon ui hyeoltu, 2008) and reaching its apotheosis in the novel *Jezebel* (Jejeobel, 2012). They have dabbled in genres beyond science fiction; for example, "A. B. C. D. E & F" (1998) is a satire of cyberspace zoology while "The Valley of Foxes" (Yeougol, 2007) reads as a period-piece horror.

Still, despite the impressive capaciousness of Djuna's imagination that has been on display over the course of their fiction-writing career, the core characteristics of their works have not greatly changed. The last two decades have seen an amazing surge of

Korean-language science fiction, as evidenced by the works of such fellow travelers as Kim Bo-young, Bae Myung Hoon, Kim Chang-gyu and Kim Cho-yeop. Yet, Djuna still comes first to mind when thinking of writers/authors/beings, Korean or otherwise, for whom the label "posthuman" is not a cliché. Djuna is still the only Korean writer whose references to Fred Astaire musicals come off as effortlessly and authentically as those to Vladimir Nabokov's or Virginia Woolf's writings. Djuna is still the only Korean writer whose complete indifference to categories such as "sophisticated" and "vulgar" or "artistic" and "pulp" or "East" and "West" feels not like some kind of belabored postmodern affectation but rather a natural outgrowth of the author's life experiences.

The word that perhaps best articulates Djuna's prose style is "aplomb." Like a cat calmly waiting to capture a mouse, their writing is inevitably shaded with cream-colored wit that's just on this side of irony, even as the brains of characters explode like toads that have swallowed firecrackers. Yet, this syntactical leanness does not prevent them from cramming numerous, epic, mind-expanding ideas into the space of a short story or novella, without any seams visibly breaking apart. Perhaps Djuna's assessment of Christopher Nolan's *Inception* is the best expression of the effect that Djuna's own stories can have on their readers:

> "[Watching *Inception*,] I had an image of a gigantic picture crumpled up and folded inside an empty walnut shell. In the multi-layered world of *Inception*, the interior is always larger and wider than the exterior. As such, the Dante-esque journey to the bottom of this layered world becomes progressively grander in scope as we move into the second half of the movie...."

What can be said about the "Koreanness" of Djuna's fiction? Most notable Korean writers I know, regardless of the "genres" they work in or how seriously they are taken by literary critics, resemble resilient plants rooted in the Korean soil. Their novels are at heart critiques or explorations of—or sometimes even frustrated screams directed at—South Korean society. Djuna's stories, which could be said to share these sentiments, have however uprooted themselves and taken flight. Some readers, upon seeing the uncanny vision of what seems to be a plant flying gracefully through the air on wings made of leaves, might at first be perplexed, before shaking their heads in self-righteous irritation and proclaiming, "That strange flying creature cannot possibly be a native species. It must be an alien transplant." Wringing their hands, they'll act as if they've just caught a huge blue lobster in the waters of the Han River ("An invasive species, what else can it be?").

To counter such claims, one could easily point to the many local "Korean" flavors in Djuna's fiction. Then again, why bother? Thankfully, we are at last entering a world in which the best and most successful K-pop artists and filmmakers no longer have to prove that they are "really" Korean or even articulate what "Koreanness" is, despite the powers that be in politics and mainstream academia who remain stubbornly committed to building fences around what constitutes a "Korean" identity. Hopefully the same is becoming true for fiction writers.

Let's listen to what Djuna has to say on this issue:

> I won't spend time worrying about [what constitutes "Korean" science fiction]. I am not saying that it's meaningless to ask such a question. I am simply saying that I'm not the person to ask it. If I were to worry about such things, I would end up sitting at the starting line like Linus Van Pelt with his shoelaces untied and not be able to write a single word. Still, I prefer to launch my stories in a geographical space that I am reasonably familiar with. That way I am less likely to commit errors. This is why many of my temporally contemporary stories are set in southwestern Seoul and the satellite cities around that area. But does this fact make these stories "Korean" science fiction? I doubt it. If I changed a few details, these stories could easily have been set in Peru, the Philippines, or Belgium. I think most science fiction stories are like that. The genre always compels us to draw on a canvas bigger than whatever neighborhood we happen to live in. It isn't really that important where an author is living at any given moment; after all, they will not be able to stay put in the same neighborhood forever.

Nevertheless, my view is that Djuna, that "mutant flying plant" who resides and works in South Korea, is actually more of a native Korean species than most of their contemporaries. Why? Because Djuna's works demonstrate that illustrating the past and present of "Korea" for readers is not their only objective. Make no mistake, this is something that Djuna does in any case—and with consummate skill, crackling intelligence and, yes, aplomb—but they also document the future, or rather, the many possible futures, of Korea. Because Djuna is a writer who lets us also encounter all these possible "Koreans" as they mutate, evolve, and progress beyond the strictures of ideology and identity (ethnic, national, cultural or otherwise), and as they ultimately redefine what it means to be "Korean."

If Djuna were to read the present introduction, I imagine they would smile (or perhaps display a digital emoticon signifying "smile") and quip, "I guess I should thank you for all this acrobatic writing... on my behalf?" or some such remark.

It is my sincerest wish that the present collection can lead to the discovery of this brilliant science fiction writer by Anglophone readers, and that these same readers will continue to seek out the many other stories by Djuna that are for now, still only available in Korean, not to mention the fabulously fun, elegantly cool, and intellectually adventurous stories Djuna will no doubt continue to produce in the future.

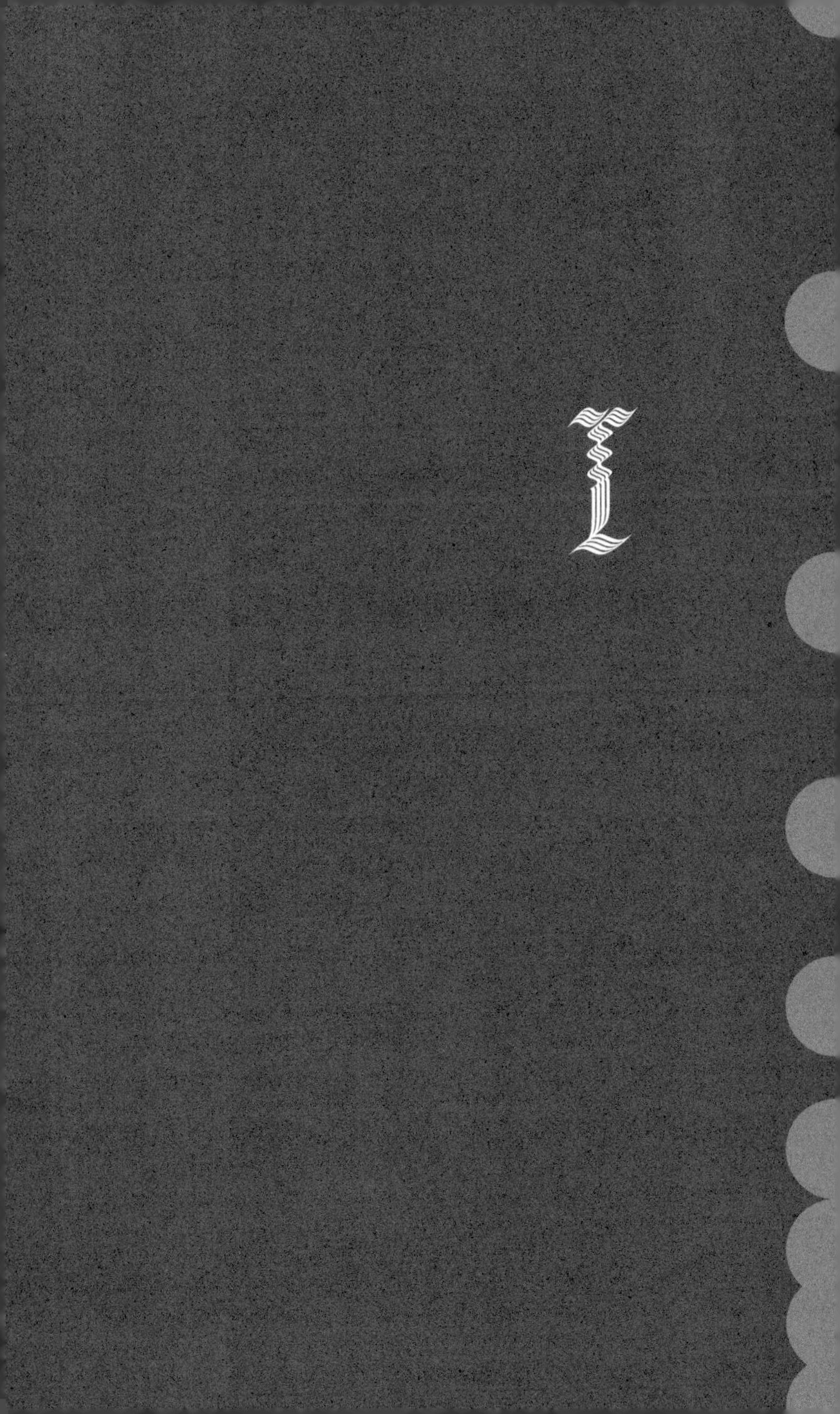

THE RABBIT HOLE

1

Yesterday evening, I discovered a secret passageway under my bed.

It rumbled like a digestive system running on a forty-two minute, twenty-four second cycle. At its smallest, it contracted to less than two centimeters in diameter, and at its widest, it expanded to between ninety and one hundred centimeters. The soft brown fur covering its interior made it feel dry and squishy like an enormous, velvet-covered hot water bottle.

Pushing my bed to one side, I threw various things in: a broken teacup, pebbles, leftover buttons. Everything bounced quietly down and disappeared. I even lowered a flashlight on a string to try and see where the hole might lead, but this too proved useless because I couldn't see past the curves of its fur-lined walls.

I didn't ask Mother about the passageway. I was curious whether she realized I had noticed it, but still I didn't ask. I understood the rules: anything Mother did not directly tell me was something I was supposed to figure out for myself.

Turning off my bedroom light, I crawled under my bed and spent an hour staring into the tunnel, which glittered dully under my flashlight. I found myself desperately suppressing a desire to jump in.

2

I was writing in this diary when Saskia came to visit.

As I hid and locked it away in my safe with the key I keep around my neck, she took dolls out one by one from her pink wagon, along with a Cinderella picture book. The illustrations were splendid, beautiful even, but like all drawings by people from the planet Mélusine, they contained anatomical errors. Even relatively accurate depictions of human body parts looked slightly awkward when drawn by Mélusinians. This particular illustrator must have wondered why Cinderella's big toes were attached to the front of her feet and not the back. Perhaps Mélusinians thought the heels on her glass slippers were prosthetic devices designed to compensate for this anatomical flaw.

"I went to the ro-le-kang-ting," Saskia boasted as she put a new green dress on her favorite doll, Mamarolly. She meant "rolakactring." This name, seemingly designed to torture the clumsy tongues of children, refers to the playgrounds where Mothers gather together.

I called them playgrounds just now because that's all we see from our perspective. The only things visible to us in the rolakactring are games and snacks. It would, however, probably be overly naive to assume that the only thing our Mothers do in them is watch from a distance through the fog as we play.

While I wondered about the true nature of the rolakactring, Mamarolly set off on her own journey. Saskia's doll games always involve travel: Mamarolly put on a new dress, packed her bags, and headed out to meet all sorts of animals before returning home. Saskia acted out the part of Mamarolly in her nasal voice while I played make-believe with the other dolls spread out around us. Knowing what I now know, I found it difficult to enter into the spirit of the "Mamarolly game." The game became hard work and required skillful improvisation.

Mamarolly had just returned to her pink house with a new doll friend when a bell rang somewhere above our heads. Saskia's Mother appeared. Not through a door, but rather out of thin air, like an origami flower that magically blossoms in water. Saskia's toys moved neatly back into the pink wagon like a film running in reverse. Giggling, Saskia threw herself at her Mother. I stood up to say goodbye, and Saskia and her Mother went home.

As soon as Saskia closed the door, I sat back down on the sofa and began to count. One, two, three, four, five. As I moved my lips into position to pronounce "six," my Mother materialized. She, too, appeared out of thin air like a blooming origami water lily or an exploding firework. I felt her gentle, dry warmth embracing me as I told her about my latest adventures with Mamarolly.

3

To me, math is an inductive science. In a normal world, kids build pyramids of logic based on the principles of addition and subtraction. I, however, am forced to reconstruct general theories of mathematics from clues scattered throughout the books in our library, all of which were written thousands of years ago by my ancestors. None of this is easy. Most of the books I possess are fiction; I don't have even a single textbook on basic arithmetic.

Nonetheless, I have managed to become fairly competent. I can do calculus, I understand the concept of double-entry bookkeeping, and I am stumbling my way through trigonometry one theorem at a time. I also know how to apply this painstakingly accumulated knowledge to the real world. Once, when I went with Mother to a huge rolakactring on Mélusine, I was able to calculate the planet's rotation using just my wristwatch and a protractor. Yes, the whole exercise was rendered pointless by the huge clock hanging in the sky behind me, but that didn't diminish my sense of accomplishment.

I have also accumulated other rules and bits of knowledge that I only partially understand. After reading Abbott's *Flatland*, I tried using the concept of the fourth dimension to explain the existence of the Mothers. Of course, I realized soon enough that time-space was much more complex than anything ever depicted by Abbott, but this would be obvious to anyone who's ever taken a few interstellar trips with their Mother.

I will probably never grasp the true nature of the Mothers. Just as I am unlikely to ever understand that tunnel to the unknown that appeared under my bed on the second floor.

4

I often wonder if life would have been easier had I been sold to a lower life form such as the ones on the planet Endril. Those giants with soft gray fur and strong protective instincts could not have provided me with the kind of house and library that I now live in, but at least I would have understood their rough and simple world.

Yet, it was not someone from Endril who noticed me there

as I sat in my cage wearing a dirty diaper and waiting to be adopted. Instead, I was chosen by a green-gray flower with a body that constantly swayed like cloth in water. The instant one of her sight organs fixed on my face, the shop proprietor ran over to her. Pressing my ear to the wall, I listened as they haggled in Milky Way Language 42.

"I'd prefer an animal with fur," the customer said in an unusually clear and vibration-free voice.

"Species without fur are much easier to play with. You can dress them up in different kinds of clothing and sculpt the fur on their heads into different looks."

"But doesn't their skin damage easily?"

"If you take good care of it, it should last a lifetime. If you're still concerned, we also sell cell rejuvenation equipment."

"I've heard that Terrans are violent. Didn't they drive themselves to extinction? And don't they sprout patches of fur and begin to stink when they mature? I've also heard that their beauty is ephemeral, that their faces distort and grow ugly over time. What then?"

The shopkeeper's antennae shook as he smiled.

"Ma'am, please. I assure you. I would never sell an unimproved Terran. My models never grow beyond seven years old. After they reach seven, they cease aging entirely. Moreover, their inclination toward violence has been adjusted, so that they won't even kill insects. They can't kill. That instinct has been blocked on a genetic level."

5

Later, I learned that Terra is the third planet from a yellow star called Sol that's tucked away in a corner of the second quadrant of the Milky Way. My species had lived there until it went extinct four thousand years ago. Now the planet is a colony of the Salic Alliance. Seven years Standard Time equals just under six Terran years. I learned half of this from the books in the library Mother had prepared for me, and picked up the other half from neighborhood kids. That is the sum total of my access to knowledge. A library filled with Terran novels and pet children who knew no more about the world than I do.

Are we really pets, though? Our Mothers are not Endrilians. I do not believe that they keep us to satisfy maternal instincts. No matter how seemingly full of love their care for us is, no matter if it actually is loving, I know I cannot fully comprehend them. I do not even know how Mothers' physical bodies exist on this world, so how could I possibly understand their feelings?

Even pet dogs know more than I do. They at least understand that they belong to a human and are loved. I, however, do not have the slightest idea what my role here in this artificial world is supposed to be.

6

Yesterday, I got into a fight with Saskia. I don't even remember why, but even if I did, I still wouldn't have really understood. Probably one of my dolls misbehaved toward Mamarolly, or perhaps I said something blasphemous about the Mothers and rolakactring.

Before I realized what I had done, Saskia threw a pencil case at me in a fit of anger. This over-stimulated her violence control nerves, so she began to cry and scratch herself all over with her fingernails. Scared, I rushed to get the banana-flavored medicine from the cupboard and spooned it out to her. Once she had finally calmed down, she wiped her tears, collected her dolls, and went home. The Rin Tin Tin movie we had been watching continued to play noisily on the screen hanging from the wall.

I waited for Mother to scold me. She never has, but every time I make a childish mistake, I still anticipate some kind of punishment. It's funny in a way, because what would be the point? It's not as if we are ever going to grow into better adults. I am and always will be six years old. My physiological age does not reflect the time I have spent alive.

Saskia does not seem to realize this fact. To her, we are the same age. The adults will always be "Mothers," and we will always be "children." The thirty-four years I have actually lived mean nothing to her.

7

As soon as it became clear that Mother would not be scolding me this time either, I began to prepare my escape. I packed my picnic bag with ten jars of jam and ten cans of food, filled the space between them with clothing and underwear, and hid the bag under my bed. While Mother prepared dinner, I improvised two ropes out of hand towels. I tried not to think about the real nature of the tunnel or whether Mother suspected anything. Instead, I focused on the details of my plan.

That night, after Mother left my room, shutting the door behind her, I pushed my bed aside and shone my flashlight into the tunnel. It was expanding and contracting as always, its soft velvet surface writhing. While I was waiting for one of its contraction cycles to finish, I tied one end of my towel-rope to my bed and the other end to my bag of supplies. When the entrance began expanding again, I tossed my bag into the tunnel, secured a second rope to my waist, and slowly climbed down in.

The first five meters were fairly steep, but nothing I couldn't handle. After another five meters, the slope flattened out enough to crawl along without needing to hold onto the rope. Once I reached the end of my rope, I untied my bag, swung it onto my back, and continued downward.

I crawled along in this manner for about another hundred meters. No, maybe it was less than that. It's my body—I tend to overestimate distance and weight. I blame this on books. I'm so used to reading stories with adult protagonists that it's difficult for me to remember how much smaller I am than them despite being thirty-four-years old.

The tunnel curved gently at first, but twisted more and more the farther I went into it. I often couldn't tell whether I was crawling along the floor or the wall or the ceiling. It felt as though each bend in the tunnel caused gravity to pull in a slightly different direction.

The end of the tunnel flared out like the bell of a trumpet. It seemed to be opening upward, but I could not actually be sure. Murky fog obscured my view, but what I could see beyond the exit looked less like sky and more like green ground about ten meters distant.

As I continued gazing out through the fog, I realized that some kind of dense green netting blocked the tunnel exit. The thick green strands were the size of my index finger and reminded me of a story I had once read called "Jack and the Beanstalk." The tendrils looked like the limbs of some unknown lifeform. I reached out to touch them and discovered the netting was just as furry, resistant, and soft as the walls of the tunnel. The moment I touched the netting, I felt my body grow lighter. It was as if I had entered a weightless zone where the gravity inside the tunnel negated the gravity outside. Grabbing ahold of the netting, I pulled myself forward until my head stuck out of the tunnel. A light gravitational force tugged at my head.

Unfamiliar green life forms filled the space outside. Some were shaped like starfish and moved quickly; others were spherical and stationary like hot air balloons. From what I could tell, they seemed to co-exist in relative harmony.

I felt vertigo looking down at all this, but it wasn't because of acrophobia. My vision and sense of balance was thrown off by the absurdity of a world that did not obey the laws of perspective. What I had initially thought were green objects, were actually holes in the light green space.

I stared out from the tunnel for about ten minutes, hesitating. The netting appeared solid, and the green life forms did not look particularly threatening. If I could make good use of the weightless zone, I should be able to orient myself enough to get down there. But was the ground I was aiming for actually ground? And even if it was, what was I planning to do once I got there? And then what?

I turned around and started crawling back home.

8

Mother said nothing about what I did yesterday, even though I pushed my bed to one side to expose the hole and spread my bag and hand-towel ropes on the floor for her to see. By the time I returned to my room after breakfast, she had cleaned it all up and put everything back in its place, her entire body swaying with laughter as always.

Saskia came over to our house again while I was in the midst of stacking blocks. She clutched a small box, clumsily tied with a ribbon, and as soon as she entered the room, she held it out to me shyly. I untied the ribbon and looked inside. The box contained a hand-knit, or at least seemingly hand-knit, doll sweater.

The apology gift must have been Saskia's own idea. The Mothers never force moral choices on us. We need only to observe the rules of etiquette already implanted in us, which in any case did not include sacrifices such as this. Was the child maturing mentally? Perhaps. But that wasn't going to change anything.

Like a good elder, I accepted Saskia's present and hugged her to show I had no hard feelings about her temper tantrum the day before. Saskia began to cry as soon as my arms encircled her. Surprised, I stepped back to take a good look at her. I could read fear, anger, and above all loneliness on her face. For just a moment, she looked far older than six. I suddenly grew curious about her age. Although I've always assumed she was only six, I can't think of any reason why she couldn't be older. She behaves like a six-year-old, true, but so do I.

"Shall we play Mamarolly?" I asked timidly.

Saskia nodded and began dressing Mamarolly with her clumsy hands, while I laid out my dolls on the carpet and prepared for a new adventure. An adventure about a fantastical world in which Clairvoyant Bear and Crazy Rabbit could travel anywhere they wanted through a magic carpet tunnel.

THROUGH THE MIRROR

1

I want to tell you the story of my mother—a woman who suffered incessantly for thirty-eight years from the tedious biases and casual malice of faceless gangs. I doubt you'll like it. The story contains good people who suffer unjustly; a miserable villain who dies before the drama even begins; and ordinary people who, in banding together, end up perpetrating an act of evil greater than anything their petty prejudices and general callousness might otherwise have instigated. All that plus an unwanted child born of rape who craves her mother's love, even while that same mother perceives her daughter as little more than a scarlet letter. Coming from a genuine storyteller, this would be a poignant tale. Coming from an honest one, it would teach you something meaningful. Either way, that story still needs an ending. I hope someone will be able to give it one someday. Preferably a happy one in which the heroine frees herself, achieves emotional and economic security, and is ultimately able to love her daughter without pain.

But I am not going to tell you that story, for it would require an authenticity equal to the weight of its topic, and I now know that what I once thought to be true is nothing but a self-indulgent fantasy. Instead, I will tell you an entirely different kind of story, one funnier, lighter, and far less painful than my mother's. I doubt it will move or edify you. But it's the only one I can tell without lying.

2

This story starts in Mother's hospital room. Had I the courage to feign indifference and spin Mother's story into something the length of a novel, this would undoubtedly be one of its climaxes—or the ending of part one.

Mother and I were staying in the hospital after we were forced to vacate our rented apartment two days earlier. It was one in the morning. The hospital cafeteria was less than adequate, so I had been tossing and turning with an empty stomach. Giving up on sleep, I got up from my couch, took a coin from Mother's purse, and left the room. The corridor was hot, humid, and dim. The incandescent lightbulbs hanging from the ceiling flickered as if they might go out at any moment. Luckily, the moon was up, so I was able to find my way using the pale light that filtered in through the dusty windows. I listened to cars crossing on the overpass as I went downstairs to the vending machines on the first floor.

Just as I was just about to unwrap the bar of milk chocolate I bought with the coin, I heard someone behind me. Frightened, I turned around to see who it was and saw a shadowy figure standing at the far end of the hallway. I couldn't make out much, other than the fact that it did not look like a nurse or a patient. It began moving towards me. I froze in place, too petrified to move even a finger.

As the figure got closer, what had seemed so frightful from a distance turned out to be a completely normal, middle-aged woman of average height wearing a completely not normal matte gray jumpsuit. In her left hand, she held a bent rod from which dangled metal balls of various sizes. Strangest of all, however, was the way she stared at me: her face flushed with emotion, her eyes wet with tears. Almost as if she had just run into her favorite movie star.

The woman pulled me into a tight hug, catching me off guard. She was sobbing so much it was difficult to understand what she was saying. The only words I could make out were: "You poor child!"

When she finally managed to collect herself, she grabbed my hand and pulled me toward the exit. Confused and scared, I followed her without thinking.

Now, were I a more experienced storyteller, I probably would have started out by describing the hospital itself. The weirdly long seven-story building stood at the corner of a market and an overpass, which meant that its old, gray rooms were constantly filled with the noise of cars and the smell of meat from the butcher shops below. Water dripped incessantly from various spots in the ceiling. That's the kind of place it was.

But as I approached the exit, these familiar sensory cues seemed to fade away. The smell of meat disappeared, and I could no longer hear the sounds of passing cars. The streetlights beyond the hospital doors swayed and intensified.

The woman opened the door. I hesitated for a moment. When I finally stepped outside, I found myself standing in a dense jungle filled with strange gray trees whose swaying branches were tipped with luminescent white berry-like objects. The market and the city had disappeared entirely, and where the overpass had once been there now stood a huge tree shaped like an arch. The hospital was also changing. What had until a moment ago been a rather uninteresting concrete building was now covered with the gnarled bark of an old tree. Remnants of the hospital's gray walls could still be seen where the transformation had not yet been completed. The egg-shaped spaceship wobbling in front of me and the gray jumpsuited figures moving around it seemed rather ordinary by comparison.

The woman who'd taken me from the hospital continued to talk at me as she pulled me onto the spaceship. Soon thereafter, Mother, dressed in pajamas and still half asleep, was carried on board by two men. We were clinging to each other in confusion when the spaceship took off.

3

Please bear with me now as I explain a few things. That night, you see, I went to sleep still confused about what was happening to us. It was not until the following morning that the woman in the gray jumpsuit explained what was going on. It turned out she was the captain of the ship we were on. She and her fellow crew members had traveled one hundred and seventy-eight light years to rescue Mother and me.

According to her, the place we had been living until the day before was not, as I had always assumed, Earth. Neither Mother nor I were actually from Earth at all. The planet we had been living on was named Baba Yaga IV. Earthlings had given it that name when they'd set up a colony there fifteen years ago. But every single member of that expedition had soon died from mysterious diseases and accidents, and before long, all that remained of the colony were the artificially intelligent base systems and robots.

That was when people back on Earth learned an astonishing fact. The trees on Baba Yaga IV that they had always presumed were just ordinary plants actually linked up to form a single giant neural network similar to a brain. The jungle was conscious. It learned, upgraded itself, and was almost omnipotent. It could create whatever it wanted in a mere instant–even a full-sized Buckingham Palace floating in mid-air. The jungle had desires and acted upon them but, fortunately perhaps, its desires were mundane—it did not have any particularly strong ambitions.

Although she had no proof, the captain believed that the jungle had killed the colonists. The colonists would have posed an obvious threat to the jungle, and eradicating them would have been an act of self-defense. If true, the situation was tragic but not something the jungle could be blamed for.

What fascinated the Earthlings was what had happened next. The jungle began to examine their houses, machines, and libraries. It did not have any particular aim—it was probably just bored. It had time and nothing better to do. The many ways in which living organisms could be killed must have been interesting, but eventually the colonists were all dead and the jungle had to find other ways to amuse itself.

The jungle did not have much interest in natural science or the principles undergirding the Earth machinery. Its concern was purely utilitarian: it needed just enough scientific knowledge to operate the construction group's machines and access the libraries. It was not interested in the sorts of things that it could figure out for itself; it wanted instead to learn about the lives of people on Earth. And the more sensational, explicit, and simple the stories were, the better.

In that sense, the jungle was a bit like your stereotypical

middle-aged housewife. It loved American and Latin American soap operas, twentieth-century Hong Kong and Taiwanese melodramas, and nineteenth-century Italian operas. But its absolute favorite stories were those that featured beautiful female protagonists suffering from unjust social oppression.

Once the jungle had finished all the romance novels, dramas, and movies in the libraries, it decided to invent a story of its own. First it created within itself a female lead who looked like a cross between Li Li-hua and Lin Dai. Then it gave this character a plot trajectory typical of Hong Kong melodramas from that period: an unexpected pregnancy leads to an unwanted child, and that in turn forces her to work as a nightclub singer. This woman and her daughter were the only ones to be given any kind of personality in the show. The jungle was completely uninterested in the inner lives of any of the peripheral characters. After all, who stops to wonder what's going on in the heads of extras?

Because the machines left behind by the colonists were still connected to the Ansible network, the people of Earth saw everything the jungle did. They recorded the jungle's melodrama and broadcast it to all their other systems. Viewers on over forty-seven planets enjoyed the show for almost two decades, and it inspired countless independent movies and edits. It even sparked a retro fashion revival.

After fifteen years, the jungle began to tire of this shy Li Li-hua-style melodrama. It wanted to experiment instead with the more exciting, sexually suggestive, and violent American-style soaps. The familiar 1960s Hong Kong backdrop gave way to 2150s Los Angeles.

Fans of the jungle's original Hong Kong drama did

not want the stars they had watched for so long to simply disappear, however. Which is why a rescue party had been sent to save us.

4

On Earth, we were treated like movie stars. We were provided with a permanent residence in a five-star hotel and since Earth no longer used money, we were given consumer privileges instead. Almost everyone knew our names, and we were obliged to appear on all kinds of broadcasts.

I liked it. The real Earth was so much nicer than the fake one I had lived on until now. It was clean, pollution-free, and filled with lots of high-tech toys. I also enjoyed the attention I received. It was at least preferable to the abuse I had suffered before.

For Mother, though, Earth was just another kind of hell. Despite what others may have believed, she was never just playing a role. Unlike the real Li Li-hua, who lived comfortably at home as a normal woman while playing tragic leads in Shaw Brothers movies, Mother did not have a private self distinct from the roles she played. Set down on 24th-century Earth, Mother was like a fish that had suddenly been transformed into a cat.

Why was I able to adapt more easily than Mother? Experts said it was because I had been more of a supporting character than a lead. My storyline was only of secondary importance in the melodrama that had occupied Mother's entire life. This meant I had been given a lot more time to myself, and as a result, had been able to develop more free will.

Scientists ran all sorts of tests on us. Strangely enough, the only time Mother looked at all happy was when our bodies were being scanned and analyzed. The scientists were the only people on this gentle planet who subjected Mother to anything resembling abuse.

Little by little, Mother and I grew apart. She couldn't understand why I had stopped vocalizing dramatically, as had been our habit, and instead talked like a normal person. Why was I no longer taking our misfortunes seriously? Why I was suddenly free from the feelings of guilt that had until recently weighed me down? Mother was not dumb, but no matter how hard she tried, she just couldn't rationally understand our new situation and always ended up retreating back into her original, fixed ways of thinking.

I suffered too. Yes, I had been given more free will than Mother. But, even so, my love for her—the love that had so long controlled my life—remained intact. It was difficult for me to imagine how my existence could have any meaning beyond my love for Mother. Difficult, but not impossible.

5

Mother is no longer with me. Five months after arriving on Earth, she took her own life using stolen sleeping pills. The doctors who had told us we couldn't die because our bodies were fundamentally different from those of regular humans were complete imbeciles. Mother and I were products of imagination. Imagination was the air we breathed. Even plain water could have killed Mother had she believed it to be poison.

Mother's funeral was impressive. A crowd of fans tracked down the crematorium and showed up in tears. When the ashes of Mother's body were compressed into a small diamond, people shrieked with appreciation. The photo of me wearing it around my neck became the second hottest piece of news on Earth.

Fans seemed to enjoy Mother's death. In truth she had been of no use to them on Earth. All they had wanted was a good old-fashioned, tragic heroine, the kind that no longer existed on Earth. Mother's suicide was the perfect conclusion to the drama they craved.

Immediately following her funeral, I fell into a state of severe anxiety. It's true that when we had first arrived on Earth I had, for a brief period, been unable to focus my attention on her. But my love for her had not faded in the least. She was forever a part of me.

My first thought after she died was to return home to Baba Yaga IV, but the city where we once lived had been replaced by the set for a new American-style series that was already attracting fans. I wanted to go back and tell the stars of this new drama about the jungle. I wanted to exhort them to find their freedom, but they were unlikely to handle the news any better than Mother had. In any case, my consumer privileges did not include the use of spaceships. I was an alien to be studied and observed; they did not want me to leave.

I was visited by numerous specialists doing research on the Baba Yaga melodrama. They would ask me detailed questions about what Mother and I had felt at different points in the storyline, and why we had acted certain ways in specific situations. I also appeared occasionally on talk shows and met with members of our fan club. I found it all very tedious, but I always answered whatever questions and requests were sent to me. I figured this was the only way I would ever feel closer to my home. Only a few months before, I had cursed and spat and screamed at the place, wishing it buried in a landfill and forgotten. I could hardly believe that I now missed it.

While recovering from Mother's death, I tried integrating into the 24th century. I studied history and culture and received occupational training. But no matter how much I tried to acclimate, I couldn't fully adapt to this world. I was an alien modeled after a 20th-century Earthling and living on 24th-century Earth.

The only thing for me to do was to rebuild myself on the model of a 24th-century Earthling instead of a 20th-century one. It was not easy, because to me, I hadn't been modeled on a 20th-century Earthling. The jungle had been aware of it, but I had just been me. In order to act a 24th-century Earthling, however, I had to take on full artistic responsibility for myself. I had to consciously, constantly fake it, and I gradually began to despise myself.

6

From here on out, the story takes yet another turn. I'm not sure you will like this plot twist, so if you already feel you've heard enough, you should probably stop here. Know, however, that even if you do stop reading, you won't be able to remain forever ignorant of what's going to happen to me. So you might as well keep on reading. Unlike the misfortunes I wrote about above, what I am about to tell you might be of some use.

As I was walking back to my hotel room alone, after a party arranged by my fan club to celebrate the third anniversary of my arrival on Earth, I found myself thinking about something the club leader had said: "You know, you haven't changed a bit in these past three years."

It was true. I was still fifteen years old. Growth and aging were not biological imperatives for me, they were processes I could choose to enact or reverse. And I hadn't felt any particular obligation to age since coming to Earth.

Scientists had learned a great deal about my physical body in the three years since I had come to Earth. According to them, I was basically a plant imitating an animal. I was incapable of photosynthesis, and I needed to eat three meals a day and excrete waste, but these functions were later, externally-imposed additions to my design. They were not part of my original form.

As I cut through the park in front of my hotel, I wondered if there might be some way for me to return to being a tree. Maybe if I reverted to an unthinking tree, I would no longer feel so uncomfortable. But that was just a useless fantasy. Baba Yaga's trees were not unthinking. How else could I have been endowed with the ability to think?

But if that were true, then I had inherited all the powers of the jungle.

I stopped walking. It was so obvious. Being on a planet one hundred and seventy-eight light years away didn't change the fact that I was connected to the Baba Yaga jungle. Like Earth's Ansible system, the Baba Yaga system was completely unaffected by distance—or at least that was what the scientists on Earth said.

Was the Baba Yaga jungle watching me right now? Was I an envoy for them? An explorer? Or perhaps I was meant to be a conqueror?

A rush of energy flooded my body. I felt like I could do anything I wanted.

I closed my eyes and thought of Mother. When I opened my eyes a few moments later, I saw a translucent balloon-like object in front of me that gradually began to resemble the top half of Mother's body. Eventually, unable to bear its own weight, it fell onto the grassy ground and disintegrated.

I rushed breathlessly back to my hotel. Getting into bed, I pulled the blankets over my head, closed my eyes, and concentrated. This time I did more than picture Mother's appearance. I strained to recall every single detail from our fifteen years together, conjuring up her very being.

Inside the blankets, a warm body began to take shape. The Mother I had missed so much over the past three years was appearing before my eyes. Only this newly created Mother no longer looked pained. She was younger and more beautiful than ever, and her eyes brimmed with love. I pulled her into an embrace.

7

A short while ago, I promised to give you information that might be useful. I'm going to fulfill that promise now.

Can you guess what I've been doing over the past three years? I've been spending my time eating, excreting, breathing, getting my hair cut in salons, and clipping my finger and toenails at home. Earth's scientists have been careful in their quarantine procedures, but they haven't caught on to how Baba Yaga really works. They only worry about microorganisms, not the scraps of material shed from my actual body. Meanwhile, tiny pieces of me have spread all around the world. And not just this world—they've spread to all human-occupied systems.

Most of these fragments remain linked to me. Where do you think the new body I created for Mother came from? From the hotel room itself, which was already filled with

Baba Yaga jungle particles sloughed off from my body. Shall I tell you something even better? Billions of these particles have taken up residence inside the bodies of everyone who's ever inhaled or otherwise ingested them. Which means I can now control their brains and nerves. So far twenty-eight planets have entered my system. I can command obedience from them without even lifting a finger.

Please don't do this, you say? For better or worse, it's already happened.

Did you hear about the island that suddenly appeared in the middle of the Pacific yesterday? That was me. I'm planning to rebuild my hometown there. Then I'm going to bring back everyone who made life so difficult for Mother and me. Some of them I'll bring back just to set Mother's mind at ease; others I plan to punish as I see fit. Then, once I've finished with that, I'll start remaking Earth and all its space colonies.

Keep your tributes. I have no interest in lording over the universe. All I want are a few small changes. I spent the last three years hoping to acclimate to 24th-century Earth, but nothing I tried worked. The only option I have left is to change the world to fit me instead. Resistance is futile. You lost your free will a long time ago.

What are my ultimate plans, you ask? I'm not sure yet. I'll start by fixing a few things I don't like. After that, I'll have plenty of time to figure out what to do next. The Baba Yaga jungle has never had ambitions suitable for ultimate plans before either.

No matter. We'll create those ambitions soon enough.

MEMOIR OF A JOSEON BRIDE

1

May I tell you a story? It is the story of what happened to me in 1842, the year I turned nineteen by the Western reckoning. Ah, I already see disbelief on your face. Nevertheless, perhaps you might consider setting your doubts aside for a moment and indulging me?

Have you heard of a country called Joseon? That is where I was born. It is a small, peninsular country between China and Japan that became a Japanese colony at the beginning of this century. Who knows what its fate will be once the war ends. I have heard its people are still fighting for their independence.

I wish I could tell you more about Joseon before starting my story; however, I left the country one hundred years ago, and it is insignificant in world affairs. Most people do not even know of its existence, and those who do tend to be uninterested in learning more. It is thus difficult to find books to supplement my own fading memories and knowledge. To me, Joseon will forever remain that small neighborhood where a young girl whom others called strange lived for nineteen years.

For the first fifteen years of my life, I lived with my father.

My mother left this world as she brought me into it. My father, a scholar, was a member of the yangban, the Joseon ruling class. He was curious and clever, but also woefully incompetent and poor. All he knew how to do was read, write, and discuss books. I never once saw him do anything that might put food on the table. It was amazing that we did not starve to death.

My father was a Catholic. I am not sure we would have survived the persecution of Joseon Catholics in 1839. But, conveniently enough, my father died just before the difficulties began, and his friends burned his dangerous books as soon as his funeral rites were concluded.

My future looked bleak. I had no relatives, and none of my father's friends were in good circumstances. Yet, fortune found me just in time. A yangban household a day's walk from the hut where I lived decided to take me in as their daughter-in-law.

It sounds like a Cinderella story, but it was not. It is true that the household was far wealthier than I would have dared to imagine. However, the man my father's friends had arranged for me to marry was deficient in the head. Some said he had suffered a childhood injury, others said he had been poisoned by bad medicine. I do not know which explanation was true. Nearby families were understandably reluctant to give up their daughters to such a man. I, however, despite my uncouth manner and upbringing, was the educated daughter of a yangban household. The family therefore settled on me as an adequate bride for their son.

I do not mean to speak ill of my husband. He was no more or no less than the village idiot: dull, dirty, good-hearted, and innocent. His libido was too robust for his childlike manner, but I could hardly blame him for that. My only worry was that I might give birth to a child as stupid as him. It was a ridiculous thought, but before Father Mendel came up with his theory of genetics, were Westerners capable of understanding such things either?

We lived together for exactly eight months. His death was an accident. He and the neighborhood children were playing with a ball made from a pig's bladder when a wagon coming down the hill ran over his head, crushing his skull. His family was both sad and relieved. Despite being a precious son and younger brother, he had been a burden. My husband's mother was the only one who seemed truly grieved by his death. She also seemed to resent me for no good reason, though she did not let it show.

Most of the family pitied me for having become a lonely widow at such a young age. In truth, however, I lived quite happily for the next few years. I had not disliked my husband. But he had been a dull, annoying, and beastly person. And besides, why shouldn't a woman like living without a husband? I had a room of my own. For the first time in my life, I was clean, warm, and well-fed, and could sit by myself and do whatever I pleased without being interrupted. And yet they pitied me. Did they really not know how truly wretched life outside our gates could be?

Our compound was quite large, palatial even, and of all the people in it, I had the least to do. The slaves and hired laborers did all of the hard work. Father was a famous scholar. His sons, all of whom lived in the compound with him, were likewise influential in the region and just as busy as their father. Mother and the women below her were always occupied with the considerable amount of housework required to maintain such a large household. I was the only person who did not quite fit in any of these categories, and so was more of a hindrance than anything else. When the women under the aegis of my mother-in-law gathered together to work, I was quietly excluded. The slaves likewise ignored my directions and would not let me join them. Everyone pitied, scorned, and avoided me.

I did not care, for I was good at keeping myself amused. Growing up in the hills without any friends, I had never had much choice in the matter. It was easy for me to find new things to do.

For one, the household had plenty of books to read. To be sure, scholars' homes always had many books in the men's quarters, but I was neither interested in nor allowed to read those. Our household, however, also held over four hundred volumes in the women's quarters, a huge collection by Joseon standards. Many of the books were handwritten copies of fiction and one, a sixty-volume novel set in China, had supposedly been written by the mother of Elder Sister, the wife of my husband's oldest brother.

I also turned my attention to bards at one point. These bards were the Frank Sinatras of Joseon. They sang of the brave rabbit who deceived the king of the sea, the wife who tricked her adulterous husband, and other old tales. I enjoyed their songs so much that once I even climbed over the compound wall and snuck out to a nearby village to see a performance. When I returned to my senses and went home, I discovered that no one had noticed my absence. I wish I could recreate those old Joseon songs for you, but the rhythms and melodies were never easy to memorize, and it has been so long since I heard them. Wolfgang Amadeus Mozart and Cole

Porter have supplanted them in my mind.

When I had time left over from these occupations, I drew pictures on scraps of paper collected here and there. These drawings were nothing like what Joseon people were accustomed to. My artistic and technical inspiration came from a miniature portrait of a girl done by some eighteenth-century French painter and twelve sexually suggestive copper etchings I found in a booklet that must have come from roughly the same time period. I found both items amongst the junk left behind by my grandfather, so I presume they must have passed through the Qing Empire. Most of my father's books had already been carted off or burned by his friends, but these two items and a small ceramic statue of the Virgin Mary I took and brought along to my in-laws' house. I longed to see more of these "pictures of pretty women," but pictures of women of any appearance were hard to find, so I made do with what I had.

I was not entirely friendless. Among the many people living in the palatial compound I had two friends, the twin girls who were the result of a relationship Second Brother had had with a government courtesan while on an official posting in the Joseon capital of Hanyang. Their mother had died of illness only a few months before I arrived, leaving them effectively orphans. Like me, they too had no real role to play within the family, and the three of us lived together in our own separate building. I acted the leader and took them around the household to play. When it suited me, I taught them how to draw pretty women and imitate bird songs by blowing through reeds.

I should probably pause for a moment here to explain a bit more about my father-in-law. During the four years I lived in that household—except for those final weeks—I hardly ever saw Father, and talked with him even less. As was typical for rich yangban households, the large external walls of our compound enclosed a number of individual buildings separated by walls and doorways into different living quarters. The men's and women's worlds were thus physically isolated from one another.

Father was a philosopher. Actually, all yangban scholars were philosophers, but even amongst this select group, Father was quite famous. He had written a number of books and could boast many disciples. I once snuck into the library and tried to read one of his books. Though I lacked the context needed to fully comprehend it, I understood the book to be Father's attempt at explaining the difference between humans and beasts, a question that had deeply concerned him at the time. To me, having grown up in the hills, it seemed obvious that the answer would never be found by sitting indoors and redefining the meanings of Chinese characters. If you truly want to know how beasts differ from humans, shouldn't you just go live with them?

2

In the summer of 1842, Father was bedridden with illness. He was seventy-two years old by the Western reckoning and had already lived a full life. He should have been allowed to die in peace, but his family saw things differently. Father's followers were enormously distressed. I am not entirely sure of the details, but they seemed to need him alive for a mess of complicated political reasons. Famous and important people were not allowed to die simply of their own accord.

Numerous physicians visited the household to no avail.

Watching from a distance, I saw Father slowly wither and waste away. Elder Brother also grew thin. He had a reputation for filial piety, but now that I think about it, that was not the only reason. He must have been very dependent on Father to have worried so much about Father's health. For there is no other way to explain what happened next.

Several days after Chuseok, the autumn moon festival, a suspicious box was delivered to the house. I snuck a glance over the wall of my quarters and saw that one of the two delivery men had a brown face and wore strange clothing I had never seen before.

When morning broke, four physicians descended upon the household and kicked the women out of the kitchen. I soon smelled the familiar smell of medicine boiling. There was however one particularly pungent odor I had never before encountered. As the medicine continued to boil, the unusual odor faded away until I wondered if I had imagined it. I remained curious, however.

Several hours later, the ingredients from the box had been reduced to a dark liquid. Elder Brother poured this into a bowl and took it to Father's room. The physicians followed closely behind, leaving the kitchen empty. My curiosity getting the better of me, I entered the kitchen. The twins followed at my heels like shadows.

Most of the medical ingredients I saw scattered around the kitchen, such as small pieces of twigs, roots, and berries, were familiar to me. Half were things out of Father's own cabinets that he took for minor illnesses. The only strange and unfamiliar thing in the kitchen was a pile of what looked like brown leather bands that lay spread out lengthwise on the cutting board. This was the source of the pungent odor.

I picked up one of the bands and examined it more closely. It appeared to be a thickly sliced piece of root peel. Twisted back into its original shape, it resembled a snake coiled around a stick. Red liquid seeped out from its fleshy inside when I turned it over. I dabbed my finger in the liquid to taste it. It was sour. Then with my front teeth, I took a bite from where the liquid had seeped out. It tasted of pear and radish, with an added a tinge of iron, like blood. Without thinking, I and the twins each took a piece of the peel and ate what was left of its flesh. We did not stop to wonder why it was the only non-dried ingredient in Father's medicine, or why it had been added to Father's medicine in the first place. It smelled and tasted good, so we ate it. In retrospect, it was quite a foolish thing to do.

I ate dinner and went to bed to the sound of men talking near Father's room. I felt rather tired, but assumed this was from all the tension in the household.

I awoke to Elder Sister's worried face peering down at me. At first, I thought I was dreaming. Elder Sister was a renowned poet, and by my standards, the most beautiful woman in the compound. Naturally, I modeled some of my pictures of pretty women after her. Her face thus frequently appeared in my dreams. Her large, hungry eyes and the way her mouth turned upward slightly at the corners led some to ask whether she might not be more alluring than was entirely appropriate for a lady from a respectable family. This was not something Elder Brother ever complained about, however.

I was not dreaming. Elder Sister had indeed come into my room, and was wiping my forehead. The shock of this realization startled me awake, but it was nothing compared to what she told me. She said that the twins and I had slept for three and a half days since that evening. I had spouted nonsense in my sleep and turbid sweat had oozed from my pores. Elder Sister had wiped the sweat from my face, but it had dried and stuck to other parts of my body, making me feel as if I were covered in some kind of thin membrane.

Also, Father had passed away while we slept.

The funeral of a family patriarch was an extremely important affair for Joseon men of the yangban class, one that involved much more than the interment of the corpse. The dead man's sons were all expected to resign from their various positions and build a mud hut in front of his grave where they would hold vigil for three years. During this period of mourning, they were not allowed to bathe or have sex. People's opinions about this custom differed, and not everyone followed it, but for Elder Brother there was no real choice. He needed to uphold his reputation as a filial son and set an example for Father's enemies and followers alike. Furthermore, Father's various political and scholarly battles were all suspended when he died, and Second Brother was forced to quit his government post and return home. As I already mentioned, the timing of all this could not have been worse.

Funerals were men's affairs. Women played only a supporting role, providing the loud, wailing expressions of filial piety and grief required by the noisy ritual. Neither the twins nor I were required to participate, We had never been considered members of the family, and besides, we still had not completely recovered our senses. While the funeral rituals took place, we holed up in a corner of our separate building playing marbles and reading the new stories that the old book merchant had brought us a few days earlier. But the marbles kept slipping through our fingers and all three of us kept accidentally biting our tongues, which made reading out loud rather difficult. We lost five days in this half-drunken state. At one point, a physician visited us to ask about our symptoms and the root scraps we had eaten. I am not sure he learned anything from us.

Little by little, the world returned to normal. For me, at least, because I was neither wife nor mother to anyone, and had no particular contact with the men in the compound. People were still gossiping about Father's death, but that was no concern of mine. My body recovered, and I learned a lesson from the affair: avoid medicinal ingredients brought in by suspicious men to save dying old people, even if they look tasty. And I thought that was enough.

Until Father came back.

3

On the fifteenth night after Father's burial, I was woken from sleep by the distant sound of someone pounding on the main gate accompanied by the low-pitched rumble of a man's voice.

It was after midnight, and someone was pounding on the gate and yelling, "Open up!"

Annoyed, I crawled out from under my blanket. This man was shouting so loudly that I could hear his voice all the way in my quarters. Why was no one from the slaves' quarters responding? And more to the point, why was someone disturbing us in the middle of the night?

Still yawning, I made my way to the main building. Something was not right. Through the open inner gate of the compound, I could see the women of the household whispering together in the entryway with the slaves and hired laborers, yet none of them went to open the outer gate. Each time they heard the pounding, they briefly froze.

Once the night air had brought me to my senses, I realized why.

It was Father's voice.

The people in the entryway were scared and confused. Many Joseon people believed in ghosts even though that belief clashed somewhat with their Confucian worldview. Yet, the ghosts they believed in did not pound on doors and ask to be let inside. The people of Joseon knew nothing about "premature burials" or catalepsy. What they experienced that night was more than just frightening: it simply made no sense.

Mother was the first to move. Nearly in tears, she walked out through the inner doorway, crossed to the main gate and, with the assistance of the old family steward and a slave, unbolted the latch. As soon as the bolt had been fully withdrawn, the gate creaked loudly open.

Father's corpse stood in front of the gate. It stood firmly and glared in our direction, but we all knew it was a corpse. It emanated the horribly unpleasant aura of a dead thing.

Despite this, Father looked far healthier than he had in the last few months of his life. He had gained weight, and a bulging stomach was visible between the edges of his dirty open robe. The ends of his fingers were covered in dried blood and all his fingernails had fallen off, probably as he had clawed his way out of his coffin and through the earth above.

Father staggered forward through the gate and headed toward the men's quarters. He sat down in the main hall and began to shout the same short word over and over. After three or four repetitions I could finally make out what he was trying to say: "Drink!" Upon a gesture from the old steward, one slave immediately rushed out of the room. Meanwhile, Mother sent two slaves out of the house. Later I learned that she had sent them to check on her sons, who had been holding vigil in the hut next to the grave.

The slave returned with a bottle of alcohol and a cold meat pancake. Father grabbed the pancake with his bare hands, took a large bite of it, and chewed three or four times before spitting it out onto the floor. He then gulped some alcohol straight from the bottle, but he could not tolerate that either. He spewed the alcohol out and threw the bottle to the floor. The only thing he seemed able to keep down was the well water hastily fetched by Mother.

No one spoke. Father's three sons were the ones who should have been talking to him to figure out what had happened, but not one of them had come home. Had they seen Father rise from his grave? If they had, why had they not followed him back home?

The brothers' absence was perplexing. Father's return home fifteen days after his burial was, on the other hand, unexpectedly easy to explain. The unusual medicine he had eaten before dying had, belatedly, worked. It was a strange idea, but plausible, because Joseon people did not demarcate life and death as neatly as their more religious counterparts in the West. My own father had taught me some of the Bible and, being reminded of the story of Lazarus, I was perplexed by Father's return. In the Bible, had not Jesus been the only one who could bring people back from death? Did it happen more often than I thought?

More troubling was Father's beard. It had been gray with

one or two strands of black mixed in, but now the hair around his mouth had all turned black. Or so it looked under the lanterns brought by Mother and the steward. And speaking of suspicious occurrences, the stains on his fingers also bothered me. They were not dried mud. More like some sticky dark red substance.

Several hours passed without much change. It was like watching a tedious but ghastly drama. Father kept trying to force his stiff tongue and lips to say things to us, but we were unable to make out any words. When we failed to understand, he grew angry, spitting at us and throwing things. We could never have imagined Father acting this way before.

Unable to stand it anymore, Mother finally ran up to Father. She moved her lantern across his face and screamed in a trembling voice. "Where are my sons, you old man! My sons were at your grave, where are they now?" Father shook his head as if to indicate his own bewilderment. Of all the people in this ridiculous scene, he seemed the most confused.

Another loud noise came in from the main gate. I feel I should let you know at this point that I might repeat certain descriptions as I continue this story. The main gates of Joseon compounds were always loud. It was not that they were poorly made or anything like that. To the contrary, it was a deliberate ostentation. As I recall, every time something decisive happened in that household, the main gate would always sound with a loud and upsetting *creeeeeeak*.

The gate had only been closed, not bolted, and now the three sons Mother had just been worrying about opened it and entered. Since all the lanterns were pointed at Father, his sons looked like shadows at first. But it took only a moment to differentiate them. Each brother was slightly shorter and fatter than his elder, and with the three of them standing in a line, we could tell them apart by their silhouettes.

Mother ran towards them, relief on her face, but just before reaching them, she froze and dropped her lantern. The lantern's paper wrapping caught fire, and in the resulting blaze of light I could see them clearly for the first time. Blood oozed from their mouths and necks, staining their clothing, and their cloudy pupils were visible only through eyeholes torn in the greasy gray membranes that covered their heads. They stood in the gate like scarecrows and glared at the family and slaves.

I quietly backed away. I did not understand what was happening. But there were four corpses walking around, so my top priority was to stay away from them and protect the children. Although there were four people in the household young enough to call children, I am of course referring here only to the twins.

I had barely managed to retreat to the inner gate before it started. I was unable to witness the events for myself since everyone's backs blocked my view, but putting the pieces of the story together from what I heard later, it seems that Third Brother, the laziest and dullest of the sons apart from my dead husband, had been the first to attack. He threw his mother to the ground and bit into her neck. Chaos ensued. Like starving foxes in a henhouse, the brothers and Father began to attack everyone trapped inside the compound walls. Screams filled the night and blood spurted from torn arteries. The slaves were helpless when faced with this onslaught. For them, the mere idea of standing up to yangban men was unthinkable. I thought I glimpsed one large young man run toward the shed and grab a pickaxe, but I cannot be sure he ever swung it.

I ran, sprinting off as fast as I could through the women's quarters and toward the room I shared with the twins. They were still asleep when I opened the door. As I shook them awake, I felt someone grab my neck. Twisting around, I saw it was Second Brother. He threw me to the ground and, holding my chest down with both hands, sunk his teeth into my neck.

I thought that was the end. To my astonishment, however, Brother let out a cry and pulled away. Something that looked like steam rose from the mouth that had just bitten me. He stood back a few moments before attacking once more, this time biting one of the twins, but again he immediately screamed and withdrew.

His cries drew the attention of his brothers, who rushed over to us, their mouths gaping open like children with stuffy noses. Inside each of their mouths I could see a pair of long, sharp teeth. These were not human canines. They were the fangs of venomous snakes.

The scene of moments ago repeated itself. First and Third Brother attacked me and the twins just as Second Brother had. They too screamed and drew back as soon as our blood touched their lips. Since all three bit me in the same way, I was able to distinctly feel their new teeth touch and enter the holes in my neck.

The three brothers circled us, growling. I had no idea what to do. Were it not for the twins, I might have considered slipping out of the house, over the wall behind my building, and away into the hills. But it would be impossible to do that with the twins, and I could not imagine abandoning them and running away by myself.

Second Brother grabbed my neck once again. This time, instead of biting me, he dragged me out of the building by the scruff of my neck, as if I were a sack of rice. The cries of the twins behind me indicated they were being subjected to the same treatment.

Bloody corpses lay strewn across the yard in front of the men's quarters. They looked different somehow in the dawn twilight. The corpses of the slaves and hired laborers were covered in blood, their necks torn, but the bodies of family members had much smaller neck wounds that were covered by a viscous liquid. Had I had time to check, I am sure I would have found a pair of needle-like punctures at the site of each family member's wound. The brothers had unconsciously divided their prey into two groups, food and family. When biting family, they had released something from their fangs and into the victim's bloodstream. The twins and I had been a meal for them. I got chills when I thought about it later. Me, I could understand, but why the twins? Were they not Second Brother's own children?

Father sat in the main hall rubbing his bloody hands together and stared at me. His face was ghastly, yet I found myself beginning to relax because, unlike the three brothers who were behaving like beasts and could not be reasoned with, Father still at least resembled a human. I enfolded the twins in my arms and stared back at Father. I did not speak. Words seemed unnecessary given the circumstances.

Father opened his mouth, but again I could not make out what he was trying to say. Just as his consonants and vowels seemed to be coming together into something approximating speech, they were torn apart by screams. It was not only Father; his three sons also cried out in agony. I blinked, confused. It took several seconds for me to understand what had happened.

The morning sun had risen over the wall to the compound and was now shining into the hall.

4

Vampires. They were vampires.

To Westerners, no more explanation is needed. But for me a hundred years ago, that convenient word did not yet exist. I had to reason everything out for myself.

To begin with, how had Father come back from the dead? It had to have been because of the medicine he took before he died. But if that were the case, then why were the twins and I still fine? Why had only Father changed? Was it because he had taken the medicine too late? Or perhaps the root peel was meant to be eaten raw as we had eaten it, and its effect had been reduced or altered when mixed with other ingredients and boiled into medicine for Father.

Moreover, why had Father turned into a monster who hid from the sunlight and drank blood? Back then, I had a theory. Joseon men were pathologically averse to bodily injury. There was however one exception to this general rule: when your own parents were sick. Back then, it was the fashion to cut your own finger and feed the blood to your dying parents. People were praised for following this unhygienic trend, and I assumed that Elder Brother must have done it too. Even had he not wanted to, he knew that he must perform to the expectations of those around him. And who knew what would happen if an old man on his deathbed drank the blood of his sons mixed with a suspicious root?

Do I still believe that theory? I am not sure. Blood and medicine do not seem a sufficient explanation for fangs and fear of sunlight. I cannot even say with certainty that

Father and I had ingested the same thing. As I have already mentioned, the root bore an uncanny resemblance to a snake. We had only eaten the skin, but maybe there had been something else, something inside the root, that Father had eaten instead. Something that could survive hours of boiling and then continue to live on inside a human body. Maybe the fangs that now jutted from their jaws belonged to that thing, whatever it was.

If so, what had happened to me and the twins? Perhaps the peel we ate had acted like a vaccine. Cowpox had not yet come into use in Joseon as a kind of smallpox vaccine, but I had heard of the concept from my father. Anyway, it was clear that Father and his sons had turned into monsters and were unable to drink our blood.

Not that this made our situation any better. As soon as the sun rose, Father and his three sons grabbed us and rushed us into a storeroom in the slaves' quarters. They blocked the windows with straw mats, then draped the remaining mats over themselves like raincoats and ran back out. They soon returned dragging their wives and children. I was forced to wait in the storeroom with the vampires' glowing eyes until the sun went down. When the twins and I needed to use the toilet, they made us leave one person behind. We were being held captive, each of us a hostage for the other two. Despite knowing they would not drink our blood, we did not feel safe. They knew that none of us would run away without the others.

When the sun went down, the three brothers forced me to help deal with the corpses. We moved the twenty corpses to the foot of the hill behind my building and covered them with dirt and leaves. It was not a pretty sight. The brothers had all grown incredibly strong since becoming vampires, and could now toss corpses over the wall with ease, yet they were still clumsy and had difficulty with shovels and pickaxes. Fingers and toes stuck out here and there from under the mound of dirt they had thrown over the bodies. The satisfied expression on their faces as they looked on their own shoddy work was unbearable. In my irritation, I grabbed a shovel from one of them and piled on more dirt to cover up the protruding digits.

Despite the horror of the situation, I found myself gradually able to relax. Moving my body had helped put my mind at ease and, more importantly, these people, who had behaved liked beasts on the previous night, seemed to have returned to their senses. Their speech was still clumsy, but at least they were talking with one another. They also appeared to be making an effort to suppress their violent urges.

When I returned to the compound after burying the corpses, I found that Father had come out into the men's quarters and was engrossed in reading the ten or so open volumes scattered about around him. His brain seemed more alert now than when he had been alive, and he had fully recovered the use of his tongue. When the three brothers announced themselves, he simply waved a finger toward the storeroom, his gaze still fixed on his book.

In the storeroom, the brothers' wives were now all awake. Aside from their relatively clean clothes, they were in much the same state as their husbands had been the day before: they were starving beasts. Third Sister, who had been pregnant, looked the worst. Elder Brother, always the devoted husband, ran over to his wife. He endured quietly as Elder Sister bit his neck, but barely any blood came out.

What they needed was living food.

The men left without a word. I remained in the storeroom. The twins were fine, with no new bite marks on their necks. I later learned that Father had yelled at his sons' wives to control themselves. They must have been more sober than they looked to have obeyed such an order in their current state. Perhaps women changed differently from men, or maybe the difference lay in whether a vampire was first, second, or third generation. Or both. I am not sure. Even though there are many parts of this story that I still cannot fully explain, this is not a fictional story and I refuse to simply invent things.

Mother and the children looked seriously unwell. Third Brother's four-year-old son seemed to have already died from the membrane exuded by his pores, which had blocked his nostrils and mouth. His brother, just a year old, did not look likely to make it either. Mother was struggling, too, and made an unpleasant snoring sound with each labored breath. Perhaps the poison the men had injected into them had been too strong.

An hour or two passed. I heard the sound of the gate again accompanied by hushed voices. One female and one male. And the sound of an infant crying. I thought I knew them. They were the young tenant farmers whose son had been born five months earlier. I knew the woman's face because she often came to help with housework.

What should I have done? I still wish I had screamed to warn them of the danger. They still would not have been able to escape, but at least I would have tried. Who knows? Had I done something, perhaps many more people would have survived.

But I did not. At that moment, I was fully one with the

vampires. I even smacked my lips and sat with bated breath in the dark storeroom. I returned to my senses when the storeroom door opened and the woman came in carrying her child, fright on her round face, but by then it was too late. I held the twins tightly to me, pressing all of our heads into a corner of the room, until the sounds of the couple and their child writhing and screaming faded and eventually stopped.

I again heard the storeroom door opening. I turned around and saw moonlight shining through the open door and onto the corpses of father, mother, and infant, which had been tossed on top of each other into the center of the room and formed a small mound. The women were leaning against the walls of the room, fixated on the food they had just killed. They were all shaking badly, as if the human blood they had just imbibed were some sort of powerful drug. As always, my eyes sought out Elder Sister. Her blood-smeared face had turned a pure snowy white, and I remember it being surprisingly beautiful.

It was Elder Brother who had opened the door. He rushed to his wife and fell to his knees, burying his face in her skirt. Elder Sister stared at her husband coldly before shaking his hands off of her thighs. He moaned. I took the twins by their hands and left the room.

Father stood outside the storeroom. He had wrapped up the book he had been reading and now held it in his hand. The other two brothers stood awkwardly behind Father's shadow. Once everyone had emerged, Father shook his head and spoke. "This is no way to live. My children—we cannot go on like this."

He was absolutely right. If they wanted to survive, they needed a regular supply of food, and their food was the blood of the living. However, they could not just summon a nearby tenant or slave family every time they grew hungry. Doing so would be as foolish as eating their own arms and legs.

One commonsensical alternative was to leave the village every night and go hunting for food. But even on the longest night of the year, how far could they really go and still return before sunrise? Were these bookish scholars and sheltered wealthy ladies even capable of hunting people? Their reputation was also an issue, of course. No matter how hungry they might be, hunting people was simply not something that yangban did.

To survive, they needed to develop a system for regularly summoning new outsiders to the household and then disposing of the corpses without leaving any evidence. Because they were only able to go out at night, the vampires could not accomplish this alone. They needed an assistant. Someone who knew their situation and could walk around in the daytime.

They needed me.

5

The household bustled incessantly for the next five days. First, the compound had to be restructured. The vampires could not sleep in the storeroom forever, so they bought coffins to use as beds, placed them in their own rooms, surrounded the coffins with black lacquer screens, and boarded up all the paper windows. The storeroom too needed to be improved for the continued occupancy of the twins.

We also had to dispose of the corpses. The tenant farmer couple and their child were buried in the hill behind my building with the other corpses. Third Brother's remaining child died the following day. The corpses of the two boys were laid outside together, where the sunlight reduced them to piles of white ash and bones. These remains were then placed into two jars and buried in the family grave Father had dug himself out of just a few days before. The site already contained the corpses of the slaves that Mother had sent to look for the brothers, and whom the brothers had eaten. Second Sister hated to put her children there with the slaves, but there was no other choice.

It was important that they secure space to dump future corpses as well. At the foot of the hill near the compound lay an old cave that had been buried in an avalanche. All they needed to do was excavate an entrance, and they suddenly had enough space to store several years of corpses. They dug up the previously buried corpses and relocated them to the cave. Those bodies all would have been exposed by the first rainfall anyway. The cave was a better site.

Slaves borrowed from nearby yangban households handled most of the house repairs. After the sun went down, Father and Second Brother would come out to lead them, but during the day I had to manage everything myself. There were of course questions about why the household had neither steward nor slaves, and why I was the one handling this work, but Second Brother spun plausible lies to hold them off. Some had gone to visit relatives, others had gotten sick and gone home to convalesce. Although these excuses now strike me as pathetic, they had sounded quite plausible coming from Second Brother's lips. He was after all a yangban politician, and the greatest asset of politicians everywhere is the ability to lie without batting an eyelash.

It was five vagrants gathered from the village who dug out

the cave entrance. Second Brother had found them sleeping near the compound with only bamboo mats for blankets and brought them home. I probably do not need to tell you that they all became food for the household as soon as they finished the work.

The family gradually became familiar with their new bodies. Every five to six days, they each needed to drink two to three liters of blood to satisfy their hunger. Because Joseon people were rather small, this meant roughly two had to die to feed three vampires. In other words, many of the victims from that first day had died unnecessarily.

The expression I just used, "satisfy their hunger," is not entirely accurate. They were always hungry. They needed fresh blood not when they felt hunger, but when they began to suffer withdrawal symptoms. Blood was more a drug than a food to them. They ate it to avoid losing their senses and turning into beasts.

Serving up their meals was my job.

I brought their food mainly from the villages in the area, although if need be I could also reach the nearby city within the four nights and five days that I was allowed to be gone. They were all men, mostly homeless beggars and itinerant traders. I selected them very carefully. The sick, the elderly—people with no future and no one to miss them. I thought it was almost a kindness to let them die with stomachs full of good food and drink.

When traveling to gather sacrificial victims, I disguised myself as a man. Lest you mistakenly picture this as a scene from Shakespeare's comedies, let me assure you it was quite common back then in Joseon, because women were not allowed to travel alone. Growing up in the hills, I had often disguised myself in this way. I could play a very convincing fifteen-year-old boy, and most people never caught on.

Sometimes a man would realize that I was a woman and try to force himself on me. A few of these men even tried to have me without realizing I was female. I was scared when it first happened, but I found them surprisingly easy to subdue. I had been growing gradually stronger since eating the root, and it seemed I would soon be just as strong as my in-laws. I simply needed to learn how to use my new strength. My strength was two or three times that of a man, yet my weight and height had not changed. Over the course of several fights, I learned how to avoid the disadvantages of my slight frame and developed techniques for focusing attacks on my opponents' joints. Usually, my attackers ended up moaning on the ground, their arms and legs broken.

I grew more cunning and bold. My sympathy towards my victims diminished every time I was attacked. I still preferred the sick and the elderly, but I felt no need to be generous toward bandits who attacked me for no reason. I would show them a few coins, make them respect me, and convince them to follow me home like loyal dogs. By the time we reached the compound, the exsanguinated corpses of the men who had previously followed me there would have already been hidden away in the cave.

As I continued this job into a second month, I became more and more an accomplice to the vampires. At first, I thought I had no choice: I had to do it to save the twins, who remained imprisoned in the storeroom. But as the dead began to pile up, I began to think less about the twins' safety and more about my own guilt. I may as well have killed them all myself. The crimes I was committing twisted into a tight noose around my neck. If everything came to light, how would I plead my case?

Even more concerning than the fact that I was committing these crimes, was that I had begun to enjoy it. With an inhumanly strong body and enough money to do anything I wanted, I had the power to control people's fates, and that made the world more interesting. I took further pleasure in enjoying, with the help of my disguise, all the privileges accorded only to men, and sharing in the knowledge that men kept to themselves. Thinking about my in-laws at home treating the beggars as lords while I was enjoying every luxury on the outside brought a smile to my face.

6

Would you like to know what Father was thinking over the course of those two months? As I mentioned earlier, Father was a philosopher. He had lived life in accordance with his concern for questions such as: What are humans? What is humanity's place in the universe? What is the proper way to live? Would a person of that sort, once turned into a vampire, really just abandon those questions and concern themselves only with basic survival needs?

Of course not. In fact, that period was the most philosophically important period of Father's life. This was only to be expected. Father had just experienced something that no one else had ever experienced before, something that completely upended his previous ideas about the world. What else was there for a philosopher like him to do in such a situation, if not to amend, revise, and supplement his previous theories in light of his new experiences?

I wish I could share with you the details of his

philosophical investigations. Unfortunately, nothing he wrote has survived. Moreover, despite enjoying every freedom offered to men when I was outside the compound, within it I was still only a woman and unable to participate in the discussions. Even had I been allowed to join the discussions, I would not have been able to fully understand what was said.

Even so, I will try to explain as best I can. There is a pair of Chinese characters, 理 ("i" in the Joseon language) and 氣 ("gi"). Though not the sort of characters whose meaning can be defined with any real precision, they approximate the ideas of "principle" and "energy." Joseon intellectuals attached considerable importance to debates over the definitions and relative weights of these terms. To certain intellectuals, in fact, i and gi were the sum total of philosophy.

Before becoming a vampire, Father had regarded i—principle—as the more important of the two. He was nonetheless considered open-minded in comparison to a now-famous former disciple who had split with Father and founded his own extreme faction.

However, after dying, digging his way out of the grave, and living off human blood, Father concluded that his previous stance had been absurd. He now went in the opposite direction and placed an extreme emphasis on energy. Having determined this new direction, he reconfigured all his related ideas accordingly.

What was most chilling about Father's new worldview was not its arrangement of concepts, but rather the conclusions he came to. I am unable to follow every link in his chain of thought, yet it seems to me his philosophical arguments existed to serve one and only one objective: to justify his own existence as someone who killed and drank the blood of his fellow humans. It did not matter which of the two concepts took precedence over the other. Either one could serve for the creation of a new class system that placed humans beneath vampires.

When I put it that way Father seems like an evil villain, yet that was not the case at all. He was an intellectual. He did not set out to create a philosophical system benefitting vampires just because he was one. He was not a terrible scholar and disdained such selfish and naive desires. I think perhaps his philosophy had more to do with the following questions: Now that I have been reborn in this way, how am I to comprehend the differences between my current remarkable existence and my previous one? How do I fit into the universe, and how must I behave?

Like most scholars, Father wanted to disseminate his new discovery and increase his influence. He chose the most straightforward way of doing so. One by one he summoned his friends and followers.

The first person Father invited was a fellow scholar who lived not far from the compound. They were childhood friends who had grown distant due to diverging philosophical views, only to reconcile in the last few years of Father's life. This man had cried the loudest at Father's funeral, and his eulogy had been the most magnificent.

I do not know what happened that evening. I was playing with future prey in a house of leisure at the time. Once I familiarized myself with the procedures for entering these places, nowhere was better for distracting my prey. More than anything, I could listen to music in them. The house I frequented had a beautiful courtesan who played the gayageum zither with exceptional talent, yet the drunken customers were too busy fondling the pubescent bodies of the girls to recognize the artist in front of their eyes.

As for what happened that night, it is not difficult to imagine the scene. The scholar no doubt was surprised to see that his supposedly dead friend was still alive. Seizing upon this, Father would have related his experience and explained the philosophical propositions he had been entertaining. Was his friend able to accept these propositions? Impossible to know. In any case, Father must have ended the discussion with his teeth in his friend's neck.

Need I mention how annoyed I was when I came back with just enough food for everyone only to discover there was now an extra mouth to feed?

7

The villagers gradually grew suspicious as winter approached.

It was unavoidable. No matter how carefully we planned, the presence of vampires could not stay unnoticed forever. Especially a large household of vampires.

The sudden disappearance of the three brothers from the hut at the family gravesite had generated only mild gossip. But after the household slaves, hired laborers, and tenant farmer family all disappeared, and strange construction started up at the compound, people began to worry. Despite Second Brother's best efforts to contain the gossip, a rumor began circulating that the compound had been struck by plague.

The spread of that particular rumor was slowed by the rise of other rumors. Some people noticed that the family compound was visited by suspicious characters every five days. This happenstance of course gave birth to a rumor of its own, but one which could not be reconciled with the rumor of plague. When the nearby scholar suddenly became our long-term guest, suspicions coalesced into a third rumor that accorded with neither of the previous two. The rumors could easily have been stitched together into a coherent story had anyone been familiar with the concept of vampires. Without that, however, the pieces of the story made no sense.

In the meantime, the number of house guests kept increasing. Father knew it would be impossible to keep up this state of affairs forever. He meant to turn as many of his colleagues as possible into vampires and take control of the area before the secret was out. After that, he must have planned to overthrow the state and create a vampire utopia. It was not a selfish plan. Father had no desire to make himself king. The First Opium War had just ended that year in defeat for the Qing Empire, and the Joseon people also felt their world slowly collapsing. They were willing to do anything to stop the collapse, including turning their entire ruling class into vampires.

I do not know how realistic the plan was. The men Father gathered at the compound were all cut from the same cloth as himself: philosophers, gentry, retired officials. There was not a soldier, merchant, or diplomat among them. They were all the type who talked a great deal but had no real experience. The constant chatter that came from the men's quarters at night was quite a nuisance.

I had no interest in their scheming. All I knew was that if they did not each get three liters of blood every five days, they would lose their senses and might harm the twins.

I told Father that I could no longer do it alone. A few girls at the house of leisure knew me by sight. The talented zither player had gone so far as to ask my name. No one missed the itinerant traders and beggars, but I heard that some of the vagrants I had taken were now sought by their friends. Even given four nights and five days, there was a limit to how much I could do. I needed a better system.

Father was persuaded by the extreme rationality of my proposal. The plan had come easily. Unlike what had happened in our household, our new guests had not murdered all their slaves when they became vampires. Although these new vampires had no desire to reveal their new identity to the slaves still living in their households, through an appropriate delegation of tasks, they could, without risking exposure, procure plenty of food for our compound.

Yet, Father saw this as an opportunity to do more than just obtain food. If they must kill and eat people anyway, could not the choice of food be a political one? He could eat people whose absence would be beneficial to his grand plans. In other words, his political enemies.

It had probably been Second Brother's idea. It was too realistic and opportunistic to have come from Father. Moreover, like most plans conceived by high government officials, it was weak on details. I had entertained similar ideas myself. Yet, if the disappearance of just a few vagrants had led to their friends running around spreading rumors, would it really be possible to assassinate rapacious politicians?

Ultimately none of this mattered. The plan of father and son was destined to collapse before it began. I will return to that story later. For now, let me tell you what was happening elsewhere in the compound.

I may have made it seem as if the vampires were excited by their new bodies and powers. However, Father and Second

Brother were exceptions. The others shared neither their excitement nor their sense of purpose.

Mother, for example, was a brainless corpse. She did not regain her senses after becoming a vampire. Her incessant, loud breathing was the only sign she was still alive.

Third Brother and his wife acted out and complained the loudest. They had both been gluttons, and furthermore Third Sister was pregnant, and yet all they could hold down now was water and blood. They could not even smoke tobacco. Third Brother was used to spending his leisure time outside of the compound walls, but now, going out during the day was simply impossible. They were in such a foul mood that they could not muster the energy even to mourn the death of their sons. The one and only thing they did as vampires was complain about food. Not once were they satisfied with what I brought them. Every time they would complain it was too thin, too dirty, or too old. Third Brother pleaded with me to bring a young woman or child and even named a specific person from the village that he wanted. I ignored him, of course.

Second Sister became a fervent follower of Father and her husband. She threw herself into it so enthusiastically that she eventually assigned herself the duty of turning all her relatives, even the most distant blood kin, into vampires. Her first target, naturally, was her only son, who was away studying in Hanyang. She wrote dozens of impassioned letters to him and to her other relatives, but I intercepted most of them. When not writing letters, she seemed to be writing a book about the virtues that vampire women should uphold. That book was probably lost at the same time as Father's books.

Most wretched of all were Elder Brother and Elder Sister.

Elder Sister was the only vampire in the household who suffered existential anguish. She could not accept the fact that her life now depended on killing other people. Nor could she forgive her husband for making her that way. To her, Father's new philosophy was nothing but empty words. Her conviction was simple and firm: murder was wrong no matter what the circumstances. She could not abandon this belief just because she had become a vampire.

Only later did I learn Elder Sister was a Catholic. When I searched her room, I found a rosary made of birch and a book by Father Pantoja with its cover missing. Knowing she had come from a family that firmly resisted Western culture, I wondered how she had become a believer. I remembered how once, when a slave was caught thieving, she had stopped Father from having the slave beaten to death. Elder Sister had also played a large role in bringing me into the household. Several of the Chinese poems she wrote gave off the same air of longing for absolute truth as that of European Catholic poets. She also loved donkeys and sometimes wrote poems about them. I think of her whenever I read the poems of Francis Jammes.

Unlike Father, Eldest Sister found herself caught in a trap from which she could not escape. Given her Catholic convictions, Elder Sister was a more devout follower of principle than Father. Father, in contrast, could with relative ease change his beliefs from energy theory to the position that "we must accept nature the way it is." Therein lies the difference between religion and philosophy. If Elder Sister refused to drink blood, she would lose control of herself, turn into a beast, and likely harm an innocent person. Yet, even in these circumstances, the Church would not permit her to end her own life. She had no choice but to suffer drinking the minimum amount of blood needed to remain sane. Needless to say, that was not a solution either.

Elder Brother said nothing as he watched his wife. He loved her deeply. Even with their two daughters married off and gone, his feelings for her had not lessened. His wife's pain was his own. He cursed himself for having made his wife a vampire, but curses were not a solution.

How romantic, you might think. But it also showed how weak and easily swayed Elder Brother could be. He had lived his whole life pulled this way and that, whether by his father the renowned philosopher, or by his wife the headstrong artist, and so had never achieved anything for himself. That was Elder Brother.

Elder Sister, on the other hand, was neither weak nor indecisive. She soon found a solution, albeit an imperfect one. She broke through the weakest point of the walls imprisoning her.

It was an early winter morning and the ground was dusted with powdery snow. I had covered the dead beggars' corpses with straw mats and was busy washing away the bloodstains with hot water. The rest of the household, having sated themselves, was fast asleep. Elder Sister, however, had not consumed so much as a drop of blood the previous night. She spent that morning crouched behind the boarded-up doorway of her room. When the first ray of sunshine broke through the clouds, she ran into the yard. Elder Brother ran after his wife a moment too late, and only managed to catch the hem of her dress before she was incinerated by the sunlight. He wailed as he watched his wife burn to a pile of white ash and bones. His own right hand fell off at the wrist, its bones pinned under hers in a pile just beyond the shadow line of the eaves.

8

I have been mocking the people of the household for losing their sense of reality. Yet, I really have no right to mock them, for it was my mistake that led to the secret getting out.

It was not entirely my fault. It was bad luck. I was caught by someone with extraordinarily keen powers of observation. Surely one must guard against such people, you say? But is it so easy? They say the longer one's tail, the easier it is to trip over. The secret was bound to be exposed someday.

The clever man who put all the clues together was a military officer working at the topocheong judiciary. His job was somewhere between that of a military lieutenant and a police detective. And he was smitten by the talented zither player I mentioned earlier. Naturally, he made a habit of frequenting that establishment. Although I never met him directly, for we never happened to visit the place on the same day, I had heard something of his existence from the courtesans. He, in turn, learned from the courtesans about a young yangban lad who visited the place in the company of unseemly friends.

Thinking back now, the officer must have envied me. He knew nothing of music and found the zither performances boring and tiresome. The zither player would have mentioned me to him, for good listeners were uncommon in such a place. How foolish I was back then. I ought to have remained silent on my visits, yet I found myself unable to resist telling her the Chinese legend of the zither player Bo Ya and his encounter with Zhong Ziqi, the only man in the world to truly understand his heart. I even painted for her one of my unique portraits of pretty women that were clearly influenced by the eighteen-century French model. When I then rented a room and said I would be sleeping alone, I could not but have stood out. Realizing this, I thought to find a different house of leisure the next time, but try as I might I could not get her music out of my mind. How starved I was for music in those days!

Joseon leisure houses were not open to outsiders. To gain admission to the house with the zither player the first time, I made use of someone who was familiar with the place to learn the procedures. My introduction was through an old man who had been wandering around homeless for many years, but nonetheless had frequented such places until only a few years earlier. The madam of the house had known this old man for a long time, and when one day the officer mentioned me, the madam mused: "I haven't seen the old man since that day. Maybe he lucked into some good fortune."

Normally, such a statement would have meant nothing. But the officer knew that several vagrants had recently disappeared. What if the old man had disappeared in the same fashion? What if others had gone missing as well? What if all these disappearances were connected? The officer asked the madam about the missing vagrants and ascertained that they had disappeared from the village the day after staying at the leisure house and never been seen again. He then toured the surrounding area questioning residents and discovered that two more vagrants had disappeared in similar fashion.

The affair was not his business. Those people were all better off gone. But the officer was gripped by jealousy and curiosity toward me. On the next fifth day, he went to the leisure house to meet me, but for the reasons I described earlier I did not appear. Instead, the slaves of Father's friends were out and about finding people to feed their masters.

I was in the compound with the twins searching for a way to escape. Since Elder Sister had died, I had even less reason to remain in the household. However, Father and Second Brother both knew of my plans. Someone was always guarding the twins, and a new bolt was installed on the storeroom door.

Perhaps still uneasy even after taking these precautions, Father decided to send me away again. This time I was to check up on the slaves sent out to procure food. How was I supposed to manage the many slaves whose faces I hardly knew, and who had all headed off in different directions? But that was precisely the point. My presence bothered Father, so he was ordering me out of the house.

I wandered aimlessly for several days, spending Father's money freely, until I heard the familiar sound of a zither. Although I had not intended to approach my regular house of leisure, habit had drawn me near. Like a bobby-soxer unable to afford a ticket to a Sinatra concert, I stood wretchedly outside the wall and listened to the music flowing from within.

That is when I ran into the officer. He recognized me at once. He might not have known me had he had seen me anywhere else. But here, in the middle of the night, standing with an obvious expression of longing on my face just outside the residence of his unrequited love, I was a precise match for the romantic rival he had long imagined.

He demanded to see my hopae. These were rectangular strips of wood, inscribed with name and other particulars, that all Joseon men carried for identification. Rather stupidly, I carried my dead husband's hopae. Normally a man's hopae was returned to the government upon death, but Mother had kept my husband's for sentimental reasons. I had taken it from her room to use as an accessory when I began to disguise myself in his old clothing.

Needless to say, the officer was not deceived by the hopae I held out to him. The merest glance revealed that the age did not match. Furthermore, my husband's name and death were well-known in the area, because Father was an important public figure, and because the accident itself had been quite unusual.

He took me to the local jail. Because I was not yet suspected of anything except the false identification, I was provided a cell all to myself. The cell next to mine held at least ten convicts who sat shackled by their ankles, exchanging lice and fleas. The officer stood in the hallway congratulating himself on his intelligence and vigilance, and demanded to know my real identity. When I said nothing, he left with a growl that he would be back the following morning.

As soon as my eyes adjusted to the dark, I explored my cell. The first thing that caught my eye was the writing that sparkled in the moonlight along the wall. I approached and saw carved into the wall a Chinese poem in regulated verse that compared its author to the famous patriotic poet Qu Yuan. The idea was unoriginal, but it was a good poem, brimming with honesty and power.

It was clear that the poem had been carved very recently. What then had the wronged poet carved it with? I carefully searched the straw-covered floor until I found a large nail, its pointed end worn to gleaming bare metal. I bent the nail into a hook by propping one end against the wall and stepping on the other, then inserted it into the lock of my cell door and jiggled. The lock opened on the third or fourth try. This was a skill I had perfected over years of practice opening the cupboards in the main hall to steal honey.

I waited until the jailers dozed off, then cautiously opened the door of my cell. The noise caused one jailer to startle awake. I ran toward him and pulled out the ornamental knife I carried in my sleeve. Holding the blade against his throat, I dragged him along with me until the jail was out of sight. A swift kick to the derriere from the top of a bridge left him floundering in the stream. It was rather mean of me, but the second male lead of Elder Sister's mother's novel had done that to the villain in the twenty-fourth volume, and I had always wanted to try it myself.

I thought hard while running back to the house. The officer would not give up. Running away was proof that I was hiding something. He had found me carrying the hopae belonging to the son of the area's most renowned scholar. It was only a matter of time before he would come to the compound to investigate the truth. Would that be my chance? Or would it bring disaster? I did not know. It was clear, however, that I had to find a way to save the twins before he arrived.

Dawn had already tinged the sky a dark red by the time I arrived back home. It was time for the vampires to take refuge in their boarded-up bedrooms. Yet, to my surprise, the main gate was open. I saw someone short and stocky walking about. It was Third Brother. He was holding something dark and glistening in his hands.

It was a half-eaten human liver.

"I was hungry, I was really hungry," said Third Brother innocently, his face covered in blood.

I ran into the compound. Just inside the entryway, my foot

caught on a corpse and I almost fell. It was one of the slaves of Father's guests. The skin of its belly had been lifted like the lid of a pot and the organ cavity was empty. I could see all the way to its spine. Five more corpses torn open in similar fashion lay strewn around the yard, and three or four vampires were feeding on the organs of each. The arms of one of the corpses still twitched, though it was probably just post-mortem muscle spasms.

Father stood like a statue in the main hall and gazed down at the scene in rage. Just as I arrived, he bellowed at the vampires in the yard, "Stop! Do not eat meat! You must not consume anything except blood! Do you wish to devolve further into beasts?"

9

I felt nauseous. I wanted to vomit, but I had not eaten for hours and only bile came up.

I covered each corpse with a straw mat from a pile we kept to one side of the yard. I was short two mats. I grabbed bundles of paper from the library and spread them out to cover the upper halves of the final two corpses. It was a terrible waste, as paper was in short supply in Joseon. But it was my way of registering protest against the vampires who, having eaten, could now comfortably retire to their coffins.

I watched expressionlessly as oozing blood gradually turned the paper red. I then turned my attention to the storeroom into which Father had retreated. I ran toward it and tried to shove the door open, but the bolt was secure. I grabbed a poker lying by the door and stabbed at the boards covering the storeroom windows. It was no use. I hurled at the storeroom all the curses I had learned in town, but not a peep came from inside.

I considered opening the main door of the compound for all to see. I also considered stopping passers-by and showing them everything. But had anything really changed? The vampires had killed and fed on people before. The only difference now was that they were no longer just drinking blood. From a certain perspective, this was actually preferable. Until now, vampires had been the most wasteful carnivores in the world.

Even so, I was not going to help them clean up those corpses.

I went to my building and changed into women's clothes. Though still not hungry, I went to the kitchen, cooked rice and prepared the most appetizing side dishes I could out of the available ingredients. After eating my fill, I left a tray in front of the storeroom door for the twins. When I went back later to check, the food was gone.

I returned to my building and began to toy with the saenghwang that had been lying in my room. I did not know how to play the instrument properly, so I just made sounds. I was preoccupied with terrible thoughts and did not have the presence of mind to draw or read. When I tired of the saenghwang, I went into Elder Sister's room, took out her best pipe and tobacco, and began to smoke. Before long the pipe stopped up and I had to search Elder Sister's drawers for a cleaning brush. That was how I found Father Pantoja's book and the rosary.

The officer still had not come. He must have been kept away by circumstances I was unaware of. Perhaps his superiors did not believe him. Perhaps he was unsatisfied with the evidence and was gathering additional witnesses. Perhaps he was afraid of approaching the compound. Or perhaps merely driving away his rival had been enough.

It being winter, the days were short and cloudy, and it grew dark as soon as the sun went down. I listened as coffin lids were raised, screens scraped against the ground, and doors opened. Family members and guests crawled out from their rooms. Half of them rushed toward the corpses I had covered with straw mats. The remaining half sat in the main hall and licked their lips as they watched the others eating human flesh. Soon three or four more had joined the group of eaters. Nowhere could I see the intelligence that they had briefly shown as vampires. They were devolving into beasts.

Until a few days earlier, all they had been able to consume was water and blood. Now, however, they were flesh-eating monsters. This meant that the vampire stage was unstable or transitory. Back then I did not understand why the more recent vampires regressed simultaneously with the household's original ones, but now I wonder if the regression itself was not contagious.

The storeroom door opened. Father leaned halfway out and gestured for me to come in. I unsheathed my knife and, holding it with the blade pointed backward, entered.

Elder Brother lay sprawled in the middle of the storeroom floor. His throat had been cut all the way to the bone, but his head was still alive, as evidenced by his blinking eyes. In his left hand, the only hand still attached to his body, he held a scrap of old paper that appeared to have been torn from a book.

Father held in his right hand the sword that he had clearly just used on Elder Brother. In his left hand, he held a book with a singed cover. Father pointed his sword at the twins, who were bound tightly together and crying in the corner of the storeroom. Then he held the book out to me.

"Read."

While keeping hold of my knife with my right hand, I took the book with my left (that was extremely rude of me, but neither of us noticed the breach of etiquette). I looked at the open page, but it was too dark to make anything out. I stuck the knife back into my sleeve and used a flint to light the oil lamp.

I picked up the book and began to read. It was a handbook of home remedies that Elder Sister had inherited from her family. I had heard that the book was written by her grandmother, but this was the first time I had seen it for myself. One corner of the page had been ripped out–probably the scrap of paper Elder Brother still held in his hand. The rest of the page described an ordinary folk remedy for colds: a decoction of bellflower root mixed with honey.

This was so unexpected that I raised my head and looked at Father. He was just as surprised. Disconcerted, he began to look back and forth between the book and me. I continued reading only to find that the next page was also a discussion of cold remedies with summaries of the effects of quince tea and the juices of radish, pear, and ginger.

That is when I realized what was really strange about the situation.

Father was not the one reading the book aloud. I was.

Father was illiterate.

To understand what I mean by this, you need to understand the Joseon writing system. In Joseon, people wrote not in the Joseon language they spoke, but in classical Chinese, similar to how medieval Europeans wrote in Latin. Several hundred years before my time, a king invented an alphabet for writing down the Joseon language. Commoners and women, who could read little if any classical Chinese, were then able to read and write their own language using the new alphabet. This alphabetic system, called eonmun, was that in which most of the books in the women's quarters were written.

I had assumed that all men could read eonmun. Elder Brother clearly could. Whenever he left home for even just a few days, he would write love letters in eonmun to his wife. But I had never seen Father read or write anything in it. Until now, I had assumed that this was simply because he disdained novels and other eonmun works as writing fit only for women, but in fact he simply could not read the script.

My shaking hands flipped page after page of Elder Sister's book. The content grew more bizarre the further I got. The book had started out as a compendium of home remedies. But gradually, curious asides began to interrupt the introductions to berries and herbs, and by the halfway point, the book had turned into a disorganized encyclopedia of the strange. No wonder I had never seen the book before. It was nothing more than the ramblings of a crazy old hag.

About three-quarters of the way in, I found what Father must have been looking for. A passage began with, "In the kingdom called Burma can be found human-eating monsters who are unable to tolerate the sunlight. Though once people, they became monsters after consuming an improperly prepared concoction of the boa-root medicine of immortality. To treat them,..."

I stopped. Father stamped his feet and urged me to keep reading. Elder Brother moved his lips soundlessly from where he lay fallen on the floor, a pleading look on his face.

Now I understood. The household had always been proud of

its thousands of books, but the truly special books were the ones in the women's quarters, specifically in Elder Sister's room. Elder Brother, ever the devoted husband, had read his way through most of them, which is how he had found the book detailing the effects of the boa-root. Yet, he had thoughtlessly skipped over the page about the root's side effects and how to treat them. Only now, long after most of the household had turned into vampires, had he gone back to read it.

I do not know what had transpired between Father and Elder Brother. But I knew one thing for certain: I held in my hands the key to Father's plan. If I read him the information on that page, Father would conquer Joseon with a group of immortal and sunlight-immune vampires. The treatment for their condition was, moreover, absurdly simple, but I would not in a million years dream of revealing its details here.

I sunk deep into my thoughts. Until now my hands had been tied by concerns for the twins' safety. I had been letting those concerns dictate my course of action. However, it was imperative that I now look at the big picture. Giving Father the treatment information would indeed guarantee safety for the twins and me, because as soon as the vampires were cured of their sunlight allergy, they would no longer need us as hostages. Nor could they feed on us: we were immune. And yet, what would happen if the vampires conquered Joseon? I had never considered that possibility before. I had always viewed the vampires as dangerous but somewhat pathetic beings. Were they to gain immunity to sunlight, however, they would become far more dangerous.

I tried to imagine a world in which Father's plan succeeded. Joseon would become incredibly powerful. It might even conquer the whole world. What would happen if this unknown country nestled next to China were to become the center of world power? It was an enticing possibility to many in Joseon, and for a time to me as well.

It was not what I wanted, though. I did not wish to see Joseon values and Joseon culture conquer the world. My skin crawled at the thought of a ruling class forever made of men like Father and my brothers. Some worlds are fated to die and do not need to be saved.

I tore out the page about the boa-root and touched it to the flame of the lamp before Father had a chance to react. It took only an instant for the page to burn to ash. Now the secret of the boa-root existed only in the heads of Elder Brother and me.

Father shrieked. He stamped his feet some more, growled, and waved his sword over the twins' heads in an attempt to intimidate me. He soon realized his threats would not work and turned instead to the art of persuasion.

What followed was an eloquent speech. Or at least that is how I remember it. Father managed to flawlessly compress his philosophy into succinct sentences that built up into a tempting proposition. The amount of flattery he squeezed into his words was truly astounding. But I should not have been surprised. Where else could Second Brother's political acumen have come from?

I was not persuaded. I did not even listen to the second half of his speech. I merely nodded along, pretending to listen while I waited for an opening. When Father began to wrap up a beautifully-told tale based on an ancient Chinese fable, I pulled the knife out of my sleeve and stabbed him in the left eye. He screamed and clutched at his face, and the sword he had been holding fell to the floor.

I picked up Father's sword and ran to Elder Brother. Seeing me, he closed his eyes and clenched his left hand. I hesitated for a moment before dropping to my knees and chopping at his throat with the sword. It only took two cuts to sever Elder Brother's head, which then wobbled across the floor toward Father. The old man looked at it, momentarily uncomprehending, then stamped down. The head exploded like a watermelon. No longer showing any sign of reason, the old man paused there with his left foot soaking in the smashed brains of his son. A single blow from my sword severed his head and both hands, which were still brandishing my knife. His head fell backward onto the straw matting. I recall saying something like the following to his head as the remaining eye continued to glare at me: "The problem is, Father, I could not understand a word of what you were saying."

I ran over to the corner of the room where the twins were still crying and unbound them. Though exhausted and shaking from fright, they were uninjured. They seemed to have been fed enough and were not emaciated. We still had to figure out how to escape from the vampires-turned-monsters on the other side of the door, but at least I was now free of the heaviest of the burdens I had been carrying on my shoulders.

As we prepared to leave the storeroom, I heard a familiar voice from outside. The first time the voice spoke it sounded hesitant, but when it repeated itself, it was filled with confidence and authority.

"Open up!"

The officer had finally arrived.

10

I still wonder how the officer spent that day. He arrived at our household at the hour of sulsi, which is seven to nine in the evening according to Western time. He would have needed four or five hours to gather his subordinates and travel to the compound. Earlier that day I had cursed him as a lazy coward, but considering the distance involved, he had in fact moved with surprising speed. That he brought with him so many armed troopers showed that he had managed to convince his superiors of the seriousness of the situation. He was competent in addition to being quick.

Not that the extra men were of any help.

After ordering us out a fifth time, the men outside of the compound fell silent. The men had stilled their horses and were straining to listen for noises inside the compound.

I was about to call out when I noticed two black shadows peek over the compound wall. The night was dark, and even from that position the police would not have been able to clearly see what was happening in the yard. But, at the very least, they would have made out that people were moving around on top of corpses and doing something to them.

Moments after the shadowy forms disappeared from the wall, cries rose from outside the compound and the gate began to quiver and creak. Several minutes later the bolt snapped and the gate opened. That was the last time I ever heard the unpleasant squeak of the compound gate.

The officer dismounted from his horse and entered the compound with torch-wielding troopers at his sides. The people inside hesitated for a moment, confused, then lunged at the intruders as if they were hunting dogs who had just heard a whistled command to attack. Gunshots rang out.

Spears flickered in the torchlight. Blood and screams flew through the air.

I wanted to run, but it looked like we would not be able to break out through the main entrance. The slightest misstep could get us mistaken for the enemy and killed. I wanted to explain to the police what was happening, but I never got the chance.

One of the troopers tottered in our direction. We started toward him to ask for help but recoiled when we saw blood spurting from his left shoulder. His face held the same vacant, beastly expression as the other occupants of the compound. He had been infected.

Gripping my sword in my right hand and a torch picked off the ground in my left, I ran with the twins into the men's quarters. I set fire to the door, screens, and books. As soon as the beams caught fire, I ran to the main building and set it alight as well. Finally, I dropped my lit torch into the open coffin where Mother still lay breathing heavily in her comatose state. What I did certainly cannot be called euthanasia, but someone had to end that dreadful existence.

When I at last arrived in the main hall, the first thing I saw was Third Sister crawling toward me on her hands and knees. She was groaning. A long sticky streak of blood trailed behind her. Her belly, which until yesterday had been mountainous, was now deflated. Looking past her to the room she had just exited, I saw a creature about the size of a dog drop wetly to the floor and bound off into the darkness. I would rather not say what it was.

The twins and I ran to our quarters. I strapped on the pack I had prepared a month earlier for precisely this occasion, then the three of us climbed over the compound wall. The twins had no more difficulty in crossing the wall than I, for ramps of earth and straw matting had been built on both sides to facilitate the disposal of corpses.

We followed the base of the hill in the direction of the village. We had to warn all the neighboring villagers. I had thus far managed to spare these people by feeding vagrants to the vampires in their stead. Perhaps they would get lucky and the police would finish off all the vampires at the compound. But maybe not. The least I could do was warn the villagers to prepare.

Language was a problem. How could I describe the monsters to these villagers? They were not even vampires anymore. Even now I do not have a good word for them. Ghouls? I have read Galland's *One Thousand and One Nights*, but its description of ghouls does not quite fit. What I faced were living corpses that ate people and infected their victims, turning them into fellow monsters. Is there any word for such creatures?

The more serious problem was that most of the monsters were yangban. How could I convince the villagers to stand up to yangban? Supposing they fought and managed to kill all the monsters, how could they later justify their actions to others?

"Ma'am, what is happening?"

Someone called out to me. I turned to see an old slave from a neighboring yangban household whose master had become a guest in our household just a few days earlier. Worried by the flames and noise coming from the house where his master now lived, he had come out to see what was going on. There was a crowd of people surrounding the compound now, though no one made a move. They had come to help with the fire, but the unusual sounds coming from inside had given them pause.

That is when I noticed another familiar face among those watching the fire. It was the daughter of one of the nearby tenant farmers. She was nearly fourteen and very pretty. This was the girl that Third Brother had repeatedly asked me to bring to him as food. Her face glowed brightly in the light of the flames coming through the main gate of the compound.

Realizing the danger she was in, I placed myself between her and the compound and readied my sword. I was just in time. A dark, fat shape ran out of the compound toward us. I cut through its neck as it stretched a sticky right hand out toward the girl's carefully braided hair. The headless body tottered and fell sideways, spraying foul-smelling black blood on the hem of my dress. I looked down and saw Third Brother's head had broken through a thin layer of ice and lay trapped at an awkward angle in the mud beneath. His round face gazed idiotically up at the space between me and the girl.

"Monsters! Arm yourselves! Run!"

The officer screamed at the crowd as he ran out of the main gate chased by two monsters who had until just moments before been his subordinates. He did not have the presence of mind to realize that his two orders contradicted each other, but it did not matter. The villagers, having just witnessed the scene, understood immediately what he meant. They all ran. A few soon returned carrying farm implements to use as weapons.

I do not know how many of the villagers survived, how many became monsters, and how many died. While they fought, I was busy gathering women and children to lead to safety. I considered joining in the fight against the monsters, but in retrospect, I am confident I made the correct choice.

The monsters were a plague. Had I joined in the fight without proper preparations, I might have ended up further increasing their numbers. By then, at least half of the officer's troops had already been killed or infected, and the situation was getting worse. It was not a time for throwing the dice. Saving people had to be my priority.

The sky was brightening by the time we finally arrived at the village on the other side of the hills. Only one of my group died. She was an old woman with bad legs, and had been bitten in the arm and neck by two monsters who had followed us. I had been forced to behead the old woman as well as the monsters. Thankfully, no one questioned me about it. They had seen her begin to change.

I told the chief of the neighboring village the whole story and entrusted my group to his care. I do not think he really understood. I hoped that the officer had survived the night. If not, perhaps a few yangban whom Father had not yet turned would survive and explain to the officials what had happened. Otherwise, the whole incident was liable to be misconstrued as a peasant revolt.

The twins and I slipped away as the villagers busied themselves preparing breakfast for their exhausted guests. We still had plenty of energy, and I had no intention of entrusting my fate to the Joseon justice system. How could I possibly explain my situation to them? I was not innocent by any standard.

My destination was the sea. I intended to find a ship that could take us away from Joseon. The gold I had stolen from Mother and now carried in my pack would buy us passage.

It was not until evening that we found a small, dilapidated inn devoid of visitors where we could spend the night. The twins fell asleep as soon as they lay down in our corner room, but sleep did not come to me. I sensed someone watching us from outside the inn, and thought I heard faraway sounds that could have been the death cries of people or the howls of beasts.

We resumed walking at the break of dawn. I had no idea which road to take or where I might find a port. I knew that the sea was to the west, but I was not always sure where west was. Clouds obscured the sun that day, and it was at times impossible to confirm our heading.

And someone was following us the whole way.

We arrived at the sea on the afternoon of the third day. The coast was a vast expanse of mud, with no sign of people anywhere. We started to make our way south, thinking that we would eventually run into a village or port.

When the dim sun sank beneath the horizon, the world instantly went dark. I pulled my sword from the cloth wrappings on my back. I knew the thing that had been following us would now attack.

The creature jumped out from where it had been hiding in the brush at the edge of the mud. It bounded on all fours like a wolf at first, then rose to run on two legs. Its skin was blackened as if by fire, and its head and facial hair had also been burnt away. What little clothing had survived the flames barely held together.

Ignoring the twins, the monster ran straight for me. I swung at its neck as it neared me, but one of my feet sunk into the mud and I missed. The monster knocked me to the ground and attempted to bite my neck. I kept hold of my sword as we struggled, but was unable to bring it into position to take off the monster's head.

Suddenly the monster screamed and fell on its side. One

of the twins had dropped a small boulder on its head. In the ensuing confusion, I stood up and tried once more to stab the monster, but it grabbed my foot and knocked me down again. I lost my grip on the sword and it fell to the side. The thing pressed its two hands into my breast and bared a mouth full of yellow teeth. I saw a half-broken fang hanging from the upper-left side of its jaw.

A gunshot rang out and a small hole appeared in the monster's blackened forehead. The thing reached up and touched the wound, uncomprehending, and collapsed sideways. I grabbed my sword and cut through its neck. The severed head rolled down toward the sea. In the instant before it disappeared into the water, the head hit a rock and bounced up into the air, giving me a momentary glimpse of Second Brother's face.

The twins shouted and pointed toward the sea. A large and strange trident-shaped ship floated there not far from the shore. I saw a burly man approaching us with a rifle. He was clean-shaven and wore a black hat over his curly light hair.

The man's name was Patrick Brody, and he was second mate of the Mary Embry, a clipper belonging to Robertson & Company. The ill-fated ship had set sail from Hong Kong to Singapore several days earlier, but a mutiny had brought it far off course, into the Joseon sea.

11

The twins and I were given free passage on the Mary Embry. Having just suppressed the mutiny, Brody and his crew had only come ashore to replenish their stock of fresh water, but we put them in a difficult position. Confronted with native girls who sat in their boat and refused to leave, what could they do but take us on as passengers? They did not know there were no more monsters on the shore.

When we arrived in Singapore, we were sent to the missionary husband and wife, William and Charlotte Bunbury. I tried to explain to them what had happened to us in our village, but it was not easy. I had thought we might be able to communicate in writing through a Chinese interpreter they brought over, but the interpreter did not even know the meaning of the characters for yangban, which was to me the most basic of written words. Unable to convey my meaning in words, I attempted to relate my story through a series of several dozen drawings. The husband and wife liked these drawings, but neither believed nor understood them.

I studied English frantically, devoting all my time and energy to the language. A year later, I could speak it fluently, but still no one believed my story. I gave up and instead began to draw my special pictures of pretty women. These sold well. When people grew curious about the origins of my style, I showed them the miniature portrait I still kept in a locket around my neck.

The Bunburys died of cholera in 1858 and the twins and I inherited most of the wealth they had accumulated in Singapore. We took the money and left for Malacca. After six years there, we went to Hanoi, then Phnom Penh, then Manila, then Hong Kong, staying a dozen or more years in each place. In 1932 we went to Honolulu. I left the twins two years ago, for reasons I cannot share with you here, and passed through the American mainland on my way to this country. It was my first time seeing snow in one hundred years.

Over the decades, I have learned English, French, Vietnamese, Cantonese, and Pekingese. Every thirty-one years

I shed my skin, and every twenty-nine years I grow new teeth. The twins and I still look as if we are in our twenties or thirties, and most Westerners think we are even younger. Whatever was in those scraps of root we ate over a hundred years ago has survived across time and still lives inside our bodies.

I have written down my experience multiple times in every language I know. I wrote it as a memoir the first time, and thereafter as fiction. I tried out many styles, each retelling becoming more and more imaginative. The first fictionalization was a gothic tale imitating Ann Radcliffe. The most recent one was a horror story overflowing with bloody adjectives in the style of *Weird Tales*. None of my accounts have been published; I never even tried to publish them. Who these days would be interested in something that happened in old Joseon?

I cannot guarantee the accuracy of the memoir you have just read. When I left Singapore, I lost the original memoir that I had written in the Joseon language, and my memories have gradually grown to resemble the tales I have written since. I no longer even feel like I am from Joseon. Joseon is the least proficient of my languages. I cannot read books in it anymore. I do not know the words Joseon people use for airplanes, communism, chocolate, or radioisotopes.

I still dream about what I experienced there, but these days my dreams take place in a monochrome Western mansion, like those built in the sound stages at Universal Studios, and the characters all have the faces of Hollywood stars. Perhaps I should write a movie script of my story adapted to a Western setting and sell it to Hollywood. I want to be played by Joan Fontaine. The day I arrived in this city, I saw Hitchcock's

Rebecca at the Eglinton Theatre.

Yet, I doubt Hollywood will ever be ready to depict the truth of the cruelty and inhumanity I experienced over a century ago.

PENTAGON

1

Corpses are just clumps of rotting protein. See them often enough and you get used to them. This is especially true for those of us in the profession. It doesn't matter what kind of shape a corpse might be in, it's just not going to faze us. Have you ever seen a body that's been flattened? I have. It was my last murder. I pulled him out of the industrial press and polished off a cucumber sandwich while searching the pockets of his mangled remains. Don't get me wrong; I'm not telling you this in order to brag. I'm just trying to explain the mindset that comes with the work I do.

Yet, I had difficulty remaining calm or objective when I saw the corpse of Kim Wu-sik. A heat gun had penetrated Kim's head and chest, leaving only a tiny hole in each. His corpse was so neat and tidy it should have been entered into a beauty contest for morticians. I hadn't even known him that long, but I guess there are always exceptions to every rule.

Department Head Choi sent the reporters and members of the Integrated Police Force away into the conference room before starting to debrief us.

"Kim Wu-sik died approximately thirty minutes ago," he began. "He was struck twice from the front as he was turning around, probably just as he was getting coffee from the hallway vending machine. No one witnessed the hit, and there are no CCTV cameras in this area. It's a total blind spot. I trained you well, that's for sure.

"The doctor was killed in his office, most likely while trying to stop her from escaping. She shot him in the head and chest also. No, there's no need to go in there to see for yourselves. He's already been carted away. But I've got the photo that bitch left pinned to his chest."

He pulled out a two-dimensional printout of a black and white photograph. Though slightly out of focus, it showed the corpses of five children who'd burned to death in a factory in Jin-am. It was a terrible accident, but it hadn't really been our fault. Anyone else in that situation would have done the same.

"Something similar was found on Kim Wu-sik's corpse. As if she were preaching to us. But why? Why is she suddenly doing this?"

He turned to look at us, his voice getting louder. His question was clearly not meant to be rhetorical. Someone had to volunteer an answer. I cleared my throat.

"We're not sure. She did suffer more surgical trauma than the rest of us. Perhaps that's what's behind all this?"

"Surgical trauma? Are you kidding me? Trauma is what caused that bitch to start shooting holes in the heads of her teammates? Right after we spent so much money bringing her back from the dead? What kind of trauma causes that?"

I didn't have an answer. Fortunately, before he could start in on me again, Dr. Pavel Zaminov appeared in the hall like a messiah.

"The IPF are throwing around blame again," Zaminov said, "Go talk to them. I don't have time to deal with idiots like that. Why haven't you kicked them out yet?"

Choi swallowed a curse and followed Zaminov into the conference room. The door wasn't fully closed, so we could still hear Choi's voice. At a loss for what to do, I sat down on a bench. I looked down and saw a drop of saliva suspended from Kim Wu-sik's open lips. I closed my eyes.

The argument between Choi and the IPF heated up. The IPF wouldn't cede their jurisdiction over the investigation no matter what Choi did. Once they started nosing around on their own, it wouldn't be long before their communications networks distributed the following intel:

> *Name:* Nguyen Tu Le
> *Age:* 32
> *Height:* 158cm
> *Occupation:* Preschool teacher
> *Weapon:* Heat gun.
> *Wanted for:* The murders of Kang Mun-gu, neurosurgeon at Uicheon City Hospital, and Kim Wu-sik, third secretary of Foreign Affairs. Committed the crimes while hospitalized following a car accident. Fled the scene.

A smile appeared on my face. That bullshit wouldn't convince anyone. No matter how dumb the IPF was, there was no way they weren't going to find this suspicious. Damn. Damn Choi, damn the Politburo, damn Nguyen, damn the Pentagon Plan, and damn Lazarus Kolton.

2

Nguyen Tu Le was small, thin, and somewhat shabby-looking. Whenever she tried to form our usual wide grin, her small mouth would get stuck halfway. Her ill-fitting hospital gown made her look even more tiny and helpless.

After the surgery, she was kept away from the rest of us. When they brought all five of us together in one room so we could meet one another, you can imagine how surprised we were at the sight of her. Disgusted, really—that was our initial reaction.

"Must be hard to piss." Mikhail Perelman snickered. He'd already begun to speak with a fake Russian accent. It was a stupid pretense. He didn't know any more Russian than the rest of us.

I had no idea what Choi and the others were hoping to learn from us. We all knew quite a lot, but we didn't know what any of it meant.

They forced us to keep talking. Judging by the number of times they asked the question, what seemed to interest them most was the final accident that pinned us under the burning roof. But we couldn't be certain—they had no reason to show us their cards so easily. Perhaps that was just what they wanted us to think.

Ahn Jae-ho talked the most. That guy would open his mouth at the drop of a hat and never shut up. It was as if all the energy that should have gone to his two amputated arms had instead been rerouted to the tip of his tongue. In the right setting, I could be fairly talkative, too. But whenever I felt the slightest inclination to speak, he would beat me to the punch. I didn't like him. Mostly because he was always imitating the way I speak, but also because he would inevitably spill small, private secrets we wanted to keep hidden. He was like a tape player we couldn't shut off.

Our examiners were unfailingly polite. They always referred to us formally as "Mr. Ahn" and "Mr. Perelman" as if we were meeting for the first time. "So, Mr. Perelman, let's talk about the oil tanker explosion last April... Mr. Kim, which employees of your former syndicate do not appear in this photograph? Mr. Yoon, did you see a light on the second floor of the building when the final accident occurred? Wait, please, Mr. Ahn, I'd like to hear what Mr. Yoon has to say about this...."

Sometimes Nguyen would pipe up in her clear, slightly wavering voice. Unlike Perelman, she didn't try to fake an accent. Nor did she pretend, like Ahn Jae-ho, that nothing out of the ordinary had happened. She talked simply and naturally, without pretense. Mostly she confirmed what Ahn Jae-ho and the others had been saying. But sometimes she raised her voice. When Ahn Jae-ho proudly recalled the time he'd killed Edgar Chen from the Basic Human Rights Commission, she sprang out of her seat and cried out:

"That's all wrong! Why can't you tell the story straight? You shot that guy the instant he walked out of the factory! Did you ever even consider talking to him? We shot him like a dog."

I was shocked, not because she had shattered our professional dignity, but because she had addressed Ahn Jae-ho directly as "you." By the end of her little outburst, she had switched back to "we" again, but it was clear that she had decided to pull a Pontius Pilate and was washing her hands of everything that had happened in the past. It was as if she were telling our inquisitors: "Look, I'm not to blame for all that."

One week later, she shot the doctor and Kim Wu-sik full of holes and fled the hospital.

3

Try as they might, neither the IPF nor the Politburo were able to find Nguyen. The radio chip she'd been implanted with was discovered in a sewer near the Dudinstev Theater. Extracting it must have left a sizable wound in her left arm. Not that this piece of information helped them in any way. The methods used by the police and Politburo are glaringly obvious to those of us who've plied our trade for sixteen years. If I'd been the one to escape from the hospital with about a thousand credits in cash and a charged heat gun, I would've slipped silently into the cracks of Uicheon and found a comfortable place where I could hibernate like a dormouse. The pursuers are always at a disadvantage in such games.

In the end, we were not released from the hospital. They said it was because we were still suffering from unforeseen aftereffects of our surgery. But they tightened their surveillance and reduced our unsupervised free time. If the three of us that remained even so much as gathered in the same room, our pagers would instantly ring.

Guilt by association, that's what it was. All the trust we had built up over sixteen years of loyal work collapsed the instant Nguyen murdered those two. If she was capable of going off script like that, so were we. The integrity we had shown over the years no longer mattered.

"Why do you think she did it?" Perelman whispered to Ahn and me at lunchtime. One of our guards had just left. The other was still there, but a bit too far away to restrain us without being obvious about it. They were still trying to be discreet about the new restrictions placed on us.

"She hated us," I replied. "We're evil, we cheat, we help murderers, and we're horrible racists. The world would better off without us."

"Hah. And she thinks she was better?" Ahn Jae-ho waved his prosthetic hands in protest.

"She probably does," I replied. "Two months is a long time. Long enough for a person to change from head to toe. Maybe she changed while we didn't. Well, we changed, too, but not as much. I hate my work, too, just not as much she does. Anyways, I've already given these people all the information I'm ever going to. As soon as I can get my affairs in order, I plan to find some way to quit. Not that I'll be able to run very far with this fat body of mine."

There must have been a note of exasperation in my voice because Perelman and Ahn frowned, unhappy. But I didn't bother listening to whatever they were saying. Instead, I thought about retiring and about the absent escapee, Nguyen. These thoughts were interrupted by a sudden summons and we were led back to our isolation rooms.

The questions became more direct after Nguyen's escape. They began: "If you were her..." Our examiners wanted us to tell them how she might have escaped and where she might be hiding. Now they gave us more information about what had happened, and forced us to think and talk like her.

Our examiners became more aggressive in their questioning, and a rougher group from the Politburo joined in as well. They dropped the courtesies and formalities.

"Okay, let's go over it again," Department Head Choi spat out while glaring at us from between his propped-up feet. "You all agree that she's not likely to leave the city. You also agree that she is probably planning to retaliate against the Politburo. Then what? Perelman thinks she's going to spill everything she knows to the Unity Government or the media.

But there are no signs thus far that any of our secrets have been leaked. Ahn thinks she's looking for revenge–direct, physical revenge. But he has no idea how she's going to go about it. Yoon, you think she'll stay hidden and wait for us to abandon the search. But we've already looked in all the hiding places you've suggested. Did you all really used to work together?"

I shrugged. "She knows what we know. She also knows that the Politburo is getting information from us. She would have taken all of this into consideration before escaping. With all due respect, sir, sitting here and chastising us is not going to change the situation. We don't have a telepathic connection to her. All of us have changed a lot over the past two months, and she barely ever revealed her true self to us. Besides, even if we did have access to all her thoughts, how would that help when we don't have a good grasp of the situation out there on the ground..."

"What are you trying to say?"

"Maybe we should go out and search for her ourselves."

This really was the best plan given the situation at hand, but Choi and his Politburo pals wouldn't buy it. After a loud argument, they rejected our suggestion and gave us a new problem and various experiments to work on instead. Perhaps I shouldn't have mentioned telepathy. Two of the researchers were obviously parapsychologists.

"What is this, an exorcism?!" Dr. Zaminov complained. He protested to the Politburo, but they didn't listen.

The "exorcism" ended sooner than expected. Seventy-six hours after Nguyen had escaped, the IPF had a lead on her whereabouts. A woman fitting her description and sharing some of her movement patterns had been caught on camera near a building in District 24 North. Her half-exposed left arm was tightly wrapped in a compression bandage. She was rusty. For her to be exposed that quickly meant her skills must have deteriorated over the last two months.

That lead didn't result in her capture, though. By the time the IPF broke into the building, she was long gone. Moreover, because the IPF had successfully tracked her down first, before the Politburo got involved, we lost all our remaining value. We were no longer simply untrustworthy, we were now useless as well.

So they put us back into solitary confinement. I actually preferred this to the pathetic pretense that we hadn't been their prisoners for the past months. It was hilarious, really. I couldn't help a snort of laughter. They had saved us from death? For this?

When Dr. Zaminov entered my room, I had been comfortably settled for a while watching black and white movies from the previous century on a monitor squeezed into one corner of my cell. A tall woman with a round face was pointing a gun at the bartender and demanding a passport or something like that in old fashioned English. I wasn't sure who was the bad guy because I'd started the movie in the middle.

I never got the chance to find out. Dr. Zaminov turned off the monitor, pulled up a chair, and sat down.

"Shall we talk?" he asked.

"What's there to talk about? I've already heard enough excuses."

"Excuses? I haven't made any excuses. All I've done is explain the situation to you. I'm the one who saved your life. Do you have any idea what you looked like when you first got here? You were a charred 32-kilogram lump of meat. Shouldn't you at least say thank you to the person who was able to bring you back from something like that?"

"I would be thankful if you had saved me from dying. But I was already dead by then. Am I supposed to be thankful that, instead of letting me stay dead, you forcefully implanted me into this ridiculous body?"

"Yes. You should thank me because if you had died, you would have gone straight to hell."

"Since when have you ever believed in an afterlife?"

Zaminov seemed to lose interest in our war of words. "It's the idiots at the Politburo who are responsible for the state you're in. I warned them when they first implemented the Pentagon plan. Those fools think people are just pieces of hardware and software. If the hardware breaks, rip out the software and implant it in new hardware. But that's not how all this really works. Hardware and software are always interdependent. Those Politburo imbeciles underestimated the influence the body has on the mind. You could say that's why Nguyen did what she did. Did you know she's pregnant?"

I snickered, which might have been what caused Zaminov's face to wrinkle in disgust.

"I'm not joking," he insisted. "She's ten weeks pregnant. She diagnosed herself ten days before escaping, but we didn't find out until yesterday. Pregnancy is a big deal, especially for someone who used to be a man. It must have been quite a shock to her. A little while ago, I ran the simulation of Nguyen's actions again using this new data. What Nguyen actually did was nothing compared to what the computer says she might be capable of. The rest of you have it easier...."

"So what? Are you really going to tell Choi that Nguyen acted the way she did because she's pregnant? Do you think that's going to make him let the rest of us go? Are any of us better off than her? Perelman turned into a ridiculous Russian, Ahn has no arms, and look at me... Hah! Do you have any idea how shocked I was when I woke up? I never imagined a human could be so obese, least of all myself!"

"You're not that fat."

"Whatever. I'm definitely fat enough that I'd rather die again than be stuck in this body."

"Do you know how hard it is to procure brain-dead corpses? Do you think we just pick them up from 24-hour convenience stores? If we had a choice, do you think we wouldn't have chosen better looking bodies? We did the best we could! They could have been so much worse! Just lose the fat and you'll be fine! Even attaching new arms to Ahn isn't a problem."

"Just lose weight and I'll be fine? Sure. And how are you planning on compensating me for having turned my life upside-down? Not once have I ever questioned my work. But now every time I close my eyes, my mind seethes like a bathtub full of dry ice."

"Don't blame anyone else for that. The mental upset is probably due to memories that were left out during the transfer process. That's something that happens even to people who haven't had surgery."

Zaminov stood up and straightened his body. "Please calm down. I came here to ask for help. Ever since Lazarus Kolton died, I've been struggling to figure out how to carry out the Pentagon Plan. It doesn't matter that you belong in hell. I just couldn't let the opportunity to do this experiment slip away. I have to do whatever I can to keep you all alive until I've gathered enough data. I can't just feed you to the Politburo. Trust me, I'll figure out some way to hold them off. Please loosen up and try working proactively with the Politburo. You've been too uncooperative thus far. Choi says that if you'd tried harder, you'd have known that Nguyen would be hiding in that prefab building. Why didn't you just tell them everything you knew?"

"We had no idea that place existed. It must have been left out of the memory transfer process."

"Okay, okay," Zaminov conceded. "I need to go now and meet with the others. In the meantime, please reconsider your position."

4

That night I had a dream that I'd had fifteen times over the past two months. In it, my body sank slowly into a gelatinous and sticky red sea. The further I sank, the harder it was to breathe. I felt the pressure increasing and tried to scream, but sticky liquid clogged my throat. Previously, that's when I had woken up. This time, however, the dream continued. The water filling my throat began to solidify. Then, inexplicably, I felt it tap against my body.

I woke up gasping. Ahn had climbed on top of me and was blocking my mouth with his prosthetic arm, a frightened expression on his face.

"Quiet!" he spat out in a hoarse whisper.

I nodded and sat up as he quietly slid off my bed to the floor. Neither of us made a sound. Outside the room, however, it was louder than Beijing International Airport. I heard sirens, phones, and people running through the hallways.

"What's going on?" I mouthed the words silently.

"Nguyen," he replied in the same way.

"What?"

"She came back, and not just to say hi either. She split the skulls of Choi and Perelman, and then disappeared again."

My throat suddenly tightened. "Perelman's dead too?"

Ahn nodded. "She was targeting Perelman all along. You remember that video of her from the District 24 North building? Well, apparently it was all a trick, but the IPF and Politburo used it to update the profile of her movement patterns and appearance and then combed Uicheon thinking they'd catch her there. Meanwhile, she dressed up as a nurse, came back to the hospital, and *BAM!* cut Perelman's brain out of his head. That dumb-ass Choi happened to be in Perelman's room at the time, so he got the same treatment. She even left another copy of that photograph. If she'd been able to disable the alarm for a bit longer, we would have died, too!"

Had he been speaking out loud, I would barely have been able to understand him. He was quaking like an aspen. Suddenly I noticed the small shock pistol in his prosthetic hand.

"How'd you even get in here?" I asked.

"The doctor opened my room. He's been trying to save our lives. He disabled the floor alarm and gave me the code to your room. I'm not sure how he learned it. The gun I stole from Choi. He didn't know that I figured out his personal code yesterday. I have a shock pistol for you, too. Here. Hurry up and get dressed."

"Why?"

"Why? Can't you see what's going to happen to us if we stay here? Do you really think the Politburo is going to let us go? Why would they let us live? They've already pumped out whatever information they were hoping to get from us, and now we're useless to them... Didn't you always dream of being important? Well, congratulations. You and I are now both incredibly important. The information in our heads is dynamite, and all we'd have to do to set it off is talk. If we went over to the Syndicate or Unity Government, there'd be trouble at the Politburo. They won't risk it."

"What are you saying we should do? Leave the city?"

"There's a better way. We need to find Nguyen before the Politburo does."

"Are you crazy? You want me to run in this body? No thanks. Besides, Zaminov has no choice but to keep us alive. The fact that she's preg..."

"The doctor can't stop the Politburo from killing us. As for going to the Syndicate, that's ridiculous. It doesn't matter what we give them, they're never going to forgive us. And you know just as well as I do that the Unity Government can't be trusted. The Politburo is the only faction we can depend on. So we catch her and hand her over to them. It's not impossible. For starters, we're in a better position to find her than anyone else. Besides, she's only just left the hospital. This is our chance. So come on. Please. Maybe you think it'd be easier to just die, but I don't want to die. And there's no way I can catch her without you. These stupid mechanical hands don't do anything I tell them to."

"But how do we get out of here?"

Ahn clucked in exasperation. "Right now, the hospital is half-blind. Nguyen shut off the central computer sensors when she came in. And the doctor and I have already taken care of the alarms on this floor. We can get out if we hurry. Are you getting up or not?"

Moving quickly but awkwardly, he collected my clothing for me with his creaking prosthetic hands. I pulled my heavy body up with some difficulty, got into the clothing he tossed to me, and pulled on my shoes. As soon as I was ready, he put his eye to the small glass peephole in the door and looked out. Apparently, he deemed it safe enough. He opened the door and gave me the signal to move.

We must have looked like geriatric Boy Scouts as we moved clumsily through the corridor. Ahn's prosthetics creaked every time he moved his body, so he wound up pulling off his left hand and shoving it into his coat pocket.

Our new bodies were sloppy and tottering, but at least they did what we asked of them. Thanks to the disabled security system, we were able to make our way into the closest stairwell without being detected. We ran down the stairs, ignoring the security cameras on each landing. When we arrived at the basement, we followed the laundry chute and hid ourselves between dusty boxes on a transport conveyor. Then we waited. I couldn't help but wonder who'd cooked up this crazy plan, Ahn or Zaminov.

We took advantage of an opening at the transport conveyor's second node to jump over to the hospital trash conveyor, and then managed to hop off that conveyor only moments before all the garbage fell into a high-pressure transport pipe. I took a look around while trying to catch my breath. We'd been deposited in the City Sanitation Department's Comprehensive Trash Center #224, which was about a kilometer from the hospital. I struggled to gain control of my trembling legs, and then followed Ahn out.

The stench of morning trash filling my lungs was a welcome change from the hospital sanitizer I'd been inhaling non-stop for the past two months. My overweight body meant that even a short walk left me panting, but I worked diligently to keep up with Ahn.

"How did Nguyen get out that first time? She went through the sewer, right? But that's been blocked off now. Any idea how she got out this time?" I asked Ahn, almost completely out of breath. We'd reached the first intersection of District 12 South.

"She used the sewer again. She's just thumbing her nose at everyone. She had a tool to get through the barrier placed there by the inspectors. It's a solid lead for us to follow. Don't you remember?

"What?"

"Those barrier neutralizers aren't something anyone can just make themselves. But she left the hospital with only 2000 credits and couldn't possibly have bought one. So how did she do it?"

I knew what he was thinking. It was something I'd guessed on some level even before escaping from the hospital.

The doctor had been right. We hadn't told our interrogators everything. We definitely weren't entirely honest agents. For instance, instead of handing particularly effective weapons over to the Politburo, we'd hidden them away and done deals on the black market. Even talkative Ahn had kept his mouth shut about this side hustle of ours. We'd never really dealt with neutralizers, but they were easy enough to cobble together using parts from the weapons we'd stored away. Nguyen must have made a visit to our secret warehouse.

"She won't be there now, though," I said with some effort.

"Whether she's there or not, the warehouse should probably be our first stop. We're already at the corner of the first intersection of District 12 South. From here, it's just a ten-minute walk."

Ahn took the prosthetic hand out of his pocket and reattached it to his left arm. He opened and closed both hands. Smiling goofily at me, he said: "Thanks for coming with me. I was worried you might not come."

"Why would you think that?"

"Because we've changed so much. Ever since that damned surgery, our whole world's been turned upside-down.

Ahn continued to blather on about our surgery as we climbed to the top floor of the seven-story building where our warehouse was located. Only when we got to the door of our warehouse did he finally stop chattering.

We hesitated for a while before trying the lock. The code hadn't been changed. We opened the door and went in. Piles of junk were scattered everywhere, but there was no one there. Ahn was right, though: someone had visited the place. There was an indentation in the cot in the corner, and several boxes had been opened. Nguyen must have slept here for a day or two.

"She's rusty," Ahn complained. "Look at how she opened this box. She ruined these perfectly good parts. Two months of rest and she's already this out of practice?"

"It's not just two months of rest. Her body isn't listening to her. And it's not just her body either. Think of how hard it was for us to get here in our new bodies. We just ran here like kids playing detective games, breaking all the rules. All of us are rusty. We're not who we used to be."

A dull clang drowned out my sigh. The middle part of Ahn's right prosthetic hand had fallen onto the metal floor. As he bent over to pick it up, his belly shifted forward and he lost his balance and fell to the ground. Because he had no way to catch himself, he rolled like a log all the way to the wall, where he lay giggling. The sound of his laughter mixed with a strange groaning noise, then both faded and he went quiet. I got a blanket from the corner and covered him. I didn't dare move him onto the cot. I collected some felt fabric from one of the boxes, threw it onto the cot for myself, and burrowed inside. It creaked under my weight.

As I warmed up, my head grew clearer. Instead of falling asleep, I stared at the ceiling and tried to figure out what was wrong. The answer came to me before I could even count to five. I sprang off the bed, rushed over to Ahn, and shook him awake.

"Get up! Quick!" I said.

Ahn rubbed his eyes with his good prosthetic and looked up at me. I continued to talk as I grabbed him and pulled him up.

"We're such idiots! Nguyen fed the IPF a fake file! She's meticulous enough to have been planning this for a long time—isn't it possible that she used a neutralizer on purpose in order to lure us here? We're confused right now and our bodies are a mess. We came here thinking we'd be able to catch her, but we don't have the strength for that kind of thing anymore. She lured us here because it's the best way to get rid of us without the Politburo interfering...."

I didn't finish the sentence because I heard muffled footsteps outside. Light and bright steps, like those of a child. I readied my shock pistol. Ahn gripped his in his good left prosthetic hand and stepped behind a wall.

There was a rattling sound and the door opened. A small, slender shadow appeared in the doorway. We would have taken cover and waited for her to draw closer, but our new bodies weren't capable of such a reaction. Like scared new recruits, we plastered ourselves against the walls and began firing our shock pistols in all directions. The dull pops of the guns echoed around the warehouse, making it sound as if an earthquake had struck.

The shadow stood for a second, then stumbled forward and fell to the floor. We breathed a sigh of relief. Holding our shock pistols, we approached the door.

For a moment, I didn't trust my eyes. The place where she had fallen was empty. There was nothing there.

"A hologram projection! Fucking shadow play!" screamed Ahn.

Before the words were out of his mouth, we heard the thin, slightly wavering voice of a woman. It came from the other side of the warehouse. We fired in the direction of the sound. Soon we heard the sound of return gunfire. The first shot cut Ahn's right prosthetic hand off at the base, causing it to bounce to the floor. The second smashed my left shoulder, and the third skimmed Ahn's head.

We ran out the door like a pair of frightened idiots. We no longer had the physical courage required to hold our positions. It had died with us in the fire two months ago.

Two more gunshots rang out as we reached the staircase, and Ahn fell with a strangled cry. I somehow managed to stop him from rolling down the stairs, but his spine was broken and the back of his skull had caved in from the impact of the gunshot.

I laid him on the stairs and ran downward. When I reached the sixth floor, I opened the red box on the wall and set off the alarm. Fire doors descended to the floor as the alarm shrieked.

Other people working in the building opened their doors to see what the commotion was. "Call the ambulance and the police!" I screamed at them. "There's a wanted murderer on the seventh floor, and somebody's hurt up there!"

People retreated back into their rooms, whispering. Soon the alarm died away, only to be replaced by the sound of sirens. Someone must have called emergency services.

A short, dark-skinned young man, one of the few people who hadn't gone back to their rooms, approached me.

"Do you need a doctor? I'm a doctor. Well, not a clinical one, but perhaps I might still be of some use?"

I led the doctor up the stairs to Ahn's prone figure. After examining Ahn for a moment, he shook his head and said, "He's already stopped breathing. Is he an important person?"

I nodded half-heartedly. Deep in thought, he asked, "Are you two Politburo? You are, right? That ring on his finger is from the Politburo, isn't it?

"Yes."

He rubbed his hands excitedly. "Aha! I knew it! That means there might be crucial information in his head! I have an idea. Most of that stored information will remain intact for a while, even though he's dead. This kind of thing is my specialty... You probably haven't heard about something called the Pentagon Procedure before, but it's a medical procedure invented by Lazarus Kolton of Boulder University that's never actually been performed before. Let's see, how do I explain it? Despite all of our advancements in science, we still haven't been able to figure out how to read information directly from a brain. All we can do is store the information that's found there. The Pentagon Procedure takes information out of a dead person's brain and moves it into a partially replicated brain that's then implanted into a brain-dead body. Of course, a lot of information gets lost during this process, but we're working on ways to work around that problem. For example, instead of transferring information from a single brain to another brain, we've been experimenting with transferring it into several brains—all of which can then work together to fill in any memory gaps. Five brains should be sufficient for full memory recovery. This is why we've called it the Pentagon Procedure. Of course, having five copies of the same person might make things a bit complicated, but that's a small price to pay if the information in that person's brain is important enough. Ask your boss about it... Hey! I'm being serious here! Why are you laughing?"

I was trying to force back my laughter, but with little success. Doing my best to keep a straight face, I managed with difficulty to stand up.

"Sorry. But we've already tried that, and the drawbacks far outweigh the benefits. If you're looking for someone to sponsor your little games, you'll have to look elsewhere."

5

I left the building before the paramedics and police arrived. Settling myself in a secluded nook outside, I squatted down to watch. They brought Ahn out and loaded him into an ambulance, but I didn't hear any shouts or gunshots. It seemed Nguyen had escaped again.

I knew there was no time to lose, but I also didn't want to move. So I sat there on the ground, my legs stretched out. When passersby began giving me curious looks, I crawled into an alley so as to draw less attention to myself. Waste water from a 24-hour laundromat ran through a pipe that emptied into a sewer in the alley, so it was actually quite warm back there. It looked like I could use the paper and boxes that lay around the alley. I pulled some of them to myself and laid down for a nap. Even the ache in my shoulder had become more bearable.

That's when I heard a metallic click. A still-warm cylinder of metal had been placed up against my neck. I looked up. Nguyen's pale face filled half my field of vision. She didn't look shabby in the least now. She was as sure of herself as the fourth horseman of the Apocalypse on his pallid steed.

She waved her shock pistol at me and spoke. "Get up."

I shook my head and eased my tense body back to the ground. "Nope. That's not going to happen. If you want to kill me, kill me now. I'm not moving an inch."

She snorted. "What do you take me for? Do you think I'm like you? That I would kill you without first figuring out your intentions?"

"Isn't that what you've done so far?"

"If all I wanted was to kill the four of you, I would have done it before escaping from the hospital. But I'm not like you. I've been trying to talk to you this whole time, but everyone has either sneered or started shooting at me without bothering to listen to what I have to say."

I rested my back against the wall. "Okay, I'm listening.... Why did you kill Kim and Ahn and Perelman? Not to mention Choi and that other doctor?"

"Because you're all horrible people. Don't you get that? You're child murderers, rapists, arsonists, and scammers. You monsters didn't even bat an eye at setting fire to a factory full of children. You don't deserve to live."

"Tell me something I don't know. What about you? You were one of us until not long ago."

Nguyen spoke with the staccato precision of a machine gun. "I changed. I'm having a baby and starting a new life. But how can I possibly start over and wash myself of my past if all of you are still around, waiting to drag me back into the filth of our past. To start anew, I have to eliminate every part of the past. It isn't enough for only one fifth of us to repent."

"But all of us have changed, not just you," I protested. "Do you really think I was this lazy two months ago? Or Perelman that stupid? Or Ahn that talkative? Think about it. None of us are the person we were two months ago. You didn't kill three-fifths of Kim Eunsu, you killed three completely different people!"

"People are always changing. Just because they changed doesn't mean they're different people. We all have the same memories and experiences. We all have to be responsible for our own memories. You'll probably say that Kim Eunsu committed all those acts and he's dead. But... fuck. Why do you try to deceive your conscience with that sophistry? You did all that stuff yourself. All the memories of those actions are stored in your head. And still you're lounging around here pretending you're innocent! One last question: do you regret your crimes? If you sincerely regret them, I'll let you live."

I had grown bored of her sermonizing. All I wanted to do was crawl back into the trash and go back to sleep. Why the fuck should I repent? What would I gain if I did? There'd just be one less person trying to kill me, that's all. Someone would eventually drag me out of this warm trash heap whether I repented or not.

I shook my head. "No."

Nguyen's sepia-colored face, visible through her disheveled hair, flushed red. She was extremely beautiful. I had never in my life been considered handsome, so I was glad that at least one of my new selves had been put into a good-looking body.

I watched as she tossed away her shock pistol and pulled out a laser cutter. I was glad that she was kind enough to kill me when I was too lazy to do it myself. I felt fully relaxed, more so than ever before in my life. This was perfect. Self-harm and suicide without the bother of fighting my own will. My brain held on to that thought as my head fell from my neck and rolled toward the sewer drain.

UNDER THE SPHINX

1

It was chance that introduced me to *Under the Sphinx*. Having just learned that Robin Cook's novel *Sphinx* had been made into a movie, I looked it up on IMDb and noticed an entry for a movie titled *Under the Sphinx*. Curious, I clicked on the link and discovered it was a 1946 production directed by Henry Vince. The names of two cast members appeared on the page: Harriette Holbein and Julie Benson. According to their filmographies, each had appeared in only one film: *Under the Sphinx*. That was all the information there was.

Listings of this kind are so common on IMDb that I sometimes wonder whether the movies they describe really exist. Not that it is ever really possible to confirm one way or the other. Besides, it's not like those are the only errors on IMDb.

At any rate, I soon forgot all about the movie and lived peacefully and uneventfully until one day, about a year later, when I again came across *Under the Sphinx* while loitering on IMDb. To my surprise, the movie's page, which had previously only contained the names of the film's director and two lead actors, now also contained a short synopsis and listed the names of additional cast members and the director of cinematography, someone named Peter Landon. The private detective in the movie was played by Jonathan Murray, an actor who had also appeared as a socialite in Hitchcock's *Saboteur*. That's what had led me from Hitchcock to Vince's movie, though I can't remember what made me click on Murray's name. It had probably just been an accident.

The synopsis was written by someone named Chloe Barry (chloe@darkhorse.com). It read: "Miriam Blake realizes her husband has been unfaithful and hires a private investigator to look into his relationship with the young typist Rosalind Hunter. When the investigator ends up murdered, the police become suspicious of Miriam's relationship to the murdered man." Harriette Holbein played Miriam, and Julie Benson played Rosalind.

Okay, a suspense flick. But that introduction didn't give any clue as to how the story would progress. The fact that Julie Benson's name was listed so prominently seemed to indicate that the core of the movie might be the relationship between Miriam and Rosalind, but that was merely a guess. Also, why was the movie titled *Under the Sphinx*? I wanted to know more, so I clicked on Chloe Barry's name and sent her an email asking whether she might be willing to add more details of the movie's plot.

Almost immediately, the email bounced back with an error message: the address did not exist.

This was not especially surprising. People were always changing email providers and addresses. Still, when I visited the *Under the Sphinx* page again a month later, something about it felt off.

The movie's listing had expanded greatly in the month since I had last checked on it, and the list of crew and cast members was now as long as that of more recent movies. Twenty-four people had rated the movie, giving an average score of 8.1. What did this sudden increase in information signify?

The following Tuesday, I revisited the page and once again found new material had been added. This time it was a photo. The photo showed the two women played by Holbein and Benson looking at each other in what appeared to be a study. Holbein—and here I'm merely guessing it was Holbein because she seemed older and was wearing more expensive clothing—held a pistol in her hands, though it wasn't aimed at anyone.

I followed the URL of the photo back to the homepage of a woman named Olivia Evans (http://www.o_evans.simplenet.com/ movies.html). The image appeared in a section of her website titled "Movies I Like." Aside from *Casablanca* and *I Walked with a Zombie*, I did not recognize most of the movies she listed there. She appeared to be a fan of 1940s Hollywood B movies. After downloading that image and a few others, I quietly left her page.

It was in my dream that night that I figured it out. I had a bizarre dream in which I walked through old movies, though *Under the Sphinx* was not one of them. Bette Davis passed by me at just the right moment, and when I asked her whether she had seen Harriette Holbein, she grabbed my hand as if she felt sorry for me and led me to José Ferrer, who was dressed as Toulouse-Lautrec. Wielding his brush intently, he painted Holbein perched atop a small sphinx. Except that the woman posing for him was Virginia Woolf.

That's when I woke up. It was still just four in the morning. I scrambled to my computer and opened the still from *Under the Sphinx* in Photoshop. It was not bad, but as I turned up the levels, certain details began to stick out. The picture was a composite—well-done for an amateur, but not professional-level. After smoothing out the inconsistencies, I went to Olivia Evans's homepage and sent her an email saying the photo was good, but I had found a few problems and was sending her my revision. I addressed the email to "Chloe Barry" (Chloe and Olivia, wasn't it obvious?). I remember writing very respectfully, because I assumed that whether the recipient's name was Chloe or Olivia, she would have a strong sense of fair play.

A reply arrived from Olivia Evans the following morning. She wrote frankly and openly, probably realizing that I'd already guessed the truth.

Her real name was Olivia Evans; Chloe Barry was a pseudonym she used from time to time. And there was of course no movie titled *Under the Sphinx*. One day, she'd been bored and sent a movie she'd made up to IMDb as a joke, only to find that lo and behold, those idiots had put it up. Enjoying her own joke, she'd added to the stub bit by bit until she finally even uploaded the fake photo, which she'd created in Photoshop from images clipped from 1940s film magazines. She did not know the identity of the women she had assigned the roles of Holbein and Benson. The women themselves couldn't have recognized their own faces, which Evans had liberally distorted into more interesting expressions.

And the links? Those had been a clever trick as well. Olivia had chosen B actors and staff whom no one would care about and connected them to *Under the Sphinx*. She'd assigned *Under the Sphinx* to the production company Monumental Pictures because, she said, it had been engaged in a legal fight with

Warner Brothers at the time. *Under the Sphinx* could very well have been one of the many movies Monumental Pictures had never released. The movie's cast and crew were all people who could plausibly have been caught up in those circumstances as well.

Satisfied with these explanations and impressed with how skillfully Olivia Evans had managed to fake an entire movie, I wrote her a warm reply. She seemed to think her prank was more original than it actually was, however, so I also pointed her towards other websites that might be of interest: John Price's imaginary library page (http://www.meow.co.uk/~-jorgeborges), which lists books that only exist inside of other books, and Emilia Sarton's "Balkan 2" page (http://www.users.aol.com/emilia/balkan2), which provides maps and histories for imaginary countries on the Balkan peninsula that appear in English novels.

2

Since I do have a job, and my internet browsing is not restricted solely to IMDb, I nearly forgot about *Under the Sphinx* after that. I was too busy with weekly work deadlines to think much more about it. Had Olivia Evans not sent me a follow up email, I would never have known what happened next.

Her message was simple: "If you have a minute, visit http://www.wind.com/~dizzy/movies."

The URL led me to a movie site run by someone called Dizzy who was writing close analyses of homoerotic elements in Hollywood movies—including, to my surprise, *Under the Sphinx*.

Dizzy's section on *Under the Sphinx* provided much more

detailed information than anything Olivia had ever posted on her page. It briefly outlined the collapse of Monumental Pictures and talked about the various movies that had been buried in the process. Dizzy also gave more background on the director of *Under the Sphinx*, Henry Vince, one of the artists ruined by Monumental Picture's bankruptcy. Noting "regretfully" that Vince was not gay, or at least did not seem to be, Dizzy claimed that he was a forgotten genius.

After mentioning a few of Vince's other films, Dizzy jumped straight to *Under the Sphinx*. Dizzy claimed there had been two different versions of the film: a 98-minute cut and a 119-minute one. The 98-minute version—the one meant for the official release that never took place—never explains the relationship between Miriam and Rosalind. The unofficial 119-minute edit, however, includes a kiss scene between the two leads reminiscent of the one with Greta Garbo in *Queen Christina*, and contains dialogue clearly explaining the situation. Vince had apparently created this 119-minute edit as a first draft without any thought of actually releasing it. Then he cut the film to 98 minutes, holding onto the excised footage for his own personal records.

Dizzy's website contained three images from *Under the Sphinx*. At 640 x 480 pixels each, they were much larger than the one Olivia had created. In the first, Harriette Holbein and Julie Benson are looking down at something outside the frame. The second shows Harriette together with the private detective. The third appeared to be a video capture of Harriette Holbein in closeup.

As before, I used Photoshop to play with the levels, contrast, and so forth. I tried everything I could think of to figure out how the photos had been stitched together. It was useless. They seemed to be real photographs. I then went to the video store and borrowed *Saboteur* to see whether the private detective in the photo was actually Jonathan Murray. And it seemed to be—someone who looked like Murray really did appear in *Saboteur's* party scene.

An e-mail is not going to be adequate for something like this, I thought. I prepared my desk with an English-Korean dictionary and notes on idioms, and sent Olivia a chat request. She accepted almost immediately. Without a word of greeting, she asked:

–So?

–It's weird. Those photos look real to me.

–I emailed Dizzy.

–What did you ask?

–Just whether he'd had actually seen the movie.

–Hah! ...And?

–Dizzy said he had borrowed a video cassette of the movie from a friend. That's where that third still is from. But he doesn't have a copy of it now, and he's lost contact with the friend. The other two photos were taken from magazines, but he doesn't know which ones.

–Such an elaborate lie. Dizzy's post is interesting too.

–But it's my movie! Mine! Why is he interfering with my little joke?

–Aren't you happy that it's taken on a life of its own?

–No. You haven't looked at Vince's IMDb, have you?

–No. What's up with it?

–There are four more movies on it now. One of them is a new entry I just created, but the two others were probably posted by Dizzy. Why is he interfering with my joke? I've got to set him straight right away.

Then she left the chat.

Two days later, she forwarded me an email saying simply: "Look at this."

> Dear Chloe,
>
> I believe there may be a misunderstanding. *Under the Sphinx* is a real movie. It's true that it's hard to find, but there's a video tape of it out there somewhere, and plenty of other material on it besides. If you have time, take a look at the *Under the Sphinx* IMDb. You can also visit Olivia Evans's film site at http:// www.o_evans.simplenet.com/movies.html and Coilboy Cult's film site at http://www.coilboy.com. If you have trouble believing internet sources, then try reading Brian Stevens's book *Forgotten Bricks*. It provides detailed information about many of the forgotten movies made by Monumental Pictures.
>
> Best,
> Dizzy

3

Forgotten Bricks was not easy to find in Korea, so Olivia faxed me the relevant passage.

The collapse of Monumental Pictures narrated in *Forgotten Bricks* was just as tragic as Dizzy had described. What drew my attention, however, were the various falsehoods inserted between the truths. I gradually began to doubt what I was reading. Had Olivia really made up the film? Stevens certainly did not seem like the kind of person who would waste his time playing along with someone else's internet joke. Yet, he wrote with the utmost seriousness about Henry Vince and Harriette Holbein, two entirely fictional people.

According to Stevens, Vince and Holbein had been lovers until 1950 when Holbein broke it off because Vince had become a drug addict. After the breakup, Vince stumbled around for a few years before dying of an overdose in 1954. The two had made four movies together, yet not a single one of them had ever been given a proper release. It should have taken roughly four years to make four movies, but all of them seemed to have been filmed in a very short stretch of time between 1945 and 1946.

Stephens wrote that Holbein had probably been far more interested in writing than in acting, which she had never taken seriously. He believed Holbein had written the scripts for three of the four movies she made with Vince, including *Under the Sphinx*. Stevens's conviction on this point seemed wholly disproportionate to the evidence he provided. I couldn't help but wonder if he might not have had some kind of a crush on Holbein.

–All of this is fake, fake, fake!

This time Olivia was really mad.

–Holbein is fake! She doesn't exist! I created her face from models I found in furniture advertisements! Vince is fake, too. I created him by combining the names of my little brother and my dog. Benson is
fake too. I gave her the name of my best friend in high school, and I made her face by stretching and shrinking the photo of someone whose name I've forgotten who played a minor supporting role in some old movie!

–Stevens doesn't seem to be joking around though.

–But I'm telling you the truth! You have to believe me!

–What about the photos?

What upset Olivia the most were the photos in Stevens's

book. One was an extremely beautiful portrait of Harriette Holbein; another showed Holbein laughing together with Henry Vince. And then there were the two stills from *Under the Sphinx*.

–Something must be wrong with them! I'll send you the originals so you can see for yourself.

When I received the originals from her, it did not take me long in Photoshop to conclude that the dull, impersonal faces from the 1940s magazines could indeed have been distorted into faces resembling those of Harriette Holbein and Julie Benson. But, even if that were true, where did those other pictures in *Forgotten Bricks* come from?

–I have no idea. But they're fake, too! Fake!

Olivia was outraged. So much so, in fact, that when I went to check out her website later, I found she had completely deleted the section on *Under the Sphinx*. She had then gone on all the major message boards and posted that *Under the Sphinx* did not really exist.

The rebuttals came quickly. Most were from people who claimed to have seen the movie themselves. Among them was someone called Jellybean who took extreme issue with Olivia for, among other things, demeaning the memory of the great actress Harriette Holbein. Later I found that this person had created a superfan page dedicated entirely to Harriette Holbein and her work (http://www.sirius.com/~jellybean/Harriette.html).

Jellybean's Harriette Holbein page contained no fewer than thirty-four photos of Holbein. Some I had seen before, but most were new to me. And many came from movies other than *Under the Sphinx*.

I sent an email thanking Jellybean for the cool webpage

and asking how they'd managed to see the movie and get ahold of the photos. Jellybean explained that they'd seen the movie on video a while back, but no longer had a copy of it. As for the Holbein photos, some had been sent in by people on the internet, and the rest had been scanned from a 1940s movie magazine called *World Screen*. I asked for a scan of the magazine cover, and Jellybean obliged. I checked this image too, and as with the others, I could find no hint of it being fake.

One week later, Olivia sent me another link (http://www.fys.uio.no/~jorgen/Sphinx). This was the first website I'd seen dedicated to *Under the Sphinx*, and to my surprise, it contained a 30-second AVI clip from the movie. When the 4.5 megabyte download finally completed, I played the clip. In it, a woman who looks like Holbein sits on a bed next to a woman who looks like Benson. They are talking about the way a sphinx sits, and their dialogue sounds like the kind of thing that would only make sense if you've watched the movie from the beginning. The actors could have been other people dressed up as Holbein and Benson, but to me at least, the AVI clip seemed real.

I sent an email to the site's owner, Jorgen, to ask where he had gotten the film clip. His reply surprised me: he said he had a tape of the movie. I asked whether I could buy a copy, and he replied that he would be happy to send one to me for the cost of a blank tape and shipping.

I ran breathlessly to Citibank, made out a money order, and sent it to Norway. Two weeks later I received the tape. I put it in my VCR and hit play. For those of you who might be wondering how that was possible: there are multi-system VCRs capable of reading both NTSC and PAL tapes.

The quality of the film was, in a word, shit. It looked like it had been transferred to tape from a 16mm film. The picture flickered annoyingly, and the sound quality was horrible, as if the audio had been recorded on an Edison phonograph. The dialogue was at times almost impossible to understand.

Still, the movie itself was interesting. Really interesting. Though surprisingly modern, it also felt like an authentic noir film. Holbein and Benson were both so fabulous that I wondered how they could possibly have been forgotten. The jerky camera movement was reminiscent of Samuel Fuller, albeit with a character of its own. I couldn't help but think how uncomfortable all this would have made audiences from the 1940s feel. Imagine how 1940s audiences would react to the Wachowskis' *Bound*. *Under the Sphinx* would undoubtedly have elicited a similar reaction.

I sent a thank you to Jorgen as soon as I finished watching the film. I also asked how he'd come into possession of the tape. The story was relatively simple. An Australian friend possessed a 16mm copy of the film and had copied it onto tape for him. This friend did not have an email address, but Jorgen kindly offered to get in touch with him for me.

The next day, I received an email from Jorgen with a cute jpeg detailing how he'd gotten his copy of *Under the Sphinx*. According to the diagram, Jorgen had received the tape from his Australian friend, who had in turn inherited it from his uncle, a former broadcast cameraman. Most of the movies in this uncle's collection had been copied without permission from 16mm tapes at the television station (which, incidentally, used to belong to a young Rupert Murdoch). Most likely, in its early years, this Australian television station must have bought the old movie reels during the liquidation sale that followed Monumental Pictures' purchase by WB. If this was indeed the case, the original film of *Under the Sphinx* might still be somewhere in Australia.

Jorgen's Australian friend asked the broadcast station and received a surprisingly quick reply. The station still had the film! This information was of course immediately added to Jorgen's site.

It was around this time that the world officially recognized the existence of *Under the Sphinx*. I should have known it would happen when *Forgotten Bricks* author Brian Stevens appeared on CNN to discuss Monumental Pictures. Needless to say, the movie he devoted the most attention to was *Under the Sphinx*. Soon it became trendy to circulate bootleg tapes of the movie. The film's Australian premiere in Sydney was widely reported in the news, and Vince, Holbein, and Benson were being discussed daily on Usenet. What had happened to Holbein and Benson was another popular topic of speculation. When someone discovered Benson living in Ireland, the media converged on her privately-run nursing home to interview her. According to Benson, her film experience had been little more than "some fun I had had when I was young and immature." I could only imagine how awkward all that media attention must have been for her.

It was at this point that Olivia Evans wilted. If she was right, the entire world was conspiring to deceive her. But how could such a thing even be possible? Then again, what other explanation could there be for the fact that someone she'd created in Photoshop was now walking around in real life?

She even began to talk of supernatural phenomena. What if Vince, Holbein, Benson, and the movie *Under the Sphinx* had actually existed all along and she had merely discovered them?

What if her mind had simply downloaded the information from whatever extra-universal space it was being stored in? Were this the case, the fact that she had named her dog Vince might just be further evidence that information had already been present in her unconscious.

In the end, though, Olivia Evans was much too practical to truly believe in such fables. The last email she sent me was quite serious, tragic even. "I don't know if the world out there is trying to fool me or if we're dealing here with something supernatural," she wrote. "All I can say is I know for a fact that I'm the one who created *Under the Sphinx*. No matter what other people might believe, that will never change." This dignified and somewhat touching declaration was, however, somewhat undermined by the lack of confidence revealed by her postscript: "Do you believe me?"

To which I replied: "I believe you."

4

Perhaps you think my answer was a lie, intended merely to console Olivia Evans. But it wasn't. I really do believe her to be the original creator of *Under the Sphinx*. Moreover, my conviction is far stronger than Olivia's, because I know something she does not.

You probably have never heard of Professor Choi Minseung, a scholar of Korean literature who passed away last year, but he was my uncle. And it's precisely because of this family tie that I ended up getting involved with the business I'm about to relate, despite it having nothing at all to do with my profession.

In his final years, Uncle used to amuse himself with Joseon dynasty tales of the strange. His primary interest lay in works of fiction that were banned during that period. One of these was *Legend of the Golden Crow*, a tale whose title and description are the only things about it that had survived. My uncle used to lament the loss of *Legend of the Golden Crow* every time our family would get together to celebrate Lunar New Year or the Autumn Moon Festival. And indeed, judging from the description, the tale seemed to have been an awfully interesting one.

Following the conclusion of my uncle's funeral, however, a double-sided photocopy of this much-lamented lost tale was found bound up with cord in his desk drawer. The original was nowhere to be found. This discovery threw the world—or at least the little corner of the world to which my uncle had belonged—into an uproar. Two months later, the copy's original was found, and no one ever again challenged the authenticity of the tale.

I can't comment on the literary or historical value of *Legend of the Golden Crow*, but the plot is truly fascinating. It is an adventure tale about a woman reborn as a golden crow who travels between this life and the next, and really is a fun read, with an over-the-top story and erotic descriptions that appeal even to a modern-day layperson such as me.

What intrigued me most, however, was the condition of the copy.

The copy had clearly been made on the copier in my uncle's house. Much like fingerprints, all copiers have their own unique characteristics, such as scratches on the glass or cover that show up on every copy. The top left corner of my uncle's copy machine bore a scratch that left a mark resembling the letter ㄱ on whatever we copied. That mark was visible in the corner of every page of the photocopy of *Legend of the Golden*

Crow.

Copiers can also have temporary fingerprints, such as a bit of ink from a ballpoint pen, that remain on the copier glass until wiped off, and can help identify the day a copy was made.

At the time, we had thought my great aunt was dying, and the whole family was gathered at his house to prepare for her funeral. But sometimes a person who rushes around making preparations for someone else's funeral dies before that funeral has a chance to take place. That is what happened to my uncle, who died peacefully after a three-day illness. Meanwhile, the great aunt my family was always fussing over is still alive and complaining of her illness a full year later.

While I was there at my uncle's house peeling fruit, carrying tea, and pretending to be busy, I received a message on my beeper reminding me to finish an important work assignment that day. I entered my uncle's room with his permission, but because his printer was broken, I ended up having to bang out my work on his electronic typewriter. When I finished, I went to make a duplicate on his copy machine so I could send the original to my company. But the machine jammed up, and I had to pull paper out of it several times in a row. Some toner must have gotten on my thumb because one corner of the glass ended up with a smudge. This mark, needless to say, appeared clearly on all the copies I made that day.

The same mark shows faintly on the first two pages of the photocopied version of *Legend of the Golden Crow* that was later discovered in my uncle's study.

My uncle collapsed just three hours after I made my copies, and it was obvious he had not had a chance to touch the copier during that time. This meant that someone else had brought

Legend of the Golden Crow into his house at some later point, then copied and hid it amongst my uncle's things.

It's not that unusual for such photocopies to be discovered in the studies of literature scholars. Moreover, other note-books found in my uncle's study provided plausible enough explanations as to how a copy of this rare story might have ended up in his home. They even explained the later discovery of the copy's original. If not for my little misstep with the toner smudge, nothing about any of this would have seemed the slightest bit unusual.

I was thus convinced that *Legend of the Golden Crow* is a fabrication. And if *Legend of the Golden Crow* is a fake, then there's no reason why *Under the Sphinx* could not also be a fake, despite all the evidence for its existence. Obviously, it's difficult to compare the forging of a book with the forging of a movie and its actors. Yet, aren't the two cases similar?

Here, I can't help but entertain an elaborate conspiracy theory, namely, that a worldwide secret organization dedi-cated to the fabrication of movies and novels might very well exist. But wouldn't the people involved have better things to do? Wouldn't people capable of mass-producing masterpieces like *Under the Sphinx* put their talents to better use elsewhere?

I began wracking my brain to come up with a theory that made sense, and that is when I thought of you.

5

I do not usually remember or save the email addresses of people I've met only once, but I made an exception with yours. I can still recall your ridiculous online sermon. But I did not connect you and your beliefs to *Under the Sphinx* until now.

Shall I summarize the arguments you were making? You

first asked, "What is history," and answered that "history is no more than words written down on pages and broken shards of pottery." History wields influence only through records, you argued. What would it matter if someone insisted that the French Revolution had never really happened, and that the records of it in history books were the fabrications of a worldwide conspiracy? Our modern society exists on the basis of the belief that the French Revolution did in fact happen. As long as our historical records say that the French Revolution happened, whether or not it actually did is irrelevant.

"What, then, is historical truth?" you asked. "Something we cannot directly prove." In which case, the French Revolution really is no different from Roswell. Again, why bother ourselves about what is true and what is not?

I argued against you then, and I still want to now, even though I don't remember what my counterarguments were. It was clear, however, that no matter what I thought, my weak arguments would never sway the likes of you. It was also clear that people like you would feel no qualms whatsoever about manipulating the past in order to prove their point.

Yet, what could possibly be the point of fabricating works of art from the past? Once I happened to read a strange article from a religious news group, and it contained enough similarities to your arguments that it's distinctly possible you or one of your friends was its author.

Anyway, according to that article, human history has a purpose. But that purpose is not, as classical historicists would have it, to arrive at an ideal stateless society. The purpose of history is to produce what is necessary for each moment in time. If a particular age has not fulfilled its potential, it can be considered a failure. And it's our job to make up for any such deficiency. To take an example at random, suppose that noir films from the 1940s failed to depict lesbians. It would then be our—no, your—responsibility to make up for this inadequacy at a later date.

Even if you claim your position is not deterministic, it reeks of eschatology. You are like those people who rush around trying to complete all you can before the world ends.

In truth, you disturb me. You shamelessly push your opinions on me under nicknames such as Oedipus and Horace, and there's something sinister about how you brazenly took advantage of Olivia's creation and twisted it toward your own goals. You knew all along how she would react.

I just read that additional clips from *Under the Sphinx* have been discovered by Henry Vince's estate, and that there are now plans to restore a "director's cut" of the movie. Even though I no longer believe in the existence of Vince or Holbein, and I very much doubt the identity of the old woman who calls herself Benson, I can't deny that I felt a flutter of excitement at the news.

However, may I ask what you have done to Olivia Evans? Why is it that the new biography of Harriet Holbein lists Chloe Barry as a co-author?

II

THE BLOODY BATTLE OF BROCCOLI PLAIN

1

Yeon-ah dumped Cheongsu on the second floor of the Jongno Burger King.

Cheongsu wanted to say something, but the words just wouldn't come out. He cleared his throat and shifted about uneasily while looking down at his untouched bag of onion rings and coffee. His clothing was soaked from a sudden rain shower, and he couldn't think clearly because of a summer cold. Two days earlier, he'd been fired from his job. His mind and body could not have felt any worse. It really was not the day to get dumped by his girlfriend of four years.

"Why?" he finally managed to get out.

"You really don't know?" Yeon-ah shot back, tiredly.

"No, I don't. What's the problem?"

"That is the problem."

"Is it because I was fired? I can always ask my uncle for a new job."

"I already told you that has nothing to do with it!"

"Then why? What the hell did I do wrong?"

"Forget it."

"Forget what? I don't understand why we have to break up!"

Yeon-ah gathered her handbag and stood up. "Please don't make a scene here," she said coolly. "You're embarrassing enough as it is. Not that you ever understood that either..."

Words continued to pour out of her mouth, but Cheongsu neither understood nor remembered them. His memories of her cut off abruptly at that precise moment. Or rather, the world itself paused at the moment. An alien who happened to peer into Cheongsu's head just then might have thought that the planet called Earth was little more than a small rock consisting of the second floor of a Burger King and the section of Jongno visible through its windows, and that its only inhabitant was the large man sniffling into his still-hot coffee.

2

This is neither the time nor the place to be thinking of his ex-girlfriend. Cheongsu needs to focus on putting out the fire on his ass.

That is not a metaphor. Cheongsu's ass really is on fire. A patrolling Cooper noticed him wading through the marsh toward the Olivier and gave him a warning shot in the rear with its laser rifle. The shot did not tear Cheongsu's spacesuit, but it did ignite the flammable, translucent goo of the marsh. Now Cheongsu is running about with his ass on fire like Yosemite Sam. In theory, his Russian-made spacesuit can easily withstand this level of heat. But theory aside, why is his backside starting to feel hot right where it touches the inside of his spacesuit?

As soon as he drops into a shallow ravine and out of the Cooper's line of sight, Cheongsu begins to drag his butt across the grassy ground. Finally, he manages to extinguish the fire. It leaves a black scar on the rear of his spacesuit, but Cheongsu can't see that. The wound to his dignity, however, is all too obvious.

After calming himself down, he climbs carefully out of the ravine and quickly snakes his head out from behind the boulder he's using as a shield. He can't see the Cooper. Oh, there it is. He begins to count all the different Coopers circling the Olivier's perimeter while marking time on his watch. If his calculations are correct, there are five Coopers on patrol. He doesn't have a chance of getting to the Olivier no matter which way he tries to go.

And inside of that Olivier sits the Adjani he rode in on.

Until just two hours ago, things had looked promising. The Adjani had landed in an open area about a kilometer from the ravine. Its signal lights had indicated it wasn't planning to leave the planet for at least four days. Lured by the blue fields outside the window of his capsule car, Cheongsu had grabbed his gun and canteen and set out to explore. He'd only gone about a hundred meters when a sudden whoosh made him turn around. The Adjani had swallowed up Cheongsu's capsule car and was now flying away from him.

The signal lights on the Adjani hadn't been lying. It wasn't leaving. The Adjani had merely decided to spend its time on the planet resting in the bosom of the Olivier about a kilometer away from its original landing site.

Cheongsu curses the Adjani with every word he can think of. He grinds his teeth, swings his fists at the air, and kicks at the innocent ground. He acts as if the Adjani has just violated his rights.

Once he's exhausted himself, he goes back down into the

ravine. He's overcome by an impulse to commit suicide. All he needs to do to bring his suffering to an end is open his helmet and pull on the trigger of his pistol. Pulling the trigger might not even be necessary. What are the chances he can survive this planet's atmosphere?

Even if he does, he still has no way of returning to Earth.

3

The first contact between Earthlings and the alien spaceship occurred at 4:23 PM Korean Time on April 1, 2009. The spaceship, looking like a stingray extravagantly decorated with gems, had descended from the sky without warning. It landed cheekily right on top of the cars on the road in front of Anyang Station, and began flashing signal lights indicating it planned to stay for at least twelve days. Amidst the din of horns from the sudden traffic jam, small mechanical creatures exited the spaceship's mouth. These creatures unfolded menacing pincer legs and laser rifles, and began to slice up and devour the vehicles blocking their way. One driver became so angry about losing his new car that he forgot to be afraid and kicked the spaceship. The creatures diced and ate him too.

It took the alien invaders only eight days to construct a colony occupying most of Anyang and part of Gwangmyeong. Using the resources they had consumed, they made more of themselves and began to build large metal structures. At first, the invaders were no larger than baby strollers, but they grew until the largest of them were the size of dump trucks. They also began to vary in shape. On the eighth day, they constructed five loosely-packed projectiles, each resembling a ten-meter-diameter soccer ball, and launched them into the sky. These landed on the outskirts of Hamheung, Kuala

Lumpur, Brasilia, San Diego, and Glasgow. Two months later, the invaders had expanded to twenty-four colonies and were seemingly content with that number.

In the meantime, Earthlings tried to stop the alien invasion in all the usual ways. They tried dialogue, they tried violence. Nothing worked. The invaders didn't seem to think the Earthlings were worth engaging with. They cared only about raw materials for building their colonies. To the extent that Earthlings could serve as those raw materials, they too would be ruthlessly assimilated. People liked to assign unnecessary political motivations to some of the invaders' actions, such as the sudden attack on the Blue House early in the invasion. But to the invaders, the Blue House had been no more than a convenient source of subcutaneous fat for use as a lubricant.

As soon as the invaders ceased expanding their colonies and began to keep to themselves, Earthlings started to study them. This was relatively easy. The aliens had no interest in Earthlings. The spaceships didn't complain when spray-painted, and the mechanical creatures didn't react when kicked. Living alongside them wasn't too different from living alongside moving cars. People were safe as long as they followed a few rules.

Earthlings discovered that the aliens could be divided into two basic categories: spaceships that flew through the sky and mechanical creatures that worked on the ground. The behavior and appearance of these two types were so different that they appeared to have entirely different origins. The flying machines were extravagant and beautiful, with fixed, unchanging forms. The terrestrial machines, on the other hand, were entirely practical, with specific functions and individualized designs that were temporary and contingent. It wasn't uncommon for a terrestrial machine to have four legs and two wings one day, and eight legs and no wings the next.

Because they were easier to observe, the terrestrial machines were the first to be subjected to a taxonomical analysis. Although each type of terrestrial machine appeared in many different forms, the functional role of each type was distinct and persistent. Type As were responsible for manufacturing and construction. Type Bs destroyed things and killed people, and delivered the resulting raw materials to Type As. Type Cs acted like extremely cautious soldiers who concentrated solely on passive defense. Type Bs and Cs provided the materials and protection necessary for Type As to build the structures that came to be recognized as Type Ds. It was obvious that Type Ds were, like their colleagues, living creatures endowed with artificial intelligence.

This taxonomy was important. It showed that the invaders were not simply a single entity working in concert like an army intent on obeying orders. Instead, they were a group of individuals who had chosen to cooperate with each other for their own personal benefit.

For a while, people called the machines whatever they liked. Type B machines alone were referred to using dozens of different monikers ranging from the fairly straightforward and descriptive "Starfish" or "Soldier Ant" to the flashier "Butcher," "Slaughterer," "Crashhead," or "Megatron." South Koreans like Cheongsu just called them "Myeong-bak fuckers" after their despised president.

It was Wendy Hobbs, a graduate student at Glasgow University, who gave the machines their common names. In a series of viral videos uploaded to YouTube in December of

2009, she assigned the name of a male movie star to each category of terrestrial machine. Type As, the builders, were called Guinnesses. Type D machines, the building-like structures, were called Oliviers. And Type Bs and Cs, the soldiers, were called Waynes and Coopers respectively.

Hobbs's own experiment showed that the spaceship-type aliens could likewise be divided into four categories. Type As were the largest of these flying machines and did not descend to planets. Type Bs, fish-shaped spaceships like the one that first landed on Earth, shuttled between planets and the Type As in space. Type Bs all carried within them Type Cs, small flying machines that looked a bit like Cartier brooches and served primarily to gather information and collect samples. Type Ds were the depots that would appear in orbit above planets once the terrestrial machines dropped off by Type B shuttles had established themselves.

Hobbs named these flying machines after women. Type A spaceships were called Garbos, Type D depots were called Dietrichs, and Type Bs and Cs were Adjanis and Deneuves respectively. These names made some people uncomfortable at first, but as is usually the case in such situations, popular opinion ruled the day. (The fact that Hobbs herself was beautiful and resembled Hannah Murray probably played a part in this.)

Strangely, it took quite a while longer to settle on a name for the aliens as a whole. Not knowing where the invaders came from, people seemed reluctant to name them. This was not too much of an inconvenience, however, since the third-person plural generally sufficed.

What experiment did Hobbs conduct? Like Columbus and his egg, it was simple and ingenious. Taking advantage of the invaders' lack of interest in Earthlings, Hobbs built a simple camera robot and placed it inside an Adjani. When the Adjani returned to Glasgow two days later, she retrieved the robot. On it were images of a colony being constructed by the invaders on Olympus Mons. Hobbs had managed a trip to Mars for a mere £700.

Hobbs's experiment ignited a worldwide trend. Robot stowaways were soon flying on Adjanis out to all parts of the universe. The one in three or so that returned to Earth carried photos of places that did not—could not—resemble anything in the solar system. Some seethed with strange life forms the likes of which Earthlings had only ever seen in comic books.

Many Earthlings boarded Adjanis and left for space. A few were scientists or soldiers sent by governments, but over 80% were just normal people hoping to strike it rich. They wrapped themselves in low-quality, privately made spacesuits, sealed themselves up in beat-up old cars, and flew off to the stars.

The machines were no longer invaders. They were now guides leading Earthlings out into the universe.

4

Four local days later, Cheongsu is still alive. Hunger has begun to cloud his mind as his emergency rations run low, but he's alive nonetheless. The air is breathable, and the temperature, which fluctuates between 21 and 25 Celsius, is ideal. The air and water are no doubt teeming with microscopic life that Cheongsu has never encountered before, but so far nothing has interfered with his bodily functions.

He's set up camp in an old abandoned bus he stumbled across three days earlier while walking along a stream. The loud fluorescent lettering on the side of the bus is still legible: "Hope Church Extraterrestrial Mission 2011." Cheongsu has no idea how the bus came to be here, or where its passengers might be, or why the Waynes haven't eaten it yet. But he couldn't care less. He's grateful just to have found a sleeping bag and a place where he can shelter from the rain.

Unfortunately, the bus has no food to offer him. He's now down to just four sticks of beef jerky and five energy bars. If he hadn't made a habit of carrying emergency rations after the massacre on planet Purify the year before, he probably wouldn't even have those.

He walks out of the bus and gazes across the plain. It's hard to believe that he's dying of starvation in a place like this. The landscape is as beautiful as Teletubbyland. The meadow, dotted here and there with tall trees from which peach-like fruit hang, resembles a well-managed golf course. The mushroom-like things sprouting from the ground around the trees look delicious as well.

The tastiest-looking of all is the animal that Cheongsu has named "broccoli." Covered with soft green fur, these plump herbivores are dumb, slow, and easy to catch, and can be found all over the plain. When night falls, a pack of three or four carnivores resembling green dogs come out and catch one broccoli each to eat. When day breaks, the herd appears no different from the day before, and the remaining broccoli show no concern at all for their missing relative. The plain resembles a vegetable garden more than a hunting ground.

The problem is that Cheongsu can't eat any of it.

Over the last four days, he's tried everything that looks edible. He's picked and eaten the fruit, he's sampled the mushrooms, he even plucked one of the plants and ate its leaves and roots. But despite their delicious appearances, they all tasted horrible and upset his stomach terribly, causing him to vomit and giving him the runs.

Finally, he tried a broccoli. He selected a suitably small one, climbed onto its back, and, not knowing where to strike first, stabbed his knife in at random. The broccoli gushed blue blood and died. He dragged its corpse onto the bus and cut it apart. The results were disappointing. The broccoli didn't have any meat. The tough leathery honeycomb structure that made up its outer casing enclosed little more than blue blood, green jelly, and innards that resembled rubber hose. He tried eating each part, but all it gave him was another bout of vomiting and diarrhea. It seems nothing on this planet is edible no matter how he prepares it. The only thing his body accepts is water from the nearby stream.

Cheongsu wants to cry. He could, even, since no one is around to see him. But he doesn't. Instead, he spits curses at all the lifeforms on the broccoli plain as they enjoy their usual, languid serenity. His vocabulary has improved immensely over the past three years as he travelled about exploring the stars. Now he can curse in five languages, and his Korean cussing is more proficient than ever.

But no matter how many curses he hurls at the broccoli plain, it remains as serene and beautiful as ever.

Cheongsu gives up and breaks off half an energy bar for breakfast. He then checks again on the Olivier, inside which is resting the Adjani he'd hitched a ride on to get to this planet. He also checks whether a new Adjani he could ride on has arrived. Boarding an Adjani in just a spacesuit without a capsule car would be suicidal, but at least death by freezing or suffocation would be quicker than starving away on the broccoli plain.

After confirming that the Adjani still remains enfolded in the Olivier's embrace, Cheongsu explores a new part of the plain. He has begun surveying the area around the Olivier, carefully checking one sector at a time. If missionaries from Hope Church had managed to find their way to this planet, maybe others from Earth had too. Who knows, they might still be alive. Even if they were dead, they might have left behind a few cans of tuna.

Cheongsu climbs upward along a hill to the north. When he finally gets to the top, he nearly cries out for joy. On the other side are three round tents that closely resemble yurts. Three or four humanoid figures stand in front of them. Throwing himself to the ground so he can't be seen, Cheongsu takes out his binoculars and aims them at the tents. A man and two boys come into view. One of the boys is showing the man a crayon drawing of an airplane in his sketchbook. Then Cheongsu notices the red scarf wrapped around the boy's neck. His body grows cold with fear.

Commies!

5

Cheongsu has never been a hardcore anti-communist. He doesn't know much about politics, and never cared about the people starving or being executed in North Korea. His "commie" doesn't even have political connotations. The group of South Korean escapees he'd belonged to had simply needed an epithet for North Koreans, and "Commie" had been the obvious choice.

To understand his attitude, it's important to know what happened in North Korea during those first few years following the alien invasion.

The aliens hadn't singled out the North Korean system for attack. Hamheung received the exact same treatment as Anyang and Glasgow. Waynes destroyed factories and houses, clearing sites for Guinnesses to build Oliviers. Several months later, Adjanis popped out of the Oliviers and flew up into the heavens.

Many thought it was the North Korean government's response that had caused the tragedy. If only the North Korean government had bothered to pay more attention to its quarantine system rather than encouraging hundreds of astronauts to fly into space in the name of the Dear Leader, they could have avoided the worst of it. Or so people said. But was North Korea really any different from any of the other places the invaders had colonized? Had any country completely prevented their people from sneaking onto Adjanis and out into the universe? North Korea was in fact best equipped to control its populace, in theory anyway.

In the end, the disaster that occurred in North Korea wasn't caused by humans. It was bound to happen somewhere, and North Korea just drew the short straw.

According to the classified documents discovered later, the first signs of impending disaster were detected on August 16, 2009, when five pilots belonging to the DPRK space force returned to Earth after successfully planting a North Korean flag on an alien planet seven hundred light-years away. Four days later, all five suffered simultaneous seizures and collapsed. Two died that night; the remaining three ended up brain-dead.

They'd caught an alien virus.

Contrary to rumor, North Korea had actually taken great

pains with its quarantine system and been researching all the potential dangers of encountering alien microbes. But even the best preparations would have proved insufficient. Every day, hundreds of Adjanis crawling with new microbes landed on the planet. In August 2009 alone, over three thousand new varieties of viruses were discovered. Sooner or later, people would have caught a deadly space flu. That North Koreans caught it first was pure chance.

The "space flu" rapidly spread throughout North Korea. By the time the country finally requested international assistance on September 8, 2009, more than 27,000 people had already died. Frustratingly, the space flu manifested a variety of different symptoms and could be transmitted in several different ways. Some suffered sudden heart failure, some died when their lungs filled with blood, and still others suffered from erupting livers. It looked as if North Korea was simultaneously suffering every possible disease that could be caused by an alien virus. The only common denominator was that prepubescent children suffered the lowest rates of mortality.

While international scientists conducted research on those who managed to flee North Korea, people continued to die within the country's borders. By January 2010, the death toll in North Korea was estimated at 420,000. By May, it had surpassed three million. The government had completely lost control by this point, and everyone who was not yet infected was trying to escape. Most were shot dead at the Chinese border or at the DMZ. Those attempting to escape by sea didn't fare much better. No country in the world was willing to accept North Korean refugees. All everyone wanted from North Koreans was for them to die and take the fucking virus with them. Everyone was glad this calamity had taken place in the world's most isolated country.

North Koreans didn't all die, however. At the beginning of January 2011, three hundred thousand North Koreans remained alive. Seventy percent of them were children under the age of twelve and suffering from malnutrition, but at least they were alive. Although they showed no signs of further susceptibility to the space flu, eighty thousand more died by the end of the month—from biochemical weapons sprayed by North Korea's neighbors in a misguided attempt to halt the spread of the virus.

Knowing what we do today, this attack on North Korea seems lazy, foolish, and cruel. We would eventually realize that the so-called "space flu" was merely the result of the cosmic virus network that we would later name the "Linker" virus adapting to the local environment. It was only because the Linker virus adapted by trial and error among the isolated North Korean populace, killing many in the process, that the rest of Earth was spared any serious harm. By January 2011, the Linker virus could coexist harmlessly with humans and had nearly completed its merge with Earth. The massacre of North Koreans with biochemical weapons had been completely pointless. But does it make sense to measure the actions of people back then by the standards of today? How can we understand the terror everyone must have felt at being confronted with the fact that their species might become extinct?

6

The man Cheongsu has in his sights is named Jinho. Jinho had been nobody, just a worker at the Hamheung Wool Textile

Factory, before the alien invaders had landed in Hamheung. He was childless and had been living alone for three years since losing his wife to pneumonia. He was healthy, but lacking ambition or the initiative to go against the wishes of others, and had lived a dull, boring, and essentially worry-free life. He wasn't happy, but that wasn't particularly unusual for someone living in North Korea.

The aliens destroyed the factory where he worked, and when the contagion arrived, it devastated the city of Hamheung where he'd lived his entire life. Yet, despite all of this, he was less unhappy than before. He was finally free of the oppressive system under which he had lived. Although Hamheung had been destroyed, Jinho found the Oliviers that rose up like skyscrapers all around him to be much more beautiful than the collection of old buildings they replaced. The fear of death intoxicated him. Each day was a thrilling adventure.

Jinho spent the first few months after the invasion like a lone wolf. He stole canned food and rice from a destroyed military base and built a greenhouse and vegetable garden on the roof of a still-standing apartment building. Every morning at the hour he used to go to work, he would head outside, collect discarded corpses, burn them, and then disinfect the surrounding area. When the hour marking the end of his former workday arrived, he would head outside to fill his sketchbook and camera with images of the invaders.

For a while, Hamheung was practically a ghost city. But it didn't stay that way forever. People began to arrive. Most were just stopping by on their way to the border, but there were others for whom Hamheung was their final destination. As reports about the chaos at the border began to filter back, people who'd passed through hoping to escape returned and decided to take up residence in Hamheung's abandoned apartments and factories. From there, they watched as Oliviers sprouted up like Towers of Babel and Adjanis swam like stingrays through the sky. A path out into the universe opened before their eyes.

It was the only escape route available to them. People organized into groups and cobbled together spacesuits and capsules out of whatever materials they could find. The spacesuits could barely hold air, and often they only had a single suit per repurposed bus "capsule," but this didn't stop them. In groups of twelve, they would enter a nearby Olivier, board an Adjani, and fly out into the universe along the routes established by North Korea's Space Army.

At first, Jinho just watched. He had no intention of leaving Hamheung. Observing the invaders through his apartment window was enjoyment enough. Sometimes he drew pictures of the places he imagined the escapees were traveling to.

When the massacre of January 2011 began, he had no choice but to change his plans.

At first, he'd thought the new wave of deaths was merely a resurgence of the space flu epidemic. But this time most of the victims were children, all of whom were suddenly stricken with difficulty breathing before dying. Children had been relatively unaffected by the space flu, so whatever was happening to them had to be something else. People started talking about the bombers that flew over Hamheung every night. The rumor was that the outside world had decided to exterminate all potential carriers of the virus.

People grew frightened. They stopped preparing spacesuits and capsules, and crowded into departing Adjanis with nothing more than masks for protection.

Jinho was afraid as well of course, but he wasn't one to fly out into space without the proper precautions. Even if the mere act of boarding an Adjani was a suicidal move, there were ways to mitigate the risk. He'd already pieced together a spacesuit for himself out of a safety suit scrounged up from his factory. The only other thing he needed was a capsule, which he built for himself by modifying an abandoned Whistler sedan.

The day Jinho left Earth, he selected two girls and two boys from among the many lost children wandering the streets to take with him. He didn't ask their names and tried not to remember their faces. He had no intention of becoming attached to them. He only wanted to give them a chance. Even though it might lead to a gruesome death, this was still their only chance to survive.

7

Cheongsu retreats to his bus. He locks its door and hunkers down next to an aluminum cross mounted behind one of the seats in the back. Nervously fingering the bottom half of the cross, he stares through the dust-covered windows.

What the hell are those commie bastards doing here?

He knows the question is rhetorical. He somehow found his way to this planet, as did a group of missionaries, so what was to stop a bunch of commies from doing the same? Still, why did they come here?

He wonders for two seconds whether he could take advantage of the situation. To survive this far from the Olivier, the North Koreans must have brought ample supplies with them. Either that, or they'd figured out some other way to survive on this planet. Under normal circumstances, he would probably just approach them and ask to share some of their food. After all, no military demarcation lines or soldiers or police stand in his way.

But there's nothing normal about the circumstances.

To Cheongsu, commies aren't human: they're monsters, clusters of bacteria, vectors for the space flu. When they first began to flee out into the universe along the Korean route, the North Korean refugees carried with them sickness and death. Two space colonies died out completely after accepting North Koreans into their settlements. After months of trying different approaches, everyone concluded that the only solution was to kill all North Koreans on sight and burn their bodies. Any place North Koreans had stayed for more than a month would be abandoned and the settlers would move to a different continent if possible. If no other continent were available, they would leave the planet.

Such extreme measures turned out to be an overreaction born of ignorance. Space travelers who left Earth before the completion of the Linker network merger were bound to contract the space flu sooner or later. The North Korean escapees had merely accelerated this process. In fact, one of the colonies obliterated by space flu hadn't had anything to do with North Koreans at all. The virus had simply caught up to them.

Those people should never have gone out into space like that in the first place. Why the hell had they left without taking adequate precautions? Had they even bothered to consider the impact their behavior might have on themselves and their fellow Earthlings? Of course not. Those first space travelers were all reckless idiots. It was a miracle that over 20% were still alive five years later. And that 20% survived only because the invader's universe proved unexpectedly hospitable.

It was all thanks to the Linker virus.

From 2009 onwards, new strains of alien viruses kept popping up one after another, but it was not until 2013 that a fuller picture of what was happening came into view. It turned out that the millions of viruses that collectively came to be called the Linker virus were all connected—not by shared biology, but rather by function. By reorganizing their hosts' DNA as well as their own, these viruses were able to merge with their local environments while tapping into a larger Linker network that extended throughout the universe. Any attempt to destroy or control the Linker virus would have been akin to an amoeba trying to take on the entire human race. Adapting was the only option for humans.

Cheongsu himself has survived thus far only because the Linker Virus facilitated modifications to his body. Over the course of several years, he metamorphosed into a space traveler and gained the capacity to acclimate to the different biological or gravitational conditions of other planets with relative ease. If he can avoid starvation on this planet, eventually his body might adapt enough that he'll be able to digest the broccoli.

Cheongsu has already dragged his slowly transforming body through several hundred different star systems. He'd wanted to return to Earth someday, but circumstances made that impossible. War, illness, mutual fear, and the fickleness of the Adjanis prevented North Korean escapees and South Korean colonists from going any direction but forward along the Korean route. Unlike the Scottish and Brazilian routes, which branched out in every direction, the Korean route was a thin, closed loop that wrapped around the Milky Way. No matter how hard the North and South Koreans tried to steer clear of one another, their paths always crossed. Once on the Korean route, they were stuck.

Actually, that's not quite true: Cheongsu passed at least two crossroads in his travels. At one point, the Korean route intersects with the Brazilian one, which would have returned him to Earth. The other branch he had encountered was unmapped, and all he knew was that it would have taken him further out into the Milky Way instead of back toward Earth. But it would at least have saved him from dealing with any more North Koreans.

Cheongsu hadn't been able to take advantage of either opportunity because he was too busy fighting his enemies to observe the comings and goings of the Adjanis. Though he had originally fled into space to avoid mandatory military service, the number of combat hours he'd racked up along the way would have astounded even the most battle-hardened Vietnam War veterans. As far as he was concerned, the Korean route was nothing but war. He and the others didn't know they could stop fighting—they had left Earth too soon. News of the Linker virus was beginning to spread along the different routes, but it never managed to catch up with Cheongsu and his enemies.

Over time, Cheongsu grew inured to death and violence. Back on Earth, people had told him he was a good fighter, but he had never thought that gave him the right to kill a person. Yet, he'd learned to kill people coldly and indiscriminately during the course of his travels along the Korean route. Even children. It was the only way to survive the war. He had no idea why half the North Korean escapees were kids in their early teens, and he didn't want to know. He was only interested in killing them.

The further Cheongsu and other escapees pushed the frontier of the Korean route, the fewer people they encountered. Yet, the paucity of combatants did not make the conflicts between the North and South Koreans any less horrific. To the contrary, no longer able to hide behind numbers or modern weapons, the two sides now engaged in hand-to-hand combat, knifing and spearing each other so intensely that they forgot why they were killing each other in the first place. The South Koreans transformed into zealots, and the masks they wore were no longer just for protection from contagion—they had become a symbolic accessory, like the cross or the South Korean national flag. Sometimes North Korean escapees would disguise themselves as Southerners by wearing masks, which infuriated Cheongsu much as a devout believer would be angered by an act of religious sacrilege.

The fury Cheongsu now felt was not much different from that. He might use catchphrases such as "danger of infection" to try to justify his way of thinking, but the truth of the matter is that he's come to loathe the very existence of North Koreans. If he is to remain on this planet, he's going to have to kill them.

8

In the afternoon, while going to fetch water with two of the children, Jinho discovers Cheongsu's presence when he sees the fresh footprints of an unfamiliar man near the stream. He isn't surprised. He has always known others would someday find their way to this planet as well. But is this man a friend or an enemy?

He sends the two kids back to the tents with their buckets, then slowly follows the footprints upstream. It isn't difficult to figure out where the man is hiding. The bus. It's the only shelter in the area. The South Korean missionaries who it had once belonged to had come to this planet hoping to spread the gospel, but had instead ended up being used as fat and protein in the manufacture of lubricant and memory circuits for the Guinesses and Olivier. When Jinho and the kids first arrived, they had lived for a week off the leftover biodiesel in the bus's tank.

What should he do about this new man? Jinho crouches between the grazing broccoli and thinks things over. First, he has to figure out who this newcomer is. It would be great if he turns out to be North Korean, but what if he isn't? There don't seem to be other people with him, but Jinho is exhausted and doesn't have a proper weapon.

Also, he's sick of killing people.

Until he landed on the planet that the North Korean Space Army had proudly named Limitless Prime, he'd had no idea that things could turn out the way they did. His worries had been about the unfamiliar atmospheres of alien planets, not about other Earthlings. How could he have imagined that other colonies already existed on a planet the North Korean Space Army said they had conquered, and that all the other colonists treated North Koreans like vermin? No one had warned him.

So he ran. He stole a capsule car and weapons, loaded himself and the kids into an Adjani, and fled. As he traveled, he learned how to read Adjani signal lights and how to secure food on unfamiliar planets. By browsing through an English-Korean dictionary he found on a stolen tablet, he even learned how to tell lies in crude English: "I'm not North Korean. We are not dangerous." But the farther he got from Earth along the Korean route, the fewer foreigners he encountered, and the South Koreans weren't fooled by his lies. No matter how much he watched and re-watched the South Korean dramas stored on the stolen tablet's hard drive, his attempts to speak with a South Korean accent were met with gunshots and curses.

As he fled from planet to planet, the number of children following him kept growing. He'd started out with four, but left Limitless Prime with seven. At the next planet, the number shrunk down to three, and at the one after that, it ballooned up to eleven. Since then, the number of children had continued to fluctuate, but never again dropped below ten.

Jinho doesn't really know why he keeps bringing children with him wherever he goes. He's not some courageous philanthropist or altruist. In fact, he doesn't even particularly like kids. But ever since Limitless Prime, he's come to think of protecting children as his duty. It had been a mistake to take children with him when he first left Earth.

He doesn't regret it. Fleeing would have been easier without the kids, but then he would be stuck all alone on this planet thousands of light-years from Earth with no real reason to live. At least this way he knows why he has to keep forging on: for the children. No matter what, he has to make sure the kids survive. And in order for that to happen, he has to survive as well. What could be more obvious than that?

On the other side of the broccoli flock, a flash of reflected yellow light glints and disappears: someone has opened the door to the bus. Jinho quickly ducks his head down. Then he peeks back up. Carefully taking out his binoculars, he examines the area around the bus. A big man emerges and looks around. Jinho notes that the man's hair is long like a woman's, and half the man's face is covered by a ragged mask. The man is carrying a serious pistol in one hand.

This is exactly what Jinho was afraid of. Not only is the man an enemy, he's armed. Still, it could be worse. Attacking Jinho and the children won't be particularly easy even if he knows of their existence. They have the numbers and the experience. The man is probably alone, and he'll probably not attack until he's had some time to adapt to the ecology of the planet. He might just be waiting to fly away on the next Adjani.

Several different plans begin to form in Jinho's head. They could flee before the man notices them. There's nothing tying them to the Olivier. In fact, the farther away they can get the better. The only reason they were even there was because they'd found abandoned tents nearby and the stream was a good source of water. But they could erect their own shelters elsewhere, and there might even be caves in the mountains to the north. If the situation with the man ever got truly dangerous, they could always make the first move. They didn't have any bullets, but just showing their three rifles to the man might be enough to scare him off.

Jinho really doesn't want to leave this planet. Why go somewhere else? Here, they can at least live like human beings. They can't expect the conveniences of civilization, but there's enough to eat and drink, and the weather is good. With a little more experimentation, he'll soon figure out how to make clothing from the fur of the sheep-like broccoli. Then he and the kids can start a farm. Yeah, that's how he'd like to spend his days.

Then Jinho grows pessimistic. Even if his plan worked, how long would it last? Say he gets this thug to leave—how long would they have until someone else showed up? Not many had come to this planet yet, but that was probably just because they'd been too busy fighting. The war between the North and South Koreans would eventually end, and everyone knew which side was going to win. Jinho and the children would be hunted into extinction.

Jinho slowly retreats. Just as he's reached the edge of the broccoli herd, he hears a scream, probably from a young broccoli that has been kicked in the gut. This happens a lot. But the sound catches the long-haired man's attention, and he turns his gaze to the broccoli flock. Which is how he discovers Jinho looking back at him.

The two men stare at each other in silence for a moment. Although the long-haired man is holding a pistol, he doesn't look like he's about to shoot. He's too far away to hit Jinho, and probably doesn't have enough bullets to waste on a warning shot. He's just as much at a loss about what to do next as Jinho is.

He's alone, Jinho thinks. Moments ago, Jinho hadn't been entirely certain, but now he is. The man acts like he's alone. He probably got separated from his companions. This makes him even more dangerous. Jinho has seen people in such circumstances do all sorts of crazy things.

Jinho wants to say something. He wants to tell the man to leave them alone, to please just go away. He opens his mouth, but no words come out. His mind floods with the memories of his previous failed attempts at dialogue.

Retreating from the flock in silence, he heads back north to where the children and tents are waiting for him.

Although the sun has already set, they are gathered outside the tents. He counts them out of habit. One, two, three... There are only thirteen of them. One is missing.

The oldest of the girls, Hyeonhwa, steps forward. Jinho stares at her ears. Looking directly at her face has become difficult for him. At fourteen, Hyeonhwa is already starting to become a woman, and Jinho hates how his body responds to her blossoming figure.

"Uncle Jinho, Yeongwu disappeared," she says.

Yeongwu is a year younger than Hyeonhwa. Jinho had discovered the boy amidst the chaos on the planet Chang Yeongsil and added him to his group. Yeongwu is anxious and violent. Jinho doesn't know whether Yeongwu has always been that way, or if it's the result of having witnessed the murder of his parents. Most of the others dislike Yeongwu, but they wouldn't wish for him to disappear. In a place like this, everyone is thankful to have one more person around.

"Who saw him last?"

The kids all look at one another and shake their heads. Jinho enters the tent he shares with Yeongwu and two other boys. One of the rifles is missing. Has the kid taken it? Why would he do that when there aren't any bullets?

Then a terrifying thought flashes through Jinho's mind. How does he know there aren't any bullets left? He doesn't have any himself, and the kids said that they were all out. But how does he know the kids were telling the truth? How does he know Yeongwu in particular hasn't lied to him?

Jinho grabs his hunting knife and spear and rushes out of the tent. Selecting two fast boys to accompany him, he runs down the path that he and the children have tread into the ground. Jinho does not know where Yeongwu has gone, and he lacks the skills of a storybook hunter to track him down. All he can do is imagine where he himself might go if he were Yeongwu and lusting to kill someone.

As he and the two boys near the midway point between their tents and the bus, they hear the bang of a gunshot. The roar of the blast is soon obscured by a second shot. The broccoli wail loudly at the commotion at first, but soon grow quiet again.

Jinho orders the two boys to hide behind a boulder and stay perfectly still. They obey. After making sure that they are fully hidden, he walks slowly in the direction of the gunshot.

About fifteen minutes later, Jinho finds Yeongwu's body lying face down next to the flock of broccoli. Blood from a bullet hole in Yeongwu's back has stained the ground dark. His pants have been pulled halfway down, and Jinho can see his underwear is wet with urine.

Jinho cannot stop himself from cursing. The fucker has carved out and taken the meat from Yeongwu's thighs.

9

Two vacuum-cleaner-size Waynes stare at Cheongsu. Their red eyes are devoid of emotion, but Cheongsu feels as though they are looking at him reproachfully.

"Get lost," Cheongsu says, waving his hands at them.

The Waynes don't budge. Cheongsu picks up a rock and throws it, causing them to draw back a few centimeters before retreating. No, they're not retreating; they're just continuing to go about their business. They pass by Cheongsu and his bus again a short while later on their way back to the Olivier, each carrying an arm they must have cut from the child with their sawblade hands. So that's what they were so curious about. They had just been wondering where he'd gotten his hunks of meat from.

The Waynes on this planet are small, much smaller than Coopers. The biggest are only about the size of a large suitcase. Back on Yi Sun-sin, a planet named for the legendary admiral, Cheongsu had seen Waynes nearly the size of dinosaurs crush colony buildings under foot and chew up mountains with their jaws. Yi Sun-sin had been a rough place. This planet is peaceful, though, and there probably isn't very much for Waynes to do here. Maybe once they'd finished building that one Olivier, they'd be done with all their work on this planet.

Cheongsu uses scissors to cut up the meat in front of him into pieces so small they no longer resemble meat. When they've all been transformed into fingernail-sized chunks, he places them on the bus's dashboard on the driver's side. One day he's going to have to eat them. Maybe tomorrow. All that remains of his emergency rations is half an energy bar.

"Why shouldn't I have done that?" he mutters to himself. He hadn't done anything wrong. The boy had shot first. Killing him had been an act of self-defense. Sure, taking meat from his thigh had been a bit extreme, but so what? Was he supposed to just starve to death in the midst of all that broccoli while clutching his shrunken stomach? It's not as if he'd killed the boy in order to have something to eat; he'd simply taken a piece of him after the fact. What was so terrible about that? It was certainly no worse than what the green dogs would have done to the boy's body if given the chance. Why should they have more of a right to live than him?

Cheongsu boards the bus and inspects the boy's rifle. There's one bullet in the chamber and nine in the magazine. Between the rifle and his pistol, he has thirteen shots.

How many commies are there? If he assumes four to a tent, then there could be twelve. Possibly more. And they would come for him soon. They must know by now that one of their own had died. The dead boy's parents might even be among them. If their kids carried rifles, what sorts of weapons did the adults carry?

The guns he has aren't going to be enough. He needs other weapons.

Looking around the interior of the bus, his eyes fall on the large aluminum cross that's attached to the back of the driver's seat. Using his pocket knife, he removes the screws that join the two pipes into a cross. He tosses the shorter pipe away and inserts his hunting knife into the longer one, then stomps on it to secure the knife in place. He hefts his new handmade spear and waves it around. The tip is a bit heavy, but nothing he can't get used to. During the course of his travels, he's had to improvise all sorts of weapons. A spear made from a cross is a luxury.

If only he could flee. But that's not an option this time. The Adjani that originally brought him here has already left, and although he searches the landing area around the Olivier every night, he has yet to see any indication that another Adjani will be arriving anytime soon. It seems unlikely. Cheongsu has seen enough Oliviers by now that he can read their personalities. And the one here on this planet definitely does not seem like the social type. Other Olivers he's encountered were more like construction site foremen or merchants, but the one here is clearly enjoying its solitude as it continues to investigate the secrets of the universe. Meanwhile, he's stuck on this old bus preparing to fight a bunch of infectious commie scumbags.

He suddenly finds himself thinking about his old ex-girlfriend, Yeon-ah. Why now? Is it because he knows he has little chance of surviving the fight that awaits him? No, it's only because there's nothing else to do. He can't let himself fall asleep. He has to occupy himself with some thought or another.

Still, why can't he call up an image of Yeon-ah's face anymore? Or her voice? Surely, even if he's no longer able to remember what a woman he dated for four years looks like, he should at least be able to remember her voice.... But why can he no longer recall the face of any woman at all right now?

10

"I can't let you kids die," Jinho says to Hyeonhwa. He gazes one by one at the faces of the sleeping children huddled together in his tent. Before arriving here on this planet, he hadn't been able to tell them apart, much less remember their names. Their faces had changed too often, and he'd lost too many to death. But things are different now. Not only does he know each child's face and name, he knows their nicknames, their hometowns, their favorite foods.

Not one of them can die. Yeongwu shouldn't have died either. Even knowing that Yeongwu had placed them all in danger, Jinho couldn't hate the dead kid. The kids were no longer fungible to him. While they had once been just a faceless group of bodies, now he saw them as individuals.

"At sunrise tomorrow, pack your things and run for the mountains to the north. No matter what, you have to leave this plain. Don't even think about fighting. You can't risk getting slaughtered like Yeongwu."

"Uncle, what about you?" asks Hyeonhwa.

"I'm not going there to die," Jinho lies.

Before leaving, Jinho leaves his treasured notebook with Hyeonhwa. In it he's recorded all the various survival techniques he's learned over the years. Hyeonhwa understands what the gift means, but she doesn't protest. She only cries, covering her mouth and pressing on her throat to stifle the sound.

Armed with an empty rifle and a hunting knife, Jinho slowly makes his way toward the bus. About an hour after he crosses the southern hills, the bus comes into view. He hides himself in a nearby flock of broccoli so he can assess the situation. A nasty vinegary smell permeates the plain. The green dogs must have just made a killing. The other broccoli are quiet and relaxed. They know that they can spend the night in peace after one of them dies. Whenever the green dogs approach, the broccoli push the weakest among them out to the edges of the herd. The green dogs don't hunt; they merely accept the sacrifice offered to them.

Jinho detests the broccoli.

Jinho continues to creep along using the broccoli as cover. When he finally reaches the bus, he slowly makes his way rearward and pushes on the second window from the back. That window never closed properly, he remembers.

The bus is empty.

He ducks almost instinctively. As his head drops, a sharp metal object flashes past the nape of his neck. He rolls away only to find Cheongsu standing before him in a homemade spacesuit.

Having missed with his spear, Cheongsu clenches his teeth and pulls out his pistol. Just as he starts to pull the trigger, Jinho springs and knocks him down. Cheongsu attempts to maneuver his larger body back on top of Jinho, while Jinho continues to hold Cheongsu's pistol hand down. Two bullets are discharged in quick succession. Cheongsu manages to place the barrel of his gun against Jinho's temple, but it slips across Jinho's sweaty brow and behind his ear. They hear the last bullet shatter one of the bus windows.

Realizing that Cheongsu's pistol is now empty, Jinho draws his hunting knife. His first swipe grazes Cheongsu's left forearm but doesn't do any real damage. Cursing, Cheongsu runs toward the bus to retrieve his spear. Jinho attacks again, this time slashing Cheongsu's ankles. Cheongsu falls, and Jinho raises his knife to deliver the final blow.

All of a sudden Jinho goes deaf and feels a crushing weight slam into his chest. Still holding his hunting knife, he looks back and forth between Cheongsu and the rifle that had, until recently, belonged to him and the kids. When had Cheongsu picked it up? Had he been carrying it on his back? Had it been hidden under the bus? The hunting knife falls from Jinho's hand. A bubbling sound comes from somewhere in his body. He tastes blood in his mouth.

Cheongsu limps over to the aluminum spear that is now sticking awkwardly out of one of the bus's window frames. He grabs it and stares at his enemy. The black blood flowing out of Jinho's pierced artery soaks his pants, his chest, and the ground beneath him.

As Cheongsu raises his spear to finish Jinho off, Jinho says something.

"What?" Cheongsu asks.

With all his remaining strength, Jinho repeats himself: "Spare the children," he says, spitting blood with each word.

Sorry, Cheongsu thinks, I can't do that.

11

Cheongsu sets about dismembering Jinho's corpse. He decapitates Jinho, skins his body, and cuts off as much meat as he can. He smashes Jinho's bones at both ends with a hammer to get at the marrow. He throws the rest of Jinho's remains behind the bus. Before long, a Wayne comes by and carries the scraps off. Human meat must be more useful to the machines than broccoli meat.

Jinho's last words linger in Cheongsu's mind. "Spare the children." What did that mean? It meant that Jinho was the only adult of his commie group, and that the remaining children didn't have any real weapons.

Good. He's got the advantage now. The magazine of his rifle is still half-full, and he's got enough food for the time being.

He heads out to hunt the children. Wearing his spacesuit and shouldering his rifle, he attacks their tents at dawn. But he's too late. The tents are completely empty and there's no sign of the children. There's only one place they could have gone: the mountains about four hours' walk from the bus.

For a while, Cheongsu goes out to the mountains nearly every day. He combs through all the places they might be. He discovers footprints and where they bury their shit. He sees drops of blood and pieces of a torn sleeve. But he can't find the kids themselves. Instead, he runs into an eight-legged lizard monster that almost kills him, and wastes three of his precious bullets killing it. Its meat is inedible, of course. Cheongsu still doesn't know about the edible watergrass and waterberries, the foods which Jinho and the children discovered on the day they arrived on this planet. He continues to subsist on his human jerky.

As Cheongsu weakens, he becomes increasingly scared. He uses up his remaining bullets one by one without managing to hit any of the children. Each time he fires his gun, he imagines them counting how many bullets he has left.

The children eventually stop hiding in the mountains and return to the area around the bus. At first, the only traces they leave behind are faint, timid footprints. Then, one day, he discovers that the boys have pissed on the tires and scrawled nasty graffiti in charcoal on the side of the bus. The kids also begin to break the bus's glass windows one by one.

Cheongsu stops going into the mountains. He surrounds the bus with a makeshift alarm system consisting of wire and metal scraps and hunkers down inside. Whenever he sees human-like shadows outside, he throws stones and screams curses.

He's hungry, and his stomach hurts. There isn't much dried human meat left, and some of it has gone bad. Only about three days' worth of food remains.

Then, one morning, he wakes up to find that the rifle magazine has disappeared. He'd been cradling it while he slept.

Staring wildly at his vandalized alarm system and shredded spacesuit, he's forced to admit that the tables have turned. This thought somehow relaxes him. For the first time in a week, he leaves the bus. Realizing that the weather has grown colder, it occurs to him that it has been autumn until now.

He takes a folding chair from the bus and sits down outside, gazing at the broccoli that are gathered as always on the field. Chewing thoughtfully on a piece of Jinho's breast meat, he thinks about the man he killed. Why had that commie come to attack him instead of running away with the children? It's a mystery to Cheongsu–but not one he will be given enough time to solve.

The sun sets. He's just finished the last of his jerky and is nodding off when he feels a chill. He opens his eyes again.

He's no longer alone. More than ten children surround him. Two hold rifles. Cheongsu looks around at all of them, then focuses on the girl who looks like their leader. Her gaze is cold and expressionless.

She silently raises her hand. One by one, the children pull out the weapons they've hidden behind their backs: hunting knives, bayonets, awls, wooden spears. Even bags of stones.

They torture Cheongsu to death without wasting even a single bullet.

12

No Adjanis came to the plain following Cheongsu's death. For the next seven hundred years, the Olivier meditated in silence. Waynes and Guinnesses, now shrunk to the size of puppies, still emerged from the Olivier every now and again to scrounge up raw materials for repairs, but their appearances became increasingly rare.

The children survived. After killing Cheongsu, they obeyed Jinho's final instructions and moved north. There they built houses and found new kinds of food to eat. They wove clothing from grass and made shoes from broccoli leather.

When they came of age, they had sex and bore children. Born with DNA altered by the Linker viruses, their offspring had light green skin and didn't know how to smile. When night came, they would wail at the sky and hunt naked for broccoli.

Forty years after the death of the last of that first generation, the population had increased to five hundred, and was evolving rapidly. Every ten years, a generation would manifest adaptations that were even better suited to the environment of their isolated planet. Their lifespans shrank, as did their bodies and brains. They lost intelligence and language, but gained new senses and the ability to fly. Taking on the green color and nasty sour smell of the plains, they beat their new wings and spread across the entire planet. Not one of them passed onto their descendants the memories of Jinho, Cheongsu, Earth, or any other worlds.

When the Olivier finally ended its meditations and space travelers began arriving once more, they found nothing resembling a human being.

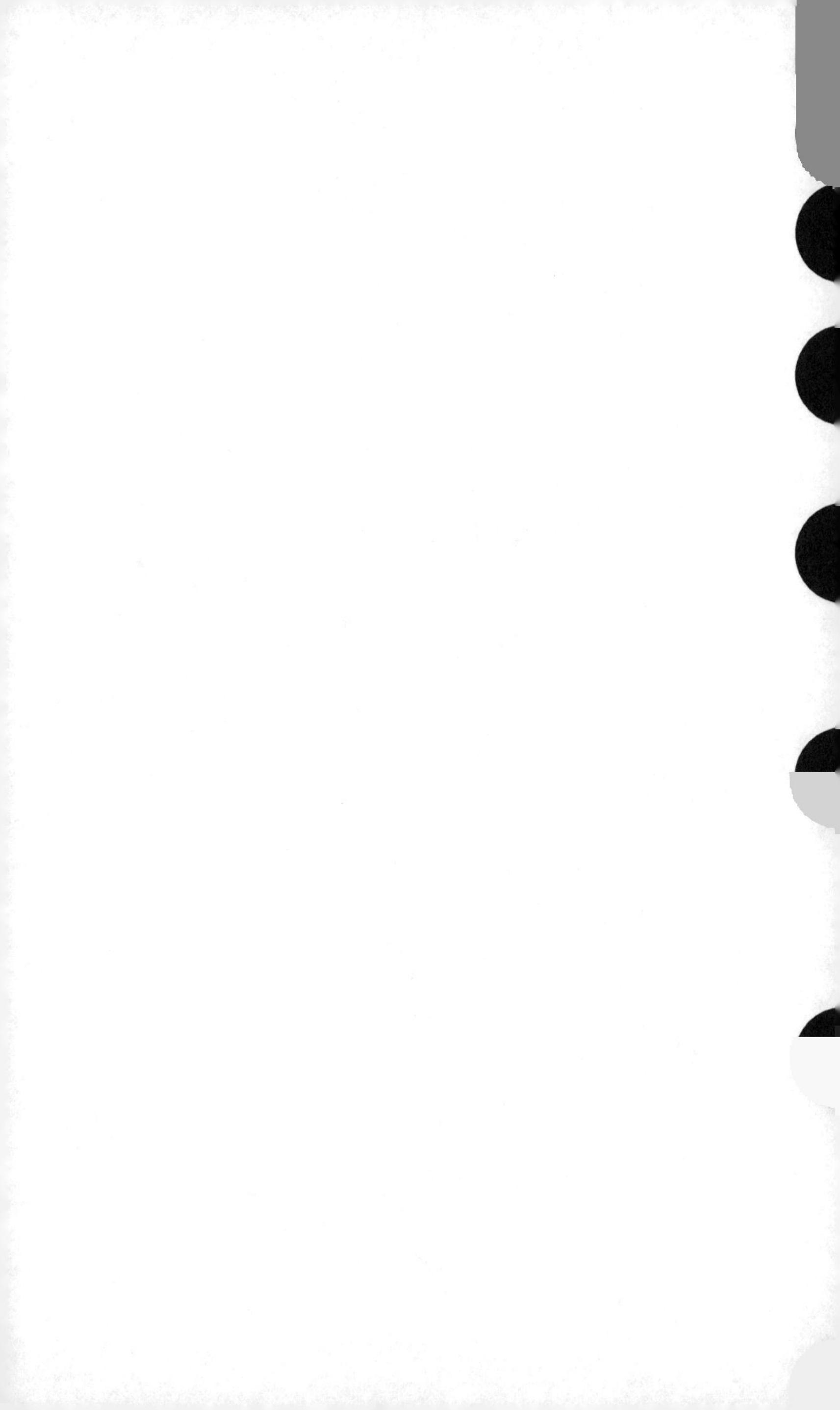

SEA OF FOG

1. MATTHIAS BOLTZMANN

At 9:05 in the morning on April 2nd in Year 92 of the standard calendar, a brilliant sapphire-colored Adjani arrived at the shore of the northern continent of Hańska e outfitted in a thin layer of ice that sparkled like a cocktail dress. Though it was almost solar noon, clouds threatening heavy snow had darkened the day into night. Twelve German men and twenty malamute dogs rattled out of the Adjani in a capsule car with a broken wheel. As soon as they had disembarked, the Adjani flew off toward the other shore of the ocean without even a goodbye.

The men and dogs were all wearing masks, but they didn't plan to keep them on forever. Their bodies and immune systems had already been changed by the Linker virus during their thirty-three-year journey along the Scottish Route and could handle this environment just fine. Hańska e was a bit colder than their hometown of Tubingen, but aside from that, it felt just like home.

The village they built on the coast consisted of five stone houses surrounded by a stone wall. They did not leave room for village expansion—they were old men. All of them were over sixty, and Hańska was the end of their travels. This is where they would live out the rest of their days.

As time went on, the men passed away one by one. The first death occurred the day after the village was completed. One of the men entered his individual dwelling and overdosed on sleeping pills. Four days later, a man fell into the sea while carving steps into a nearby glacier and died of exposure. Two others succumbed to a native disease. Five men built a boat, set sail for the equator, hoped to arrive at a southern continent that may or may not have existed, and were never heard of again. One man went fishing and was eaten by a native fish. One man died in his sleep.

The only person who did not die was Matthias Boltzmann. Boltzmann waited and waited, but death seemed to be deliberately avoiding him. Though he grew younger and healthier with the passage of time, the virus did not restore him to the beauty of his youth, when he had been said to resemble Dirk Bogarde. Instead, as his body rejuvenated, it grew unevenly and sprouted gray hair all over. He ended up with the stooped body of a long-armed, 2.2-meter-tall sloth.

One century passed and then another, but Boltzmann still did not die. He continued to occupy his old room in one of the original stone houses, gazing out at the sea, grumbling and complaining. The stone wall had long since disappeared, and the village he and his friends had once built now sat at the edge of Ewelina, a city with half a million residents. The planet itself was populated by over four million dogs who walked on two legs and spoke both German and English fluently.

They were all Boltzmann's children. Within the context of the Linker virus's games, their evolution was the easiest to understand: two related species, isolated in an alien environment, exchanged genes. Once the resulting lifeforms evolved fingers and bipedalism, they no longer needed Boltzmann's help. Their minds and bodies evolved in directions of their own choosing. In the Linker Universe, the evolution of a species was rapid and frequently reflected the species' will. When they began building the city of Ewelina, many of Hańska's dogs could still remember a time when their ancestors had walked on all fours and were only able to bark and growl.

Boltzmann's relationship with the dogs was asymmetrical. Though he felt both fierce love and loathing for his descendants, he tried to hide his feelings behind a sullen silence. The dogs, however, felt little more than a simple respect for Boltzmann. They recognized and honored him, but they did not accept him as one of their own. He was like a living but unapproachable bronze statue.

On a winter day one week before his three hundredth birthday, Boltzmann went to city hall and applied for a one-person electric boat.

"What are you going to do with it?" The employee asked.

"Go south." He answered.

"Why now? City hall is preparing your birthday party."

"What use is a birthday party? I'm going south."

"You're not planning to kill yourself, are you? We need you, sir. You're the living history of this planet."

"Don't treat me like a library. Where's the key?"

His application was rejected. His complaint to the mayor was likewise rejected. Disappointed, he went home, only to find five dogs from the Defense Force in front of his house. They said it was part of the preparations for his three hundredth birthday, but he did not believe them. They were there to watch him. He had said one wrong thing and now he would be treated like a prisoner.

For the next several days he pretended to help with the city's preparations, giving lectures at schools and signing a new likeness of himself in front of city hall. But at night he went home, descended into the basement that he had once unsuccessfully tried to make into a cellar, and dug a tunnel to the outside.

The night before his birthday, Boltzmann took advantage of a lapse in the vigilance of his watchers to escape through his tunnel. He ran to the harbor, jumped into a two-person fishing boat that he found languishing in a corner, and fled south. When the fireworks rehearsal for the next day's celebration began, he did not even turn around to watch.

2. MAMA KEPPEL

The funeral was held at the city landfill, the only place in Ewelina where it was legal to cremate a corpse. Mama Keppel had wished to be buried at sea like the dogs on Hańska, but she was an alien, and the dogs could not risk the possibility of her genes polluting Hańska should her ashes be dumped at sea.

No one knew what disease Mama Keppel died of. The dogs knew nothing of biology beyond what pertained to the ecology of Hańska. They had little opportunity to learn about the dynamism of the Linker ecology, and even had they understood certain aspects, the knowledge would have been of little use. Mama Keppel had been healthy in the morning, and then her body temperature dropped, her heart rate slowed, and she just died. There had not been time to do anything about it.

Aside from the landfill employees, fifteen dogs attended the funeral. Three were the city employees in charge of us, the remainder were members of the Boltzmann Academy. After the ashes were collected, placed into an urn, and handed over to me, the dogs came up to me one by one to express their condolences in antiquated English that sounded like a nineteenth-century novel. One even offered a handshake, but, as usual, the radial symmetry of the Hańska dogs' five fingers made it difficult.

I entered the landfill with the urn. It was time for me to leave, I thought. Now that my employer was dead, I had no reason to stay any longer. Nor did the dogs want me to stay. They did not enjoy having humans at their side. We were like the second coming of Christ. Everyone said they were waiting for us, but when we came, we were an inconvenient presence that no one actually wanted around.

I went home to make arrangements for the items left behind by the deceased. There really was very little beyond some items of clothing and decorations I would send to a museum. All of the information Mama Keppel had managed to collect on Hańska could fit into two library cubes. The dogs of Hańska lived quietly. Their origin story was their only tale that wasn't simple and boring.

We had known this before we even learned how to get to Hańska. It was the first thing Kristina Buechner warned us about. That place has nothing but stupid old dogs, snow, and ice, she said. Why on earth would you want to go there?

Nevertheless, Mama Keppel had been enchanted by Kristina's story. Mama Keppel loved dogs, which meant loving the vestiges of an old species that had been eliminated by the spread of the Linker virus. And this two-legged dog had appeared in front of her and told her that somewhere along the Scottish route, two-legged, talking dogs had continued canine civilization.

She had to go and see for herself. Even if it really was as boring as Kristina said, visiting Hańska would give meaning to the rest of her life. I was a well-known guide on the Scottish route, and so she hired me. It took us two years of changing Adjanis and Garbos to find Hańska. In the end, we passed through one hundred and eighty-four planets and moons along the way.

Was she happy during the eight months she lived on Hańska? I don't know. The Hańska dogs allowed us little freedom. Our house was no different from a prison, and when we went out, we had to wear masks and gloves. Needless to say, they also collected and incinerated all of our waste and excretions. Yet, even in that environment, Mama Keppel always remained positive and cheery. The dogs who attended the funeral did not do so merely out of politeness. They truly did want to pay their final respects to their departed friend. They did not feel the same about other species as they did about fellow dogs, but they did feel something.

I hung my legs over the edge of the couch and read Mama Keppel's unfinished draft on the library cubes. She had worked on the book regularly over the eight months as if it were a diary. It was as long as *War and Peace*, but, as for the content—it seemed Mama Keppel had never set out to write an orderly, logical report.

Let's read it from the beginning. Instead of starting with Boltzmann and Kristina Buechner, she opens with her own seventy-sixth birthday party, which is a way to reminisce back to her eleventh birthday party, which in turn is little more than a window to recalling memories of her first pet. She then spends the length of a decent French novel in philosophical exploration of the existence of pets before the word "dog" even appears, much less any mention of Hańska or Boltzmann. Or rather, she does mention them, but without naming them. Instead, she hints at them vaguely, so that they appear as a kind of leitmotif that can be read between the lines. Only when Kristina Buechner appears in her world do these words suddenly ring out with the force of a trumpet call.

The story became slightly easier for me to follow from that point because I had witnessed the events described in person, but reading her book became more difficult. It doesn't seem as if Mama Keppel ever considered simply describing reality. Rather, she embellished, abstracted, and exaggerated everything that crossed her mind. Her description of Kristina Buechner as a proud Russian aristocrat who took refuge in Paris in the early twentieth century astonished me. When I realized that Mama Keppel's guide, whose description as a taciturn, tough persona she had obviously modeled on Clint Eastwood, was me, I nearly split my sides with laughter.

I never for a moment thought to ridicule her for the inaccuracy of her book, though. She viewed the world from her own perspective, and her book reflected that—nothing more, nothing less. So what if it wasn't true? We are no longer in the age of Darwin and the HMS Beagle. No one looks to explorers for objective information. All discoveries are personal experience, and in a book like this, people give more weight to the perspective of the author than to the informational content. Would it ever really be possible to learn anything from Hańska? Apart from the fact that they walk around on two legs, Hańska's dogs are unexceptional. Just like all the other beings in the Linker Universe.

3. SOPHIE MOZART

Mayor Sophie Mozart had casually proposed that we have dinner together one day, but this turned out to be far easier said than done, as I had to be kept isolated from the dogs. Not wanting me to feel inconvenienced by that requirement, the dogs constructed a glass box to enclose my side of the table. While trapped inside, I exchanged formalities with the five dogs attending the dinner and ate slices of meat from a native sea creature that looked, at first glance, like the cut-off legs of a Chippendale chair. It felt as though I had landed in the middle of a scene from *Get Smart*, the Earth sitcom Mama Keppel had liked almost as much as the writings of Marcel Proust, but I found it impossible to laugh. Not out of politeness, but rather because I was playing a part in it too.

Though I've been calling them dogs, the inhabitants of Hańska were more like anthropomorphized bears. In the process of evolving into two-legged, talking animals, their bodies and faces had grown rounder and shorter, their arms and legs had grown thicker, and their tails had receded until they almost disappeared. Parts of their bodies bore little resemblance to anything that could be found in dogs or humans or bears: their radially-symmetric fingers and their rounded, split tongue that looked like Mickey Mouse's ears, for example. In fact, there was no real reason to go on calling them dogs. Genetically speaking, they were already a new species.

Our conversation went pretty much as expected. "Since

Mama Keppel is dead, there's no reason for you to stay here any longer," they said. "If you would like to, of course, the city will do its best to cooperate with you. However, is it really necessary for you to stay? We will continue to cherish the memory of Mama Keppel even after you leave, so you need not worry about that." By the time dessert came out, their suggestions became a little more concrete: "A research vessel will be leaving Ewelina the day after the summer solstice and will arrive at the shore of the south pole in less than half a month. It can drop you off next to an Olivier and protect you until you board an Adjani and leave Hańska." Apart from details about days and names, all this was almost exactly as I had expected. I agreed without thinking too much about it, and this seemed to put them at ease.

When dinner ended and I made to exit the glass box, Mayor Sophie suddenly grabbed my hand. This was unexpected. Even wearing masks and gloves, the dogs did not like to touch me. There was something she wanted to say. Something personal and secret. Were I more astute, I would have realized that this might be the case when I had first received the dinner invitation. There was no need for a formality such as this dinner simply to notify me of what they had already decided.

"I have a personal favor to ask." Sophie said.

I looked around. Everyone else had already disappeared. This was awkward: I had never before been alone with a Hańska dog. There were always two or more of them and Mama Keppel had always been at my side.

"I understand if you are not willing to accept this charge, but there is something important I need your help with."

"What is it?"

"I would like you to take my daughter Wilhelmina with you."

"To the south pole?"

"No, to the world outside. Into the universe."

I was astonished. For starters, it had never occurred to me that Sophie Mozart might have a daughter. She was the beta female of Mozart pack. I had naturally assumed she would not have children.

To understand this requires an abbreviated explanation of how the Hańska system works. Mama Keppel would have intertwined the information gradually over one hundred pages of her story, but I don't have the energy for such games.

You might think it strange that I referred to the mayor as Mayor Sophie rather than Mayor Mozart, but apart from the deceptive pervasiveness of the antique proper nouns they use in imitation of German culture, the society created by the Hańska dogs was quite different from the old culture of Earth. One of the most obvious differences was their "pack" culture. Mozart was not Sophie Mozart's "family name," but rather her "pack name," so to call her "Mayor Mozart" would be meaningless. A third of high-level positions in the Ewelina city government were occupied by the Mozart pack, as were all the dogs I had just eaten dinner with. It was therefore useless to refer to anyone in the city government as "Mozart."

Seventy percent of Hańska's dogs belong to a pack. These range in size from five to one hundred members, and resemble families as well as trade guilds, with occupational affinity being more important than bloodline. In elections, votes are tallied for packs rather than individuals. Sophie Mozart had been named mayor because she was the beta female of the Mozart pack.

Why was the beta named mayor instead of the alpha? I can explain that too. Packs are typically mixed-sex, but this is not always the case. Mozart was a female pack. And in female packs, internal politics are somewhat complex. The female alpha controls and manages everything related to household affairs and pregnancy, but this means that she's sometimes unable to realize the pack's actual objectives. Therefore, occupational leadership is often delegated to the second in the hierarchy, the beta, and, in turn, most betas refrain from bearing children out of respect for their alphas. This is not of course an iron-clad rule; there are exceptions. It's just that I had never imagined Mayor Sophie might be one. She had never seemed like someone who might allow herself to be an exception.

"Does she want to go with me?" I asked carefully.

"I'm not sure. But I have to send her. She knows that."

"But... Why?"

"She is like you. A hermaphrodite. The doctor confirmed it last week." Mayor Sophie pronounced the archaic term "hermaphrodite" carefully, as if chewing on the word. As if it were a curse.

I now understood the situation. Her daughter was being exiled because she was a mutant. It did not matter to the Hańska dogs what the specific mutation was. I think Kristina Buechner had said something like that. What was the reason she gave again? Ah, yes. Because they were thought to dream different dreams. Kristina had talked about how, when she was still just an eight-year-old puppy, her pack had taken her to the hospital after she had told them about her dreams. After analyzing her brain, she'd been told that her dream must not spread to other dogs. Then they'd sent her away to the south pole, where there was an Olivier. Kristina never told me what that dream had been about.

This obsession with genetic identity had begun when

Boltzmann fled, leaving a dog-only world in his wake. The inhabitants of Hańska were proud of the fact that they were dogs, and they feared the possibility of turning into something else. These fears were probably exacerbated by the fact that they still remembered their own process of evolution. Just like breeders on ancient Earth, they managed bloodlines closely for purity. Yet, rarely were the choices they faced as extreme as this one. In total, fewer than four hundred Hańska dogs had ever left their homes because of mutations. According to the Hańska records, anyway.

It would be really worrisome if Willie Mozart's abnormality was real. The dogs of Hańska were afraid of virgin births and hermaphrodites. This wasn't just paranoia. Why had the Linker Universe become a breeding ground for mutants, if not because of such genetic changes? I've always thought this was likely why they accepted Mama Keppel more easily than they did me. Mama Keppel was really a woman. Never mind the fact that being such was both an abnormality and a handicap on her home planet of Sylvanus.

I later learned about Sophie and Willie's past from another member of the Mozart pack. Originally born into the Shanghai pack, which specialized in cooking, Sophie had worked frantically for ten years in order to attain her position as the beta of the Mozart pack. Willie was her child from when she had been in Shanghai pack. I tried to ask my interlocutor, who'd been born and raised Mozart, what this signified, but all she gave by way of reply was a polite smile.

4. WILLIE MOZART

Willie Mozart and I arrived at Boltzmann Harbor at 4:15 in the morning. The kid must have woken up at 3 am, because she kept falling asleep in the car and nearly fell down when we finally got out of it. She was twelve years old according to the Hańska calendar, or about eleven years old according to the standard one. She didn't look particularly strange. To me, all Hańska puppies looked cute, although I had no idea of the dogs' own standards for cuteness. The mayor followed us into our assigned cabin and I gave both mother and daughter some space so they could say their goodbyes. I didn't hear anything that sounded like crying. At exactly 5:50 in the morning, the mayor disembarked from the ship, and we departed on time at 6:00. The mayor stood awkwardly on the shore, looking away from the boat as she pawed the ground.

The kid lay down on a bed to try to sleep while I arranged our luggage. Most of it was mine. Hańska dogs barely ever wore clothing except for when it was particularly cold or hot. The only things the kid had brought with her were an insulated suit that could cover her whole body, an ice vest, three sets of gloves, a small puppy doll, and a small tin box on which had been printed her initials: W.M. I turned the box over gently. From inside, I could hear the sound of small, heavy objects like pebbles hitting one another.

Spending time with the kid was easier than I had expected. I had steeled myself to deal with a crying puppy who just wanted her mother, but my new roommate could control her emotions fairly well. She looked depressed and tired, but didn't seem to have any intention of discomfiting the dogs around her by revealing her emotions. Life as a Hańska puppy was never particularly happy. They knew where they belonged in the pack hierarchy.

How would she change when she got to a different world? I didn't have any plans whatsoever. In the Linker Universe, possibilities were almost limitless. Willie could find herself some foster parents or enter an institution, or she could meet Kristina Buechner. There was no need to worry about any of that in advance. The Linker Universe always had extra space.

When in the ship's cabin, the kid spent most of her time reading books, usually books about the ocean. It didn't matter to her what kind of ocean it was or what planet it was on. As long as enough liquid came together in one place, the kid found it fascinating. When not reading, Willie walked around the ship, checking out the ocean through each and every window. The ocean seemed to soothe her heart.

Sometimes she would ask me about the world beyond Hańska. I talked about Kristina Buechner and, boasting only a little, described the diversity of the Linker Universe. I also talked a lot about oceans: the ocean dyed red with iron oxide on Sylvanus c, the ocean held together by centrifugal force inside the wall of the first planet of Anna Karenina B, the ammonium ocean of Salome h, and many, many others that I had heard about but not seen with my own eyes.

When I finished with my stories, Willie would talk about Hańska's ocean. She seemed to know every possible story there was related to the Hańska ocean ecosystem. She didn't much care whether these stories were true or not; the stories just needed to be interesting. Were she still alive, Mama Keppel would have loved this kid's ocean, with its abundance of sea monsters and ancient sunken civilizations.

Examining the paleontological evidence left from its Darwinian era, the possibility that ancient native civilizations or sea monsters had ever existed on Hańska was actually quite low. The Linker Universe should have been fertile ground for sea monsters, but over the last few hundred years, only four or five of the reclusive monsters have actually had their existence confirmed with photographic evidence. As was the case with old Earth's sea monsters, the rest seemed to exist primarily in people's imaginations. Instead of going out into the universe, Hańska's dogs seem to have projected an imaginary universe down into their own oceans.

I will probably discuss this in more detail later, but the monster stories Willie told me were not entirely fictional, and in fact, would cause us significant difficulty. At the same time, I do not mean to say that Willie's fantastic stories were true. Throughout the course of our lives, reality sometimes collides with our imagined fictional worlds. These discordances illustrate the limits of our imagination, but they do not mean our fictional worlds are real.

5. OLD SHATTERHAND

Old Shatterhand was a scientific research vessel with a displacement of 300 tons. Its all-male crew of seventeen belonged to the Surabaya M pack. The female Surabaya F pack worked at the oceanic research institute in Ewelina. These packs would get together during the spring mating season and at the year's four seasonal festivals, but other than that, they barely met. Surabaya was a relatively young pack. Even the oldest estimates put them at younger than 200 Hańska years—200 years ago was when Hańska's dogs had stopped clinging to European pack names.

Old Shatterhand's main duty was periodic research into the marine ecology around the northern continent. Hańska relies on the ocean for eighty percent of its food, so this was important work. From time to time, the city government would pay researchers an additional stipend to go further afield to the equator or the south pole. This was something of an ordeal for Hańska dogs, born as they were with thick fur coats.

Hańska has only two continents, one at each pole. The dogs lived at the edge of the ocean on the northern continent. They kept away from the southern continent, which was only a quarter of the size of the northern. Interference from the Linker machines prevented communication between the northern and southern hemispheres, so the southern hemisphere seemed like a completely different world. Aside from exiles, only scientists, cartographers, and historians ever visited the place.

The rest make sense, but why the historians? They were Boltzmann Scholars. They believed that there might still be things left by Boltzmann somewhere on the southern continent. It was important for these scholars of what they called Boltzmann Studies to learn and master everything about Boltzmann's life. They did not glamorize or deify Boltzmann; they tried to see him for who he was. They exposed and displayed his shortcomings, mistakes, and crimes without attempting to defend them. Every aspect of Boltzmann was important to them. Sometimes they conducted earnest debates on topics like "Why did Boltzmann steal his coworkers' coffee on planet Ingersoll?" Although there were no Boltzmann Scholars on Old Shatterhand, all of the crew nonetheless dabbled in Boltzmann Studies to some extent. They all had their own opinions about Boltzmann's disappearance, and they were willing to come to blows in defense of these opinions. It was the closest thing Hańska had to a religion. Or perhaps it was closer to soccer fandom.

The spectacle of seventeen males growling around together

on Old Shatterhand was new to me. I had never before seen a Hańska pack made up entirely of males. Until then, I had only ever encountered mixed or majority-female packs. Women held the largest share of the city administration.

The most particular thing about the all-male group was their language use. They were constantly cursing, though their curses were not mere imitations of human ones. To the dogs, the curses of Earthlings sounded like emotionless, absurd poetry. Instead, the dogs cursed in Wolfish, a language inherited from their ancestors and imprinted into their genes. Old Shatterhand rang with the growls and howls of Wolfish mixed together with human language. Even if most of the sounds had no particular meaning, they still gave me chills when they woke me in the middle of the night.

I gradually came to understand the ship's atmosphere. Old Shatterhand was definitely not a happy little family. The Surabaya M pack was slowly breaking apart from within.

On the surface, the reason for this was that the ship's captain, Augustus Surabaya, was infuriatingly lazy and incompetent. That, at least, is what the crew believed. Augustus Surabaya's alpha position in the pack could be attributed entirely to high-level political connections he had within the Ewelina city government. The pack's current beta male, Sigfried Surabaya, had ascended to First Mate only two years after joining the pack thanks to his personal connection to the captain, and was even less popular.

Waldemar Surabaya was the de-facto alpha championed by most of the crew. Waldemar had a large body that was paired with a good personality and reputation. His only shortcoming was a lack of ambition. The crew was quite upset by the fact that he wasn't interested in challenging the ship's captain and claiming the alpha position for himself. I, however, understood his choice well enough. He was already the de-facto alpha anyway, so why would he give up all the benefits the pack enjoyed from leaving Augustus in the alpha position? But according to simplistic calculations of the crewmembers, Waldemar should become the alpha no matter what.

Most of the Wolfish growling I heard at night were arguments related to this topic. When I learned what the ruckus was about, I grew even more alarmed. The government administration had warned me that all sorts of things happened in all-male packs. But Old Shatterhand was the only research vessel capable of going to the southern continent that the Ewelina government could commandeer, so they had had no choice but to put us on it.

The only thing that put my mind somewhat at ease was the fact that, because we were travelers leaving for outer space, the pack had no reason to get rid of us regardless of what we might witness. There was no way we would ever go back to tell the Ewelina government about something the crew had done. This thought was actually not that comforting, but it was the first card I would play were something to happen.

6. ADELBERT ESTRELLA

For a week, Old Shatterhand sailed south at a relaxed pace. Our trajectory was arced like a bow because we were riding the Basler current that drew a crescent between the northern continent and the equator. When we reached the equator, Old Shatterhand would leave the Basler Current for the Kohler Current that curved in a similar fashion down to the southern ocean. Our route was like a vehicle track carved into the surface of the ocean.

The equator divided Hańska's ecosystem in two. Linker evolution had proceeded in entirely different ways in the north and in the south. Although the federation of city governments in the north had declared the southern continent to be Linker machine territory, dogs regularly sent boats to the south. They felt they had to know what was happening on the other side of their world.

Having been born on a desert planet, I was the only one aboard who welcomed the warmer weather as we headed further south. The dogs began grumbling when the temperature reached a mere twenty-two degrees Celsius. They turned on the air conditioners and wore ice vests to prevent heat stroke. Yet, the temperature rarely exceeded twenty-five degrees. The tropical sun I had been waiting for was often covered with clouds and fog.

That fog also covered the place where we rescued Adelbert Estrella.

At the time, I was discussing sea monsters that I heard about from Willie with Waldemar Surabaya. More specifically, we were talking about whether the evolution of the morak, a fifty-meter long sea snake monster with ten long tentacles, was possible in the Linker Universe. Even though Waldemar was the cause of all the violence that erupted on the ship, he was nevertheless pleasant to speak with. He was like the eye of a typhoon, tranquil and serene.

Just as our discussion reached an apex, the ship's horn rang out, producing not just any old sound, but rather a song in Wolfish. To my ears, the blast from that horn sounded far clearer and more certain than the Wolfish growls of the Surabaya pack.

Stop. Caution. Something's out there.

Planting myself on the deck, I looked around but didn't see anything. However, the dogs, whose noses and ears were far more sensitive than my own, seemed to sense something. I closed my eyes and concentrated all my energy on listening. Between the sounds of the waves, I did finally hear something: a rescue signal in Wolfish. Someone had learned of our existence in the midst of all that fog and was crying out for help.

The ship moved slowly in the direction of the sound. Soon, a small oblong boat came into view. Something like a dog's head stuck out from between the ropes of the black net that covered it. It was the dog whose cries we had heard. A strong vinegary smell wafted up to greet us as we drew near.

Two crewmembers descended and rescued the survivor, bringing him up into Old Shatterhand. As I mentioned before, the survivor's name was Adelbert Estrella. The Estrella pack was a maritime research pack much like Surabaya, though with a slightly different focus. Until two days ago, the Estrella pack had been at the Bachmann Deep, four hundred kilometers south of the equator, researching the deep-sea fish of that unique ecology. But what could possibly have happened to Adelbert Estrella's colleagues? They've all died, he said. How? Monsters. It was also the monsters that had sunk their ship.

"A morak?" someone asked.

"It wasn't just one species," he replied. "I actually saw at least three, all new. One looked like a whale, another like a dinosaur. I thought at first that one of them was a Guinness-made submarine because it was well over fifty meters long. But they were all living creatures. Look at the boat I was on. You can still find fluids and bits of skin from them on it."

"You're saying the monsters just attacked your ship?"

"Yes. For no reason. They just swam up from the ocean depths and rammed us. We were completely unprepared. We were sitting ducks. The ship sank in less than thirty minutes, and most of the crew became fish food. I was lucky."

A cold fear gripped our ship. Hańska dogs liked stories about sea monsters. But hearing about them directly from a dog who had actually fought the monsters in this remote ocean and barely escaped alive was a different matter. Old Shatterhand was an old ship and no sturdier than the Rhodes. If the monsters had sunk that ship into the Bachmann Deep along with its Estrella pack crew, they could sink us too.

The Old Shatterhand crew immediately set out to try and confirm Adelbert's story. The boat was raised on deck and samples were taken for the lab. Adelbert also had video and photo files of the monsters. He had shot them on a moonless night, so the quality was terrible, but, even so, it wasn't difficult to confirm the existence of the monsters that had attacked the ship.

The dogs met in the mess hall and began to growl. What should we do now? Was what happened to the Estrella pack just an unfortunate accident? Should we simply continue on our way? Or should we take the attack as a declaration of war against dogs and head back north? I felt the latter suggestion to be an overreaction, but then again, existing pack politics were interfering with the discussion. When the captain and his beta supported the first option, the others naturally felt they had to support the second. The second option really would have won out had not Waldemar stood up and voiced support for the captain's position. It won by only a single vote.

As soon as the voting was over, the crew members returned grumbling to their various positions on the ship. Only the captain and his beta remained in the mess hall. Willie and I had been watching from the back of the hall, and as we left to go back to our cabin, I saw the beta put his hand on the captain's shoulder and say something to console him. I did not share the Surabaya pack's feelings of hatred and disgust toward the pair, so, to me, the scene seemed merely pitiful.

That was the last time I saw either of them alive.

7. WALDEMAR SURABAYA

It was not until eight o'clock the next morning that the Surabaya dogs realized their captain and beta were missing. At first, no one was overly concerned about their absence. But when there was still no news at lunchtime, the dogs began to wonder if something bad might have happened. They searched the boat from top to bottom to no avail. Old Shatterhand was now a boat without a captain.

The atmosphere on the boat grew strange. It was no secret that the captain and the beta had been unpopular. Up until a few days ago, the rest of the crew had growled at them as if they might kill them. However, now that they had actually disappeared, the dogs were unsure what to do. They would have felt better if the two had been murdered in public for all to see. Yet, as it was, everything was too ambiguous and confusing for them to accept the disappearance and relax. Had the captain and the beta died in an accident? Had they killed themselves? Had they been murdered? Having a known murderer on board would have been far easier to endure than the possibility that a murderer lay concealed in their midst.

There was only one solution: to elect a new alpha and let

him worry about it all. Waldemar Surabaya was elected by a unanimous vote. Once he had been officially named the new alpha and captain, he insisted on not holding an inauguration ceremony until they had fulfilled their duties and returned home. He also refused requests to hold a new vote on whether or not to proceed with their journey. So we continued on toward the southern continent.

Willie and I shut ourselves in our cabin and whiled away the hours guessing at the fate of the captain and the beta. The most likely suspect was, unsurprisingly, Waldemar Surabaya. Hańska dogs were capable of all sorts of heinous deeds to occupy the position of alpha. Was Waldemar really any different? Still, it didn't fit his personality. We simply couldn't see him as the kind of dog who would go to the trouble of murder just to be alpha. It seemed much more likely that one of his followers had acted alone. If so, then who? That's where our hypothesizing came to a dead end. We did not know enough about the rest of the crew to go any further.

Old Shatterhand now rode the Kohler Current. The days were gradually getting colder, and as the temperature fell, the fog around the current grew thicker. This southern ocean fog was far worse than the fog we had encountered prior to crossing the equator. It looked almost as solid as a gray brick wall. Even older crew members who had visited this area dozens of times before appeared uneasy at the weather. Their keen ears and noses were of no help in relieving their unease. Rather, all the information stimulated excessive imagination. They heard water, groans from unidentified animals, wind. And they noticed the odors of everything. This data, which would, in normal times, have been part of their natural environment, now bore down on them like monsters.

The third day after entering the Kohler Current, Waldemar realized something ominous. The current was moving in a strange direction.

The ship had already deviated from its course by about one hundred kilometers. Waldemar immediately ordered everyone to get the ship back on course as he tried to understand what was going on. But there was not much they could do. The ship was already well within the Linker interference zone, so the crew could not connect to their satellites and had no way of communicating with city officials in the north. All they were able to do was gather as much information as possible from their surroundings.

So far, they had figured out only one thing: the cause of the fog. It was the colder-than-usual surface temperature of the water. This piece of information was too random to draw any real conclusions from. However, the realization that they were in Olivier territory led them to one hypothesis worth entertaining. It seemed clear that something the Linker machines were doing had led to large-scale environmental changes. The shifting of the Kohler Current and the cooling of the ocean were both the result of this. If caused by the melting of nearby ice, then the coldness of the ocean might also be evidence of warming. That would be the perfect environment for rapid Linker evolution. In other words, the idea that sea monsters might suddenly start jumping out of the sea and sinking boats such as the Rhodes did not seem that strange after all.

It would not have been surprising had some dogs again begun to advocate returning north. Yet, the atmosphere on Old Shatterhand was now rather tranquil. Though the dogs were uneasy and fearful, no one deviated from the consensus.

Ever since Waldemar had ascended to the alpha position, the emotions of the pack members had stabilized. They were not loyal followers of Waldemar, nor had they forgotten their suspicions about the disappearance of the captain and beta. It was not Waldemar that they wanted, it was pack stability. They were satisfied that the leader they recognized as alpha was now alpha. One could not expect Hańska's dogs to exhibit the sort of devoted loyalty that Earth dogs had been famous for. Hańska dogs were always coldly realistic and opportunistic.

Old Shatterhand found its way back to its original route, but the situation there was not particularly different. They found a location marker, but that was all. The southern ocean was no longer familiar to them. The tastes, smells, sounds, and shapes of things were all different, and the fog was thicker than ever.

One day, a huge, winged shadow swept over the ship and disappeared. The crew cried out in alarm at the time, but later collapsed into laughter. It was just an Adjani that had come out of the southern continent's Olivier. It had to have been an Adjani. No matter how much the Linker virus might have changed the southern ocean, such a giant flying creature could not possibly have been born there, in that place. Everyone teased the crew members who had been unlucky enough to be up on deck that day.

The very next day, a huge sea monster rushed toward our ship. Someone rang the emergency alarm and the crew grabbed all the weapons they could find and ran out on deck. It turned out that this so-called monster was in fact just a gigantic Hańska whale. Though larger than average, the whale was of a known species, and it was a gentle species that subsisted on plankton.

While crossing the sea of fog, the crew continued to experience episodes such as this. They would see unknown sea monsters in the fog and cry out, only to realize that what had appeared to be a fantastical creature was actually something quite familiar to them. The repetitive anxiety and despondency brought about by these disturbances left the crew ever more paranoid.

Willie Mozart seemed the most relaxed dog on the ship. She accepted all the things that were happening as if they were just adventures in one of her books. She would wander around shooting photos, recording audio, and jotting down everything in her notebook. Returning to our cabin, she would read Herman Melville's *Moby Dick*, carefully comparing our experiences with those in the story and looking for similarities. She was disappointed not to find anyone on the ship resembling Captain Ahab.

If we extend the comparison to *Moby Dick*, Waldemar Surabaya would be not Ahab, but rather Starbuck. He was rational, cautious, and avoided unnecessary risks. Yet, Old Shatterhand was not a whaling ship, and no one knew what might meet us in that new ocean. As such, Waldemar's rationality and caution were, in fact, completely useless. No matter if we were captained by an Ahab or a Starbuck, fate alone would dictate whether the ship met a sea monster.

8. MONSTERS

The first trace of the sea monsters was the pumice.

What seemed to be thousands of gray stones appeared in front of Old Shatterhand. They were each one to two meters in diameter and resembled peach pits in their shape, density, and pocked appearance. Sometimes stone of this kind formed in the stomachs of sick Hańska whales, who then vomited them out. But it would have taken more than a few sick whales to regurgitate so many stones of this size. These were clearly the discharge of an entirely different creature.

As soon as we passed by the floating stones we were confronted with something like an island floating on the surface of the ocean. On closer inspection, it appeared to be the jumbled wreckage of a sunken ship. Something like seaweed tied the wreckage together into a single mass, and half-inflated, transparent balloons floated around it. We saw nothing living or moving inside. At first, everyone thought a Guinness must be playing a joke on us. But the construction was too poor for that. Crucially, it did not seem to have any function at all. It seemed nothing more than a knot of scrap metal floating on the ocean surface.

The third thing that met us was the corpse of a huge animal. It looked to be around sixty meters long, making it about ten meters longer than the largest Hańska whale ever found. What remained of the corpse was a backbone extending from the head to the end of the tail, a left fin with exceptionally long fingers attached, and a tail. As we watched, the corpse suddenly flitted under the water, tail first, and then resurfaced a few moments later. Flesh disappeared from the tail. Something around fifteen meters long, with a tail and a rounded body, was moving beneath the corpse.

"Look, there's something there!" Someone said.

The crew broke into Wolfish laughter and looked happier for a brief moment. Actually seeing a monster turned out to be preferable to imagining one. They began joking around and hitting each other with their fists and lightly biting one another, perhaps due to the sudden surge of adrenaline.

"Attention!" Waldemar stood in front of the crew. "We are now only 320 kilometers from the southern continent. We could reach it before midnight if we were to proceed at maximum speed. Needless to say, we are not in a rush, and so let's not startle whatever monsters are lurking beneath the surface. Anyway, given that it is already too late to retreat, let's put our fears aside and continue onward as planned."

It wasn't a particularly stirring speech, but it resonated with the crew nonetheless. To be fair, they didn't really care what Waldermar said, it was the calm and optimistic way he said it that mattered. The crew responded to the responsible attitude of their alpha and began to move about in an orderly fashion. They had never displayed this sort of enthusiasm when Augustus had been alpha.

The general excitement did not include Willie, Adelbert Estrella, or me. Waldemar was not our leader and we did not have any responsibilities on Old Shatterhand. Even had we wanted to do something, they would not have let us squeeze our way into their pack. As the pack grew more cohesive, we became more and more of a burden.

While the crewmembers rushed about, we gathered in a corner of the mess hall to eat an early dinner and drink tea. As we drank, Adelbert Estrella told us his view of the situation. He thought that some kind of contagious gigantism had piggybacked on the Linker virus, and explained to us how this could be possible. His hypothesis sounded reasonable. Yet, he did not have the passion of a scholar, and his logic unfolded extemporaneously. It seemed like he was saying whatever came to mind in the moment just as a way to make conversation.

I thought it all a bit strange. He had just barely escaped being eaten by sea monsters and was facing another attack by monsters. Shouldn't he be afraid or angry or excited? Adelbert talked and acted as if he had no interest in the monsters. Or, more precisely, it seemed he was more interested in something else, even though I didn't yet know what.

Yet, what on Old Shatterhand could be more interesting than monsters large enough to sink the ship? Old Shatterhand was an ordinary research vessel. There were no particularly sensitive secrets or special research to be found onboard. The only thing remotely strange about the ship was me, the only alien on the planet. But he clearly had no interest in me. So what was it on this ship that fascinated him more than the monsters?

That's when I noticed his gaze slip to Willie. I had turned for a moment toward the sound of shouting from the crew outside, and when I turned my head back, I found Adelbert staring fixedly at Willie, who had met his gaze. Adelbert immediately lowered his eyes back to his teacup as if caught in a criminal act. All this had taken no more than a few seconds, only an instant, really, but I was sure of what I had seen.

I pretended not to have noticed a thing and continued to sip tea and talk about the huge sea monsters I'd seen on other planets. Though most of the stories were true, I embellished a bit based on books I'd read. Adelbert had no way of confirming the truth of my tales, and, in any case, he wasn't interested. Something else dominated his thoughts.

We heard another shout. This time it was accompanied by a thunk. Something large had grazed Old Shatterhand. I went up to the deck with Willie. Only Adelbert stayed below in the mess hall.

The ship's surroundings had changed completely while we were down in the mess. Half the fog had dissipated and we saw that monsters filled the ocean around us. Some resembled giant jellyfish, some resembled giant sharks. Some resembled giant water dragons with their long necks, some resembled giant snails. Some had fins that stood up like the ears of the rabbit monsters on Velveteen Rabbit f, some had the shape of flattened fish like the mud monsters of Nostromo b. The monster that had just grazed our ship looked like a starfish covered in tiny cilia. Now, it was resting calmly in the water. Perhaps by ramming into our ship, it had already fulfilled its duty.

"Have you ever seen anything like this on other planets?" shouted Waldemar.

"Nope. This is the first time I've ever seen monsters gathered together like this." I replied honestly.

"But surely there must be examples of this happening elsewhere."

"Yes, I've read about it before. Hańska is not an isolated planet like Crusoe, so there's always a chance that this sort of evolutionary explosion might occur near an Olivier."

"What's the chance that the Linker machines themselves made these creatures?"

"Beats me, I'm not the biologist."

Waldemar barked with laughter, then walked to the other end of the deck and disappeared. His question had been motivated not by simple curiosity, but rather by a desire to show me, the space traveler, that this kind of spectacular event could also happen on his planet.

The dogs on Old Shatterhand now began to sing the closest thing to a choral piece that I had ever heard in Wolfish. Yet, this was not a song that had ever been composed before. As the fifteen wolves sang in unison, they gradually united their individual feelings into a single unified chorus, and the movements of Old Shatterhand grew more supple and organic. It was as if the ship had itself turned into a living organism as it slid gently amongst the monsters.

The dogs looked happy, but I could not feel it myself. Their song did not affect me. I checked my pad, which was synced with Old Shatterhand's computer. At first glance, the monsters did not appear to be following the ship closely. They seemed to be holding steady in a two-kilometer-wide circle around the ship. We were still approximately 150 kilometers from the southern continent. We had already halved the distance since the morning, but there was no way we would reach it by nightfall at the speed we were going. How many more hours would it take? Ten? Eleven? Would we be safe if we managed to reach it? How could we be sure that this Linker evolution was confined to the ocean? If the monsters here had been able to multiply this explosively over the past few years, perhaps all sorts of wild monsters awaited us on the land.

We needed to plan. The Surabaya pack dogs were undoubtedly looking for a way to save themselves, but Willie Mozart was my responsibility. We had to put our heads and hands together to prepare for the worst.

I looked around but couldn't find Willie. After confirming she wasn't on deck, I took the stairs down into the hull and headed toward the mess hall in search of her. I stopped and listened. Willie's muffled voice was coming from somewhere at the other end of the hallway. I pressed myself against the wall to listen. That's when I heard Willie say to someone I couldn't see:

"Then it was you who killed the captain?"

9. MUTANTS

I did not hear the reply. I knew, without thinking, who Willie was talking to. Aside from Willie and me, there was only one other person on Old Shatterhand who didn't belong to the pack and wasn't singing in Wolfish.

"And the beta too?"

This time I heard the reply clearly. As suspected, it was Adelbert Estrella.

"Yes."

"But why?"

"They were an obstacle. We would never have made it this far with them alive."

"But why? Both of them were in favor of coming here."

"Exactly. Didn't you see it? They did win the vote, but just barely, and with everything that has happened since then, these idiot dogs would have staged a mutiny by now and returned north. You think I've never seen this before? The only reason we were able to make it this far is because the captain and first mate are gone."

"That's not a reason."

"Was there a good reason why you were driven out of your home? Did you do something wrong? Is it because you are a girl who can also play the man's role? So what! It's not as if your genes could proliferate that easily either. It's ridiculous. Over eighty million dogs live on Hańska. If only one in ten or even twenty thousand survived, the species would still continue. Your genes have as much influence as a speck of dust in the ocean. They're just paranoid and kicking up a stink for no good reason."

"So what's wrong with you?"

Silence flowed for a moment before it was broken by Willie's innocent "Aha!"

I was not curious to know what Adelbert's abnormality was. It was just something physical that was easily concealed and could be pulled out and shown off in front of the kid. Nor was I curious about Adelbert's real name or how he had managed to survive in the south without being expelled from the planet. The important thing was his plan. It was clear that he was doing on Old Shatterhand exactly what he had done on Rhodes: pretending to be a refugee, sinking the ship that rescued him, and massacring its crew, all to conceal what was happening in the southern hemisphere. He couldn't do it forever, of course—if ships sent south continued to disappear, the north would notice. But judging from his attitude, it wasn't something he meant to do forever. Clearly something momentous would soon happen to change the fate of Hańska.

What was I to do? I was tasked with taking the kid off the planet. I had, until this point, not considered whether that was the right thing to do. Perhaps there were other possibilities I was unaware of. I could even give the kid over to the care of Adelbert Estrella and the group he belonged to. It was impossible to deny that he was a mass murderer, but, well, wars were like that. The important thing was what the kid thought. It was a real dilemma, as I had never felt anything for the Surabaya pack.

Willie's piercing scream cut short my worrying. I ran towards the cry, only to meet Willie running in the opposite direction. Adelbert ran after her, but as soon as he saw me, he let out a sound like a hiccup and turned to flee in the other direction. For an instant, I saw something like a snake wriggling between his eyebrows. I had no way of knowing what function it might have had, but it looked quite obscene. I held Willie and tried to calm her down. Meanwhile, I could hear Adelbert's Wolfish scream echoing from the far end of the hallway: a proclamation of confidence and a promise of revenge.

Running to the alarm that hung at the end of the hallway, I opened its cover and, mustering all the Wolfish I knew, typed out a message: interior, outsider, invasion, caution, danger. As soon as I finished typing the final words, the siren on Old Shatterhand began to whine and sing out my message.

By the time the siren sounded for a third time, the song that the Surabaya pack had been singing up until this point changed to match it. Now it was a song of warning and hunting. I could hear the sound of pounding paws as three or four dogs headed toward the corridor where we stood. I shouted out the name Adelbert, and they immediately understood.

Willie and I ran to our cabin and locked the door. We observed what happened next on my notepad. Eight dogs chased Adelbert through the ship, which was still surrounded by monsters. The waves grew rougher, and the fog thinner. These seemingly unconnected but concurrent events were heading toward the same unknown endpoint. I felt as if I were listening to the final movement of a symphony as it sped along toward its climax. I knew we had reached that climax as soon as I heard Adelbert cry from the top of the mast over my pad's speakers.

"Look! Listen! Bow down," He screamed, "You idiot dogs! Your world is over! Dr. Matthias Boltzmann has come!"

10. MATTHIAS BOLTZMANN (REDUX)

I went back up on deck. I could not stop Willie from following me up. It was not necessary to ask where Adelbert was pointing. Over half of the crew were at the aft of the ship. I held the railing and stared in the direction they were pointing.

A large creature was riding through the waves on the back of a much larger creature. The creature being ridden was a medium-sized Hańska whale; the creature doing the riding looked like a yellowish, eight-meter-tall monkey. Something of that size would have been almost unable to walk in this planet's gravity. The monkey's body was covered in dense fur, and, compared to its legs, its arms were unusually long. Holding on to the whale's dorsal fin, it rode slowly toward Old Shatterhand. It wasn't until it rode right up to us that I realized that I was looking at a familiar face, one I had seen many times in books and the museum. The monkey-like creature was Matthias Boltzmann. He had not died. Instead, he had survived several hundred years on the southern continent and had evolved into the King Kong-like monster that now stood before us.

It was not surprising. Even after Hańska had become a planet of dogs, no one had really explored the southern continent. Everyone presumed that the southern continent was less hospitable than the northern, but that was little more than speculation. Not much could be learned by sending historians and scientists there once or twice a year. Besides, it was Olivier territory. Anything could happen there.

Boltzmann cried out. It was neither Wolfish nor an Earthling language. It sounded like the loud rumble of thunder. Had he lost the ability to speak over the years? Or perhaps he no longer felt compelled to speak? Was there still something called reason inside that huge skull?

"Look!" Waldemar screamed. His finger pointed not at Dr. Boltzmann riding a whale, but rather at the sea around them. While we had been distracted by Boltzmann's large figure, small creatures had been gathering around him. At first, they looked like some sort of white seal. But on closer inspection, we saw they had arms and legs like bipeds, and that these ended in protrusions that looked much like fingers and toes. They wore homemade bags of leather on their backs. And they were singing. It sounded similar to Wolfish but was deeper in pitch, more sonorous, and more complex.

"Now I understand what Adelbert Estrella was trying to protect. Don't you see?" I said to the Hańska dogs. "They're all dogs. Not just those seal-like creatures. Most of the sea monsters are also related to you. They're the descendants of all the mutants you exiled here these past several hundred years. Instead of leaving on Adjanis, they stayed on the southern continent under Boltzmann's protection and evolved steadily under the influence of the other Linker viruses that rode in on Boltzmann and the Adjanis. Then, in just the last few decades, came the evolutionary explosion. Some evolved into dinosaur- or shark-like monsters, others evolved into seal-like species. But they clearly developed in concert with each other to form one intertwined group.

It's ironic, isn't it? You drove out the mutants to protect the purity of your species. That was totally unnecessary considering that you number eighty million. But it's precisely because of this useless act that the descendants of Earth mammals have been able to evolve in so many different directions in the southern hemisphere. They will continue to proliferate and evolve into the future. In a few centuries, their numbers will probably surpass that of the dog population of the Northern hemisphere. Isn't it fascinating to see how quickly their numbers increase? They either became hermaphrodites or started to reproduce asexually through parthenogenesis long ago. It's not that uncommon. The way you reproduce, you simply can't compete. The purity of your species has come to an end. Unlike the native creatures of Hańska, these creatures have contagious genes!"

I took off my mask. It didn't make sense. I had known from the outset that the mask I wore was useless, but to keep wearing it now was ridiculous. I threw the mask away and took a deep breath. The salty, fishy smell of the ocean penetrated my nostrils.

The whale carrying Boltzmann rammed Old Shatterhand. Waldemar and I fell over from the impact and rolled over to the stairs to the lower deck. A scream rang out. Adelbert had fallen from the mast into the sea. It looked unlikely that he would make it through the rush of monsters intact.

Waldemar stood back up. Grabbing a megaphone, he began to sing in Wolfish. It was a leader's song. Other songs gradually harmonized with his in a sign of submission, and Old Shatterhand started to move again. The ship sped through gaps between the monsters that followed and tried to catch us. When the monsters tried to block our path forward, the crew fired the electric cannons. Old Shatterhand's weapons were now working at full tilt.

I remained glued to the ship's aft watching Boltzmann pursue us. He was shaking his left hand in our direction. I couldn't tell if the gesture was a greeting, a request to stop and wait, or a threat. It might not have had any meaning at all.

Maybe his hand was just bored and decided to flail around a bit. However, the seals now pursuing us fiercely were a different matter. Their goal was simple and easy to comprehend. They meant to board the boat and kill us. I could now discern the weapons they held in their hands with my naked eyes. The realization that they might be able to hit Willie or me gave me goosebumps.

I looked for Willie. She crouched at the entrance to the stairs, holding tightly to the handrail. I grabbed her hand and ran down the stairs. We gathered my bag with my library cube and her precious box from our cabin, and then ran to the sealed room at the back of the ship that held the two-person emergency capsule. The door was shut, and the door lock wheel was secured with a chain and padlock, but both looked flimsy. The chain broke with a few strikes from a fire extinguisher I picked off the nearby wall. I spun the wheel with the padlock still attached, opened the door, and entered the room. As soon as Willie came in, I shut the door and spun the wheel from the inside to lock it. I did not think I was being selfish or cowardly. There were life boats on deck in any case. The emergency capsule was for VIPs, and if we weren't the VIPs here, then what did the word even mean?

I pushed the kid into the capsule, pulled myself in behind her, and closed the door. Launching the capsule required a code from the captain, but it took my pad only about three minutes to crack it. After entering the code, we just sat there and waited. I would wait to launch until the last instant, once all hope was gone for Old Shatterhand. I opened my pad and kept checking, minute by minute, how much distance remained between us and the southern continent. One hundred kilometers, ninety kilometers, eighty kilometers.

All the while, the ship shook from the monsters' strikes and from the recoil of the ship's own weapons.

A small explosion blew down the door to the room, and four seals entered through the hole. The expressions on their round, bland faces were unreadable. The first seal to enter immediately began swinging an axe at the glass window of our capsule. We couldn't wait any longer. I pushed the launch button, and the capsule shot like a cannonball along its rails and out of the ship. We flew in an arc for nearly one hundred meters before falling into the ocean.

It was still possible to see what was happening with Old Shatterhand through the capsule windows. A huge sea snake monster had coiled itself around the ship, which was already bent into an L shape and looked to be on the verge of breaking into two. Darkly colored beasts of some sort were climbing up from the snake and into the boat, and fish that had smelled blood were amassing nearby. The crew and the seals both rushed toward the bow of the ship, where the lifeboats were. A large-framed dog stood unsteadily on the bow deck and shot at the beasts and seals. It looked like Waldemar, but I could not be sure from that distance.

The metal plates of Old Shatterhand shrieked as they tore and the ship broke in half. The seals and the crew fell into the sea, which soon turned into a seething mass of blood. Could the monsters really differentiate between the crew and the seals? Would the seals still have entered the fray had they known?

Before submerging the capsule, I took one last look at Boltzmann, now no more than a vague outline in the fog. He raised himself up and pointed a finger at the sinking boat while bellowing like a train in an old film. That was the last I saw of him before he was lost to the fog entirely. His cry was buried beneath the screams of the monsters attacking their meal.

11. OLIVIER

Willie and I arrived at the coast of the southern continent the following evening. According to our map, we were about three kilometers from the south pole base. No monsters had bothered us as we'd floated to the coast in our capsule. Maybe we'd been lucky, or maybe we just hadn't been worth their attention.

When we finally arrived, the south pole base was a terrible sight. Its doors had been smashed open and a mess of bloodstains and bits of flesh littered the floor inside, along with one of the seals' axes. The base looked as if it had been left this way for more than a month.

I looked for a homing rocket to send this news back to the dogs in the north, but everything was broken or missing. No matter. They would learn what had happened in the southern hemisphere soon enough. At the very least, they would soon realize that two ships had disappeared and communication with the southern base had been lost. The next ship they sent south would not be a research vessel.

We had to hurry. The Olivier lay twenty kilometers from the base. The sleds rolling around outside were of no use to us. The temperature outside was nearly ten degrees Celsius, and the snow and ice near the coast had melted to reveal the rough, volcanic surface of the land. This was not at all what I had heard the winter weather at the south pole was like.

We walked the unpaved road to the Olivier. Or rather, it would be more accurate to say we followed the sled guide cable from the base to the Olivier. We set the capsule's alarm to its highest sensitivity, but did not discover any seals or monsters in the vicinity. The south pole was clammy, warm, quiet, and dark. It was the darkest place I had ever seen on Hańska.

As we walked along in silence, I thought about what Adelbert Estrella had done. I did not believe he had done it on orders from the seals or Boltzmann. I thought he had done it because he had been recently driven from his home and held a personal hatred for the dogs who had exiled him. I also did not believe that Boltzmann and the seals had actively used Adelbert. It was more likely that they had sunk Rhodes and Old Shatterhand merely to cover up the evidence of Adelbert's misdeeds. Adelbert had been as foolish as could be, but I thought I understood him.

What would happen to the planet now? The quiet world of the Hańska dogs would change, that was certain. Sooner or later, the monsters would cross the equator into the northern hemisphere and the DNA of the Hańska dogs would be polluted. The evolutionary pressure of this climate change would function as a catalyst for mutation. The lovely sight of Ewelina's snow-covered domes that lined up along the shore like Go pieces would not last much longer either. I knew how fragile the permafrost layer here was. Mama Keppel was fortunate she had died before learning this fact.

We arrived at the walls of the Olivier's fortress at the approach of dawn. Hańska's Olivier was a black oval tower nearly one hundred meters tall. Coopers patrolled the perimeter of the metal wall like roly-poly toys with long arms. Near a round hole in the wall was a metal gate that looked like it had been erected by the dogs. I destroyed the lock with my shock pistol and we walked inside. Two Coopers stared at us but did not seem inclined to interfere.

We ascended a slope to reach the Adjanis' nest. The insides of Oliviers are as complex as labyrinths, but we were able to simply follow the directions the dogs had drawn at each intersection. Even without directions, it would not have been difficult. Just take the path with the most Deneuves flying along it.

The inside of the nest rang with the percussive sound of what seemed to be the instrumental outro of a song–Illyrian synesthetic jazz. Or at least there was some part of it that my senses and brain recognized as such. A woman about two and a half meters tall with yellow-green skin lay on the roof of a remora that had seen better days and flicked her fingers in time to the music. As soon as she noticed us, she sat up and waved a hand.

"Guests! Where would you like to go? Wait, first, tell me where we are. "

"It's not anywhere worth staying for long. How did you come here?"

"I fell off the route at Huxley Junction. An electrical field malfunction threw me off the Adjani I'd been hanging onto, and I only just barely managed to grab the Garbo next to it. That Garbo brought me here. So what's the deal with this place? It seems a bit weird. Did you see that yellow King Kong running around with all those little rag-doll-like children on your way in? It acted as if it owned the place. I've never seen Earth descendants evolve into such large creatures before, so I stayed here a few days to observe. Are you from here?"

"No, but I do know a bit about that King Kong. I don't think those guys are in the mood for visitors right now. When can we get out of here?"

An Adjani was slated to take off in thirty standard

minutes. I was able to buy two tickets from the woman to ride the remora. As soon as our negotiations were concluded, I walked over to Willie. Still clutching her precious box, she was leaning against the railing near the hole bored through a wall that served as an entrance. Silently, we stared out at the village that Boltzmann and the seals were building at the southern end of the Olivier. Unlike the round, bright, and peaceful old cities of the northern hemisphere, the seal village was dark, rough, dirty, and savage. I did not think I would like their world. Yet, just like the cities of the north, these villages and cities were only temporary. No one could know what future was in store for this planet now that it had truly started to breathe again.

I stole a glance at the side of Willie's face. It was stiff with cold hatred and anger. Her emotions were so strong and pure that it seemed the child had forgotten that the place that had given her that hatred—her home—had exiled her.

"Ready to leave?" I asked the kid.

She turned around and grimaced. "Yes, I'm ready."

JEZEBEL

"Everything good dies here. Even the stars."

—*I Walked with a Zombie*

RROSE SÉLAVY

1

Let me tell you about the time our captain faced off against Rrose Sélavy.

It's been two years already. I suppose I don't need to say "already," given how short the years are here on Crusoe Alpha b, but the seasons change so quickly it frightens me sometimes, time whizzing by like bullets past my cheeks.

Anyway, it happened out at sea near the island of Monte Grande. Never heard of it? Well, Monte Grande is an island off the west coast of Wednesday. It's only the size of Manhattan, but it's home to Crusoe's biggest active volcano. For the past two hundred standard years, a small Olivier has been meditating near the mouth of the volcano. People say the Olivier used to be so big it could have covered the entire mouth. These days, though, it's only about the size of a small truck. It shed all its unnecessary limbs and only maintains its brain at its core. It hardly even keeps any Coopers around to look after it anymore. But, even the most inanimate of Oliviers still gets Adjani visitors, so the sea nearby is always teeming with refugees, even if there aren't nearly as many as there used to be.

Picture it: dozens of Adjanis falling like golden raindrops

through a hole several hundred meters wide that opens up in the middle of a bank of gloomy rain clouds. As the Adjanis descend toward the water, hundreds of remoras that have been circling around them like clouds of dust deactivate their gravity rings and drop away. Some of these remoras manage to land on Monte Grande's beaches; the rest simply fall into the ocean. Only a few of the latter manage to wriggle their way to shore. The other two thirds just sit there in the water waiting to be rescued. And that's where we come in. We call this a rescue ship, but it's really just a fishing boat. Only instead of catching fish, we catch people.

Sometimes I imagine how we must look to the people we end up rescuing. You can't see much from the inside of a remora that's barely managed to stay afloat, because the only window is small and obscured by dirty seawater. Nonetheless, the occupants would be able to see the other remoras floating nearby and the approaching rescue boats. One of the boats is ours, and as we close the distance, they'll be able to make out the likeness of Ms. Bette Davis in her strapless dress, looking over her shoulder at them from our ship's bow. I still don't know who first painted her there, but we regularly repaint and recoat the image to keep it looking sharp.

We draw up as close to the remora as we can without hitting it, and then I head out to say hello. I used to hang off our ship's robotic arm and swing in close to the remora's window, but these days I usually use our single-person flyer. It's modeled on the Waynes, but the wings are our original design that we built from parts they discarded. Anyway, I strap the insectoid wings on my back and fly right over.

Most of the time the remora castaways are pretty relaxed because they're expecting to be rescued. Still, the sight of me never fails to elicit gasps of surprise. And who could blame them? After all, what they see peering in at them through their remora's porthole is the face of a legendary Hollywood star. And here, let me just say that I probably look even more like Fred Astaire than Fred Astaire himself. I mean, my skin is gray as if I had jumped straight out of the film *Swing Time*. Anyhow, that's when anyone who isn't too scared starts making dumb jokes, like "Where's Ginger?" Come on, do the people who ask that really think the joke is original?

I wish we could send a different crew member, but who else is there? The navigator? Sure, she's beautiful, but that feline face makes her look like a panther or a cheetah or some other large, carnivorous cat—it sure doesn't inspire trust. If she were to tap on the window of a remora, its passengers would just freak out. The engineer would be even worse—she looks like a demon doused in molten brown glass. I understand as well as anyone how the Linker virus mutations have screwed with all our genes, but the engineer doesn't look like she's even on the human end of the spectrum. There's no getting around the fact that she looks like an alien infiltrator, regardless of what the genetic tests say. And our cook looks just like Wally Walrus, which of course rules her out. That leaves only the captain... and no one's going to believe a meter-tall teddy bear claiming to be the captain of a ship. Which is why I'm the one who has to go out and greet the remoras.

After I reassure the passengers, our engineer gets to work. We bring the smaller remoras straight up onto our deck using the robotic arm. The bulkier ones we outfit with buoys, chain to our rescue boat, and tow to Wednesday.

Actually, I guess I don't need to explain that last bit. You've already experienced it for yourselves.

By the time the rescue operation is over, we're typically left with about ten newcomers shivering like half-drowned rats on our deck. I lead them down to the recreation room where I serve them the cook's seaweed tea and fish soup. There's also plain boiled water for anyone who refuses our food and drink. After the refugees have relaxed a bit, I give them the introduction.

"Welcome to Jezebel," I say. I always begin that way. "That teddy bear over there is the captain of this old bathtub. I'm the ship's doctor. For those who don't yet know, you've had the misfortune of ending up on Crusoe Alpha b in a far corner of the Large Magellanic Cloud. This planet was colonized about three hundred and fifty standard years ago, and the fact of the matter is..."

At which point someone usually interrupts me to ask some variation of "Where's the closest Olivier?" Everybody always wants to get on the next Adjani and leave this shithole as soon as possible. Every time, I just purse my lips in an impish smile and say: "Well... as I was about to tell you, I'm sorry, but there's no way to get off this planet. The closest Olivier is right here on Monte Grande Island, but it's been meditating for the past two hundred years and doesn't function as an airport. In fact, almost all of the Oliviers on this planet are meditating. There's one Olivier on Wednesday that works alright, but there's an extremely long line of people waiting to access it. Have any of you ever seen *The Wages of Fear* starring Yves Montand? Well, that's exactly the situation we have here."

That's when a clever refugee asks something like: "What about a direct shuttle to a Dietrich?" To which I reply:

"I hate to disappoint you, but there are no orbiting Dietrichs here. Crusoe is a binary star system. That up there is Crusoe Alpha; Crusoe Beta is a red dwarf star that orbits Crusoe Alpha on a twelve-thousand-year cycle. From what I've heard, Crusoe Beta has about four Dietrichs, not to mention asteroids full of functioning Oliviers and swarms of Waynes and Guinnesses flitting around like grasshoppers. They're undoubtedly doing something productive over there. The problem is that the Adjanis really don't like it around Crusoe Beta. As soon as they start descending to the Garbo, the cheeky buggers change their minds and instead zip over here at 99.999% of the speed of light, dragging their hapless passengers along with them. I'm telling you, it's exactly like *The Wages of Fear!*

"Now, what happens next is you're going to help us recoup some of our costs from rescuing you, so please hand over your library cubes. Foreign fruit or seeds or anything like that would be even more appreciated."

2

That's the kind of place Crusoe is. Some call it Prison Planet. Others call it Constipation Planet, which I think is perfect. We get enough to eat, but shitting is a problem. Fickle Adjanis come here from all over the galaxy and drop off the remoras they've been carrying, and leave—they couldn't care less what happens to the people they drop off. All sorts of species are gathered here, but there are hardly any children being born because procreation's nearly impossible with the Linker virus constantly scrambling the gene pool. It's a shithole.

When I myself first arrived here seven local years ago, things looked bleak to me too. In the fifteen years I'd spent travelling after leaving my home planet of Maria Wutz, I'd never even imagined staying for more than a month on a single planet. I'd planned to spend my entire life traveling the Milky Way. Instead, I got unlucky and ended up stuck here on Constipation Planet with no way out and no other future to speak of.

"I tried to escape too, at first. I'd heard that three Oliviers on the planet were still functioning as airports and accepting Adjanis, though they were surrounded by greedy cities that charged extremely high entrance fees. One of the Oliviers is in the McKinsey bloc on Wednesday, where we're headed now. All refugees want to go there first, because it's the only escape route on this continent. But almost no one can afford the ridiculous fees those scammers charge. Most people settle for registering with the Refugee Assistance Association and living near the Olivier, where occasionally they get to see an Adjani lift off with its cargo of lucky passengers.

"I quickly gave up the thought of escape. After all, I didn't have a rare library cube or untainted seeds from Earth. I was flexible and adapted to the circumstances. I got my qualifications to become a doctor, and I'm pretty good at it too, but even so I'll never make enough money to pay my way off the planet.

"Anyway, that's when I met Jezebel and the captain. I was out of work and just hanging around Deronda Bay when I happened to hear that Jezebel was looking to hire a doctor. Two fox-headed refugees they had just picked up were having seizures and looked like they were dying, but the Jezebel's medical machine was on the fritz and no one on the ship knew what to do. Luckily, I knew how to treat this sort of Linker seizure, having dealt with mutants during the several years I spent on the Scottish Route. I was able to save one of the refugees, but the other one died. The captain must have liked me because he asked if I would like to stay on. I agreed.

It turned out to be a pretty good decision. Jezebel is a great boat for people who like to lounge around and don't care much for responsibility. For starters, the ship is self-sufficient. We'll all die of old age before the main battery does, and if we ever run low on energy, we can always harvest more directly from compounds dissolved in the seawater. The food here is pretty decent, too, unless you're especially partial to terrestrial food. You could waste your whole life away shut up in the projection room watching old movies on a library cube and no one would bother you.

That's what the captain himself did for a few months after he first came into possession of Jezebel. As the ship circled the continent of Tuesday and then followed the equator around the globe, he taught himself to speak Italian and play piano, and watched all of Hitchcock's films except *Juno and the Paycock* a few hundred times each. The captain sometimes tells me that was the happiest time of his life. It makes sense. On Crusoe, having a boat means freedom. For someone like the captain, who never before had the luxury of being alone, the solitude of the boat must have been the absolute pinnacle of freedom.

The captain probably would have lived out his days alone on Jezebel if all he had thought about was himself. But he loved Jezebel too much for that. Boats aren't born merely to float on water. If you really love a boat, you have to give it a reason to exist.

The captain has done a lot of things since he became captain. He's rescued remoras that landed around Monte

Grande Beach and Deronda Bay, he's searched for treasure in the sea around the continent of Thursday, and he's transported suspicious passengers to other continents. A few times, he even worked as part of a mercenary army, though never for long. The captain hated wars, but he hated hierarchical military culture even more. He'd had more than enough of that during his earlier stint on the aircraft carrier.

Jezebel usually traveled alone, and no one in the crew minded that in the least. Most of the crew resembled the captain: individualists with no lofty goals. The one exception was the engineer. No one really knew what she was thinking. But given that she turned down a chance to be a scout for the Duncan Foreign Legion in order to remain on Jezebel, she must not be particularly ambitious either.

3

Harvesting newcomers hadn't actually been the point of our visit to Monte Grande. We hadn't planned to rescue anyone at all. Adjani visits had been steadily decreasing for several months, and besides, there were already plenty of others there who could pick up the new arrivals. There was no humanitarian reason to go.

Up until just two hours prior to the Adjanis' descent, we'd been sitting together in the warmth of the boat's projection room watching *Casablanca*. As always, we booed when Humphrey Bogart appeared, gustily recited all of Claude Rains's lines from memory, and sighed each time Ingrid Bergman's round face filled the screen. Every member of Jezebel's crew was a loyal Bergman fan. The name of the ship might make you think that we preferred Bette Davis, but not everything happens the way you want it to. We liked Davis too, but Bergman always came first.

We were applauding the shooting of Conrad Veidt when the captain received a phone call. He grumbled and left the projection room to take the call.

It was Bayan Purple of the Free Ship Alliance. For some unknown reason, the name Bayan had been popular for a while on Wednesday, and the different Bayans had begun to attach colors to their names in order to make it easier to differentiate between them. We'd already made the acquaintance of seven different Bayans.

"What is it?" asked the captain.

"We need a hand," Bayan Purple replied. "We just got word that a pack of Adjanis are coming to Monte Grande tonight."

"Aren't there plenty of boats for that already? What do you need us for?"

"This has nothing to do with rescuing refugees. That's just the pretext for something else I'd like you to do for me."

"What's that?"

"I need you to retrieve a bag with a library cube. One of our clients dropped the bag into the ocean when they fell onto this shithole planet. Though the client was saved, the bag is still sitting at the bottom of the sea. That was three years ago, but we have reason to believe that the contents of the cube are still of considerable value."

"How much?"

"Enough to create or revive three or four wombs."

"You've found yourself a fortune! But why are you only fishing it out now?"

"Our client arrived right at the beginning of the Seven Day War. They had no idea what the cube was worth and zero connections on this planet. Only after working in a salaried position on Wednesday for a while did they realize the cube's value. We stepped up and found a buyer, and the buyer's got the money ready and waiting for us. Now all we need is the cube."

"You're sure the cube's still there? Some other treasure hunter might have already stolen it."

"We're still getting a signal from where it went down. Take a look at the signal fingerprint I'm attaching here. With the equipment you have on board, picking it up shouldn't take you more than five minutes. First save a few people as a pretext, then start toward Wednesday and release your submersible to retrieve the cube. Once I've picked it up and concluded the sale, I'll give you ten percent of my cut."

"If this is so important, why are you suddenly telling me about it now?"

"Keeping secrets too long is never useful, my friend."

Bayan Purple hung up. It was a weird thing to do, but in keeping with his personality. He was equal parts calculating and impulsive. If you looked closely enough, his seemingly thoughtless actions were usually based on careful calculations of some sort or other. In the end, the captain gave up watching the final scene of *Casablanca* and went up to the bridge.

As Bayan Purple had said, the job was a piece of cake. As soon as we arrived in the waters near Monte Grande, the engineer threw our submersible into the water. It took her less than ten minutes to find the library cube. The submersible brought the cube back to the surface and then attached itself to the remora we had rescued for our cover story. Once both were on board, the engineer surreptitiously removed the cube and took it into the captain's cabin while the rest of us continued the rescue operations. Everything went according to plan.

So, what was in the cube? The captain was curious, so he called the engineer over and scanned it. The encryption was easily broken, and after that it was simple enough to get a sense of the contents. Yet, we still couldn't figure out how much the information it contained was really worth. According to Bayan Purple, the cube contained information that might be able to revive dead wombs or create new ones. But this library cube might instead be part of grander plan, and the possession of the information stored on it might be more important than the content of the information was. Nothing was ever simple on Crusoe, where there were no fixed countries and over seven hundred cities that were constantly merging and dividing. Everyone knew that the only way to survive here was to watch your back.

As if to prove this point, something unfortunate happened on Jezebel while the captain and engineer were busy with the library cube.

I was the first to notice. We had gathered the newcomers together and were just beginning orientation when I noticed that one of them had gone missing. I was pretty sure I knew who it was. We had rescued one small and one medium remora that day, and it was the small remora's pilot who was missing. I couldn't forget him—the guy had almost died. At first, we thought he had died, but it turned out his lack of vital signs was just a space suit malfunction. When we opened his helmet, he was still breathing, but just barely. I managed to revive him, after which he had looked alright. Except that now, he was nowhere to be found.

I began to worry. The remora had been in really bad shape. It was taking on water and had started to sink by the time we got to it. From the look of things, the remora's defensive shield had been broken for some time. Even though it had likely remained within the Adjani's force field, who knew what might have happened to the pilot's body while traveling near light speed. What if his brain had suddenly seized when he came up on deck to get some air?

I was so worried that I ran a scan for him and discovered a signal coming from behind the boat. When I went to look, I saw something hanging off the medium-sized remora, which was attached to a buoy we were dragging behind us. I called the engineer over and she used the robotic arm to pull it up. It was the pilot's corpse. There were two holes in his shirt and burn wounds on the skin underneath. Someone had killed him with a shock pistol and tried to dispose of the corpse. But his clothing had snagged on the remora.

I was shocked. There was a murderer on our ship. But what possible motive could there be? The thirteen people we had brought on board had all flown here from different parts of the galaxy. It was highly unlikely that they even knew each other. Of course, it was possible that the murderer was one of the two people the pilot had carried here with him—maybe one of them wanted to get back at him for bringing them to this shithole. But I doubted it was that simple. All the newcomers looked dead tired; none of them looked like they had enough energy to kill anyone. Sure, the murderer could very well be faking fatigue, but if that were the case, the crime was premeditated, which meant it would be next to impossible for us to uncover the motive. Furthermore, even if we were somehow able to discover the criminal, what then? People without Crusoe citizenship have no rights here anyway. No agency would ever investigate, much less pursue a trial on behalf of a victim who had just fallen out of the sky. The Refugee Assistance Association? Not a chance.

In any case, by the time I had gone back to report this incident, the captain's room was empty. I went back up to the deck, where I saw the captain and three or four refugees pointing their fingers at the ocean somewhere to the west and talking noisily. I went over to see what they were pointing at, but there was nothing there. There really was nothing there. Really, truly, nothing at all. Which just doesn't happen in nature. It was as if someone had taken an eraser and erased what was there. There was no white mark left over or anything like that—the space was simply blank and empty. Moreover, it felt showy and absurd, but why? What could be creating such an impression?

The captain called out to me, and as I followed him down to his cabin, I overheard him muttering to himself. That's when I finally remembered why the emptiness had felt so familiar.

What the captain said was: "What could we possibly have on board that has made Rrose Sélavy come after us?

4

Now it's time to tell you the sad history of the captain and Rrose Sélavy. To tell the story right, though, I have to go all the way back to the beginning and tell you about the captain's birth.

Or, more accurately, the captain's discovery—because no one knows where the captain was born. He was discovered in the wreckage of a remora floating around Deronda Bay and taken to the Refugee Assistance Association, where he was subjected to research. How does one treat a living toy? Like a regular person? A pet? And was it male or female?

Regarding this last question, a compromise with reality was unavoidable. A small cloaca in the shape of a short plastic pipe was found, believe it or not, inside the pocket attached to the baby's stomach. Perhaps this was quite normal for the baby's subspecies, but it was decided that keeping things this way would make life difficult for the young teddy bear. So, the doctors created an anus for the baby and pulled the pipe, which could now be used exclusively for urine, out through a hole they made in the stomach pocket. This meant the baby was now able to use urinals, which effectively meant he had become a man. You all know that "man" and "woman" mean different things now than they did back on Earth. On most planets these days, "man" is just a vague umbrella term for all individuals who lack the ability to become pregnant. But even that definition isn't very precise—the White Termite Amazons of the White Lion System will never recognize themselves as men.

Anyway, the Association held off answering the question of whether he was a person or a pet. Seven months after being discovered, the captain was adopted by a wealthy, depressed old lady. Although the transaction was formally an adoption, it was in fact no different from the sale of a pet. The Association didn't care. Good luck, teddy bear.

To the baby, his adopted mother's house was a site of struggle. Had he wanted to, the captain could have eaten, slept, and charmed his way through the rest of his life there. But that wasn't what he wanted. Instead, frantic to learn how to speak, he tortured his tongue and mouth until they could form words. He taught himself to read and write, and worked hard to ensure that the people around him knew he was literate. No matter what he did, though, those around him continued to think of him as a talented pet: he was a talking teddy bear and not a person worthy of respect and dignity.

The captain immersed himself in study, choosing subjects that were as abstract and far from reality as possible. In the morning, he studied physics and mathematics; in the afternoon, counterpoint and harmonics. The captain hated his roly-poly body, and instead craved the abstract heaven of numbers and logic.

That heaven might have come within reach had he received his fair share of the inheritance his mother left when she died.

But, sad to say, you won't find that sort of justice on Crusoe. His mother's relatives, seeking to get a piece of the pie for themselves, revealed that the captain was legally categorized as a pet despite having been declared her son in the adoption papers. It was a mistake that could easily have been fixed, but the filthy leeches weren't about to let their chance slip by.

What the captain then suffered was right out of that Robert Louis Stevenson novel. The dead woman's relatives kidnapped him and sold him off to the first mate of the pirate ship Veronica Lake.

Three months later, Rrose Sélavy attacked and sank Veronica Lake off the west coast of Saturday. The captain, who managed to stay afloat by holding on to an empty wine barrel, was the only survivor; but when they dragged him in front of Hammerhead Red, Rrose Sélavy's captain, he really thought he was done for. Hammerhead Red and the whole crew actually drooled in anticipation when they saw him. Luckily, Hammerhead Red realized that a talking teddy bear would be of more use than a tiny morsel of bear meat.

So let me tell you about Rrose Sélavy itself. The ship looked like a Kitty Hawk class aircraft carrier. That's probably what it had been when it came out of the womb. You see, before the Oliviers became so fussy, Crusoe, and especially the continent Saturday, was a playground for military fanatics. They used the wombs they brought with them to make replicas of real twentieth-century military weapons and play war games. But Rrose Sélavy has gradually evolved in the centuries since. Swapping out its original diesel engine and screws for a nuclear fusion reactor and a water jet propulsion system, it equipped itself with ICBMs and was painted a brilliant pink. I don't know whose idea it was to draw a toilet with a huge red rose sticking out of it on the ship's bow. It certainly wasn't Hammerhead Red's idea. Actually, it probably wasn't anyone's idea. Like most ships made by wombs, Rrose Sélavy had a will of its own. Once you entered the pink aircraft carrier's system, it co-opted your thoughts, whether you liked it or not. That's not to say the ship had supernatural powers. That's just how strong its system was.

Like the four other aircraft carriers on Crusoe, Rrose Sélavy was legally recognized as a city of four thousand people, but it definitely did not need four thousand crew members to function. Recent advances in technology meant that a hundred or so people would have been more than enough to run the ship, even if they had to control the flyers manually. But headcount was important to guarantee legal status, so Rrose Sélavy's crew had to find some way to get people on board and keep them there. Feeding and housing four thousand was easy enough for a ship like Rrose Sélavy, but the ship needed to provide more than just food and bunks to entice people to stay. A lot more. After a while, the five ship-cities had no choice but to turn aggressive in order to provide their populations with the dignity that comes from having something to do. They manifested this aggression both outwardly and inwardly.

And so, this was where the young teddy bear, a lover of books and music who was used to the luxuries of a wealthy family, wound up. Sounds gloomy, doesn't it? But there was an easy enough solution. All he had to do was find the softest-hearted, most feminine part of the ship and play the role of a cute baby. It would not have been impossible. Rrose Sélavy was a savage place, but it wasn't all just seething men. For example, the administrative and nutrition divisions were composed primarily of women. "Feminine" women, I mean. It didn't really matter if the people were women or not as long as they were "feminine." Anyway, the captain could have left the ridiculous place in less than a year just by becoming the "pet" of someone who seemed likely to leave the city as soon as they had fulfilled their contract.

But that's not what the poor, naive bastard did. Instead, he saw his arrival on Rrose Sélavy as an opportunity to prove his worth. For the next eight years, the captain struggled mightily to carve out a place for himself on board. It wasn't entirely futile. Because he already knew mathematics and had a good foundation of general knowledge, he quickly learned how to work the machines. On a ship that whimsically reconfigured itself and mutated, having an engineer with a small body like the captain's proved useful in a surprisingly large number of circumstances. Before a year was up, the captain knew everything there was to know about Rrose Sélavy. As his value to the ship increased, his share of the dividends increased accordingly, and in this respect at least, we could say his plan was a success.

But life aboard Rrose Sélavy was horrible, and got worse as the captain's dividends increased. His colleagues bristled at the thought that this freak of a stuffed bear, who had crawled out of who knows where, was being treated better than they were. He continued to face every type of abuse and maltreatment. He almost never talks about it, so I can only guess at the details. I think the crew must have enjoyed it all the more because the captain cries easily and has no tolerance for physical pain. Then there's the fact that bruises would be hard to see under the brown fur that covers his entire body. And the captain would not have been able to complain to anyone. He must have felt as if he were confined to a male dormitory at a school from which he could never graduate.

Even more detestable to him was the role Rrose Sélavy played in the world of Crusoe. Rrose Sélavy traveled the seas engaging in battles large and small, because that's what aircraft carriers are meant to do. To the captain, though, most of these battles were completely pointless. The people of Crusoe held no ideas or convictions firmly enough to defend them with their lives. And none of the cities on Crusoe were so destitute that going to war was the only way they could survive. It seemed to the captain that the people here fought purely out of habit. The wombs laid down by their ancestors were constantly pregnant with weapons of war, and those weapons had to be put to work somehow. Those military fanatics who've been fighting toxic tank battles on Saturday for centuries are objects of derision these days, but in the captain's eyes, the inhabitants of Rrose Sélavy were not much better.

Rrose Sélavy's flawed motivations for fighting aside, the

inefficiency with which it fulfilled its role also bothered the captain. The wars on Crusoe did not have any need for aircraft carriers. In modern warfare, what use was a slowly crawling hulk of a ship that carried flying machines on its deck? Why else are there only five aircraft carriers now left out of the hundred and twenty that fought on Crusoe two centuries ago? The captain was well aware that the city of Rrose Sélavy was fast approaching its expiration date. The smartest thing for him to do would be to take his dividend and jump ship before it was too late.

But he just couldn't do it. However horrible it might be, Rrose Sélavy was the only place where he had found a way to prove his worth. What would he do if he left? He had no formal certifications, who would take him seriously? Most of what he had learned was specific to this inefficient, anachronistic war machine.

5

How were we so sure that the ship following Jezebel was Rrose Sélavy? Well, how many other idiots were there who would cover an entire ship with the sort of camouflage netting used for fighter planes? What we saw was so large that it could only have been Rrose Sélavy.

In the years since the captain had left Rrose Sélavy, its role had changed bit by bit until it became more blackmailing madame than war machine. The ridiculous camouflage netting is all part of the act. The purpose of the netting isn't to hide the ship. If you don't look closely, of course, it does indeed make Rrose Sélavy hard to see. But, the netting is much more effectual when the adversary realizes that the ship behind it is Rrose Sélavy. It makes you think the ship is some sort of invisible ghost or monster on your tail. Whether the people on Rrose Sélavy realize the true purpose of the netting is a different matter.

But that wasn't really important. Our priority was to figure out what conspiracy we were caught up in and how to deal with the situation. It would have been nice to be able to contact Bayan and ask for help, but as expected, that proved to be impossible. Rrose Sélavy's signal jammers were already flying around us, and there weren't many other boats in the vicinity. Most of the rescue boats were either still engaged in their work or recharging at the geothermal power plant in Monte Grande. The few boats we had gone out with were too far away, and even had they been closer, there's nothing they could have done to help against Rrose Sélavy. We were on our own until we could get to Saturday.

We debated in the wheelhouse. Should we just run? Or, should we fill up our empty cargo hold with ballast and submerge? Both ideas were ridiculous. Rrose Sélavy didn't carry flyers and speedboats on its deck just for show. There was no use pretending our slightly better speed or mediocre submersible capability could save us. No matter what we attempted, we wouldn't be able to hide. If Rrose Sélavy wanted to catch us, it would.

But why the hell was Rrose Sélavy chasing us? The most likely explanation was that it had something to do with the library cube we had just recovered. Yet, considering the murder on the ship earlier that day, perhaps there was some other reason. But what?

I suggested that we should just give Rrose Sélavy whatever it wanted, but the captain was not in a mood to listen. He was not going to surrender before we even knew what it was we had in our possession and who Rrose Sélavy was working for. Looking at the captain's expression, I could guess why he was being so stubborn. He would have been more flexible had it been any other ship pursuing us, but he was not going to bow down to Rrose Sélavy. Surrendering now would mean turning the clock back to the moment he'd left Rrose Sélavy seven years before. Yet, what was the use of such obstinacy when the enemy refused to parley?

"I'll visit them myself and try to talk directly with Hammerhead," said the captain. "It might not be of any use, but we have to at least try to understand what's happening and why."

What a headache. The captain had no clue what had happened on Rrose Sélavy after he'd left. But it was understandable. In his shoes, I would have tried to avoid news of the ship too.

"Captain, Hammerhead Red is no longer captain of Rrose Sélavy," I told him. "He was exiled in a mutiny six months ago."

"How?"

"It's a sad story. Two years ago, Hammerhead Red signed a five-year contract with the allied city of Grant-Burns. But just a few months later, the Church Mafia seized power there in a counter-revolution. Hammerhead Red has his principles, and proposed breaking the contract now that Grant-Burns was controlled by Church Mafia thugs. That may have been the ethical thing to do, but politically speaking it was a stupid decision. First of all, breaking the contract meant paying a huge fine for violating the original terms and thus significantly lowering Rrose Sélavy's dividends. Furthermore, the Church Mafia saw it as their opportunity to gain an aircraft carrier free of charge. They just plain infiltrated Rrose Sélavy and instigated a mutiny. Crew members who were already upset at Hammerhead Red's distribution policies rose up against him, dragged him out of his room where he'd been busy writing a grandiose political declaration, and locked him up in the storeroom. They accused him of embezzling dividend funds and kicked him off the ship. Now he's living in a tourist hotel on Parrot Island off Tuesday. Someone who visited him there said he's doing okay, apart from the civil lawsuits against him. He's not too bad off financially either, which Rrose Sélavy claims is proof he stole the money, but there's no reason to believe that."

"Wait, wasn't the Church Mafia government recently driven out of Grant-Burns in a bloodless revolution?"

"Yes, that's why Rrose Sélavy is so hard up right now. The new citizen's alliance government used the mutiny against the captain as grounds to unilaterally void their contract. As a result, not only did Rrose Sélavy lose its employer and last source of dividends, its reputation has also gone down the toilet, and internal strife is getting worse. Going there alone would be dangerous. We have no idea what sort of villains have hired the ship. Those guys are so desperate right now, they're worse than a street gang."

"Who's the captain now?"

"Uh... they said it's someone named Alfred E. Bison. Maybe you know him? They said he's been an officer there for over twenty years. But what's up with his name? Why is there a surname hanging off of it? Does he think this is Earth? Is there even another Bison on Crusoe? And what does that E stand for? Is it even an abbreviation?"

6

Mentioning the name was a mistake. Not that there was any way I could have avoided it, but still, I should have been more careful.

Actually, the captain had talked to me about this Alfred E. Bison character on a handful of occasions. I just hadn't made the connection because the captain had always referred to him as "Anemone Tongue." You could say that nickname alone is a decent description of what Alfred E. Bison looked like. The octopus-headed fellow really did have a tongue like a sea anemone, which would jump up from his esophagus and wriggle out of his pocket-shaped mouth whenever he wanted to say something. I would have liked to see it myself, but it's already too late.

There's no need to explain why the captain used that nickname when talking about Bison. In the captain's mind, Bison represented everything that was detestable about Rrose Sélavy. And for a while, he had been the captain's immediate superior. The captain used to say he learned about every dirty thing in the world while working under Anemone Tongue. He never went into details, but they're easy enough to imagine.

Maybe if I were Bison, I would have felt wronged by the captain's assessment. Bison had begun his career as a troubleshooter for Canterbury Construction Company and was obviously a typical product of the slums of Thursday. He was the type of person who grew up unimaginative, entirely preoccupied with figuring out how to survive among the other dirty residents of the slums. How could someone who has never known anything beyond that act noble or dignified, or discuss philosophy? He'd probably never even considered that others might view his existence as wretched until the new teddy bear on board threw him a glance of contempt. But after that of course, Bison used every means available to someone in his higher position to abuse the teddy bear. It was dirty and heartless of him, but entirely predictable.

Anyway, as soon as the captain heard Bison's name, he sprang into action. The situation was already dire. Rrose Sélavy was only five hundred meters away and we could already hear its flyers buzzing around us. Jezebel lurched unexpectedly and suddenly began to rise. Four flyers had attached ropes to our boat and were lifting us up into the air. It wasn't hard to guess their intentions. They meant to drop Jezebel on Rrose Sélavy's deck, overpower us, and ransack the ship. Simple, brainless, and effective—that was Rrose Sélavy's style. I'd never experienced it myself, but I had heard rumors.

I could almost hear the captain's brain whirring as the ship floated into the air. He was sorting and classifying all the information about Rrose Sélavy that he had tried to forget over the years. His plan of action automatically began to sync up with his thoughts, and the library cube that had until now been in the captain's hands suddenly disappeared into one of his pockets.

Though I was really worried about the captain, I couldn't remain at his side forever. I rushed out of the wheelhouse, put on an anti-shock vest, and began working with the first mate to figure out what to do with the refugees. Whatever Rrose Sélavy was going to do to us, we had to hide them first. The captain could deal with the library cube himself.

We finished stowing the refugees in a secret storeroom just as Jezebel was being lowered to the deck of Rrose Sélavy. But by the time we had rushed back to the wheelhouse, the captain had disappeared. We didn't know what he was planning, but it seemed we were going to have to do our best without him. We didn't need to talk it over. Although none of us had experienced anything as crazy as this before, we all knew how to act in an emergency.

Jezebel thudded down onto the deck. The shock wasn't as bad as I had expected, but the ship tilted slightly to the left. The first mate had given each of us a shock gun and a needle gun. Nine of the ten shock guns would probably be confiscated, but we hoped they wouldn't find the needle guns hidden between inserts in our boots.

We soon heard the clang of a mobile stairway being secured to the side of our ship, and six armored crewmembers climbed aboard. Walking straight into the wheelhouse, they leveled their guns at us. They confiscated our shock guns as anticipated, but nothing else. Not that the needle guns could have hurt them through their armor anyway.

The apparent leader of the group walked right up to me. He must have assumed I was the boss. Was it because I was the only man in the room? Because I looked the most like an Earthling? Because my tuxedo looks like a captain's uniform?

"Where's the cube?" The guy asked.

"What cube?" I replied.

"The library cube Bayan Purple asked you to retrieve. Where is it?"

"Ah, the captain has it."

"Where's the captain?"

"How should we know? We were all too busy taking care of ourselves. If you don't believe me, search the ship."

The leader stuck his large chin toward his subordinates. One of them left the wheelhouse and gestured to the rest of the crew who were waiting down on the deck of Rrose Sélavy. Six more of them came up to join the first six, and together they searched our ship. I definitely wasn't happy about the situation, but I relaxed a bit. They wanted the cube, not the refugees. No one would have to die. If that wasn't luck, I didn't know what was.

Of course, at the time I was totally unaware that two of the refugees had secretly left Jezebel and infiltrated Rrose Sélavy.

7

By the time our captors began lowering Jezebel to the deck of Rrose Sélavy, the captain had already slipped inside the huge ship. Knowing how to hide from the artificial eyes of its surveillance tower, he had strapped on a camouflaged wingsuit and jumped into a blind spot just before Jezebel touched down. Because the distance was too short to sufficiently decelerate, he was forced to crash right into the side of Rrose Sélavy's bridge and fall fifteen meters straight down. It didn't hurt him though. He weighed no more than twenty-five kilos and had incredibly supple joints, and thus could easily endure the fall. He had realized he was capable of withstanding such impacts while living on Rrose Sélavy. Though he had suffered there, he had also learned a great deal. Never mind that he could have learned the same things elsewhere, and without all the suffering.

He fell into a cradle where twenty-four Horlas were hanging in three rows. Tossing aside the wingsuit, he boarded the maintenance elevator in the corner and descended. People were everywhere on deck, but they were all focused on Jezebel and no one noticed him.

Theoretically, the captain could go anywhere on Rrose

Sélavy without being noticed. In his eight years on the aircraft carrier, he had altered its inner systems to suit himself. He had moved its machinery around bit by bit to make just enough room for a creature his size to hide and move around. He had done it both to make his work easier and because he needed somewhere to hide from the persecution of his coworkers. He might otherwise have died long before encountering Jezebel.

The captain could feel his emotions welling up as he ran underneath the corridors through ducts filled with neural cables and sewage pipes. He really had loved Rrose Sélavy; it was different from what he felt for Jezebel. His love for Jezebel was that of a friend or spouse, but he loved Rrose Sélavy with the ardor of a fan for their favorite Hollywood star. Now that he was free of his nasty, former crew members, his affection for the ship felt purer.

Because of this, he was all the more pained by Rrose Sélavy's current state. The captain had been a great manager. Although he himself had never fully submitted to the ship's system, he well understood its top priorities and had always been able to implement his own improvements. The five years the captain had been in charge of maintenance had also been the best years of Rrose Sélavy's long life. Sadly, the ship had slowly deteriorated in the years since the captain left. The neural system the captain had once worked so hard to optimize now stood, seven years later, unaltered and starting to decay. It was clear that whoever had succeeded him knew nothing aside from how to flatter their superiors.

After running down the winding duct for ten minutes, the captain arrived at his first destination: the twenty-first hub of the neural network. At first, it had been no more than a physical intersection, but over time the captain had transformed it into a mini control center for his own use. The official plans in the computer system still showed only twenty hubs. Sitting down carefully in the dust-covered chair, he connected the goggles he had brought with him. Twelve percent of the neural network was damaged, but that didn't prevent him from finding out what state the ship was in.

The captain focused on information about what had happened after the mutiny. He found that Rrose Sélavy had been wandering aimlessly ever since breaking the contract with Grant-Burns. The crew hadn't been able to find a new contract or accomplish anything on their own. For the last few months, they had been most concerned with securing food rations. Business must have really been terrible for the aircraft carrier to resort to self-sufficiency. They had been especially worried about procuring fruity-smelling esters. Without enough decent desserts, they would have quickly faced a second mutiny. Rrose Sélavy's crew hadn't eaten a single real fruit in the last month.

As expected, the ship's system contained no direct information about who had hired it. Leaders usually conducted this sort of business privately. The captain learned instead that four days earlier, Bison had bragged about signing an agreement with some unknown party, saying that if the mission were successful, Rrose Sélavy's future was assured. The announcement had united Bison's faction, but a cynical opposition persisted as always, and in fact, the ship's underground messaging network saw a sharp uptick in posts attacking Bison. The most popular of these posts posited that the secret contract did not actually exist and was just a fiction created to legitimize independent piracy. The captain rejected that idea, but he was forced to accept the fact that something strange was going on. No matter how you looked at it, hiring an aircraft carrier to seize a tiny ship like Jezebel was overkill. Bison's gang, though, had probably been too preoccupied staving off mutiny to realize something was off.

Figuring out the details of the contract wasn't the captain's top priority for the moment. He had to free Jezebel. His plan was simple: he would stop Rrose Sélavy's fusion reactor. If he could do that and simultaneously disable the flyers' cradle, Rrose Sélavy would be reduced to a floating island. He would of course also have to lay the groundwork to commandeer four supplementary flyers in order to lower Jezebel back into the water. By tying Rrose Sélavy up for just five hours, he could give Jezebel enough time to leave the high seas and flee into the McKinsey bloc.

At first, it looked easy. The system had hardly been updated since the captain's departure and all the backdoors he had installed were still active. As he worked, however, he ran up against a strange obstacle. The fusion reactor was being protected by something he couldn't identify. It couldn't be Rrose Sélavy's A.I. or systems specialists—the strategies protecting the reactor were too different. Whatever it was, the captain couldn't make heads or tails of it.

After some hesitation, the captain decided to try going directly to the reactor. He ran. Still wearing the goggles that kept him abreast of what was happening on Rrose Sélavy, he passed through vents, squeezed through openings next to lockers, and ran along the top of cable tubes. The search team that had boarded Jezebel to find the cube had come up empty handed, of course, and people across the aircraft carrier were starting to jeer at Bison's stupidity. Here and there, Bison's hysteric voice could be heard over the ship's comms. Bison had never been a good talker, but now he was almost completely incoherent. It was pathetic. Finding the cube had been Alfred E. Bison's last chance at securing his authority as captain.

After running frantically for twenty minutes, the captain finally arrived at the reactor. Even though normally at least one person was supposed to be on duty at all times, the control room was empty—they'd lost discipline. Still, it was good that he didn't have to use the needle gun he'd brought along. Slipping through a backdoor in the reactor's safety equipment, the captain turned on manual control. Theoretically there was nothing that could go wrong with his plan. But just as he got to the fourth of five levels in the shutoff procedure, everything reverted to the original settings. He tried twice more, but the result was the same.

The captain scanned the system again. From the outside, nothing looked unusual. But, the fact that a function as basic as an emergency shut-off didn't work meant something was wrong. He closed his eyes and thought. He tried to picture the way the system had used to look. Then he opened his eyes again and compared that image with the result of the scan. Now he thought he could see what was wrong. Some unknown entity had cleverly mimicked part of the system and was feeding off of the reactor. Its mimicry was so clever, in fact, that it would have been nearly impossible to detect without knowing what the original system had looked like. No wonder the lazy, undisciplined crew of Rrose Sélavy hadn't noticed.

The captain went back out into his secret corridors. He searched through the nearby tunnels like a laboratory rat in a maze until he arrived at a gold-colored cable connected to the reactor. Following it, he came at last to an old hideout: a small area he had cleared himself, moving machinery piece by piece in order to have somewhere to go when he wanted to cry alone.

A cylindrical machine about two meters in diameter and three meters tall had occupied the space in the captain's absence. It looked dead, apart from an apparatus at the top that was spinning like a pinwheel. However, as soon as the captain drew near, two machines the size of puppies appeared and began to shriek in alarm with their mouths open. Coopers. The cylindrical machine was, needless to say, an Olivier.

The captain's mind reeled. Why was an Olivier here? He'd never before heard of an Olivier living off a human-made machine. Oliviers valued stability and independence, and so to find one living on a human vehicle, a boat at sea no less, made no sense. Yet, here it was, right in front of his eyes. What a discovery. Talk about a big deal.

The captain began to worry. Most of Rrose Sélavy's crew were subordinate to the ship's system. They acted as if they had free will, but most in fact did not. If this Olivier was now part of Rrose Sélavy's system, what were the chances that everything happening on the ship was the will of the Olivier? It was definitely possible. Oliviers didn't speak to humans, but they did make use of them. But to what purpose?

He had no time to dwell on the question. The captain had learned what he needed to know: physically disabling Rrose Sélavy was no longer possible. No matter what he tried, the Olivier would block him. Should he just surrender? He couldn't. After a moment's consideration, he came up with another plan. He realized now that his original idea of disabling the entire ship had been idiotic. However, it would be possible to use his hub to send conflicting control signals that would prevent the ship from actual movement. But to do that, he had to move now.

Sadly, nothing ever came of the captain's plan. It was cut short simply and pathetically when the rusted floor gave way beneath him as he was running back to the hub. The captain fell awkwardly right into a gang of thugs that Bison had obviously found on Thursday. Before the captain could even get to his feet, one of them had laid a hand on him and picked him up by the scruff of his neck. The captain's earsplitting high soprano screams echoed down the hallway.

Fortunately, you no longer get called a sissy for screaming like that these days.

8

By the time he was dragged at last into Bison's cabin, the captain's face was covered in tears. He hadn't wanted to cry, but he couldn't help it. He still didn't know how to stop from crying. He had considered a nerve treatment at one point, but abandoned the idea because it seemed like that would have turned him into someone other than himself. After leaving Rrose Sélavy, he told himself that his crying was just natural. Why not cry? Alec leaves Laura! Bambi's mother dies! Everyone yells 'I am Spartacus!' Cry! Cry! Everyone cry!

Yet the captain was embarrassed beyond measure when they tossed him down like dirty laundry at Alfred E. Bison's feet. No matter how much he wiped his eyes and gritted his teeth, he was unable to hide the fact that he'd sobbed the whole way there.

Bison was laughing at him. The shape of Bison's mouth prevented most people from reading his expressions, but the captain knew them from their many years together. How he had detested that noiseless laugh.

"Ah, if it isn't the damn teddy bear!" Bison said, his anemone tongue wriggling around inside his spread lips. Every time Bison spoke, the captain couldn't help but wonder if it might not actually be the tongue speaking, with Bison merely serving as its host body.

"D...d...d...don't be rude, Bison. I'm no longer your subordinate. I've got my own ship now." The captain tried his best to calm his tears and speak.

"Oh, that tin can? If you're the captain, then you must have the cube. Great. Give it to me."

"What cube?" The captain said. It was true. No matter how thoroughly Bison's gang searched him, they wouldn't find the cube. This was because it was inside one of the flying machines attached to the Horla cradle. He had programmed it to fly up above the stratosphere if he said the code word.

"What?" Bison bellowed. "Is this some kind of a joke?"

The captain slowly relaxed, his tears drying up and his head clearing, as he watched Bison's tongue writhe. No matter how tough Bison and his gang acted, as long as the captain knew where the cube was, he had the upper hand. That is, until they realized they could torture him for the information. He had to think of something, anything, and quickly.

"I'm just trying to warn Rrose Sélavy," the captain said in a rush, not quite knowing what he was saying, "because I do care about the ship. Do you really not know what you're caught up in?"

"Don't be silly."

"Are you kidding me? Consider this. We grabbed the cube out of the water only a few hours ago." Good, the captain thought to himself, this way the story writes itself. "But you got your orders four days ago. It doesn't make sense. Why didn't your client just ask you to fish it out of the sea yourself?"

Bison hesitated. The captain's words were getting through to him.

Absurdly, the moment the captain voiced the question, things started to make sense to him as well. It wasn't just a trick to deceive Bison. In his frantic effort to survive, the captain had stumbled on a conundrum that struck right to the core of the matter. Everything from the murder to their capture by Rrose Sélavy suddenly made sense. The captain's attempt at improvising a lie had led him to a plausible theory that might just be the truth.

"I know the identity of the client you're trying to keep secret," the captain said. "It's Bayan Purple of the Free Ship Alliance, isn't it?"

Bison didn't answer. That was as good as a confirmation.

Triumphant, the captain quickly added: "You're such an idiot. Bayan must have told you that the cube contains information that can revive hundreds of wombs. He then asked you to seize the ship the signal was coming from, saying he'd give you a reward for the cube. So, as usual, you immediately grabbed our ship and pulled it up on deck. And you know what happened as a result? No? You idiot! You turned our ship into a Trojan horse. What? You don't know what a Trojan horse is? Take a look outside and see what's happening!"

The captain gestured wildly in the direction of the window. It was just a trick to divert attention while he removed the needle gun from his ear, yet once again his timing was perfect. With a loud bang, the glass shattered into hundreds of small fragments that flew in all directions. Bison's crew ran out into the corridor, leaving Bison alone in the room screaming from the glass fragments that had wedged into his eyes. The captain ignored him and pushed his way out into the corridor.

How did my intuition get to be this good? The captain felt triumphant. He still didn't know what Bayan's goals were, but it was obvious he had been dragged into this whole affair so suddenly because Bayan hadn't wanted to give him time to think about it. Bayan owed him now. Provided he survived this mess, the captain would be demanding extra compensation.

Rrose Sélavy had by then descended into chaos. The crew members were too busy shooting and throwing gas bombs at each other to notice a small teddy bear slipping away. Something had broken the fragile equilibrium on the old aircraft carrier. The captain already knew what that something was. Two of Bayan's spies had been hiding among the refugees we'd rescued. That would explain the murder of the remora pilot. Thinking the pilot was already dead, the spies would have tried to pass themselves off as his passengers. However, his survival had put their plan at risk, and they needed to shut him up quickly to prevent their identities from being revealed.

The captain rushed back to Rrose Sélavy's twenty-first hub and prepared once again to escape. With the ship now in total chaos, it was no longer necessary to shut down the reactor. All he needed to do was direct the four supplementary flyers to lower Jezebel back into the ocean. Once his ship was back on the water, the captain would make his own escape by stealing an Horla and flying out.

That's when the captain realized something strange was happening. A battle siren sounded and all security systems disengaged at the same time. Someone who knew the boat well and wielded considerable influence over its system was up to something big.

It took the captain less than a minute to figure out what that big thing was. A glittering pumpkin-colored ICBM shaped like a soccer ball shot out of the ship and headed in the direction of the McKinsey bloc.

9

Jezebel was already halfway between Rrose Sélavy and Wednesday. Rrose Sélavy no longer had any spare energy to bother with us. Seen through binoculars, the area around the aircraft carrier flared as if with fireworks. It was impossible to tell who was winning from that distance, but we guessed that come morning, Rrose Sélavy's population would have sharply decreased.

We heard what sounded like a whistle in the distance and saw a flashing blue signal light approaching us from the direction of Wednesday. An airship. Below the light we could see the logo of the Free Ship Alliance. The airship stopped above Jezebel and a shuttle capsule shaped like a grain of rice descended. As soon as the capsule landed, a door opened and Bayan Purple emerged wearing a pair of pajamas. His round, pink, Genghis Khan-like face maintained a vague smile as he addressed the captain: "The cube?"

The captain had returned the cube to his pocket, and now he pulled it out and passed it to Bayan. After giving the cube a careful pat, Bayan placed it in a drawer inside the capsule.

"What's in the cube?" The captain asked.

"I told you earlier. It carries information that can be used to make several wombs. It's valuable." Bayan Purple replied.

"Is the cube really what you were after?"

"Well, I needed the cube too."

Angered, the captain drew a cell out from his pocket and held it up to Bayan, turning it to the news show we had been watching. A McKinsey bloc newscaster was screaming against a backdrop of black smoke, "One hour ago, the interstellar airport was destroyed by a missile shot by an unidentified power. Over two hundred people have already been confirmed dead...."

Bayan Purple flinched almost imperceptibly, but that was it.

"Why don't you explain what's going on here?" the captain demanded.

"It's not something you need to feel guilty about. It was a just punishment for their crime."

"What crime? Gouging people? Bribery?"

"Mass murder. The McKinsey bloc airport was a slaughterhouse."

The captain grew quiet. Anyone would have, hearing news like that.

"It was a simple scam," Bayan explained. "Everyone wants to leave this planet, so they all gather at the airport. But what do you think happens then? Whether they fly into outer space or are murdered and their corpses atomized, it's all the same to the airport operators. Except that McKinsey profits more by killing the so-called passengers and seizing their luggage."

"But why would they do that?"

"Because the McKinsey bloc airport stopped functioning three years ago!" Bayan shouted. "And it's not only the

McKinsey bloc. There are no functional Oliviers anywhere on Crusoe anymore. All the Oliviers are meditating! And the Adjanis are no longer landing either, they just fly around. Don't you get it? All the other airports simply bought time by saying their tickets were sold out, but McKinsey bloc was different. Those bastards decided to put on a show at an airport with no flyers. For three years! All while murdering people!"

Bayan Purple waved one of his arms as if he were conducting an orchestra. He seemed to want to sweep all unnecessary emotions away from himself. We weren't used to seeing him truly enraged.

"I can't tell you who I'm working for. But I will tell you that this is just one part of a much larger plan. Of course, you're probably thinking that there must have been a better way to go about this. Maybe publish an article exposing the truth, or something like that. But I can assure you that this was the best option. My client wouldn't have chosen it otherwise. They aren't the sort to engage in sloppy work."

He continued talking, and told us a bit about the two mercenaries who had infiltrated our boat posing as refugees. They'd once worked on Rrose Sélavy, and had wanted to return to the ship to incite mutiny. Bayan's price for making that possible was that they fire a missile at McKinsey bloc for him. Ah, and the reason for the pilot's death was just as the captain had originally surmised. It was heartless, but that's just the way things are here.

At that point, we stopped listening to Bayan's explanation. His stories faded into the background as we looked up into the night sky at the stars we could no longer reach.

10

Well, that's the story of how the captain faced off against Rrose Sélavy. The fight wasn't exactly one on one, but when is anything ever that clear in reality?

The mutineers on Rrose Sélavy cut off Alfred E. Bison's head and hung it from a flagpole. As for us, Bayan Purple rewarded us with over twice what he originally offered, so you could say we came out pretty well. Of course, I'm sorry to bring you the terrible news that there is absolutely no way off this shithole of a planet. But, well, there's no point in denying reality.

Ah, you're crying again. Is being stuck here for the remainder of your life really all that bad? Give it a chance. After all, Earthlings lived like this until just a few hundred years ago. Earth was nicer, of course—people there could still have kids and didn't long for any world beyond their own planet. Sure, it's different for us here, now that the Adjanis don't visit anymore. Still though, what we choose to make of our situation depends entirely on how we look at the world and what we hope for in life. You might recall the inscription on the gates of Dante's Hell: "Abandon all hope, ye who enter here." I choose to take it as a warm message of welcome.

So, abandon all hope.

SYDNEY

1

The doctor was good at telling stories. He had traveled all over the galaxy before getting dumped on Crusoe, and had all sorts of tales to tell. Whenever Jezebel submerged to avoid bad weather and waves, those with nothing better to do would knock on his door. Whenever someone came by, he would welcome them in and sit them down on an old recliner smelling of unidentifiable herbs. Then, seating himself opposite his guest on the corner of his bed, he would unwrap his bundle of stories.

People didn't believe everything he said. All sorts of things were possible in the Linker Universe, but many took advantage of this fact to brazenly boast of adventures that might not actually be true. No matter how wide and varied the universe was, a single person could not possibly have experienced everything the doctor claimed. Yet, no one ever objected to or actively doubted the doctor's tales. His stories were just stories; they did not have to be true.

The doctor's favorite story was about his home planet Maria Wutz d. Unlike his other stories, people knew this story was close to the truth. It had hardly ever changed over the course of numerous retellings to many people on Jezebel, and he even had a library cube to corroborate it.

"Maria Wutz is near the sixth junction of the Korean Route and the Brazilian Route."

That was how he usually started the story.

"It's 17,300 light-years down the Brazilian Route and 18,000 down the Korean one. The direct distance from Earth is 15,200 light-years. In the early years of the Linker Universe, it took people half a century to get there.

"Maria Wutz used to be a beautiful planet, though I'm not sure what it's like now. The first continent people settled was beautiful, anyway. Even with the unpredictable weather and severe storms caused by the huge ocean and chaotic currents, the planet maintained an exquisite harmony with the Linker virus, and exhibited the beautiful ecology of explosive evolution. There was plenty of empty land for building cities and establishing farms, and the Linker machines were really only interested in the poles. Everyone thought it was an ideal place to colonize.

"But they neglected one important fact. They forgot that the two Oliviers nesting at Maria Wutz's south pole were not to be trusted. To the Oliviers, Maria Wutz was nothing more than a temporary laboratory. As soon as they finished the experiment they were conducting at the south pole and confirmed its results, they planned to take off. What the settlers had originally thought was an advantage turned out to be anything but. Only now have people finally come to recognize this.

"I don't know what the Oliviers' experiment was either. All I know is that right before the Oliviers left, some terrible things happened on the first continent. A severe magnetic storm hit the area and broke all of the machines in the colony.

Five grain silos were destroyed by tornadoes and the colony's communications antennae all caught on fire. Twenty-two people died. Then, before the colonists even realized what was happening, the Oliviers boarded Adjanis and left the planet for some other far-away place.

"The surviving colonists understood their predicament. With no more Oliviers or Garbos in their solar system, they were isolated from all other humans in the galaxy. More critical was the fact that they had almost none of the tools needed to maintain civilization. All their electric equipment was broken and they had neither the tools nor other resources to make repairs. People who had been able to travel the galaxy until just a few days before suddenly found they had devolved into Iron Age savages.

"What could they do? Well, the settlers were optimistic. They were skilled. The majority of the colonists were members of a construction consortium, and over eighty percent of these had come from the Austrian Galaxy Development Coalition and the Nebraska School of Universe Exploration. They figured that if they all worked hard enough, they should be able to restore the colony to a mid-twentieth-century level of technology in less than half a century. And why not? They had plenty of labor power and natural resources, and adapted easily to the local ecology without any need for assistance from the Linker virus.

"What they lacked was knowledge. The electric storm had destroyed their library and most information storage devices. All that remained were twenty-two paper books and a few memory devices worth of astronomical data and personal diaries. If the settlers wanted to revive civilization on Maria Wutz, they would have to squeeze as much information as possible out of their own brains to rebuild their library.

"They invented a way to make paper and ink out of seaweed and the rotting corpses of native fauna, and immediately set to work. Half of the settlers established farms, constructed buildings, and searched for veins of ore, while the remaining half ensconced themselves in the library building and transferred everything they knew to paper. Relying solely on their own memories, they began to write a new encyclopedia from scratch. They wrote down the history of Earth, as well as all the poems and songs and foreign language vocabulary they could remember.

"The encyclopedia was of course imperfect and fragmentary. Necessary scientific knowledge could be reconstructed with relative ease, but the humanities? When did Napoleon invade Russia? What is 'practical reason' supposed to mean? Did Confucius really eat human flesh? Why is the genealogy of Jesus different in every Gospel? Where in South America did the Mayans and Incans live? The people on Maria Wutz had no way to confirm these things. Also, what was to be done about all the art that had once been the repository of human culture? Everyone knew a line of poetry or a Beatles song. But who could perfectly remember Mahler's "Eighth Symphony" or Tolstoy's *Anna Karenina*, or describe the Mona Lisa or Guernica using only words?

"Nevertheless, the people of Maria Wutz tried their best. Now and then, they achieved astonishing results. For example, one amateur pianist almost perfectly recalled the representative works of Bach, Beethoven, Chopin, and even Skryabin. Over the course of three years of desperate nightly discussions, the ten or so military fanatics on Maria Wutz managed to reconstruct a history of World War II that ran to over 800 pages. When others later checked it, they found only two wrong dates in the entire book.

"In most cases, however, the colonists had to settle for less. Instead of complete books, the library of Maria Wutz was filled with indexes of book titles and summaries. The number of indexes constantly increased, but an index does not make a book.

"It was perhaps only natural that the people of Maria Wutz soon found themselves gripped by a desire to create. A few dozen of them got together with the intention of reconstituting *Jane Eyre*, but the result was no more faithful to the novel than a movie script. Then—of course—someone came up with the idea of recreating *Jane Eyre* in its entirety, using only their imagination.

"The Maria Wutz library of indexes became a gigantic gameboard. The game was governed by a strict set of rules, of course. You were free to write your own *Jane Eyre*, but the final chapter always had to begin with 'Reader, I married him,' because that was the one sentence of the original that the people of Maria Wutz were certain about.

"Civilization on Maria Wutz developed without any particular difficulties. In less than twenty years, they achieved the comforts of mid-twentieth-century Earth while avoiding most of its mistakes. They continued to advance steadily after that, and before long, the human settlement on the first continent had grown into a secure gene pool. They left the second and third continents alone. They didn't need any more territory, and their population ceased increasing after it reached five million.

"At some point, the people of Maria Wutz began to change. Gradually, the color of their skin and hair drained away, their personalities introverted, and their ability to dream increased. They increasingly resembled the melancholic genteel class featured in nineteenth-century romantic novels.

"What Maria Wutz dreamed of was Earth. Earth, Earthlings, Earth history, Earth civilization. We rewrote Earth books from only their titles hundreds of times. We repainted Earth paintings and remade Earth movies.

"Eventually we ceased to see the reality of the natural environment of Maria Wutz. It became the moor where the Hound of the Baskervilles howled, the Schwarzwald where the Seven Dwarves hid, the Transylvanian ruin where Dracula roamed and abducted children.

"Soon even Earth was no longer Earth to us. We lost interest in what the actual Earth was like, and instead saw it as a reservoir of dreams. What did it matter who Napoleon actually was or what 'practical reason' meant? Nothing in the Linker Universe lasted forever, so why bother obsessing over the purity and permanence of knowledge? It was enough for the Earth to survive as a backdrop for our dreams. We each had our own Earth. Before long, authors of new *Jane Eyres* began omitting the line 'Reader, I married him.' Some even left Mr. Rochester out entirely.

"How else would Maria Wutz have changed if the isolation had lasted just a little bit longer? We'll never know. Sixteen standard years ago, the isolation ended abruptly when five Oliviers came to our world for some grand project on the third continent. Guinnesses built a diamond tower there that was over ten kilometers tall. And when the stowaways that had tagged along came and found us, they gave us a single library cube. That cube contained all the information about Earth that we had previously tried to reconstruct on our own.

"The instant we learned the 'truth' about Earth, we stopped dreaming. No one asked us to stop. It's just that words like 'actual' and 'true' proved more powerful than we had expected. Once we were able to read the actual novel by Charlotte Bronte, our many *Jane Eyres* felt vapid, despite the fact that several of them were even better than the original. At the same time, we weren't prepared to entirely accept the original work either. The real *Jane Eyre* was so vivid and new that its spectral presence made us extremely uncomfortable. Maria Wutz fell into a panic. The suicide rate increased and the birth rate fell, and it seemed like our upset could last for decades.

"How did I feel during that period? I'm not sure. I was barely twelve years old when the isolation ended, and I spent all my time practicing tap dancing. You see, when they gave us the library cube, I learned that I looked exactly like the legendary dancer Fred Astaire. But there were no young women like Ginger Rogers around to dance with me, and in the end, I just couldn't keep up with Astaire. Still, that didn't stop me from dancing alone on an empty stage to music by Irving Berlin that I'd copied from the library cube.

"I left Maria Wutz when I turned thirteen. I wasn't the only one. Many people abandoned the planet to travel the universe. We thought it was our only real option. The dream that had governed Maria Wutz for several centuries was dead and gone, and the only way to fill the void it left behind was for us to act in the real world. And in that real world, we had to keep moving in order to survive. We believed that if we were unlucky enough to fall back into a state of isolation, we would no longer be able to dream anything but the same old dreams we'd already seen before."

2

On that dark and stormy night in the small cafe on Isola Bella, however, the doctor told the captain a story about something else entirely.

The small room they had secured for the night was warm though not especially quiet. Despite the lousy weather, many had gathered to celebrate the winter solstice, and were cheering loudly as they set off fireworks in the rain. Pounding footsteps signaled the presence of people sheltering from the rain on the floor below. But such noise was nothing unusual to the doctor and captain.

"It was exactly one year after I came to this planet," the doctor began, "I was part of a gang syndicate called the Sistine Tour Group. I'd been a member for about a hundred days, I think. The kinds of things they did while I was with them were relatively tame, by their standards at least. We cruised around the Thursday desert in five old airships and rounded up escapees from nearby cities. Thursday was just as dangerous then as it is now. We transported people to cities—the safer ones—that needed laborers and collected our fees. People said we were slave traders, but it only looked that way if you didn't understand the circumstances. It wasn't as bad as that. It was a just a humanitarian enterprise done for profit, like how we rescue refugees on Jezebel. I'm not going to make excuses for being a part of it."

The captain knew more than the doctor did about what went on behind the scenes of such "humanitarian enterprises," but chose to keep silent.

"Those final months of the Sistine Tour Group were miserable. We rescued forty people and were bringing them back when we were suddenly attacked by about twenty Horlas with no markings on them. I still don't know who they belonged to or why they attacked us. Everyone said it was the Crimson Jihad, but they'd have nothing to gain from upending a runty group like the Sistine Tour. It seems more likely that a few gangsters had somehow gotten their hands on the Horlas and were just fooling around.

"All five of our airships crashed into the desert as a result of this attack. I don't know what happened to the other four airships, but I and five refugees managed to escape our airship just before it burst into flames. The situation was bleak. The closest city was over a hundred kilometers away in Crimson Jihad-occupied territory. It seemed inevitable that we would end up dying, either of thirst in the desert or at the hands of the Jihadists. We just couldn't imagine any other outcome no matter how hard we tried.

"We decided not to waste energy wandering aimlessly around the desert. Instead, we made a makeshift bunker in the burnt wreckage of the airship and searched for working machinery and tools. One telephone had survived, but it was a factory-produced model that only supported encryption level four, so it was worse than useless to us. The sand pirates would sniff out our transmission and be on their way by the time we ended our call.

"One of the people I had rescued, a guy who looked a bit like a shaggy weasel, told me something strange. He said that underneath the desert there was a huge lake that had formed when water filled an empty magma chamber, and he said that around the lake lived a race of people who had decided to hide out there until they could stabilize and secure their genetic pool. But Crimson Jihad geologists had discovered them, and now the Crimson Jihad was planning to attack. The weasel guy had overheard this and escaped from the city to warn them of the imminent strike, only to get stranded in the desert with the rest of us."

"You mean the Vesuvians?" the captain interjected.

"That's right, the Vesuvians. I've talked about them before, but this is the first time I've ever told this particular story. Once night fell, we followed our weasel friend into a tunnel that led to the underground lake. The entrance was skillfully camouflaged, but, well, the Vesuvians weren't native to the desert, and in the end, anyone determined enough could have found that entrance. Someone else would have, sooner or later.

"Anyway, the undergrounders had large insectoid eyes and pale, ghostly figures, and they sure weren't happy to see us. I think they were worried about gene pollution. But they pointed us to an empty spot away from them where we could hide from the sunlight, quench our thirst, and satisfy our hunger. We drank the dew from lichen and ate mushrooms we picked off the ceiling and roasted with our lighters. It wasn't comfortable, but it was better than dying of thirst in the desert.

"The next morning, five of the underground people came to us wearing masks. While pretending to ignore them, I eavesdropped on their conversation with Weasel. I was a bit uneasy. No matter how you looked at it, these undergrounders were a bit weird in the head. There's no use in trying to define 'normal' in the Linker Universe, but even so, surely there must be something wrong with a whole race of people whose actions betray a fatal misunderstanding of reality."

"Sure there's something wrong with that, but it's not unusual," argued the captain, "It would be a lot stranger if everyone saw the world clearly. Think about the Bethlehemians. And the Church Mafia... Or even the Crimson Jihad... And what about the eight million fools who elected Mephisto Beta mayor? How do you explain the continued operation of the Deronda Mercenary Army? Or for that matter, Rrose Sélavy?"

"Yeah, they're all idiots, too, of course, but the undergrounders didn't talk or act like religious zealots. Even zealots will call a stone a stone. The underground people weren't even capable of something as elementary as that. Of course a stone could be stone, but it could just as easily be a rose or god's eye or sometimes simply not be at all. They lived in their own dream world, and it was that world, not the real one, that governed everything they said and did. They were the worst group of Bethlehemians I've ever encountered. I figure it was probably because they'd been shut up in that cave for too long. In a safe and unchanging environment, that sort of mental abnormality must not be much of an impediment to survival. All they knew how to do was sit around and pick mushrooms from the walls of the cave and tell one another about their dreams. And as long as that makes them happy, great—but you'd think that under threat of bombing by the Crimson Jihad, they might have started to confront the real world on its own terms.

"Weasel spent a fruitless hour desperately trying to get the undergrounders' representatives to take the Crimson Jihad threat seriously. His failure was unsurprising, given that the undergrounders could not see reality, and we could not understand what it was they did see.

"Eventually the representatives left, and Weasel came over and vented. 'We can't fail,' he said, on the verge of tears. 'Sydney will never forgive us. No, what I mean is that Sydney's the only person who can save us. He won't abandon me.'

"I had learned the names of most people with any power on Thursday during my stint in the airship gang. But this was the first time I'd heard the name Sydney. It's too plain a name to become common here. Crusoe is like a masquerade: the more colorful a name, the better. Someone with a name like Sydney wouldn't have an easy time throwing their weight around in a place like this.

"I was curious and cautiously probed Weasel to learn more about this Sydney person, but his gibberish was difficult to make sense of. All I could ascertain was that Sydney had done Weasel a big favor, and consequently Weasel had sworn to do whatever Sydney asked of him. Sydney had then 'invited' Weasel to become an informant, and Weasel had instantly agreed. The first task Sydney had given Weasel was to report anything he heard about the Crimson Jihad's plans for the undergrounders.

"I wasn't able to learn from Weasel who Sydney was, when he had found out about the underground lunatics, or why he was interested in them. Yet, it was clear that Sydney was our only hope. If we couldn't alert him to what was happening, we'd be buried alive alongside the underground people.

"I had no choice but to help Weasel get out and contact Sydney. But how? We couldn't think of any plan other than breaking straight through the front door.

"Weasel was scared, but smuggling him into the undergrounders' village was easier than expected. When we got there, they were all just sitting around or napping or having sex, intoxicated by their daydreams. How did we manage to get past their sentries? Those poor suckers wouldn't have noticed anything even if it was moving right in front of them. To make up for their lack of awareness, they had erected a wall blocking the entrance to our tunnel, but we just climbed right up and over it. While passing above the sentries' heads, I couldn't help thinking that even if the Crimson Jihad didn't attack, these lunatics would no doubt find a way to finish themselves off before long.

"I ran through the underground village until I finally found what I was looking for: a garbage dump. It was a mountain of machinery that hadn't been used for centuries. I searched for hours to find the parts needed to make a vehicle. With assistance from a computer, it took me half the day to cobble together a scooter capable of carrying a Weasel-sized creature at a speed of about five hundred kilometers per hour. I used a remora's egg-shaped escape capsule for the body, and pulled the propulsion system out of a wrecked airship. The contraption could only move forward in a straight line and would shatter into pieces after about three hundred kilometers, but it was our only option. I was able to pull the scooter to the entrance of the tunnel without the underground people noticing, then put Weasel inside and turned it on. The scooter rattled for a moment before taking off in a big cloud of dust. I only hoped it was headed in the right direction, wouldn't run into any sand pirates or mountains, and the brakes worked.

"An entire day went by without any news from Weasel, then a second day, then a third. I presumed we had failed. Expecting a vehicle cobbled together from centuries-old trash to work properly had probably been a mistake. Gazing up at the pitch-black ceiling of the cavern while drinking moss dew and eating roasted mushrooms, I thought I was going crazy too. I began seeing phantoms. Purple clouds in the shape of Edward Everett Horton's face floated above my head. Thirteen of them! And when I strained my ears, I could hear the chirping of women's voices as they whispered to one another. I tried to imagine what the undergrounders must be seeing and hearing after eating these mushrooms their entire lives, but my head swam at the thought.

"On the fourth day, it finally happened. At first, I thought it was an earthquake. You get used to tremors like that when you live in the northern desert. But I knew it wasn't an earthquake when sand and dust rushed noisily into the cavern. The Crimson Jihad air force had finally begun to bomb the entrance. After the first hour of bombing, daylight penetrated as far as our own cavern, and we heard the sound of hundreds of four-legged tanks stomping the ground. The undergrounders began to react at last. The sounds of explosions and smell of blood wrenched them out of their dreams.

"Already dozens of them had been crushed under the tanks, but the real massacre was yet to begin. The tanks had come to clear a path, not to slaughter. As soon as the path was ready, Crimson Jihad would send in an army of bloodthirsty males carrying weapons plundered from six continents to turn the mushroom people into bloody pulp. But the undergrounders were completely unprepared, and all they could think to do was run farther into the cave to avoid the tanks. And before you ask, they weren't running to some other exit at the far end of their cave—there was no other exit. All they managed to do was make things easier for the butchers by gathering themselves together in one place.

"I and the other refugees weren't that stupid. We kept as close as possible to the entrance, and hid in a small tunnel connected to our quarters, blocking off the entrance with moss and rocks. The question was how long we'd be able to stick it out. The Crimson Jihad had come primarily for the underground people, but that didn't mean they would spare us. Slaughtering us would just be the icing on their bloody cake. Killing and destroying were the only things they knew besides eating and sleeping. We're talking about guys who'd had all their other desires surgically removed.

"As soon as the tanks moved away from us, softer but more horrifying sounds filled the air. The Crimson Jihad butchers had arrived. We heard the stomp of military boots, the clang of metal weapons, and soon the sounds of blaster shots and screams. The massacre had begun. We held one another's hands and clenched our eyes shut. Someone mumbled something that sounded like a prayer, but they soon fell silent again. It wouldn't do to let prayers betray our presence to the butchers.

"About twenty minutes later, we heard loud noises coming from the entrance. At first, I wondered if Crimson Jihad had brought in some new weapon, but that wasn't it. These new machines were quick and elegant, that much was obvious from the sounds they made. These weren't the crude weapons favored by the Crimson Jihad, they were exquisite machines designed for the pleasure and amusement of the operator. I stood up and peered out between the cracks in our barrier. A huge green centipede-like vehicle entered into the cave, the broken corpses of three or four Crimson Jihad butchers stuck between its abundance of legs. The centipede came right up to our barrier of moss and rock and, using its antennae, gently cleared it all away. As soon as the tunnel was clear, it opened its mouth and a fat gray man wearing a red cylindrical hat slowly walked out. The instant I saw the man's round face, I knew it was Sydney. I knew why Weasel had called him Sydney."

"How did you know?" The captain asked.

"He looked exactly like Signor Ferrari from *Casablanca*. It was as if a Warner Brothers cartoonist had taken a hippopotamus and anthropomorphized it to look like Sydney Greenstreet. The name Sydney came to mind as soon as I saw him, and I couldn't imagine calling him anything else.

"Anyway, he smiled benevolently in my direction and stuck out a stubby hand. 'I'm here to buy your lives,' he said. This line was the first thing the Sistine flyer group and other civil rescue organizations said when they picked up refugees. Our own leader had said exactly same thing just a few hours before the crash that had landed us in this situation.

"I wasn't sure how I felt about that, but it's not like there was anything I could do. We all accepted his offer and boarded the centipede, which then reversed out of the tunnel and made for the desert. Through its windows, we could see that other troops had arrived on the scene. Several hundred people wearing the latest exoskeletons and accompanied by an armored light tank had entered the cave. The remains of Crimson Jihad tanks and airships burned in a heap of wreckage near the entrance to the cave. Judging by the strength of the army he commanded, this mysterious Sydney was clearly much more powerful than I had imagined. The exoskeletons alone... I hadn't even imagined that the wombs here on Crusoe could produce equipment of such quality."

"So that's what really happened in the Vesuvian Incident?"

"Yep. It wasn't a natural disaster. It was a secret war. And the undergrounders were in fact rescued by Sydney, not by a civil rescue organization."

"What happened to you?"

"Well, I owed Sydney for saving my life. He eventually presented me with an IOU made out to himself. If he ever called on me, I'd be obliged do whatever he asked, as long as it didn't conflict with my conscience.

"I signed the IOU. Back then, at least, Sydney seemed like the kind of person you could trust. I mean, I'd just seen him go up against Crimson Jihad and save thousands of lives, so how could I not?

"I tried to track Sydney after that, but he's not an easy man to find. Mysterious events similar to Sydney's rescue of the undergrounders were taking place all over the planet, but I couldn't be sure that Sydney had anything to do with them. I couldn't even be sure that they actually happened."

"Wait, is this Sydney the same person that Bayan Purple mentioned?"

"Possible. More than possible. I think he is. But even if I'd asked, Bayan Purple wouldn't have told me. Everyone who has ever had anything to do with Sydney has always kept their mouths stubbornly shut. Even I would have denied knowing anything about Sydney had anyone asked. I mean, I've never mentioned him to you before either.

"But here's the thing. Remember when we were staying in Preston Harbor ten days ago and I went into the city to deliver something for a member of the Free Ship Alliance? Well, the cook had asked me to pick up some of those black strawberry preserves that Monday's famous for. So, on my way back, as I was buying them, someone dipped a hand into my pocket and then disappeared. Inside my pocket I found a copy of the IOU I had signed to Sydney with a place and time written on the back. That's why I came here today with you and the first mate."

"Are you sure Sydney sent it?"

"No. Sydney's probably dead. Look below the signature. It says the authority to call in the IOU has been transferred to someone called Spack. I have no idea who that is, but now he has the right to order me around. Once, anyway."

3

The captain and the doctor heard a knock, and the door of their guestroom opened. In walked the first mate, her tall, slender figure stooping slightly as she entered. She pulled a red plastic chain to the table and sat down without removing her still-dripping raincoat. As always, the first mate's graceful movements excited the captain, though not in a sexual way. Many people mistakenly believed the captain and first mate were a couple, but such a thing would have been impossible. Though the captain had age and plenty of experience in other matters, his mind and body were like a child's in respect to sex, and he just couldn't understand how anyone could find that sort of stimulation pleasurable. The captain's happiness was an innocent appreciation of his friend's beauty. To him, the beauty of women like the first mate or Ingrid Bergman was not much different from the beauty of the stars and ocean, or the paintings of Marie Laurencin.

"Did you find anything out?" The doctor asked.

"Yes," the first mate answered. "The funeral was for a man named Posco. They say he was a coffee merchant. He supplied the raw ingredients for coffee to seven hundred cafes on

Monday, though I'm not sure whether that stuff can really be called coffee."

"Don't complain. At least it's drinkable."

"I'm not complaining. I'm merely questioning the nomenclature."

"Any information about Spack?"

"Spack's his real son, with his genes. It's so unusual that most people here already know."

"That's all?"

"Almost. Are we leaving soon? The car's waiting."

The rain had stopped while the doctor was talking with the captain, and most of the festivities had moved to the eastern side of the city. With the crowds gone, the wet street looked forlorn and shabby. The first mate pointed toward the other side of the street. A black six-wheeled vehicle that shone as if it had just popped out of the womb was sitting outside an old antique store. Its menacing appearance was undercut by the fact that you could tell at a glance that it was nothing more than nouveau riche ostentation. The skinny figure in a black overcoat standing next to the car appeared to be a man. He opened its doors as they approached, before sitting down himself in the front passenger seat. All four passengers found themselves staring as if hypnotized at the steering wheel above the empty driver's seat as the car drove itself up the meandering streets of Isola Bella.

Their destination turned out to be a stone chateau at the top of the hill. It looked more like a government office or a school than a somebody's home. If there had been a cross on top of the main gate spire, they would have mistaken it for a Church Mafia assembly hall. They followed the person in the black overcoat inside.

The interior of the building was a mess. The new owner was in the midst of replacing the previous owner's decor. The captain grew depressed. One of Degas's wax ballerina statues, obviously brought here from Earth at great expense, was being removed with only a cheap anti-shock membrane for protection. The captain wasn't sure whether the rough rectangular metal boxes that were put in its place were part of an art installation or some sort of functional machinery.

The person in the black overcoat led them to a large reception room on the first underground level. At the center of the room stood a gray-faced young man wearing a tacky, blue, skin-tight, button-down shirt and grinning. As soon as their guide exited the room, the young man's smile disappeared. He raised his right hand, spread his six fingers in pairs, and intoned:

"Live long and prosper."

A small snort of laughter sounded behind the captain and doctor. It was the first mate. She'd neglected to tell them that the owner of this place was a Trekkie, and a hardcore Vulcan fan at that. They should have guessed the instant they'd learned his name, but to the captain, the growing popularity of the Trekkie phenomenon in the space age was even more incomprehensible than sex. Trekkies had been no more than a silly minority on pre-Linker Earth, but now they were a significant cultural group that boasted even greater numbers than the Church Mafia. It made a certain kind of sense. The Linker Universe was surprisingly similar to Star Trek, with its Hollywood stars wearing latex-masks and pretending to be aliens. The difference was that no one in reality commanded their own spaceship. The Star Trek fandom had persevered for centuries both because it was so close to reality and because ultimately, we hadn't achieved the future it promised.

Fortunately, Spack had no intention of imitating Leonard Nimoy for the entire conversation. His plump face broke out in a warm smile as he greeted his guests, and everyone was served hot tea and refreshments.

During the formalities that followed, the captain learned more about Spack and his father. If what Spack said could be taken at face value, Poscoe was little more than an ill-tempered old geezer with expensive habits who spent a fortune on wacky philanthropic causes. This lost him a lot of money, but gained him a number of friends. "Everyone was always doing things for my dad," Spack explained. Not long before, Poscoe had died from chronic heart disease. He could have undergone heart reconstruction surgery, but he decided not to. "Father decided to give me a chance to make it on my own."

The captain saw in Spack a shallow youngster who probably knew nothing about what his father Sydney/Poscoe actually thought. He was certain that Poscoe couldn't have had much hope for his son.

As soon as his guests had finished their tea, Spack began to talk business.

"There's something of mine I need back," he said. "And my father always said that there was no one anywhere on Crusoe better for this sort of work than Dr. Flagg and his colleagues."

"What is it?" The doctor asked.

"The important thing isn't what, but where. It's the last gift ever given to me by my father. While in transit here, it was stolen by pirates from Thursday, and now it's in the hands of the tank fanatics on Saturday. I have to get it back."

"Just tell us what it is."

Spack's speech slowed slightly, "Have you ever heard about the extraordinary womb manufactured on Bellocio? It bore other wombs, some of which ultimately merged together to form actual Oliviers. Anyway, this womb could copy human bodies at an unparalleled standard of detail. Not for medical treatments, mind you—these bodies were purely works of art. A year ago, twenty-four of these bodies fell onto Crusoe, and my father bought them all. He was going to give one of them to me himself as a present. I'd prefer if you could retrieve them all, of course, but that might prove impossible. It would be enough if you could just bring me just the one he'd originally intended for me."

"So what's the body?"

Silence reigned for a moment. Even the shameless Trekkie seemed a bit embarrassed. He forced a cough or two, then whispered with forced nonchalance:

"Seven of Nine."

The captain's party passed almost another hour in the house after that. While Spack gave Poscoe's papers to the doctor, hoping they might yield clues for the search, the captain appreciated the artwork and drank a few more cups of tea. Their business concluded at last, they were shown out of the house and driven by the black suit back to the harbor where Jezebel was waiting. They said goodbye to the black suit and watched for a whole minute as the six-wheeled car climbed back up the hill.

The moment they entered Jezebel's cabin, they began to giggle like crazy.

"Did you see Spack's face when he said 'Seven of Nine'?" the doctor asked the captain, who was rolling around on the floor holding his tummy. "I'd be embarrassed too. 'Please find my Seven of Nine sex doll! I'll give you anything!'"

"It makes sense," the first mate interjected. "Instead of spending money to hire mercenaries, better to use an IOU his dad left him. That way, even if something were to happen to us, there won't be any consequences for him. Anyway, he doesn't have any other use for the IOU, and it's not like he can exchange it for cash."

"So, you're saying that if we fail, he'll just use another one of his dad's IOUs to send someone else to the South Pole to fetch his Jeri Ryan doll?"

"Why not?"

"Well then, I guess I'd better find him the doll, for the next guy's sake if nothing else. Actually, I should apologize to you guys. This is my problem, there's no need for Jezebel to get involved. I can put a team together and take care of it myself."

"You can't go there without some advance knowledge of the place. You need a guide, and you're not going to find anyone as good as me."

These were not just empty words. The first mate was one of the few lucky survivors who had firsthand knowledge of what was happening on Saturday. She had endured 431 days in that absurd hell and managed somehow to emerge psychologically intact.

4

Let's talk about Saturday. Situated at the South Pole, Saturday is a small continent approximately twice the size of the island of Madagascar. It's a snow-covered desert, but the area around the pole itself stays relatively warm thanks to a live volcano and geysers. Spherical Guinnesses patrol the vicinity of the volcano. People think that some of the Guinnesses are there to control volcanic eruptions.

Back when Earthlings first settled this place, Saturday was used as an amusement park. Military fanatics from all over the galaxy declared it an ideal locale for reenacting WWII tank battles between the Germans and the Soviets, and began to import wombs designed to produce era-specific weapons. At the time, they thought they were just having some fun, and in truth it really was just a game. The tanks moved by artificial intelligence and remote control, and the ruined buildings had been constructed as ruins. Everything was fake and artificial.

But the thing is that when people spend their whole lives playing a game, the game turns into something more. The game becomes life, becomes history, becomes the universe.

Pretty soon, the playfulness of the military fanatics was supplanted by a deadly seriousness. At first, it was no more than abnormally intense feelings of violence and group affiliation. But when the Oliviers began to meditate two hundred years ago, closing down almost all paths off the planet, the situation changed drastically. The element of play disappeared entirely, leaving behind only war. The gamers started to believe they were actual German and Soviet soldiers, and began to massacre one another.

Of the many hypotheses on the origin of this change, the most popular ascribes it to psychology: as it grew more difficult to leave the planet, frustrated people began to act out in extreme ways, and what happened on Saturday was one manifestation of this. Another popular hypothesis held that Saturday's artificial intelligence system was to blame. At some point the system had prioritized the maintenance and thriving of wombs, and begun to treat human beings as consumables. In all likelihood, both theories had some truth to them, though there were probably also other factors that we didn't even know about. The Guinnesses around the volcano pretended to be uninterested in people, but what if they actually despised the tank fanatics and were trying to get rid of them? Or, for some special reason, made use of them in that way? There's no shortage of theories about the Saturday war, and most of them contradict one another. Yet, because the nature of the war is always changing, they might not be as contradictory as they appear.

Most people still believe that the war on Saturday is meant to be a faithful reenactment of real historical events that took place between 1941 and 1944, and this may have been true once upon a time. However, even if we accept that reenactment was the objective, it was never fully realized. No matter how many wombs they had, how could they ever have gathered enough people or tanks to execute a full and faithful reenactment of the Battle of Prokhorovka? And where's the fun in remaining faithful to historical fact anyway?

The daily battles on Saturday three hundred years ago were more like chess games. Initial conditions were similar or identical to historical fact, but after that it was up to the players. They could have done it all in virtual reality. But the military fanatics who came to Saturday wanted something closer to reality: real tanks, real gunpowder, real noise, real smells, real blood, and real death.

So what's the situation with the Saturday war these days? On the surface everything looks pretty much the same as before. World War II-era heavy artillery rolling across the snow-covered plain and firing shells at one another. But the motives and behaviors of the participants aren't the same as they used to be. They aren't acting like the armies of two fascist states anymore. These days they're behaving like packs of starving wolves. Their primary objective isn't conquest, but plunder. Their goal is to seize and destroy the enemy's weapons and feed the remains to their own wombs.

Although it looks straightforward, there's a sequence to it. Regardless of how much the relationship between the wombs and the human combatants has changed, the wombs retain their original programming. The wombs on both sides produce the weapons that were in use from 1941 to 1944, but they only do so in chronological order. Whenever the end of a cycle is reached, the wombs restart at the beginning. In other words, each time Saturday's calendar turns back to June 1941, wombs that have just been producing Tiger IIs suddenly begin spitting out outdated Panzer IIIs. Understanding this production sequence is crucial to all involved.

Let's turn now to the question of the first mate. She first got embroiled in the mess that is Saturday eleven years ago. She was only seventeen standard years old at the time, and like most of her peers, she was full of anger. Just because the years on Crusoe are shorter than on the standard calendar doesn't mean that seventeen equals twenty-five. Seventeen years is still just seventeen years even if you've seen the seasons change twenty-five times. Imagine being that age and wanting to reject the world and travel the universe, but being stuck forever on this imploded planet. It would make anyone crazy.

The first mate found a less destructive solution. Instead of shutting herself inside her house on Leventon Island and fighting insomnia with strange chemicals, she decided to leave home and explore, even if her explorations would be limited to the surface of this one pathetic planet. She should at least check out everything the planet had to offer before complaining about it. She was young and naïve, and still thought that it was possible to see "everything" on Crusoe.

Making Saturday her first stop was the stupidest decision imaginable.

At the time though, the first mate was like a bomb with the fuse already lit, and given her volatile mental state, Saturday was in fact the ideal place for her. It was a site of unending war where limitless destruction is permitted and there's no need to feel guilty about the death of oneself or others. Even if she died there, she would at least be able to claim that she had experienced everything there was to experience on Crusoe. She wanted to feel a blaze of glory, as did many of the other passengers on the old freighter that took them to Saturday.

Saturday has two harbors: Normandy Alpha and Normandy Beta. Some people take issue with the historical inaccuracy of these names, but most just accept them as is. As soon as you arrive in either harbor, you have to choose whether you want to join the German or the Soviet army. Then you wait in whatever barracks you've been assigned until the appointed day when a truck or an airship arrives to carry you away. The moment you leave the harbor is the moment you become part of the war.

The first mate came ashore on Normandy Alpha and chose the Soviet army. It wasn't a hard choice. Although her appearance was more feline than human, Russian cultural genes flowed through her body. She spoke Russian as fluently as English, and the works of Tchaikovsky and Chekhov always excited her sensibilities. Joining the Soviet army was the natural thing to do.

An officer holding a Russian name dictionary told her to

pick a name as she was climbing into the truck. "Nazimova," she said without even turning to the display. From that moment onward, she was known as Nazimova.

Despite having chosen a woman's name, the first mate was treated as a man throughout her 431-day sojourn on Saturday. Gender in that place had nothing to do with biology: all soldiers were men, and all noncombatants were women. The first mate was obviously a fighter, and hence a man. Saturday would not tolerate dissenting views on this point. The first mate was assigned to the Forth Division and directly or indirectly killed one hundred and twenty people and destroyed forty-two German tanks.

While fighting, the first mate gradually began to wake from her fantasies. It wasn't the cruelty and meaninglessness of war that bothered her—she'd been well aware of that before coming to Saturday, and besides, she had an aptitude for mechanized slaughter. She really did love the ugly T-34 tank that was under her command.

No, what she couldn't stand was how tawdry the fakery all was. The fake part didn't bother her nearly as much as the tawdry part, though. The imaginary world of Saturday was as tawdry as could be. For example, only a handful of people on Saturday knew German or Russian, so the soldiers just spoke English to one another in bad German and Russian accents. When writing, the Soviet side wrote English in the Cyrillic alphabet and the German side marked each "o" with an umlaut. Even the very real suffering, bleeding, and dying that took place around her couldn't hide the shoddiness of the fakery. Most annoying of all was the "Heil Hitler" that captured German soldiers would bark out. Did they even know what kind of person Hitler had been? Did they realize that their portrait of Hitler was actually Alec Guinness in costume? If she was going to kill people, she wanted them to be real, not fakes.

When her first cycle of war came to an end and the wombs were preparing for the next July 1941, the first mate decided to escape the tedious playground. It wasn't possible to get discharged or anything like that; desertion was the only "officially recognized" way to leave.

While her colleagues partied to celebrate the end of the war, the first mate silently slipped out of the tent. She threw a goodbye kiss to her tank, which had survived through to the end, and then grabbed an abandoned sled and began the 140-kilometer journey to Normandy Beta. The sled broke down thirty kilometers from her destination and she forced herself to trek the remaining distance in two days. She hid out for three days in Normandy Beta before she was able to convince someone on a freighter crew to smuggle her out. When he refused money and made sexual demands instead, requiring her to assume a demeaning posture, she beat him up and took his storage room keys and ID card. The freighter left without him, and two days later its crew discovered the first mate hidden away on a storage compartment. No one on the ship complained, though. She was a much better worker than the crewman they had left on Saturday.

5

Jezebel left Isola Bella the following evening and slowly made its way down the Eastern coastline of Monday. The next afternoon, it picked up a passenger who looked like an ordinary black Earthling. The man's name was Bo. Like most Crusoe people with single-syllable names, he was quiet and did not stand out. The only remarkable thing about him was the third eye in the middle of his forehead, but he wore a hat low on his head to hide the eye, and we rarely saw it.

Bo sat on the couch in the recreation room and stared vacantly at the wall until dinnertime. It wasn't until the cook brought him a specially prepared melon and chicken sandwich (which actually contained neither) and tea, that he reluctantly opened his mouth. He carefully chewed his food for half an hour, rinsed it down with a mouthful of tea, and only then began to talk to the crew that had been watching him the entire time.

"I arrived on Thursday about twelve local years ago, and that's where I lived until last year. I had a long name on my home planet. I was a radio archaeologist. It's a completely useless profession here on Crusoe.

"I chose Thursday because the first person I met on this planet told me that the continent, which extends north and south from its center at the equator, was similar to Africa. I understood the comment to be about ecology, and it made sense that way. But what the person had actually been alluding to was a different aspect of Africa. To them, Africa had been a place ruled by cruelty and barbarism, where one could legitimately engage in certain kinds of plunder not tolerated elsewhere. Can you believe that hundreds of years have passed since Earthlings joined the Linker Universe, yet these ancient prejudices still hold sway?

"I'd like to set straight the prejudices against Thursday. It's true that terrible things are happening there. But the idea that this is merely, as that insipid Monday poet said, 'the fate of the dark continent which shoulders the equator,' is simply ridiculous. Most of the slaughter taking place on Thursday occurs in the northern territory occupied by the Crimson Jihad, and even there, things are improving. The area around the equator is relatively peaceful—the human part of it, anyway. If you want to talk about the Linker virus monsters, that's a different story entirely. Nature is always cruel. I still can't understand how monotheists can believe their Creator is a loving god.

"On Thursday, I spent ten years working as an evolution tracker, tracking the Linker-influenced evolution of lifeforms in the jungles and wetlands. I did mostly technical work; the direct, biological work was handled by experts. Even so, I've learned a great deal over the past decade and now know as much about the ecology as the experts. The job I chose there was actually quite similar to my original profession. Evolution tracking is closer to history writing than to science. What we research is particular histories, not universal laws.

"Our salaries were paid by the Rothbart Advanced Science Research Center. Although the name reeks of bureaucracy, it's a private organization. No one knows exactly what the nature of the organization really is. Some think it's merely the plaything of some rich people with too much time and money on their hands. Others say the information we gathered was used in pharmaceutical research. We didn't care. They paid us on time, our research facilities were comfortable, and all our reports were published in open access online journals with our names attached. More than anything, we were happy for the chance to be doing something of value on this isolated planet in a far corner of the Magellanic Cloud.

"Two years ago, however, I realized something was wrong with the place. My team was tracking the evolution of an animal nicknamed the Alonzo Sabertooth. It's a housecat-sized animal that looks a bit like a cross between a sabertooth tiger and a lemur. It was the complex mating ritual that drew our attention: at least six individuals were needed to complete a single mating. Usually four females and two males participated, but sometimes there were as many as nine females. Even the simplest versions of the Alonzo Sabertooth mating ritual required at least seven steps, and omitting any one of them resulted in failure. We were convinced that a behavior as inconvenient would disappear within several generations. We were sure the Linker virus would ultimately interfere to simplify the behavior. Never mind that the Linker virus was responsible for creating it in the first place.

"But what actually happened was the exact opposite: the group sexual behavior of the Alonzo Sabertooths began to pass through the Linker virus to other species. The behavior was not beneficial in any way, and we could not understand why it was spreading. We reported all this information to our institute, and our report was published online.

"Three days after the publication of our report, a new team arrived from Wednesday and took over all research related to the Alonzo Sabertooth. Those of us who had been working on the project were summarily removed. This was the first time anything like this happened in my ten years of working there, but we didn't have anything to gain by trying to assert a right to the research. Besides, if we couldn't continue with that species, there were others we needed to track.

"The new team of experts were obviously more skilled than we were. In fact, they were able to unravel the mystery of the group sex phenomena in only seven days. It turns out the behavior was caused by a venereal disease. During the floods of the previous rainy season, a microbial parasite on the reproductive organs of the Alonzo Sabertooth had mutated and become the vector for disseminating information about group sex. The team released their report and returned to Wednesday the following day. Everything was resolved safely, and we had nothing to complain about.

"On the day of their departure, I went to the dorms to say goodbye. As I walked in the door, I overheard part of their conversation that ended with the question, 'But won't Sydney still be disappointed?' I asked who Sydney was, but they said he was just a colleague and ended the conversation. And they cast their eyes downward as if they'd just committed a crime.

"Most people would probably have thought nothing of the incident and forgotten it soon thereafter. It's possible that they really did have a colleague named Sydney who was interested in the project and would be disappointed to learn how mundane the truth was. But I knew that wasn't the case. There was probably more than one person named Sydney on Crusoe, but I was certain that their Sydney was the Sydney I knew.

"Sydney was a mysterious philanthropist whom I had met the very day I fell onto this planet. Pirates attacked my remora in the vicinity of Wednesday, and Sydney's boat rescued me and the other passengers. You said you found my IOU in Sydney's files. But I didn't write it the day he rescued us, and he certainly didn't collect IOUs from every single person he rescued. He wasn't stingy. I don't want to tell you how I came to write that note. All I'll say is that Sydney prevented me from committing a terrible mistake that would have resulted in my death and that of two other innocent people. I wrote that IOU voluntarily, same as all the other people who wrote IOUs to Sydney. To him, an IOU wasn't merely the value of a life. It was a promise that he could call upon us to help him with his master plan. Almost no one knew what his plan was, but we trusted him nonetheless.

"So now you know why I was excited. I had unexpectedly been given a chance to learn something about that master plan. Sydney had been doing something with the Rothbart Center, something clearly related to Linker evolution. Thinking back over the Alonzo Sabertooth incident, I reviewed all the hypotheses we'd rejected during our investigations and tried to imagine which could have been connected to Sydney's plans. One in particular stood out: if the Alonzo Sabertooth's ridiculous reproductive ritual could be stabilized and maintained, and even be transmitted to other species, what hope might it hold for us?

"After the Wednesday experts left, I left Thursday in search of Sydney. I was no longer willing to just wait for his orders. I wanted to join his plan myself. I finally found him at the end of a seventy-day search.

"When I spoke with Dr. Flagg yesterday, he asked how I could have possibly found Sydney in such a short period of time. It wasn't difficult. Sydney was always leaving a trail of information about himself here and there. An active searcher could acquire more information on Sydney than a secretive and passive searcher like Dr. Flagg. Sydney always left his door open to people like me.

"I worked for Sydney until he died about a month ago. I can't reveal the nature of the work I did for him. In fact, I'm not even sure whether helping you is the right thing to do. I'm very conflicted. But if Sydney said he wanted to leave those things to that idiot Spack, then I'll respect his wishes.

"I'll tell you something you do need to know, though. First, the dolls you're looking for were not seized by pirates. The idea that those kids would have been able to take anything from Sydney is absurd. I'm the one who came up with that lie. I didn't want Spack to know who his father really was.

"The set of dolls was gifted to the German army base on Saturday and received by an Officer Bruckmueller. In exchange for the gift, Saturday performed a special service for us, although I can't tell you what it was. Regrettably, Bruckmueller was run over and killed by a Soviet tank about a week ago, and now we have no legitimate way of recovering the present. That said, one of the dolls has a tracking device that is undetectable using World War II-era technology. I confirmed its location before coming on board here. It's still in the middle of Saturday and still in good condition.

"You might think all this is little more than a ridiculous farce. Just the idea of rescuing life-size female dolls from military fanatics playing war games with real guns and tanks is absurd. But you have to understand that Sydney was no fool. If Sydney was determined to give the dolls to his idiot son despite the sacrifice it might take to recover them, then there's something deeper going on here. We just don't know what it is yet."

6

There's a tree on Saturday known as the "sea thorn tree." But don't be fooled by the unassuming name: it's actually the largest organism on Crusoe. The tree encircles the coast of Saturday in a continuous ribbon seventy-meters wide. The black thorns—each about the size of a finger—that cover its branches make it look particularly vicious. Some branches were removed to create Normandy Alpha and Normandy

Beta, but this did not break the continuity of the organism. It remains connected and unified by roots buried hundreds of meters underground.

Saturday's sea thorn tree is the only organism on Crusoe with that name. Every summer the thorn tree sends out pollen in vessels that look like little yachts, even though there's no mate to be found on the planet. Still, some of the pollen has been able to evolve into other unique life forms. Blessed by the Linker Virus, these small, hermaphroditic, half-animal, half-plant yachts extend chitinous green sails as they wander the Antarctic ocean sucking up plankton-filled seawater through the twenty-two mouths positioned around the edges of their bodies.

These yachts were the first life forms Jezebel encountered in the Antarctic ocean. The free-floating yachts gently drew back from the waves stirred up by Jezebel, their bodies flinching, their feelers in constant gentle motion.

"I once lived off those things for a time," the first mate said as she leaned against the ship's railing and looked out to sea.

"Really? You mean you ate them?" The doctor asked.

"They don't taste like much, but they're a great source of protein. They're everywhere and easy to catch. There used to be fishermen who specialized in providing yachts to both the Soviet and German army bases on Normandy Alpha. I'm not sure they do it anymore, though. I hear there are fewer and fewer yachts, and more and more of a newly evolved species with fins instead of sails. Apparently, they're hard to catch and taste terrible. And the number of tank fanatics is constantly shrinking too. Fishing can't be as lucrative as it once was."

The first mate and the doctor heard a splash as a long

mechanical arm shot out of the kitchen window, grabbed two yachts, and pulled them onto the ship. Through the open window, they could hear the cook humming a tune.

"Looks like that's what we're eating for dinner tonight. Well, can't be worse than what you had in the army."

The doctor's words proved correct. The cubed yacht was pretty good mixed into the dinner salad. Someone from Earth would have thought it tasted a bit like sweet potato with the umami flavor of fish. Such a comparison meant nothing to Jezebel's crew, however. The flavors of the foods they ate were constantly changing as the ingredients evolved. In their chaotic world, cooks needed to have exceptional judgment and instincts. Fortunately, Jezebel's cook was first-rate. If she hadn't been, Jezebel would never have become what it is now. Her talent kept the crew together.

The captain, the first mate, and the doctor debated their plans over dinner. The captain suggested that they each fly to the German base in individual Horlas and get in and out as quickly as possible. The first mate said that would be tantamount to suicide. Even if they managed to successfully land the Horlas in the German base, it would be almost impossible to keep the machines hidden while they completed their theft. And if they commanded the Horlas to lift off again and fly themselves around immediately after their passengers had disembarked, the Horlas would either be discovered or run out of energy for the return trip. If anything went wrong, the innocent machines would fly away and the three of them would be left isolated in the middle of the Antarctic.

Besides, until they learned more about Sydney's plans, they should default to rescuing all twenty-four of the dolls—even if Spack only really wanted the Jeri Ryan one. Their best option would be to keep open the possibility of negotiating a purchase. If they could buy the dolls from the German army, then what need would there be to steal them? And even if negotiation proved impossible, they would still have plenty of other options.

After considerable discussion, they formed a new plan. They would take Jezebel to Normandy Beta. There, they would buy a truck in the harbor black market, disguise it as a German army supply vehicle, and start driving inland, after which point the other two would follow whatever instructions the first mate came up with. It was a feeble plan, but they couldn't come up with anything better. After all, none of them knew exactly what the situation was on Saturday. The best they could do was rely on the first mate's ability to adapt to circumstances, because she at least knew how to survive there.

Once they had settled on this plan, the doctor and first mate immediately began to prepare. While the doctor decoded the encrypted signals coming from Saturday, the first mate gathered information from the merchants who frequented the continent and sent out her own spy fliers to map the terrain.

The first mate appeared to be enjoying the work. The battlefields of Saturday had been hell to her eleven years ago. But now that she was just passing through for a few days, it was a playground. A deadly playground where a single mistake could cost her her life, sure, but what fun were games without danger? She hadn't been bored on Saturday eleven years ago either. To the contrary, after her body had adjusted and she could move about of her own accord, she had relished the war there. It was just that she had thought it meaningless and stupid to devote your whole life to that sort of fun. Most of the people who came to Saturday, though, had no interest in the meaning of life. Why would they need such a thing?

Once they finished gathering information, they began fabricating the necessary equipment for their strategy. The German army uniforms that the captain, doctor, and first mate would wear were the centerpiece of their efforts. They pulled the engineer away from fixing the ship's plankton collection unit to help them. She was always fast as lightning and accurate in her work. What would have taken the first mate and doctor at least two days, took only three hours with the engineer's help. The uniforms looked perfect. Even Hugo Boss would have been proud of them.

The doctor sighed appreciatively, but even so could not help feeling slightly repulsed by the engineer's existence. No one on Jezebel could fully communicate with the engineer. Language itself wasn't the problem—she could read and write, and she understood what the rest of the crew said. She could also ask and answer short questions. The problem was the brain that controlled and used the language. The engineer lacked the capacity for empathic communication with the rest of Jezebel's crew. Instead of empathy, she connected to the rest of the crew through mathematics and absolute music, but even in those areas she was slightly out of step with the others. For example, she was probably the only person on Crusoe who enjoyed synesthetic jazz from the planet Illyria.

The doctor and captain always wondered where the first mate had found such a freak, but the first mate never talked about the engineer's identity. Instead, the first mate often exaggerated her motherly affection for the engineer in front of her crewmates. They thought that was weird too. The engineer could be beautiful from a particular point of view, but it was hard to imagine that anyone could feel motherly affection for someone who looked and acted like her.

But it didn't matter. The engineer was smart and capable. That they rarely needed to converse with her was a testament to the quality of her nearly flawless work. As long as the people around the engineer accepted her somewhat unusual presence, Jezebel ran like a well-greased cog.

As soon as the three of them had completed the uniforms, the engineer and the first mate went back outside to finish fixing the plankton collector. The moment the door closed behind them, the doctor rushed to put on his new German army uniform. He looked over his shoulder at himself in a full-length mirror the first mate had brought in while they'd been making the costumes. A freak beyond the imagination of any sane person stared back at him from the mirror. Fred Astaire in an SS officer uniform. Giggling, the doctor turned toward the mirror in a flamboyant gesture and saluted. Sieg Heil!

7

The truck stopped. The doctor, who'd been dozing in a sleeping bag in the back, half opened his eyes. A warm wind entered through the openings in the truck's canopy. He crawled out of his sleeping bag and off the truck. His joints creaked from the two days they'd spent inside the old-fashioned vehicle.

Outside, the first mate and captain were gazing in the direction they were headed and whispering about something. The doctor put his left foot out to take a step in their direction, and was startled to find that his boots had sunk deep into thick mud. Hastily, he pulled them out and stepped to more stable-seeming ground, but once again he sunk right down into mud.

"What's happened?" He asked, standing awkwardly.

"The ice thawed! We're stuck in a bog," the first mate replied, pointing at the road ahead.

The scene before their eyes was indeed out of place in the Antarctic winter. The snow had long since melted, and the unpaved road that stretched out before them between rows of destroyed buildings was sticky with mud. A warm vapor wafted up from all directions. Only the cobalt sky indicated that it was still winter.

This was Saturday's famed Rasputitsa. There was a reason why the tank fanatics played their games here. Heat emanated up from the maze of lava tubes that lay underneath the continent's great plains. Magma flowing through the tubes regularly melted any frozen water and expelled it from the tunnels. The hot water emerged in unpredictable places, thawing the surrounding ground. Saturday's Rasputitsa was more infamous than Russia's had ever been. The Russian thaw was predictable, but trying to predict Saturday's thaw was as difficult as predicting the weather without the help of satellites.

"What do we do now? Was this also part of our plan?"

"You can't plan for thaws: they're sudden and unpredictable. It doesn't look like we'll be able to go any further in the truck. This is some serious mud. Look over there, it's flowing almost like water. It probably won't reach where the truck is now, but soon enough everything in front of us will be a river of mud."

"I said we should've come by Horla," the captain grumbled next to her.

"I thought we were finished with that discussion. Quit complaining. And besides, it isn't all that bad. We're less than ten kilometers from our destination. And it'll be a warm day. Even walking, it should only take us a few hours to get there. All we have to do is leave the road and walk through the petrified forest. The ground there is firm. We can just leave the truck here, no need to move it."

The first mate's composure stirred the other two to motion. They gathered their guns and equipment and walked into the forest. The glassy surface hidden underneath layers of snow was slippery, but even so it was better than walking through thigh-deep mud.

They walked silently through the petrified forest for two hours. Their surroundings glowed with ghostly gray light. The doctor had once read online about the fluorescent matter emitted by the Antarctic volcano. Scientists had identified its chemical constituents, but didn't yet know where and how it was created. The strongest hypothesis was that Guinnesses were deliberately creating the substance using the volcano as a chemical factory. No one knew why the Guinnesses would do such a thing, but they didn't need to pursue the hypothesis that far. It was just the sort of thing that Guinesses did. Guinesses were always choosing to do strange things that humans couldn't possibly understand.

The first mate signaled to the others from her position in the lead. The captain and doctor stopped behind her and gazed ahead. A moment later, the face of a golden-haired young man who could have featured on a Hitler Youth poster popped into view. His head was unusually close to the ground and tilted at a weird angle. As the head approached them, a right arm and left foot appeared. Next came a left arm and a left leg missing its foot, a torso still wearing clothing, and finally a second head, this one with pointed ears and blue skin.

What they were seeing was a parade of Guinesses carrying their spoils. Guinesses the size of cats were carting away the pieces of corpses they had cut up. The Guinness in front carrying the head of the golden-haired youth turned its black glass eyes sideways toward the trio of Jezebel crew members as it passed, but continued onward as if uninterested. The parade line extended almost one hundred meters, and roughly fifteen minutes had passed by the time the final, scorpion-shaped Guinness, dragging intestines wrapped in a blood-soaked military uniform, had disappeared from view.

"They left blood all over the ground," the first mate said, sticking out a finger toward them, the tip wet with dark blood.

"So?" The captain asked.

"Those people died only a little while ago. Considering the speed the Guinessess were travelling, for the bodies to still be bleeding means that the battle's nearby."

"The Linker machines didn't kill them?"

"Why would they? All they have to do is wait a bit and the soldiers produce corpses for them. Be quiet for a moment and listen."

For a brief while they stood still and listened. At first, they heard nothing but the wind. Before long, however, they began to hear the sounds of engines, roars, and screams. The clamor lasted about three minutes before it grew quiet again.

Walking slowly toward the noise, they soon reached the edge of the forest. Beyond the forest they saw a dense cluster of concrete buildings in relatively good condition. Perhaps the effects of the thaw had not reached this far, as the village was still covered in snow. A Tiger 1 chassis white with snow stuck out halfway from between the buildings. Five Guinesses sat in the middle of the road diligently dismembering the corpse of a man wearing German army clothing.

What overwhelmed the watchers, however, was not the village but the scenery behind it. A great plain lay behind the village, and strewn across it were what looked to be several hundred abandoned tanks. And in the midst of the tanks stood five black tadpole-like machines, each two-hundred meters long with dozens of thick legs. These were wombs. Because of their soft exterior, wombs looked more like life forms than machines, and they resembled the creation of an alien civilization even more than the Guinesses did. Yet, the wombs were a human invention. The most exquisitely designed of them evolved on their own and ultimately reached a stage where they merged into Oliviers. As long as they continued to function as wombs, though, they were part of the human world. It was merely that at one stage humans controlled them, and at the other they controlled humans. The dividing line was hazy, but most of the wombs on Saturday were thought to belong to the latter group.

The wombs were quiet now. That wasn't unusual, since wombs did almost nothing that directly involved humans. The wombs handled most of the disassembly and reproduction of tanks, aided by the subordinate machines they spit out." Unlike human factories, wombs were not constantly busy either. They produced for their own satisfaction, and human convenience was not among their concerns.

While the captain and the doctor focused their attention

on the wombs and tanks, the first mate examined the village through binoculars. Once she figured out what was going on, she clapped lightly to get their attention.

"I know what happened. Those soldiers didn't die in battle. They were executed by their own side. Look at the corpses. Their hands are tied up, and they're unarmed. And there's the Tiger just sitting over there. This wasn't the work of the Soviets."

"Then what about the sounds we heard?" The doctor asked.

"Those sounds are the reason why they rushed off without finishing the job. You see those fresh footprints connected to the buildings? And how the snow next to the tank was brushed away?"

The scene had been still as a painting, but in that instant it sprung into bustling motion. The tank moved backward and disappeared from view, and they saw a flash from a window and heard the sound of a gunshot. The silhouettes of people holding guns appeared briefly between the buildings, then disappeared. They heard a scream coming from somewhere they couldn't see, and then the scene grew silent once more. The silence was broken a few minutes later by the boom of an explosion. The Tiger hidden in the back had come forward again and rotated its turret. They heard another explosion and the village again filled with commotion.

The Guinesses continued to work serenely through all of this. Soon they had cut the corpses into pieces small enough for transport and each carried one off into the forest. Another parade of body parts passed in front of the Jezebel crew.

"I know why those people were executed," the first mate said. She pointed at the detached torso crawling steadily past the captain's feet. A capital letter B was scrawled in red spray-paint at the top of the uniform. "These are Bethlehemians. They're executing the mentally ill."

The doctor and captain heard obvious disgust in the first mate's voice. The first mate wasn't very political, but she was extremely sensitive to Bethlehemian issues.

Crusoe was not a particularly difficult place to live because of prejudices. On a planet where both a one-meter tall teddy bear and a two-meter tall cat-person could live out their lives without attracting particular attention, racial discrimination was an outdated concept. And oppressive gender discrimination had vanished with the collapse of the boundaries between the two sexes. Various kinds of prejudice and discrimination did exist, but most lasted no longer than a single generation. Rarely did a distinctive group exist long enough for prejudice against them to persist beyond that. Right now the Crimson Jihad was giving Thursday a bad name, and the Church Mafia was not terribly well regarded either, but sooner or later both groups would change. On a planet where it was nearly impossible to leave biological descendants, it was difficult to maintain a stable religion.

But the Bethlehemians were the exception.

Bethlehemians were not simply mentally ill. Some did act like schizophrenics, but in fact they were afflicted with an entirely different disease. The Bethlehemians' defenders, including Jezebel's first mate, would say it wasn't a disease at all. Like the engineer, Bethlehemians had a psychological structure completely different from that of ordinary people. The Linker virus had messed with their brains to the point that their consciousness no longer belonged to the realm of the human. In severe cases, no one could fully understand their thoughts or motivations. Their actions and words were imprinted with unsettling traces of otherness. Some high-functioning Bethlehemians could trick people by acting as if they were normal, but even then it was not possible to engage in genuine empathetic communication with them. On Crusoe, if you had a human brain that could communicate with others normally, then it didn't matter if you looked like a teddy bear or a cat. But if your brain worked differently, or—even worse—was different but still similar enough for the mutation to be transmitted like a disease through the Linker network, then people started to care. What if the Linker virus refined and spread the trait?

Most regions on Crusoe opted for quarantine. The Vesuvians rescued by Sydney were probably also now quarantined on an island somewhere. The engineer would very likely have found herself in a similar situation had the first mate not helped her. The people on Saturday, however, clearly did not have time for such extravagances. Though to be fair, it would be silly to expect a place which existed for the purpose of slaughter to bother with a humanitarian solution.

As the pieces of the executed Bethlehemians disappeared into the forest, the captain, first mate, and doctor began to grasp what was happening on the other side of the village. What they were seeing was not, as they had first thought, a Soviet surprise attack on a German village—the soldiers firing guns at the village were wearing German uniforms. As they continued to observe, the situation grew even clearer. Three quarters of the people in the village who were returning fire had large red Bs hanging off their backs.

8

Later, the doctor enjoyed talking in cafes and pubs about his experiences on Saturday, though the details and amount of hyperbole he used changed depending on how much he'd had to drink. People had no way of knowing how much of it was true. The captain and first mate didn't speak often about their own experiences, and never confirmed nor denied the doctor's story.

"Before we arrived on Saturday, we learned quite a lot about Bruckmueller and the things he left behind," the doctor would say.

"Everything he had, he'd procured through the network of merchants who traded with the Nazis. He was a logistics officer, and that's the most corruptible position on Saturday. After all, it's hard to stay upright when everyone around is tempting you with special offers. Our guy Bruckmueller controlled the black market within the German army. The scale and operation of the market were textbook perfect. They should've given him a medal for it. Anyway, this kind of black market was a necessity for the historical accuracy of the wargames. The system couldn't function without people like him.

"Bruckmueller was also responsible for military prostitution, which was tricky work. Unlike World War II Earth, Crusoe is teeming with aliens who have all sorts of different sexual needs. It would have been easy to solve the problem with virtual reality devices, but those were difficult to maintain on Saturday, and accepting them would have meant admitting that they weren't serious about the wargame. So they opted for sex drugs and dolls instead. Bruckmueller's work existed in a legal gray area. Like most things on

Saturday, what was legal felt illegal, what was illegal felt legal.

"Anyway, when Sydney approached Bruckmueller three years ago saying that he had a set of top-quality dolls made to resemble female movie stars from old Earth, Bruckmueller couldn't pass them up. I know I just said that Crusoe was full of aliens with every sort of sexual need, but even so, culture still exerts a major influence. Earth women, especially the top-quality imitations of beautiful movie stars that Sydney had brought, were highly desirable to most if not everyone. They would use the dolls to relieve their sexual needs and... well, actually the customers don't have to have sexual desires at all. No one would deny our Lord Captain's love for Lady Ingrid Bergman, but that didn't mean he imagined doing the bunga bunga on top of a doll that looks like her.

"But I've digressed. Getting back to the topic at hand, the important thing was that the toys Sydney had provided were of substantial value. If utilized properly, they would guarantee Bruckmueller a windfall large enough that he could escape to another continent and live in luxury, or even buy a ticket to another planet. Like most commanders on Saturday, he was in the war to make money and didn't intend to be buried there like the rest of the morons.

"And yet, when do things ever go the way we want them to? Bruckmueller would have known as well as anyone that Saturday was a dangerous place and he could lose his life at any moment. But could he have imagined that he would be run over by a tank from his own side that just happened to be backing up as he stepped out for a cigarette? Sure, the tank was a KV-1, but the Germans had captured it from the Soviets and were driving it themselves. Bo's information was only half correct. In any case, it was a stupid death. It doesn't pay to let your guard down in a place where no one cares about safety.

"As expected, the transfer to Bruckmueller's replacement was a mess. The next person in line was a guy named Steinhoff, but this Steinhoff was only able to assume Bruckmueller's title and formal duties. Bruckmueller's papers didn't yield any clues as to his informal dealings, no matter how much Steinhoff glared at them, and Bruckmueller's subordinates and customers didn't volunteer any information to Steinhoff either. They were all busy trying to grab a piece of the pie for themselves.

"Steinhoff was the first person we contacted when we arrived on Saturday. Bo hadn't wanted to hand over the critical information, but in the end he gave us quite a lot of material detailing Bruckmueller's business transactions with Sydney. Those papers alone gave us claim over a considerable number of things that Bruckmueller had left behind. We could show Steinhoff our cards and then tell him all we really wanted was assistance in retrieving one particular box. We were nothing if not reasonable.

"The problem was that we could only communicate with Steinhoff over the phone, and the overall circumstances weren't conducive to establishing trust. Ultimately our phone calls ended in mutual suspicion, with both sides preparing for the possibility of betrayal. We would have liked to contact Bruckmueller's other associates, but in the end we simply couldn't figure out how. We'd been lucky just to connect with Steinhoff.

"By the time we reached the tank-producing wombs, we were certain Steinhoff hadn't been honest with us. Steinhoff had said all sorts of things to try and put us at ease, but we knew better than to believe him. Our regular reconnaissance flyer flights revealed that the headquarters had been reinforced with more soldiers and small skirmishes were breaking out with suspicious frequency. Saturday's war was supposed to be like a board game where the two sides tried to best each other, it was not supposed to be about eliminating the enemy entirely. After all, they wanted to keep playing round after round, not end the game. The movements at headquarters indicated that something had gone very wrong. The only question was what.

"It wasn't until we witnessed the battle in the village that we fully grasped the situation. In the midst of this supposedly everlasting war between the Germans and Soviets, a third variable had appeared. And the people participating in this new faction were not playing a game. To them, the war was a violent means for achieving political ends. It was real war, as Clausewitz defined the term.

"This third faction was the Bethlehemians. Naturally, people classified as Bethlehemians could be found even on Saturday. Some had been mutated by the Linker virus, others had just been born that way. Up until a decade ago, dealing with them had been simple: if the admittance test revealed they were Bethlehemian, they were rejected; if they mutated while on Saturday, they were expelled. Yet, now the circumstances had changed. Paths between Crusoe and the rest of the universe had been blocked for several years, and fewer recruits were coming to Saturday. As both sides grew frantic for new recruits, the admittance test turned into a mere formality—and sometimes it was skipped entirely. Bethlehemians began to come to Saturday in larger numbers, and soon the Linker virus set to work and their numbers increase exponentially. They became a significant and not easily controlled minority.

"So what did the two armies do about it? At first, they just watched to see what would happen, because to eliminate the Bethlehemians from their ranks would mean incurring significant losses. Then at some point both sides simultaneously began to expel and execute them. Was it a coincidence? Of course not. The head of the two armies had secretly come to an agreement. It hadn't been difficult: the armies respected each other as opponents in the game, but they both hated and detested the Bethlehemians. Besides, it'd enhance the historical aspect of the game. What would World War II be without prejudice and violence toward minorities?

"At first, they thought the cleansing would be easy. That's why they started it. They thought they could just line up everyone who was bad in the head, shoot them, and it'd all be over in a few days. In retrospect, though, not even idiots would have fallen for that—and Bethlehemians aren't idiots. Their brains work differently from ordinary people, that's all. Moreover, many of the Bethlehemians who came voluntarily to the battlefield were high-functioning. Their defective brains would actually have been considered normal if only they'd had their own planet. If they could adequately adapt to the physical world, as they in fact could, then they weren't the type to quietly submit to violence. Indeed, everyone should have known that this type of Bethlehemian would become prevalent on Saturday. After all, they had decided to come in full knowledge of the insanity that occurred here. Beyond that, it's not like the cleansing only affected the Bethlehemians either. The test to determine whether someone was Bethlehemian was never precise, and there were plenty of false positives, which meant that more and more normal people were upset by the policy.

"Things finally came to a head when armed uprisings occurred almost simultaneously in the Soviet and the German camps. Many people died during these uprisings, but many others escaped and formed their own military force. They had a name for themselves too. The Bethlehemian Resistance, they called themselves. At first, all they had were a few pistols and grenades, but as time passed they grew into a tough force of over seven hundred soldiers and six tanks, and they even managed to somehow procure one Horla that flew well despite its damaged concealment device. They could have become a real threat, because unlike the Soviet and German armies, they never had any intention of following the rules of the game. They wanted the war to end, and they even made plans for afterward. They would expel the tank fanatics and create a city of their own on Saturday as a home for all the Bethlehemians facing discrimination on Crusoe.

"They won the battle in the village as we watched. It was a hollow victory, or at least looked that way to us, because they clearly failed in their mission to rescue their Bethlehemian colleagues. As soon as they'd won, they immediately executed all their prisoners. Soldiers on Saturday had no time for managing and transporting prisoners. To them, Geneva was nothing more than the name of an old city on the other side of the galaxy.

"Our telephone rang just after the Bethlehemians finished executing the prisoners of war. We were expecting Steinhoff, but this caller was an agitated man named Bernburg. He started screaming at us, saying he was waiting and we should come out and show our faces in the village immediately.

"Just as we were wondering where he'd got the arrogance to yell at us that like that, he added, 'I know you came looking for Sydney's things. We're also Sydney's people, and there's a lot we have to talk about.'

"Once he had uttered the magic name of Sydney, we couldn't hesitate any further. We all went down into the village.

"Except for his green face, Bernburg looked like an Arab youth straight out of the movie *Arabian Nights*. His real name was Amal Hasan Murkas, and despite the name and face, he'd been playing a Nazi commander in the Soviet-German war.

"Bernburg was not a Bethlehemian. Rather, he had been rescued by the rebels after being mistaken for Bethlehemian and almost executed by the Germans. According to him, the Resistance Army contained quite a few 'normals.' In fact, just a few weeks ago they had surpassed fifty-percent of the force. Some had joined for political reasons, but many had joined for the excitement of something new. They were those who had been lucky enough to survive the Soviet-German war long enough to grow sick of it.

"It wasn't surprising that Sydney's influence had reached all the way to Bernburg and his group. Sydney had helped them obtain their Horla and various modern weapons. Bruckmueller and Sydney might have conspired together in that too. The assistance given to Bethlehemian Resistance felt similar to what Sydney had done for the Vesuvians. It sure looked to me like Sydney was behind it.

"Bernburg told us the Bethlehemian Resistance was planning something big. The guerillas had decided to take advantage of the fact that German headquarters sat only a few kilometers from the wombs. They planned to hit the headquarters with the old tanks that had been sent to feed the wombs.

"The rescue operation we'd seen was in fact just a bonus. The Bethlehemians' real objective had been to quietly massacre the German soldiers inside the wombs and, once they'd gained control of the system, falsify the data to make it appear that the wombs were still running normally. After that they would secretly airlift biofuel and weapons, and find a way to infiltrate the German headquarters with spies and cut off their information supply. Bernburg's impassioned speech made the plan sound plausible, as if it might succeed.

"We discussed things again among ourselves after parting company with Bernburg. If Sydney had assisted the Bethlehemian Resistance, then they were on our side. That much was obvious. Maybe in his order to find the dolls hidden by the Nazi general, he had also meant for us to join the Saturday war. We did have several modern weapons that would help them. Perhaps the most useful of these would be our defensive shield generators, which could be installed into five tanks. They were only designed to withstand physical attack and were not made for modern war, but they'd be quite useful in a World War II tank battle. We'd brought them to protect the doll crates.

"Yet we remained uncertain. How much of this was what Sydney had intended? If he had really wanted us to join the Saturday war, wouldn't he have just told us that? Why make it all so complicated? Weren't Sydney's people now just following the orders outlined by a dead man? Or, wasn't it simpler if we just assumed he had died without leaving any sort of last wishes and this all was just his son's sincere desire for a Jeri Ryan sex doll?

"Then again, it wasn't so implausible after all. Think about it. Had Sydney directly ordered me to join the Saturday war, I would have come alone so as to not involve my colleagues. We three came together only because we were intrigued by Sydney's plot and the task of finding the dolls felt relatively easy. Otherwise, the first mate, with her knowledge of World War II Soviet tanks and her extreme sensitivity toward anti-Bethlehemian discrimination, wouldn't have come with me. Sydney could have predicted and planned it this way. Sydney had spent his entire life using people and built an empire that only he could see. A scheme of this sort would have been a piece of cake.

"But even if Sydney had planned all of this, what was his end goal? To establish a Bethlehemian city on Saturday? Was that so important to him? Was he himself actually a high-functioning Bethlehemian who had carefully concealed his identity? Or was this nothing more than an instrument for the realization of his real goal? That was definitely possible. When I met Bo, he hinted that Sydney's plans were all connected to some biological experiment. That experiment could involve the Bethlehemians, or it could be something else entirely. If the establishment of a Bethlehemian city had been the ultimate goal, Bo wouldn't have had any reason to keep it hidden from us.

"After talking it over, we decided to follow Sydney's plan, or more precisely to follow what we believed to be Sydney's plan. This conclusion combined the first mate's hatred of the Saturday war, my curiosity, the captain's sense of chivalry, and the excitement we'd caught from the resistance army. Had Sydney predicted that too?"

9

“As for the battle that took place two days later, I can only tell you the little bit I know. I’m not an historian or a reporter. I don’t know much about war, and I was stuck inside a tank and couldn’t see much of what was happening outside. The first mate could probably tell you more, because she directly participated in the operation. But you already know she would never share that kind of story with you.

“The Bethlehemian Resistance captured fifteen T-34s and four KV-1s in their surprise attack on the womb playground. However, the amount of biofuel they could haul to the tanks was severely limited, and they didn’t have time to switch the tanks to other more flexible energy sources, so they had to rely on the modern weapons we’d brought in contravention of the rules.

“We decided to use everything we had to its maximal effectiveness. First we attached our defensive shield generators to five T-34s. The shields prevented us from firing the cannons, so instead we installed drills of Gorman alloy on the tip of each barrel, as if we had left World War II and gone back to the mounted jousting matches of the Middle Ages. We installed the newest model of laser cannon from planet Cordova on one of the KV-1s. We also had two well-preserved concussion bombs that could break the shins of every soldier standing within a thirty-degree arc up to 120 meters in front of us.

“All the while, the German army, which was only several kilometers away, was completely oblivious to what we were doing. I know it’s hard to believe, but I’m telling you it was entirely possible. It wasn’t just because it’s harder to see what’s happening right under your nose. We were also protected by the tank fanatics' absurd superstitions regarding wombs. The fools' brains had lost their plasticity after several hundred years of repeating the same game.

"Still, the Bethlehemian Resistance planned things meticulously. They engaged in at least five types of harassment actions to distract the Germans: sabotage, false information, surprise attacks, suicide bombing, and even assassination. The last was especially impressive: they succeeded in poisoning General Guderian. I'm telling you, the real Heinz Guderian would have cursed the one they assassinated for tarnishing the name, if the two had ever met. The generals on Saturday were all petty bastards. Bastards who kept replaying the same game over and over despite knowing exactly which cards their opponents held. No one with actual brains and creativity ever went near army headquarters.

"Anyway, latent conflicts among the top brass erupted into the open following Guderian's assassination, and as a consequence the officials vying to replace Guderian dismissed the warnings they received from outside. Or more precisely, they were all waiting for their rivals to turn their attention outward, so that they could then seize Guderian's vacant position for themselves. Later, someone who had been on the German side told me that they had in fact received reports of unusual activity around the wombs, but the old fools in charge had eyes only for the prize dangling in front of them and had ignored the reports.

"The battle that took place on that dark polar afternoon was as strange as could be. Certainly nothing like it had ever happened in the real World War II. The whole thing was absurd, beginning with the ghostly appearance of the nineteen tanks behind a defensive shield. The first five of them were monsters impervious to WWII-era weapons, and the next few carried weapons that were not invented until hundreds of years after the war. Although our force was vastly outnumbered and surrounded by the Germans, that also was to our benefit. We were like a grenade clutched in the hand of the German army. If they made the slightest error while trying to dispose of us, they would destroy themselves. The Bethlehemians took advantage of the Germans' dilemma and mercilessly smashed their enemy.

"The captain and I rode in the first mate's tank, one of the five with a defensive shield and a drill. We played the role of sweeper at the vanguard. It's not an experience I would care to repeat. The interior of a T-34 is extremely uncomfortable, and the first mate's 'strategy' was simply to ram the Germans while screaming, 'Die, Nazi scum!' To our amazement she even rammed a Tiger-1, which weighs twice as much as a T-34, but with the ground swampy from the recent thaw, our T-34 had the advantage. The Tiger got stuck in the mud, and as it flailed about, we drilled a hole in its turret. Bethlehemian infantry climbed on top of the enemy tank and threw grenades inside, and as it went boom, we headed off toward our next tank or anti-tank gun target.

"By the time we finished off our seventh tank, the Germans were beginning to figure out how to fight back. Despite playing at World War II, they were modern people and knew the advantages and disadvantages of defensive shields. The shields block fast-moving objects such as bullets, but snails can walk right through. German infantry soon began to filter in through our tanks' shields. Judging by the way they adopted tai chi postures to penetrate the shields, some of them seemed to have real-world military experience from other places. We managed to shake some of them off with electric shocks, but they kept coming and we began to get worried. German soldiers actually shattered the tracks of one of our colleagues' tanks and rendered it immobile by carrying an anti-tank mine in through the defensive shield.

"As we wondered what to do, the first mate decided adaptability was best. Instead of leaving the shield on and pushing onward like a juggernaut, we flicked it off or on as needed for each situation. I piloted and the captain controlled the shield while the first mate climbed up with the laser rifle and picked off the infantry stuck to us. When the shield was on, German soldiers inside the shield were protected, but when it disappeared, they suddenly became vulnerable to friendly fire or being run over by one of their own army vehicles. Then we turned the shield back on, and anyone rushing the tank bounced off like a rubber ball. Ah, you must be wondering how I knew how to pilot a tank. Well, I always say there are two things everyone from Maria Wutz is certain to know. One is *Jane Eyre*, and the other is World War II.

"In the end, we penetrated the Germans' fence and arrived at their headquarters. After the KV-1 following us shot off the door with its laser rifle, we climbed out of our tank and entered the headquarters alongside the Bethlehemian infantry. We didn't care what happened in there. We'd already done everything we could do for the Bethlehemians, and we weren't there to occupy the headquarters. Our primary objective was to recover the dolls that we knew were hidden somewhere in the basement. While Bernburg's subordinates restrained enemy soldiers whose shins and ankles had been shattered by one of our concussion bombs, we located the basement entrance and headed down.

"Even after we'd descended to the second sublevel, the dolls' signal continued to come from below us. We double-checked the blueprints that Bernburg had given us, but they only showed two sublevels. When we scanned the place, however, we found a hidden empty space below us that could only be a third sublevel. We didn't want to waste time searching for a hidden entrance, so we decided to blow a hole through the floor. The captain just set a directional explosive in the corner and boom! Once the dust settled, we could see a wobbly spiral staircase just beneath where the floor had been. The captain had gotten lucky and blown a hole right on top of the hidden entrance. The top part of the staircase had collapsed from the explosion, but that didn't keep us from using the rest to descend.

"The third sublevel consisted of a corridor about fifty meters long with metal trailers painted black arranged neatly along both sides. The place was not as clandestine as we had expected. They'd hidden it about as well as a Prohibition-era bar. Most of the people in headquarters had probably known what was there on the third sublevel. Naturally, Bruckmueller hadn't kept all of his things down there. He must have moved the dolls down here because the headquarters housed all the top brass, who could afford expensive entertainments. It seemed that profit had been all he'd wanted from the dolls, and he hadn't much cared for them otherwise.

"We walked slowly down the corridor following the signal. We'd gone about ten steps farther when we heard a coarse yell from behind us: 'You think you can just steal them like this? What about our promise? Our oath?' We recognized it as the voice of Steinhoff from our telephone conversations. Turning around, we saw a golden orangutan wearing an SS uniform.

He limped toward us. A concussion bomb had injured his leg but, fortunately for him, the damage seemed to be minor and he could still walk. He waved an old Luger pistol in our direction, but it was more an expression of emotion than a threat.

"'You never intended to keep your promise either, did you?' I said. 'No one's been down here in a month or more. Even if you'd known where the hidden door to this secret third level was, you never had the password or key to open it.'

"'I was searching. I would have found it eventually,' the orangutan replied.

"'Sure. But, as you can see, we don't need your help. Saturday's a different place now. So how about you just forget about the dolls, grab your things, and get out of here?' I told him.

"Steinhoff ought to have understood me. Those guys were realists and he would have known he didn't have any other choice. Yet, still he continued to limp along behind us.

"The first mate suddenly stopped walking. So did Steinhoff. He feigned ignorance, but she smiled knowingly. She glanced back and forth from the trailer on her left to the orangutan behind us, and then turned to me. 'Perfume. *Women's* perfume.' She said and, pulling a cutting torch from her pocket, cut through the lock on the trailer door, and opened it.

"The inside of the trailer resembled the old fashioned boutiques you see in movies. It contained dressing rooms, wardrobes, and clothes hangers. Three women hung from the hangers like corpses, their eyes closed. One of Asian descent, one European, one African. All wore somewhat dirty bathrobes. I examined the face of the European woman, which had a metal ornament affixed around one eye. I was not a huge Star Trek fan, but I recognized Seven of Nine's trademark. I stuck out my hand to touch the ornament and immediately got goosebumps—not because of the metal ornament, but because of how disturbingly real the skin around it felt, with its downy hairs and the slight moisture of perspiration. When I was young, I tried out sex robots a few times too, but this was the first time I'd ever seen anything so realistic.

"Just then, the orangutan screamed and leapt at me, attacking with such rage that I was truly afraid he would bite my arm off. Fortunately, the first mate proved both faster and stronger than Steinhoff. A split second later, the orangutan hit the far wall. He lay where he had fallen and wept, 'Annika! Annika!'

"I immediately grasped the situation. Like Spack, Steinhoff was a Trekkie, and Annika Hanson, designation Seven of Nine, was his one and only love. Bruckmueller must have given Steinhoff a glimpse of the dolls when he first received them. How much had Seven-of-Nine inflamed Steinhoff's imagination and desire since then? Steinhoff must have despaired when Bruckmueller died, leaving the third level inaccessible. It was all so pathetic.

"Anyway, the important thing was that we'd found our prize. I grabbed the Seven-of-Nine doll's shoulders and the captain grabbed her feet, and together we put her into a protective case we'd found in the trailer. As soon as the doll was safely tucked away, the captain gave vent to his exasperation: 'I don't know a thing about sex, and in particular I'll probably go to my grave never understanding what it means to men, other than that it must be meaningful in some way. But here I can't even acknowledge that. What's the point of having sex with Seven-of-Nine if she just lays there with a vacant stare on her face?'"

10

One by one the doctor broke the locks on each trailer, entered, and confirmed the dolls' names: Grace Kelly. Zhang Ziyi, Claudia Cardinale, Nicola Bryant, Dorothy Dandridge, Meg Tilly, Carole Bouquet, Lindsey Wagner.... The dolls were all of astonishingly high quality, but the collection lacked a clear theme. It was as if someone had just bought the first page of a toy catalog.

Maybe randomness was the point, the doctor mused. It was easier to hide something among the dolls when they didn't adhere to a theme. But what was it that Sydney had hidden here? It wasn't in Jeri Ryan. A scan revealed nothing unusual inside her. She was perfect, but she was just a doll. And there wasn't a tracking device attached to her either. In fact, none of the dolls found in the trailers had tracking devices. But they'd found only twenty-three dolls in total, and the scanner still indicated a signal emanating from somewhere ahead of them.

It was time for another directional explosive. It blew a three-meter-wide hole in the wall, and hot air rushed out. Once the dust settled, the doctor and his party walked inside.

They found themselves in a spacious, domed cavern at least one hundred meters wide and extending out in front of them as far as they could see. It was as if they had entered the belly of some enormous metal beast. Despite the people-sized walkways and stairs littered throughout, it appeared more machine than building. What they were looking at was a highly developed womb network. Dirty, crudely designed machines clung like monkeys to various parts of the wombs.

The doctor immediately intuited their function. They were meant to act as some sort of brake to prevent the wombs from evolving to the point where they would merge into Oliviers. How long had it taken to complete this network? Bruckmueller must have put in an enormous amount of effort to develop it to this point. The doctor regretted his earlier scorn for the man.

"What is this?" asked the first mate.

The doctor silently pointed thirty meters down the tunnel to where a huge black pipe stuck out from a womb and continued downward until it passed out of view. Dozens of similar pipes were visible from where they stood.

"A factory," he said. "Everything the wombs produce is sent through the lava tubes to elsewhere on Saturday. Some of the products end up being shot up into the atmosphere during eruptions, others flow out into the ocean.

"I'm starting to get a sense of what Sydney's plans were. He wasn't interested in the tank fanatics or the Bethlehemian Resistance, and he didn't care about the war or human rights violations either. What he needed was the continent itself. There's nowhere else like Saturday on Crusoe. There aren't any cities filled with pesky residents who'd get in the way, and everyone in power is wasting their time on a totally pointless war game. By securing just one underground water source, he could use the entire continent as a laboratory. It's perfect.

"So how do we explain Sydney assisting the rebels? Ah, it's got nothing to do with politics after all. It's just because he didn't need the German army anymore. This German army functioned like an eggshell. It protected his plans as they matured, but as soon as they were ready to hatch, it was time to break the shell."

They slowly walked inward following the signal. The air grew steadily warmer as they descended. Cat-sized objects rolled here and there through the corridor. Although small, their pointy, aggressive appearance clearly marked them as Waynes. Each appeared distinct, but they all acted in the same way. They glared steadily at the monkeys that hung from the wombs, their legs and wheels vibrating as if they were about to lose their tempers and pull the monkeys off.

"It doesn't look like it's started yet, doctor," the captain commented as he walked past and touched each pipe in turn. "They're all cold to the touch and empty. Have they been waiting until all the German soldiers are expelled? And even if the plan commences, what's to guarantee it will work properly? The Waynes have already noticed and come inside. That means that sooner or later the other Linker machines will interfere. They'll probably create an opening for themselves to act. As far as we know, maybe all the Waynes need to do is pick off a few monkeys, and then the equilibrium will collapse under evolutionary pressure."

The scanner beeped loudly. The doctor frowned and glared at the huge metal box in front of him. There was a small door on the right side. It wasn't even locked. The doctor opened the door and stepped inside.

The interior of the box was arranged like a small bedroom, the walls an unadorned white and the floor covered with a dark rug. An old style gramophone with an amplifying horn attached sat on an end table in one corner of the room, and a trench coat hanging from a coat stand stood in the other. On the walls hung an old glass mirror and a vintage photograph of Greta Garbo taken by Edward Steichen. The middle of the room contained a plain gray bed on which slept a gray-skinned woman with gray hair wearing a gray gown. The doctor moved aside the lock of hair that was blocking half of her face from view. The moment her face was revealed, the captain rolled his eyes in exasperation and the first mate covered her mouth with her left hand to stifle laughter.

The woman sleeping on the bed was Ginger Rogers.

And, like the doctor, she was in black and white.

"Don't even think about it," the first mate stated seriously, after she'd stopped laughing.

"Think about what?!" asked the doctor.

"I don't even know. Just don't. This is a really bad joke."

"Why do you say it's a bad joke? Because I'm Fred Astaire? Because that doll is Ginger Rogers? Don't you think Sydney could have left it as a gift for me, a thank you for what I did for him?"

"But what use is it? It's just a doll. It can't sing or dance. All you can do with the doll is rape it. Fred raping Ginger. Does that even make sense?"

"Maybe it can sing."

"So maybe it can function as a gramophone. But a Ginger that can't dance isn't really Ginger.

"Why are you so certain it can't dance? Because it's a sex doll? The wombs on Planet Bellocio were apparently so advanced that as soon as they produced these dolls they merged into Oliviers. Couldn't such elaborate wombs have produced dolls that were more than just dolls? Couldn't one of these dolls be hiding more complex functionality? They had walking, dancing robots way back in the twenty-first century. There's no reason this doll can't really be Ginger. Would it even make sense to create a doll with such exquisite muscle and bone structure purely for sex?"

The doctor's voice had lost its usual cynicism. His face had darkened as if with fever, and his hands and legs quivered. He couldn't help thinking back to a few minutes before when he'd laughed at the sight of Steinhoff's anguish upon seeing Seven of Nine.

While the captain made a show of humming absently to himself and the first mate continued to grumble about something, the doctor sank to his knees and stared at the sleeping Ginger. What would the real Fred Astaire have done if he were here? The doctor could only think of one thing. Almost mechanically, he lowered his face and kissed Ginger's dry lips.

Her eyes opened.

The doctor yelped and took a step backward. All sorts of situations had flashed through his mind before he'd kissed Ginger, but he hadn't imagined that this particular one would actually come true. The scene unfolding before his eyes was both exactly what he had fantasized and totally cliche.

Ginger sat up on the bed and slipped her feet into the shoes placed next to it. She swung her head around and gazed in turn at the doctor, first mate, and captain. Her movements were jerky and awkward, and her gaze was greedy and stiff.

Ginger stood and staggered over to the end table. She examined her reflection in the mirror for a few seconds, and smiled. Turning back to face her visitors, she said in a perfect Ginger Rogers voice:

"You finally did it, Dr. Flagg."

The first mate and captain looked at her blankly. The doctor, meanwhile, wracked his brain trying to figure out why the relaxed tone of Ginger's voice felt so familiar. It took him some time to realize the answer.

She was Sydney.

Ginger turned on the gramophone and a staticky recording of "Let's Call the Whole Thing Off" filled the room. The doctor began to piece together all the information he knew. That thing was definitely Sydney. But how could it be? Had Sydney's brain been removed and put into Ginger's body after he died? It was technically possible, and might even help prevent the womb-Olivier merging. But the dolls had been stolen before Sydney died. Maybe Sydney's brain had been scanned and copied onto the blank state of Ginger's brain. Or the information might have been implanted before he gifted the dolls to Bruckmueller. In the end, it didn't matter how he'd done it; that was Sydney in Ginger Rogers's body. The doctor felt sick. However big and important Sydney's plans were, he was wrong to demean Ginger like that.

While the doctor stood there, lost in thought, Ginger put on the trench coat and headed for the door.

The first mate blocked her way. "Not until you tell us what's going on, Ms. Rogers," she said coldly.

Ginger shrugged and stepped backward. She pulled a silver cigarette case out of her coat pocket, took a long, thin, gray Gitanes cigarette from the case, placed it between her open lips, and lit it with a gray lighter. She puffed a donut-shaped ring of smoke and watched for a moment as it dissipated.

"I don't expect you to believe me yet, but you need to understand that everything I'm doing is for the future of Crusoe. The only future that Crusoe can possibly have. If you block me, this planet won't have any future at all. Do I really have to explain?

"Yes, please."

Ginger turned away from the first mate in disgust and

drew again on the cigarette.

The doctor staggered to his feet and replied in her stead. "What that creature means is a massacre."

Ginger held the cigarette in her mouth and tapped her fingertips together in a light clap. Bravo.

"One of the biggest problems on Crusoe is genetic instability," the doctor explained. "The planet has been unable to maintain the numbers needed for a self-sustaining genetic pool of any species evolved from Earth. Until now, refugees from elsewhere have kept the population numbers up, but recently fewer Adjanis carrying remoras with passengers have come. Outside pathfinders have noticed that there's something dangerous about Crusoe and are blocking people from coming here. Furthermore, all of Crusoe's efforts towards biological manipulation have been stymied by Linker and Olivier intervention. If this blockade continues, the population on Crusoe will continue to decrease and the descendants of humanity will eventually go extinct. People have always been saying this.

"The thing is, though, that it's nothing more than an extreme hypothesis. A natural decrease in both the overall population and the number of species is more likely to lead ultimately to one species becoming a majority and stabilizing as a species. There are actual examples of this. Already two species originating from Earth have stabilized on Crusoe, and both..."

"The dolphins and the anchovies!" Ginger interrupted sharply. "Mindless fish that swim around in their own piss. Do you know why they're like that? The Linker Universe operates in an entirely different way from an unpolluted Darwinian universe. In this impatient world, only ordinary and boring things survive. While we wait for natural selection to take its course, we'll all regress to anchovies and rats. In the Linker Universe, advanced lifeforms are like rare flowers. They need to be protected, cultivated, and weeded. This isn't a massacre, it's a culling."

"Who are the weeds?" snapped the doctor.

"The answer to that is always situational," Ginger replied. "In this situation, we can call the survivors flowers and those who can't survive, weeds. Of course it wouldn't do for the survivors to be people like the Vesuvians. For a while I had hope for them, but, well, they're hopeless. That's what happens when people are just left to reproduce and proliferate without intervention. Captain Nazimova here knows this from experience. Haven't you told your friends what happened on Leventon Island?

"I've been doing humanitarian work for several decades. Humanitarian survival methods were also what I was researching through the Rothbart Advanced Science Research Center. But there wasn't any solution. It's impossible for us to survive in a humanitarian way.

"The method I've chosen instead is more realistic and more likely to succeed. I'm going to spread a virus on this planet that will kill off the trivial species and give the more prevalent species, the ones that can maintain stable gene pools, a chance to survive. Many of them will die too, but at least those species will be able to reach their ideal form before their brain function drops to that of an earthworm. Now would you please move out of the way and let me finish my work?"

Ginger spoke these final words so softly that it took everyone a moment to understand their meaning. She took advantage of the moment to slip adroitly around the first mate. She moved so quickly that she had opened the door and run out before the first mate could react. By the time the Jezebel crew had rushed out of the box, she had already started down a stairway fifty meters away.

On her way down the stairs she touched the control panels installed on each womb she passed, causing them to slowly come online.

The short-legged captain soon gave up, but the first mate and the doctor ran after Ginger.

"Why Ginger?" The doctor yelled as he ran after her. "Why did you have to wear Ginger?"

"Why not?" Ginger answered glibly without turning her head. "My body was dying of heart disease. You can't possibly think I would bother fixing my old body just to remain trapped in it. Why would I stay in that old clumsy hippopotamus body when I could wear Ginger and dance instead? Don't be silly."

"But you're not Sydney! You're a copy! Sydney lived in his own body for three more years after that. If he was really doing it for the reasons you claim, he would have put his consciousness into that body before giving it to Bruckmueller. That would've been simpler and would've easily resolved the identity problem. There's a different reason why you're Ginger. A reason that the original Sydney made you forget!"

"Ridiculous. What, do you think the original Sydney loved you? That he chose Ginger so he could be with you?"

"No. Sydney wasn't so naive or sentimental. But, you were programmed to wake up when I kissed you. Why were you designed that way? Why were you programmed to wake up only when surrounded by people who would block you? Have you thought about that?"

The two of them had reached an elevated walkway that extended out like an intricate spiderweb. The doctor couldn't see where the first mate had gone. Ginger and Fred stood alone on a precarious thread of the web, trying to keep their balance.

"Why are you trying to trick me with lies?" Ginger asked.

"It's not a lie. It's the truth. And it's exactly Sydney's style." The doctor took a step toward Ginger, then froze. Ginger had pulled a small laser gun out of her trench coat.

"Think about it," the doctor said slowly, "Until now we thought we were acting in accordance with Sydney's last wishes. We assumed that when he died, he left behind some crucial unfinished business. But is that really what happened? Was it really Sydney's style to leave behind those sorts of last wishes? Sydney never thought or acted for himself, not even once. He always mobilized people to act for him. The Rothbart scientists, the evolution trackers on Thursday, the soldiers who rescued the Vesuvians, the Bethelehemian Resistance, and even me and the Jezebel crew. Don't you understand? Sydney wasn't a dictator or a mad king. He never thought he had all the answers, and he sure didn't leave any last wishes. What he left behind was a legacy. All of his people. A network of people who think and judge for themselves. That's Sydney's true legacy!"

"But what about me?"

"You're part of the legacy too. The real Sydney would have recognized the possibility of a large-scale massacre. But he wasn't crazy enough or dogmatic enough to do something so terrible without good cause. And if it really had to be done, he'd have wanted to do it himself. That's why he made you.

You're his more calculating and less inhibited alter-ego. But he couldn't create just you. He also had to create someone who could talk and debate with you. That's why he put you in Ginger's body. He needed someone who could act as a brake at the crucial moment, and he chose me. That's why I had to come here. And the answer is 'no,' period. You can't do it. We met Bo on the way here, and..."

"Who is Bo?"

"A radio archaeologist that Sydney rescued ten years ago. You probably can't remember him, because he joined Sydney's circle only two years ago. Do you understand? Your information is three years out of date. A lot has happened since then. The evolution tracking on Thursday revealed that it's possible to establish conditions under which even the most precarious traits can be reliably passed on. More research is needed, of course, but there's hope. And Sydney knew that. Think about it. Would the real Sydney have wanted to carry out the massacre while there was still hope?"

"Nonsense. If I buy into your lies, we all die. There'll be nobody but anchovies left on Crusoe."

As she screamed at him, the doctor drew out his shock pistol and pointed it at her. They stood there with pistols aimed at one another, like characters in a Western.

"Don't do anything stupid, Fred," Ginger said. "Do you really think you could shoot Ginger? Look how much your hand is shaking. At this distance you couldn't even... "

Before Ginger could finish her sentence, her upper body twisted at a strange angle and she collapsed stiffly to the walkway floor. The laser pistol she had held in her hand bounced once before falling downward and away. The doctor saw the first mate standing behind where Ginger had been, her shock pistol in her hand.

"Thanks. For a few seconds there it was like I was going to have to pull a Mike Hammer."

The first mate waved away his thanks. "You would have died in a gun duel. Those robots' nerve signals travel at the speed of light. You wouldn't have stood a chance."

The first mate searched Ginger's paralyzed body with a practiced hand. The cigarette case inside her trench coat turned out to be a remote control apparatus. Yet, no matter how hard the first mate tried, she couldn't figure out how to undo what Ginger had already set in motion. Ginger continued screaming and cursing at them from where she lay.

They didn't need to deliberate. There was only one option. The first mate and the doctor raised their stun guns and begin shooting at all of the monkeys within sight. Within a minute they'd knocked five of the monkeys off the wombs. When the doctor dropped a sixth monkey, the waiting Waynes began to react. They unfurled large chiropteran wings and flew in to attack. Soon the cave was filled with the sounds of metal claws and teeth as the Waynes decimated the remaining monkeys.

The internal state of the cave slowly began to shift as well. Wombs which had until just a few seconds earlier seemed to be venting hot water out their pipes now ceased their activities and slowly changed position. Tangled vine-like appendages now extruded from holes where the monkeys had been. Pipes began falling away from the wombs, and before long the whole structure connecting the wombs had collapsed. The elevated pathway where the doctor stood began to shake violently.

The area around them suddenly grew bright. The

Bethlehemian's Horla was flying toward them and opening a rescue net. They couldn't see anyone inside—it was being remote controlled. Before they had time to react, it swept the three of them up in its net and flew back toward the hole they'd blown in the second sublevel floor half an hour earlier. The captain was waiting for them at the entrance, the remote control in his hands.

When the doctor climbed out of the net, he looked back through the hole at the changing wombs. The wombs no longer belonged to the human world. They were slowly merging into an Olivier. Guinesses would undoubtedly come to welcome the Olivier, and the headquarters would collapse as well, so they'd better leave soon. They had no way of knowing how the Olivier would evolve and what role it would eventually play. Maybe Adjanis would come to meet the new Olivier, and maybe those Adjanis would open a new road out into the universe. Or maybe it would just enter a meditative state like the others and disappoint everyone. The doctor didn't know how it would turn out, and he wasn't going to bother pretending to know the unknowable. All he knew was that, for the time being anyway, Crusoe was now safe from Sydney's virus. Oliviers were germaphobes and wouldn't tolerate any virus that threatened the system.

The doctor didn't have any confidence in the claims he had made in front of Ginger. It was clear that the Rothbart scientists hadn't yet found an answer. That much had been obvious just from Bo's attitude. But who knew what might happen? People hounded by the fear of death and extinction would always find a way. And so what if they did go extinct? Crusoe wasn't the only planet inhabited by the descendants of Earthlings.

The doctor smiled. He drew back from the entrance and tapped out a few dance steps. His shoes didn't have tap plates attached, but the concrete dust created by the explosion shifted crisply under his feet, just like when Fred lulls Ginger to sleep by dancing on sand in *Top Hat*.

"Fools. Do you know what you've done?" Ginger yelled from where she lay in the net. Her back was broken, but her face still worked.

The doctor, continuing his tap dance, replied, "Of course we do. We just saved you from hell."

LEVENTON

1

Like everyone else on Leventon Island, I was about twelve years old when I lost the ability to sleep.

Losing sleep means becoming an adult. It means having to control your dreams from a constant state of wakefulness and thus having to navigate the contradictions between internal and external universes. It requires cultivating the strength necessary to maintain one's sense of self. You see monsters, too: a white snake that coils around your legs and threatens you with its black fangs; a Marlene Dietrich who paces the corridor every night humming "Lili Marlene;" and purple monsters who rip holes through the fabric of space, pop out, and lick your nose with their blue tongues. Losing sleep means you're forced to distinguish which of the monsters are real and which are not. Think you could? Think again.

The easiest solution was to pretend to sleep. Even after losing sleep, I continued to put on my pajamas, hug my teddy bear, climb into bed, pull up the covers, and close my eyes. Although still wide awake, I deliberately stopped thinking and created a void in my mind. That void never remained empty for more than ten minutes. It always filled with dreams of every sort, and these were impossible to tell apart from reality. I couldn't be sure that the dead people and impossible flying creatures that appeared before me were not real. Each dreamer has their own logic. The state of wakefulness merely provides a space for that logic to unfold.

It is a disease. Creatures who cannot objectively recognize the external physical world cannot survive. Many of them are chased by non-existent demons, search for non-existent food and companions, and ultimately throw their bodies off cliffs and into seas. Only those who learn how to separate the two worlds manage to survive. All the children of Leventon had to learn how to do this, and none had passed the test by willpower alone. They endured brain surgery, chip implantation, and chemical therapy, and even then, none except those who destroyed their brains ever recovered sleep. In the end, we had no choice but to live with our dreams.

My solution was war. I wanted to fry my nervous system by risking death. I went to Saturday and soaked the place in blood. I killed so many people but I didn't feel sorry for them. They had gone there to do the same thing to me.

Did it cure me? I survived on Crusoe without drugs or chip implants. The ships I have traveled on since have never been worse off because of my presence. I almost never make mistakes, and when I do, I fix them before anyone notices. People think I'm a perfectionist, but have no idea how hard I work to reach that perfection. And they have no idea what I hear, see, or think about while I'm working.

They have no idea what sounds I'm hearing right now from the white snake slithering past the doctor's feet.

2

I'm sitting with Cleïs on my lap as I listen to Hayes Blue.

For the past four years, Hayes Blue has been operating a taxonomic research base all by himself on Leventon Island as an employee of the Rothbart Advanced Science Research Center. If the tumor on his back hadn't grown beyond his ability to treat himself, he would still be alone. He isn't affected by loneliness. The genes for feeling loneliness washed away when his ancestors were still swimming in the Linker Sea. He doesn't dislike visitors, he just doesn't mind being alone. Visitors are entertaining for an evening, but loneliness is his daily companion.

"I'm saying that people like me will disappear," he says as he waves around the mixed juice cocktail the cook made for him. "My genes will not persist. However, a bloodline of single women with personalities similar to mine will survive. Sexual reproduction has no future on Crusoe. In a few hundred years, this will be a planet of Virgin Marys. Sex loses all meaning amidst the genetic orgy that occurs in the Linker Sea. Oh, that's a good phrase, 'genetic orgy.' See, I can come up with clever phrases too."

"Genetic orgy" sounds like a cleverly improvised phrase, but I know better. Hayes Blue has been researching this for years.

Hayes Blue studies the butterflies of Leventon Island. These descendants of Earth butterflies resemble hard, transparent pinwheels. Their wings and flight are so complex that at first, they seem to be an aberrant Linker mutation of the kind that would soon disappear. Yet, when one group of the butterflies chose to reproduce asexually via parthenogenesis, everything changed. Leventon became a kingdom of butterflies. The offspring never resemble the parents. Instead, they evolve in a myriad of seemingly limitless directions.

Hayes Blue is making money off of them. He collects butterfly wings in his spare moments and sells them to collectors all over Crusoe. If the Research Center hadn't bought up the entirety of Leventon Island, it would have been overrun by greedy collectors long ago. Some are already trying to raise Leventon butterflies on other islands. They have failed thus far, but eventually they will succeed. Even if they do not, they will learn something useful in the process. Hayes Blue doesn't care. He has already made enough money to live comfortably for the rest of his life, even while paying the base's expenses himself. He doesn't much like using money anyway.

I am drawn to his story. His version of Leventon Island is entirely different from the one I knew. To me, Leventon had basically been a luxury retirement home for rich elderly people with terminal illnesses. But by the time Hayes Blue arrived, most of the old people had died or left, and herds of butterflies had taken over the emptied space. The orchards and gardens I had so loved changed around the butterflies. The plants altered their fruit and branch shape to better accommodate them, and the predators grew new teeth and digestive organs for eating their wings. There were even insects that evolved to feed themselves to the butterflies and cause the butterflies to lay their eggs in place of butterfly eggs. Hayes carefully records the appearance, evolution, and disappearance of everything. Often his records are more story or narrative than scientific record. In Linker worlds, taxonomists are by necessity poets, at least to a certain extent. Hayes's research subjects are ephemeral, always flickering back out of existence moments after they appear, like Emma Bovary or Floria Tosca. The concept of species no longer applies to the Leventon butterflies. They exist only as individuals.

The door opens and another passenger comes in. It's the short, stocky man with green hair and long thick arms named Digger. The name could not have been more to the point. As a paleontologist, digging is his job. He spent the last ten years alone in the jungles of Thursday, excavating fossils of native plants. Now he is beginning a new project in the mountains of Leventon Island. The mechanical mole he brought with him from Thursday is still in pieces aboard Jezebel. Like Hayes Blue, Digger is unaffected by loneliness. When we leave the two of them on Leventon, they will each live their lives in their own individual realms, a hundred kilometers apart.

Hayes Blue downs the remainder of his cocktail, and he and Digger discuss their plans. Hayes talks about the native plant fossils he has discovered thus far and suggests areas where the mole should dig. Soon their conversation shifts to recent discoveries in Crusoe paleontology. Until recently, people thought that Crusoe had been incorporated into the Linker Universe two thousand standard years ago. Yet, recent excavations on Thursday prove that something akin to Linker evolution occurred during a brief window of time fifty thousand years ago. Was it really Linker evolution? If so, what had prevented it from spreading? Those are the questions the Research Center is trying to answer. Hayes Blue found evidence showing that Linker evolution may have occurred on Leventon Island around the same time. He presented the fossils to Digger in the hospital on Thursday, which is what led Digger to follow him back to Leventon. We are transporting them there.

Cleïs and I leave them in the cabin and go outside. It is

dusk. Two towers stand side by side at the edge of the orange-tinted sea. The towers, each over two hundred meters tall, are the fossilized remains of native plants, and came to symbolize the island itself. They were featured in the island's crest, back when it still existed.

I take out my binoculars and examine the coast. The village is still there, though unfamiliar vines cover the walls and roofs, and the pavement is cracking. The house where I used to live, which has been converted to Hayes Blue's Research Center, is fifteen kilometers inland. When I was little, I would go out to the coast for a picnic every weekend. I can still feel the sand flowing beneath my bare feet as the sea swept it away. I mean that literally. I don't mention sensations that I have not actually experienced.

Cleïs paws at my back. I turn around and see her looking up at the sky, hands clasped together.

"There's someone there," she says.

I raise my binoculars again and examine the coast. Nothing stands out. But Cleïs does not lie to me, and her senses are more accurate than mine.

I go to the wheelhouse and relay Cleïs's observation to the captain. He uses his cell to gather information from the Free Ship Alliance information network, then nods.

"A ship named Roy Neary docked here four days ago. It probably dropped off passengers before departing. It's scheduled to return after one week, so people must still be on the island."

"Doesn't the whole island belong to the Research Center now? They would have needed a permit to come. Can we ask the Research Center who the people are?"

"You know as well as I do that the Research Center is

particular about such things. Besides, we're almost there, do we really need to ask in advance?"

The captain is right. I go back out on deck and gaze at the gradually approaching shore. Soon I think I know what Cleïs saw. The traces left by unseen people in the sand, water, and air. Things that I was not able to see through the binoculars. But now I see them. Perhaps my bare eyes can see things that contact lenses and monitors filter out. Or perhaps I have been communicating with Cleïs in some unknown way.

Our ship sails slowly eastward along the coast in search of the harbor. Fifteen minutes later, it comes into view. There, on the broken seawall of the decaying harbor, a person stands as erect as a lighthouse and stares at our boat. As soon as Jezebel drops anchor and lowers its walkway, I grab Cleïs's hand and disembark. The feline face of the person standing on the seawall flashes an ambiguous smile that would be altogether impenetrable to anyone who wasn't from here.

"Hello, little sister." Aelita speaks.

"What brings you here?" I ask.

Aelita looks briefly down at my feet and her smile is replaced by a different but equally ambiguous expression. Raising her gaze to meet mine again, she calmly replies:

"Mom died."

3

The two people who came to the island during Hayes Blue's absence were Aelita and a man named Colonel Ozymandius. Until recently, Colonel Ozymandius had been a political mercenary for Larkin City, but now he was engaged in some sort of important work for the Research Center. The moment I saw his face I wished I had brought the doctor with us, even if that would have meant changing the ship's roster. Aside from his ebony skin, the Colonel bore a disturbing resemblance to Boris Karloff. Or, more accurately, he looked like Boris Karloff attempting to look like Raymond Massey. What genre of film would result from a pairing of Karloff and Astaire?

Aelita and Ozymandius had spent three days in the Research Center annex. The village itself was in ruins. Only our house, with the Research Center sign hanging from it, and the Research Center annex looked intact. Mom's cardboard coffin sat in the first floor of the Research Center. In keeping with the traditions of planet Leventon, it was a flattened cylinder. Her corpse lay curled inside, holding to its chest the preservatives that had kept it from rotting over the past four weeks.

Mom had died of a drug overdose. This was both true and an oversimplification. It would be too difficult to explain how the many chemicals floating through her blood and brain brought about her death. Only a portion of the deadly chemicals had been exogenous.

Cremation or atomization would have sufficed, but Aelita respected tradition. And we should let her. There are only a few people left on Crusoe who uphold this tradition, and anyway, there's nothing wrong with it. From dust to dust. From a ball of meat to insect food. After all, shouldn't we leave clues about the kind of creatures we were for future archaeologists to discover?

"Why didn't you tell me?" I asked.

"I tried. But when I asked the Free Ship Alliance for your number, they told me Jezebel would be arriving here in just a few days, so I decided not to bother. I thought I'd surprise you instead."

"What are the chances? I haven't been back since I left to join the tank wars."

"Yeah. But is it really that strange? Rare coincidences happen all the time. Without them there'd be no evolution, whether in a Linker Universe or a Darwinian one."

"So why'd you bring that Boris Karloff along?"

"Because the island belongs to the Research Center. They assigned him to keep an eye on me and make sure I don't cause any trouble. Besides, won't there be excavations here soon too? They could kill two birds with one stone."

Cleïs clucked next to me. Aelita glared coldly at her for a brief moment.

"Your taste for pets hasn't changed."

"She's not a pet, she's a friend."

"A Bethlehemian? Can you even talk with her?"

"Some would say we're Bethlehemians too."

"We read Chekhov and listen to Tchaikovsky. If our sleeping handicap makes us Bethlehemians, then everyone is Bethlehemian."

"Maybe everyone is."

"If you say so."

Aelita didn't want to discuss it any further. She assumed a businesslike attitude and laid out the schedule for the next two days. The Colonel had already brought out Hayes Blue's mini mole and parked it in front of the house. Tomorrow at noon they would use it to dig a plot and bury Mom in the family cemetery. In the afternoon, Aelita and the Colonel would tie up loose ends on the island, and the following morning they would leave on the Roy Neary. *If there are any outstanding issues between the two of us, let's resolve them before*

I leave. But had there been any? Even if there were, it's been fifteen years, haven't they all dissolved by now? I had no idea what Aelita thought the two of us needed to talk about.

Outside, Jezebel's crew was busy helping Hayes Blue and Digger unload their things. The captain and doctor were assembling Digger's mole. This second machine was ten times bigger than Hayes Blue's miniature model. It seemed the others had decided to spend the night in our house and attend mom's funeral the following day before we went our separate ways. They thought it was the polite thing to do, and we felt no need to correct them.

Dinner was a feast, as always. The greater the number of guests and the wider the range of palates that needed to be accommodated, the brighter the chef's artistry shone. Her banquets were symphonies that simultaneously resonated at different frequencies for each guest. Each of us could eat only some of the foods set out before us, yet the shared sauces and the scents from the other dishes made us feel we had indulged in much more than what was on our individual plates. I felt sorry for the doctor, who was busy looking after the ship.

Aside from a brief exchange of formal condolences regarding our mother, the topic of conversation throughout dinner remained the research of Hayes Blue and Digger. Despite having already gobbled up the entire Milky Way and both Magellanic Clouds, the Linker Universe had been in existence for only a short period of time. Over the last several hundred years, paleontologists had conducted excavations on hundreds of thousands of planets, but only on twenty or so of these planets had they found any evidence of Linker evolution prior to three thousand years ago. People continued to doubt the veracity of such scant evidence, and Digger and Hayes

Blue's claim of the fifty thousand years was particularly difficult to believe.

"More precisely, about 51,200 years." Digger said. "Comrade Hayes Blue's research into the geological strata on this island has made it possible for us to date the event to the nearest century. Of course, we can't yet be sure that it was Linker evolution. But we are certain that the fossil evidence here on Leventon Island is related to what we've found on Thursday."

What Digger and Hayes Blue had found were the bones and plumage of a native creature resembling a four-winged bird. Similar to many present-day Crusoe birds, the creature seems to have migrated between Thursday and Tuesday using Leventon as a stopover point midway. Until it suddenly underwent Linker evolution.

"It could of course have been something else. But the resemblance to Linker evolution is too strong for us to simply dismiss the possibility. If this sort of sudden mutation happened in the absence of any obvious evolutionary pressure, then it was due to Linker interference. In fact, we've also found traces of a virus that we believe to be a Linker virus. With a few more years of investment, our research should start to show significant results."

"Are you saying that the Linker virus itself evolved on Crusoe?" The captain asked.

"It's entirely possible," Digger replied. "What we call the Linker virus isn't any one particular virus. It's lots of different viruses that share a handful of characteristics. Of course, to create a stable Linker Universe like we have today requires a galaxy-wide network connected by faster-than-light ships. But it is entirely possible that Linker viruses evolved convergently on multiple isolated planets, and that many of these viruses disappeared due to their inherent instability. There are even people who suggest this happened on Earth. They say the Cambrian explosion and Permian extinction were both caused by a Linker virus, although they disagree about whether that prehistoric Linker virus evolved on Earth or was brought by Adjanis."

"But there's no evidence for any of that," Hayes Blue complained. "The Linker is like a master key. It fits into whatever explanation you come up with. The fossil evidence found on Leventon and Thursday is worth investigating, sure, but I can't accept this recent trend of invoking the Linker as a convenient explanation for everything. It isn't science."

"I agree we should be circumspect about possible ties between the Cambrian explosion and the Linker virus. The thing is, though, if we consider the genetic links between planets on the Brazilian route...."

Then their conversation entered specialist territory. Still, anyone paying close attention could have followed along. What passes for specialist knowledge of Linker biology isn't obscure at all. Very little is proven, and most of the data remains poorly understood.

Unlike us, though, the Oliviers and Adjanis know everything.

While eating the green dessert of unknown ingredients that the cook had prepared especially for me, I turned my gaze to the colonel, who had barely spoken. He had cautiously selected his meal, giving the impression of a picky connoisseur, and was carefully eating small portions. He must have experienced a great deal of danger over the last few years while working as a political mercenary for Larkin City.

I had heard all sorts of horrible things about Larkin.

Everyone dispersed after dinner. I followed the colonel into the ruins of a garden and sat down about ten meters away from him. We watched the stars in silence.

He spoke first. "I didn't join the Death March."

"What?"

"That's what everyone asks when I say I was a Larkin City mercenary. I was on Thursday three years ago, but I was on the opposite side of the continent. I won't deny that we did bad things, but nothing as flagrant as that. The Death March really was a strange accident."

"So, what did you do there?"

He took the pipe out of his mouth—I didn't even know what was in it—and put it in his pocket, then walked over to the terrace bench where I sat. The large full moon hanging in the sky behind him made him look like the depressed monster out of a black and white horror film. After asking my permission, he carefully wiped the seat next to me with a handkerchief and gently sat down.

"Have you heard of the 'Word Worm'?"

"No."

"I'm not surprised. The news circulates only as rumor; there's been no official press release. A Rothbart scientist quit the Center and went rogue. He invented something unspeakable: a brainwashing bug. Piecing together scraps of genetic material, he managed to mass-produce a parasite about two millimeters long that secretes chemicals to compel religious conviction in its host."

I laughed.

"I know it sounds ridiculous," the colonel continued, flatly. "In the Linker Universe, it isn't possible for any such lifeform to retain genetic purity across two or more generations. Everyone knows this. However, the scientist nonetheless managed to sell this parasite to Carlos del Rio, head of the Church Mafia. Was Carlos del Rio really that ignorant? No. But he fell for the inventor's claims. The inventor told him that the Word he had inserted into the bugs prevented genetic pollution. And he had reams of research to prove it. Needless to say, the Church Mafia didn't have the AI they would have needed to check all the research. Any AI that powerful would long ago have merged into an Olivier. The inventor's claims were patently ridiculous, but the Church Mafia decided to believe him anyway. They were in a tough spot back then. They had beaten back the Crimson Jihad, but only just barely, and their followers were losing their faith. Three years ago was also when the number of hardcore Trekkies surpassed the number of Church Mafia followers. One way or another, they had to go to war with unbelievers."

"Carlos del Rio wanted to implant the Word into the parasites and spread them around?"

"He didn't just want to, he actually did it. He let them loose in a mining city called Sainte-Colombe on the West coast of Thursday. Where else?"

I knew the name. Sainte-Colombe was a boomtown that had sprung up around a gold mine. One day, out of the blue, a religious war had erupted there. Or, at least, that's what I had heard.

"Naturally, the Linker virus altered the parasite. The content of the Word in the parasite's genes changed completely, but the compulsion to obey it remained. You can guess the results. The Thursday City Alliance declared that a dangerous Bethlehemian disease had broken out in Sainte-Colombe, and we were sent in to suppress it. It was all for political reasons. After we pacified the city, the Larkin City government would establish a compliant new government there and establish a beachhead on that side of Thursday. That was their plan, anyway. They didn't much care how we carried out their orders as long as we helped them achieve their political goals.

"But how does one manage Bethlehemians? We could get the Rothbart Research Center to help us make a drug to exterminate the parasite. But the parasite was merely the vector, and exterminating it wouldn't return the victims to normal. Their brains had already changed and submitted to the Word. Moreover, as the Linker Virus repeatedly diffused and re-concentrated the Word, it was becoming more violent. It mutated into something we couldn't even understand. Those afflicted ate their own children, set fire to all flowering plants, and cut down all trees over ten meters tall. Even stranger was their attitude toward language. They stopped using the words 'desk' and 'sand' and swapped the letters 's' and 'm.' They came to believe that using two consonants next to each other was lascivious, and they coughed at the end of each sentence to designate the place where the period would be. Sentences were not allowed to have subjects because there could be no doer aside from the one and only God. Anyone who violated any of these taboos was stoned to death.

"So what we were supposed to do with them? Eighty percent of the city's population was already infected. Distinguishing the remaining twenty percent was practically impossible. Healthy people also threw stones in the square when their colleagues were unfortunate enough to get caught. They couldn't be persuaded. And we couldn't declare all-out war on them either. They might have been crazy, but they outnumbered us and they had their own army. No matter how we looked at the situation, it wasn't something that a professional army like ours could solve. Nevertheless we were ordered to solve it, and they only gave us two weeks."

"So what did you do?"

"What do you think?"

I thought he would continue, but he suddenly stood up and went into the house. I sat blankly for a moment, then pulled out my cell and looked up news about Sainte-Colombe.

I had not misremembered. There had been a war in Sainte-Colombe. The news reports explained it as a war for territory between the extremist Church Mafia and a Crimson Jihad killing squad that had come down from the north. A mercenary army from Larkin City had ended the war by unleashing chemical weapons on the Crimson Jihad forces occupying the city. 210,000 people died in the process—more than twice as many people as had died in the Death March. The corpses were incinerated and a new government was set up with the help of Larkin City. Most new inhabitants of the city came from Larkin.

The colonel had found his solution within the allotted two weeks.

4

We held the funeral at noon. Digger dug the grave using Hayes Blue's mini mole. As the mole's screw burrowed into the ground, it deposited one flat cylindrical clump of earth after another onto the surface. Digger excavated to a depth of eight meters, then reversed and extracted the mole, leaving a hole two meters in diameter for the grave. We used Hayes

Blue's crane to carefully lower the cardboard box containing Mom's corpse into the hole and spread flower petals on top. The others seemed to expect an elaborate ceremony, but we don't do that sort of thing.

Mom and young Aelita stood at my side throughout the funeral and watched everything. Most people experience this sort of hallucination only in their dreams and forget it upon waking. I am not so fortunate.

Mom had come to me with young Aelita in tow at around two that morning. At first, she didn't even know she had died. She acted as if Aelita and I were little kids who could still sleep. She tried to wake me from where I had been laying on the bed staring at the ceiling. She then scolded Aelita for whining and pulled some new clothes for me out of thin air. Meanwhile, the sounds of a village performance of Tchaikovsky's "Andante Cantabile" floated through the half open window on a gentle breeze. As soon as I told Mom that she had in fact died, the Tchaikovsky and gentle breeze disappeared. Mom and little Aelita, however, remained.

Mom looked depressed. The village that had until recently been bustling was now a ruin, and the few relatives she had left were scattered across the planet. Mom recited lines from poems and novels in an attempt to find literary solace, but the noise of the mole pounding the dirt back into place over her grave rendered such efforts useless.

Once the mole had replaced the final clump of dirt, the surface looked almost as if it had never been disturbed. We left a black rock on the grave in place of a tombstone. There were two clumps of dirt left over from the burial, which Digger took away to use as raw data for his research.

Aelita went back to the house with the colonel to finish

paperwork. Mom and young Aelita followed them. Mom complained to Aelita about the funeral, and young Aelita grabbed the hem of Aelita's coat and whined. Aelita couldn't see either of them, but she may have had another Mom at her side, invisible to me, making similar complaints.

The others began to disperse. Digger and Hayes Blue loaded the dirt samples into a wagon. The captain and cook sought out the shade of the trees to avoid the rays of sun that had just begun to poke through the clouds. Cleïs, who had been at my side as Digger began to fill in the hole, was nowhere to be seen.

I went to look for Cleïs. More accurately, I used Cleïs's absence as an excuse to get away from everyone and spend a moment alone. I opened the east gate of the cemetery and walked aimlessly toward the beach.

The path to the beach was resplendent with color. Leventon butterflies that had hidden from the morning showers were now reemerging and flying up into the sky. They glittered like slivers of gemstones falling from a jeweler's table. Some looked like real butterflies, some looked like flowers. Some resembled earrings or brooches, others resembled pinwheels, and still others appeared in strange shapes so irregular that it was hard to believe they were possible. At least as many butterflies crawled along the ground as flew in the sky. Some of the crawlers displayed surprisingly quick footwork, but the rest looked deformed. Each of the brilliant creations that now sparkled in the Leventon sky owed its very existence to four or five of these earthbound failures.

The predators of Leventon preyed mainly on the failures. Even as I walked along the path, several dozen salamander-shaped creatures caught and ate some of the Leventon butterflies that wriggled along the ground. When I listened closely, I could hear the faint crunching of butterfly wings in their mouths. I could also see them spit out pieces of broken butterfly wings from the small orifice located beneath their chins. This process was what had created most of the glittering sand that made up Leventon's unpaved roads. If the butterflies stick around long enough, they will cover the island with a geological stratum of glittering wing shards.

As I watched the butterflies, I thought of Cleïs. High-functioning Bethlehemians are like these butterflies. They hadn't adopted the techniques of flight from their Earth ancestors, but they had managed nonetheless to fly up into the sky in their own way. Just as the Leventon butterflies cannot teach their method of flight to Earth butterflies, Cleïs cannot teach me what is going on inside her head. The twenty percent of her brain that functions like a normal human's enables the little communication we can have. Most of that twenty percent is occupied by an understanding of numbers, music, and physics. Some people say that's sufficient, but I'm still curious about what Cleïs is seeing and thinking on the other side of that incomprehensible barrier.

When I arrived at the end of the path, I discovered Cleïs sitting hunched over in the sand. From the back, she looked like a broken, abandoned statue. She didn't move a muscle as the waves lapped against her ankles. She was staring as if hypnotized at something in front of her.

At first, it looked like some strange sea creature. A glittering, transparent head the size of a baseball, with stuff that looked like eyes, brain, and muscle inside. Closer inspection revealed it was a machine. A machine doing a relatively skillful imitation of a living creature, but a machine nonetheless. It was watching Cleïs with four small black eyes hidden behind a transparent protective membrane.

I took my cell out of my pocket and opened the camera. When the machine heard the startup chime, it turned its expressionless face, looked back and forth from the camera to me, and fled into the water.

It was a Linker machine. A Guinness or a Wayne. Probably a Wayne. Its sleek imitation of sea life made it hard to identify from appearance alone, but that physical mimicry couldn't disguise the particularly animalistic and aggressive movement characteristic of Waynes.

Fascinating. The bodies of terrestrial Linkers were tools that mutated to suit their objectives. But the Linker machine that had just disappeared seemed nearly perfect and complete. Its appearance was more that of a flying type than a terrestrial one. It was also strange to find a terrestrial Linker in the sea. Didn't they hate the water?

Something quite unusual was happening in the seas around Leventon Island.

5

Hayes Blue was not in the house. Digger said that Hayes had taken the samples to the Research Center and then gone straight to the dig, saying he had something interesting to show us. The dig was one hundred kilometers away. Given the condition of the road and the capabilities of the vehicle, he wouldn't return in time for dinner.

We ate without him. When we had finished the meal, I showed the others the video I had taken at the beach that afternoon. They were interested, but didn't have much to say. They weren't sure what to make of the discovery either.

The captain was the first to speak, "Remember when I

infiltrated Rrose Sélavy five years ago? I discovered a parasitic Olivier living on board. We all thought that Oliviers don't board other ships, but that turned out to be wrong. Maybe it's the same with those Waynes. We don't know anything about them. Who knows what caprice they're capable of."

"Isn't Rrose Sélavy that aircraft carrier that sunk off Sunday two years ago?" Digger interrupted.

"Actually it disappeared," the captain calmly corrected him.

"Yes, right. Disappeared. They haven't found the wreckage yet, have they? Isn't that really unusual?"

"There aren't many people searching for shipwrecks around Sunday, because of the glaciers."

"Well, aircraft carriers transporting mercenaries don't often travel there either. Anyway, isn't it strange? A mutiny reduces the ship's crew to only a few people, and then it heads toward the north pole, where there's only one real city, and disappears. It's just unusual."

"What are you trying to say?"

"I mean that the two might be connected. Oliviers living parasitically off of ships, and Waynes living in the water. Both are connected to the water. And both have quit their usual terrestrial ecology," Digger declared.

The captain was quiet. I knew what he was thinking: it really was possible. But what was the use of knowing that? We understood nothing about the Linker machines' motives or plans. Even if the two phenomena were connected, that would just be one more incomprehensible mystery to us.

"We think of the Linker machines as if they were gods." Digger continued. "The Oliviers, at least. They're the epitome of refinement, the last stop of the evolutionary train. We act like they're gods and manifestations of the Platonic ideal. And the Waynes, Coopers, and Guinesses are angels helping these gods.

"We can't give up on these definitions and distinctions yet. Why not? Because we don't know anything about the Linker machines yet. We don't even know why the terrestrial and flying types are different. The names and classification were just the random creation of some Scottish film fanatic hundreds of years ago, and we treat them as gospel. It's not normal!

"And, why the hell are Oliviers the omega of everything anyway? They're just tin cans with computers inside, nothing more. They're smarter and more knowledgeable than us, but that's all. The universe doesn't have to take the path of the Oliviers. There are clearly other roads we could go down instead."

"Where are these 'other roads'?" The captain asked. "We've explored tens of thousands of solar systems over the last four hundred years and haven't found a single alternative path."

"We didn't travel to any those places by ourselves," Digger argued. We rode Adjanis to all of them. They only show us the places they want to show us. The tens of thousands of places you're talking about sound like a lot, but they're only a tiny fraction of the yellow solar systems spread across the galaxy. The Linker Universe doesn't cover the whole Milky Way, and somewhere out there in the rest of the Darwinian universe. There are surely advanced civilizations that have beaten back the Linker attack.

"We don't even have evidence that the Linker Universe is as homogenous as we've assumed. In fact we've already recorded plenty of observations that contradict our preconceptions on that point. The Wayne we just saw living in the water might be another one of these contradictory exceptions. And other things we see that seem unexceptional could nonetheless be exceptions too. It's just like how 'We smurfed the smurf' can mean several entirely different things. What appears to us as a group of Waynes could in fact be an entirely different species."

Digger concluded his speech with a commanding wave of his thick arms and contrastingly delicate hands. He blew air into his cheeks as if exasperated by our lack of excitement, and sat down.

"In that case, does your Linker virus evolution hypothesis reflect these ideas, or contradict them?" I asked.

"You could argue either way. My theory might be right, it might not. But I'm sure about one thing. The Linker machines don't want us to come anywhere near the truth. Up until a year ago we had decisive evidence that could have revealed for certain what happened fifty thousand years ago. But they destroyed it. Even worse actually, they plundered it from us."

"What are you talking about?" The colonel, who had until now been listening quietly, suddenly interrupted. His voice was stiff with sudden emotion that sounded to me partly like annoyance, partly like anger, and with a hint of curiosity mixed in.

"I didn't write about it in the reports," Digger spit back. "But I've never lied to the center. I left all my research findings in there. I simply neglected to mention a few things."

"Like what happened to Pangloss?"

The colonel got up, strode over, and stood in front of Digger. With Digger huddling in a chair and looking up at him, the colonel looked larger than ever.

"Yes." Digger replied in a small, somewhat fearful voice.

"What happened to him? Did he die?"

"It would have been better if he had."

"You mean he's still alive?"

"I wouldn't say that either. Can't you see what I'm getting at?"

The colonel flinched and took a step backward. Digger, regaining the initiative, fixed his posture and gazed at us for a moment before raising his voice.

"Let me explain for those who don't know. Pangloss was an archaeologist at the Center. When I discovered fossil evidence implying independent Linker evolution in the Monsophiad Jungle, he traveled from Wednesday saying he would assist me. The Research Center thought he disappeared along the way. But he didn't disappear. He arrived and spent three days with me here. More precisely, he spent the time in the abandoned building across from my dorm.

"I don't know for sure what Pangloss did during those three days. He seemed less interested in my fossil evidence than in other things. His vehicle was filled with strange equipment. He engaged only half-heartedly in fossil research, and instead dragged his equipment around doing whatever it was he was trying to do. When I asked him about it, he never gave a straight answer. He was obviously hiding something. Otherwise, why would he have arrived early and started conducting his own experiments without telling the Center?

"I didn't probe further. I didn't think it was very important. The Center is crawling with weirdos, and when someone calls himself Pangloss, it's impossible to take him seriously.

"On the morning of the third day, I happened to overhear

Pangloss talking on the phone. I knew who it was on the other end, too. It was Bo, an evolutionary tracker specialist that I had briefly worked with before. It's hard to forget that monosyllabic name. That and his three eyes.

"My curiosity was piqued. It seemed Pangloss was working not for the Center, but for some other group that had a foothold in the Center. Pangloss grew agitated as he talked. He worried about the lockdown as if it were something new. He even spoke of the possibility of war with the same tone of voice. If someone else had heard him, they would have thought he was a refugee newly arrived on Crusoe.

"After eating an absent-minded lunch, he took his vehicle out again and disappeared. But this time, I knew where he was going. I had attached a tracker to his vehicle that morning. I walked after him and found him easily. I knew all the roads the vehicle could travel on, and I also knew all the shortcuts through the jungle."

Digger paused for a moment and frowned.

"Have you ever seen a person merge?"

Satisfied by the comprehension he saw finally dawn on our faces, he continued:

"I had only ever heard stories about it. For something that happens so often, there are very few records. As far as I know, the entire Crusoe library contains only two videos of human merging. One video shows the second human merging recorded on Earth back in the early days of the Linker virus. The other was.... I forget where. Both are short and the details of the process are hard to make out. They each end in a momentary flash of light.

"What I saw was different. There was no light, and it wasn't quick. At first glance, it looked like Pangloss was coated with gold. Looking closer, I saw that what covered him were flat machines, each about the size of a finger. They held onto his upright body with their legs and wrapped him in white, thread-like stuff that they pulled from their own bodies. He writhed, but that was it. He couldn't even fall over. All he could do was bend and bob, up and down, forward and backward.

"At first, I thought it might just be Waynes harvesting him for resources. But I realized there weren't any Oliviers in the vicinity. There were plenty of protein and fat sources nearby, and the machines were only attacking his brain and spine. Then I noticed the expression on Pangloss's face. His face was distorted with fear and pain. Yet, it relaxed and grew peaceful as the golden insects pulled his skull open and exposed his brain. When they finished wrapping the extracted brain and spine into a larval shape that then began to move by itself, the remnants of his face looked almost blissful.

"After the insects disappeared, I checked Pangloss's vehicle. It functioned normally, but all the strange items Pangloss had brought with him were gone. It looked like he had been secretly excavating in this area. But all the holes he had dug were completely empty. It wasn't that he hadn't found anything, it was that some sort of machine had meticulously cleaned the holes out afterward."

"Why the hell didn't you tell us?" The colonel shouted.

Digger blinked slowly and answered calmly, "Like I said, I wasn't obliged to tell the Center everything. Our relationship was straightforward. They funded my research, I shared my findings. That was all. What Pangloss researched was his affair. It wasn't my business.

"And since you've brought it up, should we talk about

the things the Center kept from me? When they sent me to Monsophiad, did they tell me what had happened there? Twenty-seven research trackers killed each other by poison, gun, and knife. but the Research Center didn't say a thing. Instead they just cleaned it up and sent me there because I was ignorant of the whole affair and could be the mouse in their experiment.

"How did I know? Comrade Hayes Blue told me. Don't underestimate us outcasts. We're still capable of making friends, forming alliances, and exchanging information. The Center obviously had some ulterior motive when it sent lone researchers with similar interests to the site of each mysterious group massacre."

He turned toward Aelita, who sat tense at the corner of the table. He extended a long index finger and pointed at her.

"What happened on the island that day?" he asked.

6

For a moment, all was quiet. The spirits came out into the silence. Mom, young Aelita, and young me were now all inside our home. Ghostly feline faces bumped their heads against the window as they spied on us from outside.

"Do we really have to talk about this again?" the captain broke the silence. "We all know what happened on Leventon and who Vladimir of Leventon is. As for what happened in the Monsophiad Jungle, this is the first time I've heard about it. But the Leventon Massacre is not a secret."

"But is what we know really what actually happened? There's obviously some deeper reason why the world doesn't know what led that guy to suddenly turn guns on his family and relatives. Vladimir led a normal, healthy life for half a century before the massacre. Did he suddenly lose his sanity? Or was there some other reason?"

For a brief moment it seemed as if Aelita were resisting Digger's questions with all her strength. But she knew she would have to answer sooner or later.

"Uncle Vladimir was just lazy." She shrugged and began to explain, "Most people on Leventon were like that. Uncle Vladimir was different only in that he kept making excuses for his laziness. And in the end, he believed his own excuses.

"Some were true. We were imprisoned on Leventon. Entrusted with that ridiculous mission of protecting the gene pool. Not a single one of us bought that story, though. There were at most only thirty people left in the village, and we were all cousins. We were caught in a tiny gap between inbreeding and Linker chaos.

"We should have just given up at that point, but we didn't. Instead, we rewrote our reality and our memories. To us, Leventon Island appeared still in its heyday, bustling with hundreds of residents. I have fond childhood memories of frolicking around with many other children, even though in reality, Alla and I were the only children on the island at the time. Any children who hadn't gotten caught in their dreams like we had would have recognized the reality of the situation and grown up.

"You're wondering if there weren't any solutions? Of course there were. If we wanted to differentiate reality and dreams, we could get a chip implanted or take drugs. If we wanted to live a productive life, we could call the Free Ship Alliance and ask them to send a ship. That's what Alla did. Then she went to the south pole and joined the tank wars.

"Uncle Vladimir didn't do any of that. He made up his

mind that Leventon Island was a prison from which he could never escape, and within that prison he played the martyr. He spent his days bragging about how smart and talented he was, and complaining about how the island's isolation and his responsibility to protect the gene pool had ruined his chances at life.

"He was talented. He was cultured and multilingual like most of us on Leventon. He wrote several books. I remember one of them, a zombie parody of *Wuthering Heights* set on a Caribbean island in the nineteenth century.

"But were his talents ever useful? He could play every instrument in the viol family fabulously, but there isn't a single human orchestra on Crusoe. Like most people on Leventon, he was fluent in Russian, but no one else on Crusoe uses the language. Even the Soviet soldiers at the south pole talk like Ernest Borgnine. Uncle Vladimir knew as well as everyone else that off the island, his talents would be completely useless.

"We relaxed when he threw himself into butterfly research. It looked somehow like productive work. The Rothbart Center even said they would pay him a salary. It made sense: the islanders wouldn't accept any outsiders, and the Center wanted a researcher of their own on the island. That's what we believed, in any case. If they kept him busy, we wouldn't have to listen to his complaints and could bury ourselves in our own fantasies.

"Back then, Leventon was not the butterfly heaven it is today. At least, what we now call butterflies were at the time only a small group of bizarre creatures that lived near the quarry. But once Uncle Vladimir discovered and reported them to the Center, the butterflies multiplied rapidly. For a while we wondered if it was his doing. But the Center said it wasn't, and I believe them.

"It took him a while to get used to the work. Evolution tracking is often said to be a job for amateur enthusiasts, but even in that light, he was a bit too enthusiastic. His precision suffered for it. His early reports contained too many baseless hypotheses and poetic descriptions. He sent rough hand-drawn sketches more often than photographs, and most of the sketches were based on his daydreams rather than real butterflies. The Center soon admonished him to only report things he had actually seen, attach photos, and stop with the sketches. Funny enough, he was proud of the warning. He didn't realize that they were calling him incompetent. To him, the warning was nothing more than the complaints of fools who couldn't understand his artistic talents.

"After that, he wrote reports that met the Center's standards and learned how to use the elaborate machines it had left him. But his attitude toward research did not change. To him the butterflies were more than just mutants affected by the Linker virus. They were a surface manifestation of some greater poetic order that we couldn't see. While he carefully researched the wing shapes of the butterflies, he searched for a pattern among them. More than once he thought he had really succeeded. Yet, every time, my mother—who was calmer and far more intelligent than Uncle Vladimir—demonstrated that the patterns were totally vague and meaningless. But these disappointments never caused him to abandon the search.

"Think what would have happened had my mother just let him be. No one would have listened to his suggestion, and it would've remained just a strange but harmless idea. Exactly like everything else he had done in his life.

"Instead he went down a different path. He gave up trying to think like a scientist and turned into a mystic and pantheist. Leventon's butterflies became objects of religious worship. They were both gospel and iconography. Suspicion and skepticism disappeared, leaving only irrefutable truth. Yet, what was that truth? Nobody knew.

"Surprisingly, he found comrades on the island. The first person he convinced was Aunt Nadyezhda. And after she fell under his sway, gradually others began to join as well. A month later there were fifteen believers in the butterfly religion. And the contagion even spread to our illusions. It became common to see Uncle Vladimir, his followers, and hundreds of spirits together chasing after flocks of real and spirit butterflies.

"Mom and I began to worry. It's true that we had our own problems. We couldn't differentiate reality from daydreams. Yet, precisely for that reason, we looked at everything through rational, skeptical eyes. We couldn't have survived otherwise. Not a single religion had set foot on Leventon in over one hundred years. The lack of religion conflicted with our desire to create and live peacefully in a theme park modeled on Czarist Russia, but even so, we just could not accept religious belief. Yet, despite our aversion to it, a mysterious new religion had suddenly arisen on the island and was growing fast. This new phenomenon was strange and worrying. It was also a matter of self-esteem.

"Mom naturally thought it was a disease. Everything that happened to the people on Leventon was a symptom of disease, so it was easy to assume this was too. But that aside, what could we do about it?

"In the end, we sought help from off the island. We contacted the Center behind Uncle Vladimir's back. They turned out to know much more about us than we expected, and also seemed interested in researching and solving this problem. They promised to send a medical team and mercenaries. They had a science vessel at a research facility nearby, so we would only need to wait two days.

"We had severely underestimated Uncle Vladimir.

"I don't know for sure how it happened, but somehow the butterfly believers eavesdropped on our conversation, and word of it soon reached Uncle Vladimir's ears. He thought and acted logically. If a medical team and mercenaries came from the outside, his belief would be finished, and that would mean the end of his world. He had to prevent this, no matter what. He had to kill the doctors, the soldiers, and, most importantly, kill the people who had brought the outsiders to the island: us.

"I was surprised but grateful that not everyone had completely bought into his lunacy. At least two of the believers rebelled against him. Aunt Nadyezhda was one of them. She was also the first person he killed. I've forgotten who the second person was. But obviously he eliminated that rebel as well.

"After eliminating the opposition and consolidating his power, Uncle Vladimir gathered his people together and marched toward our house. Along the way he visited the houses of others who had not yet been infected and shot each of them dead with his rifle. By the time his group reached us, the only mentally intact people left on the island were my mother and me. Although "mentally intact" is a funny way to describe us.

"Fortunately, we finished preparing just in time. We had guessed what was happening when we heard the hunting rifle shots from several kilometers away. We ran to the basement and grabbed our self-defense heat guns, then left our house on bicycles. We headed to the harbor thinking we could leave the island on a yacht. That's as far as our plans went. A few hours earlier we couldn't have even imagined leaving the island. We hadn't even known where to find the closest harbor.

"When we arrived at the harbor, we had to revise our plans. Uncle Vladimir's people had beaten us there. While he had been killing people and marching on the village, other believers had set to work on the boats. They burned some of them and pushed the rest out to sea. We heard cackles of laughter through the acrid gray smoke."

Aelita suddenly stopped talking. She looked at the point in midair where her spirits must have been standing. While she did this, my Mom spirit encircled Aelita's shoulders and neck with both arms and whispered something in her ear.

"And?" Digger pressed.

"You all know how it ended," Aelita replied coldly. "Mom and I survived. If we hadn't, I wouldn't be here talking to you now, and I wouldn't have appeared on the news. Isn't that obvious?

"The fight was not as lopsided as it seems. They had many people, but only three imitation Winchester rifles. We had two freshly-charged heat guns. Since none of us were experienced shooters, the modern weapons had the advantage, in distance combat at least. We needed only two other things to hold them off: a fortress to protect our bodies, and the courage to kill the friends and relatives with whom we had shared food and daydreams until just a few days earlier. We chose a shack on the wharf for our fortress. The other thing, we had to find within ourselves somehow.

"It was Mom who shot Uncle Vladimir. He dropped to the ground but remained conscious as all the others died and angry spirits wailed around us. Uncle Vladimir had holes in his stomach and chest, and about half his body below the waist was gone, but he wasn't dead. When Mom approached and held the muzzle of her heat gun to his forehead, he smiled as he spoke to her.

"'Nina, Ninotchka, you should have seen the butterflies. You should have seen the writing on their wings. If you hadn't been so rash, we could have read the name of God.'

"That was the last thing Uncle Vladimir, or at least the living Uncle Vladimir, ever said to us.

"The Center's boat arrived the next day. They disposed of Uncle Vladimir's body and seized his cell and computer. They collected Linker virus samples and gathered butterflies. On the third day, two researchers carrying ordinary butterfly samples got into a fight, and one was stabbed and severely injured by a knife. The next day, a mercenary was chased off a cliff by an unidentified winged monster. He fell to his death.

"That was when we began to suspect that the symptoms Leventon residents had experienced for half a century might not actually be particular to the island.

"We sold the island to the Center. Not for the money, but because we wanted them to figure out what had happened here. But they didn't do anything except send a single taxonomist to collect butterflies.

"We grew restless and angry, and contacted the Center many times. But all we got by way of reply were meaningless equivocations and diplomatese.

"Ultimately we chose to circumvent the Center. We found out that various for-profit groups were involved in the Center's operations. So we just had to find one who would send us back to the island. We chose Larkin City, and several relatives who had already gone there introduced us to Colonel Ozymandius. He was infamous for the massacre on Sainte-Colombe, but that didn't bother us. In fact we felt a comradeship with him because of it. We were all mass murderers: me, my mom, Uncle Vladimir, and even my little sister Alla, even though she wasn't on the island at the time.

"I say I came back to the island for Mom's funeral, but that's just a convenient excuse. One way or another, I had to come back. Somewhere on this island are clues as to what we are and who I am."

7

The colonel didn't flinch from our gaze. He tapped on the small glass on top of the table with his index finger as he looked at us with sad eyes.

"The Center was not wasting time," he said. "We were merely being extremely cautious. The Center was convinced that the massacres on Monsophiad and Leventon arose from the same cause. And we did not think it a coincidence that both incidents occurred around the same time. It would have been dangerous to send more than one person. We didn't know what had caused the people to behave as they had, but we knew that it acted among human social networks. The center couldn't give preliminary information to researchers either. Prejudices might influence observational results. Of course, we couldn't conceal the Leventon Island Massacre itself, but we could cover up anything that happened later among the Center's people.

"You're correct that Hayes Blue and Digger were research subjects. But it isn't true that the Center just abandoned them to danger. They were safer alone than with companions."

"But couldn't they still have lost their minds when alone in that situation?" The captain asked.

"If they had, the Center would have noticed the symptoms. They would have immediately sent a medical team to evacuate them. But nothing like that happened. Both were fine for several years. Isn't that obvious from how they figured out the scheme and formed an alliance? What better evidence could there be?"

Digger had been fuming while the colonel spoke. He finally pulled himself together and asked, in a trembling voice, "So, what did the Center learn from their experiment on us?"

"Well, what do you think?" the colonel seemed to be enjoying himself now. "Linker-like evolutionary phenomena occurred in two places fifty thousand years ago. At first glance, they seem distant, but biologically they're connected. But because one happened in the middle of a jungle and the other was on a remote island, it took a while for people to reach these sites. When people finally did arrive in these places, they all became psychologically disturbed. Was it the Linker virus? No, it makes no sense that the Linker Virus would be confined to such small areas, nor that it would have spread so slowly over a century.

"You want to know the Center's official stance? Okay. I'll tell you. They believe that fifty thousand years ago, something containing the Linker virus fell to Leventon Island and the Monsophiad Jungle. And whatever it is is still active. It is probably a drastically different species from the Linker machines we know.

"The new information we just saw today also fits this hypothesis. Is the Linker machine we saw in that video just now really one of the known species? What about the Linker machine Digger saw in the Monsophiad Jungle?

"Now surely you understand why the Center was so cautious. Linker machines do not interact with us. They use us, eliminate us, or merge us into themselves. Yet, what happened on Monsophiad and Leventon seem like attempts at communication. If so, then this is the first opportunity for contact that we've had since entering the Linker Universe."

"Except for the Giacometis," Digger broke in.

"Calling that 'contact' seems a bit embarrassing. But if you insist on being precise, we can call this the first opportunity for 'serious contact.'

"Anyway, the Research Center had to act with extreme care. We had to treat both our unknown target and ourselves with the utmost caution. The powers behind the Center had to keep each other in check and maintain a fixed distance from one another at all times. Not all of them accepted the situation, of course. There were people like Pangloss. As a matter of fact, we thought his disappearance was fortuitous. Never mind that I've just learned from you that that's not actually what happened.

"Center employees all brought their own methods to bear on the problem. I and my coworkers chose art criticism as our tool. We investigated all of the writing and art created on Leventon over the last century. Using machines to speed up and translate the texts for me, I read over ten books a day.

"We learned about all sorts of strange phenomena. Did you know that sixty percent of the people on Leventon who attempted to write genre fiction were male, but ninety-five percent of the protagonists in their fiction were female? And that eighty percent of the genre fiction produced had metamorphosis and resurrection or waiting as a common theme? You can't imagine how many diaries I read by writers who were desperately trying to expand their horizons but kept returning to the same themes. Even considering the mental illness that afflicted them, their stories were all disturbingly similar. Someone else was behind all the stories, a ghost-writer whom the named authors were entirely unaware of.

"Today this is obvious. Surprisingly, though, everyone I've met from Leventon believes that the buildings and designs here are faithful to tradition. But they aren't. The culture of planet Leventon wasn't nearly as dull and depressing. No planet could have such a simple culture. Like sleeplessness, the island culture had been injected into the Leventon Islanders after they settled on the island. The goal of protecting the gene pool had probably come from the same source.

"Don't you see? You may have lived like aristocrats in decadent luxury on this island, but you were actually being used by some unknown power the entire time. To them, you were livestock or tools. Although I don't know whether they used you as batteries, radios, typewriters, or what."

"Then what about Uncle Vladimir?" Aelita spoke softly. It sounded more a confession than a question.

"I'm not sure. There must have been some reason for it. Perhaps the butterfly religion was the conclusion of a century-long conversation. Or maybe it was the subject of another conversation. They must have gotten tired of the old conversation after continuing it for one hundred years."

The colonel took out his pipe, stuffed an unidentified blue capsule into it, and began to smoke as if he had nothing more to say.

I quietly considered what he had said. His story had a plausible logic, but something was missing. What was it that made his words ring hollow? Was it that the story itself had holes, or was it that he'd purposely left out some crucial information?

Yet I was unable to concentrate on the problem. My thoughts flowed past the colonel further and further back into time. My past, Aelita's past, Mom's past, Leventon Island's past. I tried to sort out the parts that were definitely real, and failed. Had "real" even meant anything to us? Hadn't we given up on that distinction when we accepted the phantoms as neighbors?

I looked at the spirits already filling the house. Most were women and children. The children ran from room to room while the adults leaned against walls, sat on chairs, or walked around hand in hand with friends and shouted at the kids. Their voices were soft, like a radio with the volume turned low, and it was difficult to make out words.

I could not distinguish their faces, and the number of spirits was deceptive. There seemed to be more of them than there actually were, a mere dream of a crowd. Leventon Islanders had invoked all the phantoms of the past to enliven life on the island and fill the void left by the fact that they no longer bore children and could not maintain the gene pool. Aside from Mom, young Aelita, and young me, they were all copies of copies of copies.

Was there any difference between them and me? They had dominated my life ever since I slept my last sleep. Just because

I had managed to get my body and brain off the island did not mean I had managed to detach my dreams. They were always with me, although their faces and shapes changed. They were with me on the deck of Jezebel, on the snowy battlefields of the south pole, and on the killing fields of the Death March.

Had I ever really left the island? Amidst this filthy reality, dirtied by dreams, how many spirits had I killed and resurrected?

I stood up. I needed to calm myself. Tea, or anything else. Just warm water would be fine.

A knock sounded at the entrance. Bang, bang, bang—precisely spaced almost like a clock bell. Again. Bang, bang, bang.

"Comrade Hayes Blue?" I asked, but no one replied. I walked through the gradually dissipating crowd of spirits toward the door, but hesitated before opening it. The door did not have a lock. Hayes Blue could have just opened it himself and entered.

I heard a dull thud, followed by the receding sound of something scraping against rock.

Then all was quiet again.

Slowly, I tried to open the door. Something heavy was blocking it, preventing it from swinging open. Digger ran over and joined his strength to mine. It wasn't until the door was fully open that we could see what had blocked it.

It was the decapitated corpse of Hayes Blue. Red blood still flowed up from where his neck had been severed. I looked out at the yard and saw tracks. Something wide and heavy had dragged itself through the butterfly dust all the way into the distant forest.

8

I pulled the sprawled corpse of Hayes Blue inside. Digger fetched a sheet from the laundry basket in the utility room to cover it. The blood flowing from Hayes Blue's neck stained a crescent into the white sheet, as if the headless corpse were smiling.

"A merge." Digger said.

I looked outside. Hayes Blue's vehicle stood at the edge of the yard. Nothing else was there. Aside from the phosphorescing spirits of the island, that is.

I heard Cleïs singing. It was nothing but a walk up and down one octave in the Dorian mode, but it sounded to me like an elegy. She squatted on the sheet in front of Hayes Blue's corpse. Her left hand danced over dips in the wood floor where blood had trickled.

I closed the door. I turned around and surveyed everyone's faces. The captain was standing on a chair to make up for his small height, a most authoritative expression on his face. Digger looked triumphant, clearly expecting us to take his advice. Aelita displayed the mournful expression of a protagonist from a nineteenth-century gothic novel. The cook's face showed her smile, seemingly the same as always. The colonel, as impassive as a statue, stared at the space between Hayes Blue and me.

"I am sick of all the scheming." I said. "Ever since I first left Leventon, everyone I have encountered has been scheming. This planet is full of shoddy actors pretending to be leaders and manipulating others like puppets. Is conspiracy a mandatory part of the curriculum in Crusoe's schools? Why can't anyone speak frankly? 'I need your help,' 'I hate you,' 'I'm going to kill you...' If you'd simply said what you meant,

I would've been able to do something more useful than waste my time out in the world playing a clumsy detective.

"I'm talking to you, colonel.

"You all heard the colonel's short speech a bit ago. And you must have noticed that something was missing from it. Aelita probably knew from the start. I'll tell you what it was. If the thing on Monsophiad and Leventon used human networks like tools, and if that usage ended up being lethal to the humans involved, then what are we doing here right now?

"A little while ago, comrade Digger told us about how the researcher Pangloss ignored orders from the Center and snuck into Monsophiad. The colonel immediately grew angry. But what we're doing here is far more serious than what Pangloss did. Does the Center really know that we're here?"

"Are you saying I killed Hayes Blue?" the colonel asked.

"No. I don't think the scheme was that sophisticated. He was probably going to be assimilated by the Linker machines somewhere out there, along with the information about the things he brought to show us. It's a natural phenomenon—an accident that you plotters could not have perfectly predicted, just like Pangloss's involvement and merging. Don't you understand? No matter how carefully you try to plan, it's impossible to account for all the variables on Crusoe. Especially when dealing with Linker machines. It's almost impossible to carry out a plot on this planet without something going wrong."

"The success rate can be high."

"That's why you used the funeral as an excuse to bring us together here, isn't it? You wanted to activate the network and draw out whatever was behind it so you could meet it directly.

We were human antennae."

The colonel didn't reply.

"I'm wondering what you stood to gain from this," I continued. "Let's see, what could it be? Your motives obviously weren't pure, this wasn't about first contact with a different intelligence. Were your objectives military? No, I don't believe you're that naive. Were you planning to make money out of this? No, that idea is just as silly as the others. So what the hell is it? Don't make me stand here playing Nancy Drew. Just tell us."

Cleïs screamed then, shocking everyone into stillness. She slowly approached the colonel. She put her nose up to the colonel's mouth and chin and sniffed, as if trying to smell his breath. She began to sing. It was a hymn. I couldn't remember the title but it was clearly a Christian hymn. One of those popular, cliche songs used in church scenes in old black and white movies.

The colonel flinched. He stepped backward as if he had just been exposed as a criminal, but the back of the chair hampered his retreat. The chair legs scratched unpleasantly on the wood floor as he continued backing away.

"You're infected!" I screamed. "Why didn't we realize it? The colonel was infected by the Word Worm on Sainte-Colombe. Of course the Word must have mutated into something less obvious. He would have been instantly detected had he swapped the letters "s" and "m" and left out subjects. What the hell is it that you believe now, Colonel?"

"The Trinity! Atonement! The purity of the Word! The perfection of the Word! The spread of the Word! Genesis and Armageddon! The One God!" The colonel gasped.

"Seriously? Even the Church Mafia doesn't believe that

stuff anymore. Aren't you a scientist? How can you say stuff like that?"

"How could I ch-ch-change my b-b-beliefs?"

It was the first time he had stammered. All sorts of emotions simultaneously splashed across his hitherto expressionless, statuesque face. Fear, joy, scorn, rapture, delight, anger, excitement. Had I not seen it with my own eyes, I would not have believed a single face could hold all those emotions. His face looked as if it might tear itself apart.

I thought I was now finally beginning to understand him. The Word Worm had planted in him a belief that could be neither destroyed nor altered. His belief was likely more conservative and principled than that of the Church Mafia, but it was equally baseless. Yet, he remained a scientist and knew that what he believed was a heap of nonsense, arbitrarily created by the environment and the bug in his brain. Since leaving Santi-Colombe, he had lived in a world of insanity.

Aelita approached the colonel where he lay gasping and staring at the ceiling. She stroked the colonel's face and head until he began to relax and breathe deeply, then looked over to me.

"I didn't know either. I was aware that the colonel was hiding something, and I knew that the Center was engaged in some sort of scheme, but this is Leventon. It's our home. I had to come."

"Even after you saw what happened to Uncle Vladimir?"

"So? You came back too."

"But I didn't know the real reason."

"Yes, you did. After leaving the island, we all changed. You, me, and mom. We still saw and heard things that weren't there, but it wasn't the same as it had been on Leventon. We dreamt different dreams. Something had been speaking to us when we were on the island. I needed to confirm what it was."

The colonel shook off Aelita's hand and stood up. He staggered to the middle of the room and pulled a short-barreled shock pistol from his pocket. He didn't point it at anyone or wave it around. He just stood holding it.

"Can you hear it?" He put his left index finger to his mouth and whispered. "They're coming back."

9

We stopped moving and devoted all our attention to listening. We heard wind and rustling leaves, and the rattle of the misaligned window. We strove to make sense out of the background static.

Something was hidden in the noise.

Bit by bit we began to distinguish them from the sounds of the leaves and twigs. We made out the pats of footsteps, the creaking of metal joints, and the sounds of breathing and sighing through metal pipes.

The sounds surrounded the house.

Something banged against the door. The captain yelped and sank into his chair. Embarrassed, he stood back up on the chair and forced his tears to stop, then tried to fill his face with strength so that he wouldn't look cute.

No more sounds came from the door. Instead, we heard footsteps and some large, round thing scraping against the bushes as it circled the house. A large shadow glistened dimly in the light from the room as it slid below the crystal window.

My eyes followed Mom's spirit. Mom had gotten up and walked along the walls of the room and kitchen. She smiled and stepped lightly as if dancing. Her steps matched the growling sounds of the monsters outside with almost perfect rhythm. Bending slightly, she stroked the necks and shoulders of the people inside.

Suddenly, Mom stopped and stood still, right behind the colonel. She stared at me as she slowly wrapped her arms around him. Her right hand slid into his gray suit and her left hand tickled the nape of his neck. She opened her mouth wide and bit into his neck with unrealistically long fangs.

A metal pipe clanged outside. Mom's spirit disappeared. The colonel flinched and lifted his shock pistol. He waved it around for a moment, then aimed the barrel at Cleïs.

"For heaven's sake, make that demon shut up! I can't stand it!"

Only then did I realize Cleïs had begun singing again. Short sounds were coming out of her one by one, seemingly at random, with no relation one to the other. It was the kind of thing that the captain had nicknamed a Webern lullaby. It sounded more like an English carillon or the beeps of an electric signal than a song. Anyway, she was murmuring softly enough that I could barely hear her over the noise from outside. Yet, the colonel acted as if she were shredding his being with her bare hands.

"Put the gun down please." I put myself between Cleïs and the colonel. "Cleïs is not my pet. She accompanies me but she doesn't follow my orders. Especially when she sings these songs. When she does this, we just have to listen."

"Please just make her be quiet," the colonel pleaded feebly.

"She's going to sing the song to the end whether we want her to or not. Where that end is, we won't know until she reaches it. When she sings other music, we can more or less guess at her meaning, but no one has a clue why she sings these Webern lullabies. The only thing I know is that this song has some very important meaning to her. It's just that what she thinks is important may not match our ideas of what's important. Bethlehemians operate according to their own logic. She could be communicating with those Linker machines outside right now. No, really, she might be! Whatever those things are, they might have come to meet Cleïs, not you."

"No, no, that's impossible!"

"Then why don't you go outside and find out? Isn't that why you came? Why are you hiding in here like a scared rabbit? Go outside! Go see for yourself!"

The colonel stared back and forth between my finger and the doorway it pointed towards. Finally, he stood and began to walk, his gait that of a lame dancer. Rational fear fought with the fanatical sense of religious mission within his tall body. As he walked, we could hear the panting of something large and metallic waiting for him on the other side of the door.

The instant he put his hand on the doorknob, Cleïs stopped singing. The noise from outside gradually lessened. As the colonel stood in front of the door, stiff as a statue, the noise outside melted into the sound of wind leaking through the gaps around the door.

The colonel opened the door.

There was nothing outside.

The colonel mustered his courage and slowly walked out. He stopped briefly in the middle of the yard as if waiting for someone on the other side of the trees to come welcome him. He stood for one minute, then another. When there was no reaction, he began to walk again.

We stood at the door and watched the colonel from behind as he slowly walked out of the yard. We continued watching until his silhouette was swallowed up by the darkness, leaving only silence behind.

10

The Roy Neary arrived in the harbor the next day, but not one of us boarded the ship. We all stayed inside the house until three flyers from the Rothbart Center landed in the yard that evening. Only one person rode in each flyer. The Center still feared the power of the island.

Thirty search flyers scoured the island. An hour into the search they located the corpse of the colonel on an ocean bluff. He held the shock pistol in his hand and his face was mangled. There was no evidence of a merge.

No Linker machines were discovered. We shared the sound recording and my video with the Center's people, but they doubted the evidence. The tracks of the monster dragging itself through the yard could not fully explain what we had felt of its existence at the time.

Digger's planned excavation site had been picked clean of all evidence. What had happened on Monsophiad had repeated itself on Leventon. Digger was disappointed but decided to stay on nonetheless. There was plenty he could do even with just the remaining fossils.

Unsurprisingly, Aelita refused to leave the island. She met with the people from the Center, signed a new contract, and moved her things into Hayes Blue's old room. I did not ask my older sister about her plans for the future. She did not know either. To her, staying on the island was more important. She would figure out the rest later. The last I saw of her before leaving the island, she was standing with Mom's spirit in the harbor watching the spirits of us as young sisters splash and play in the water. Or at least that's how it looked to me.

After returning to Jezebel, we set off for Wednesday. I tried to focus on navigating while the cook debriefed the doctor on the previous night's disturbance. But the sea was calm, and there wasn't much for me to do. I set the ship on autopilot and went out on deck with Cleïs.

I thought about the colonel. On our way to the harbor, the captain and I debated what the colonel's real plan could have been. The captain guessed he had wanted to use the Leventon phenomenon to infect the entire planet with the Word Worm. I thought he had aimed to merge with the Linker machines on Leventon and thereby preserve the Word. Perhaps it had been both. Or maybe his plan had been something else altogether. Maybe he'd never had a plan at all. He would have failed either way. When he put the pistol barrel to his face and pulled the trigger, what had he seen? I could not imagine it. Or rather, I could not decide among the many things that I did imagine.

I gazed at Leventon as it disappeared into the fog. For years, the island had been my prison and my entire world. For a while I had fully believed it to be the only source of hope on Crusoe. A place where humans had, perhaps, truly encountered another species, however briefly. Now it was just a pile of dirt stuck in the middle of the ocean. The force that had controlled the madness and dreams of Leventon no longer existed. I was free. My dreams were now entirely my own.

Cleïs sang. This time her song was like the warbling of a small bird. I gazed out toward where her eyes met the sea. I saw something like a huge bubble filled with small lifeforms floating out there. The small eyes of the lifeforms looked like those of the aquatic Waynes I had seen from the island. By the time I raised a pair of night binoculars for a better look, the bubble had disappeared.

HOGARTH

1

The cabin was falling apart, half its ceiling gone and its three remaining walls barely standing, but Forty-Two didn't mind. She sat down at the desk made of compressed seaweed and placed a heavy stone on the pile of paper she'd carried in with her to keep it from flying away in the wind that blew through the open window frame, which had long ago lost its crystal pane. She carefully removed a single page at a time from the stack and began to write on it with her metal stylus. Once she had completely filled both sides of a page with characters, she put it under another stone on her right side. Slowly but surely, the stack of paper on her right grew and the one on her left shrank.

Sometimes she would tear her eyes from the paper as if dissatisfied and glower through the broken wall at the world outside: the dull, treeless hill covered in brown grass and dotted here and there with square buildings and cabins. The bit of ocean visible through the window frame was slightly better, but still it was nothing but sea. No matter where one went on Hogarth Island, the scenery was always about the same.

Forty-Two scratched her silver hair as she examined

her draft. She underlined the sentences she thought were important and erased others with nearly enough force to rip the paper. When more of a page had been erased than not, she took out a new sheet of paper and rewrote it. She passed three hours in this manner, and at the end of it, not a single clean sheet of paper remained.

Once she was finished, Forty-Two stuck the stylus back into her necklace, carefully tied the papers into a sheaf with a ribbon, stuck the sheaf under her arm, and stood up. The chair drew an awkward curve as she pushed it backward, and she momentarily wondered if the unbalanced angle held any significance.

Holding the bundle to her chest and dragging her slippers on the ground, Forty-Two set off for Building Twelve. Soon she heard the sound of footsteps behind her. She knew who it was without needing to look. She lengthened her stride, trying to get away without appearing to have noticed him, but her plan came to naught when he called out to her in greeting.

"Forty-Two! I see you wrote quite a lot today, as usual," the manager said.

"Yes, I suppose," she replied.

"I've always been curious, why do you write on paper?"

"Because you confiscated my cell."

"We would lend you a word processor or voice recorder if you wanted, you know."

"But I prefer paper and pen. Anything I write with a machine doesn't feel like it belongs to me. I dislike the grammar and punctuation correction of word processors as well. Without a few typos and ungrammatical sentences, writing has no personality. Have you ever read Charles Darwin's handwritten manuscripts?" She quickened her pace in another attempt to leave him behind, but he again caught up to her.

"What did you write today?"

"A horror story. About a woman chased by the ghost of her dead husband."

"A real ghost?"

"What would you do if it were? Use it as evidence that I'm a severe Bethlehemian and send me to Building Five?"

"Why do you always take my words as threats? I'm familiar with Poe, and I read the Dickens short story you recommended to me recently."

"How was it?"

"I didn't understand the ending. Is it a ghost story, or a prophecy?"

"There's no answer to that. The important part is the incomprehensibility itself and the emotions it stirs in the reader."

"Is that the kind of story you're writing now?"

"What I'm writing is a true story. It's from a record left by an early twentieth-century German doctor that I once read on a library cube. I just transposed that story to here and took out the psychological analysis."

"Here? Crusoe?"

"Yes. Port Amman on Tuesday. I visited there once."

"Why Port Amman of all places?"

"For the sake of my readers. Think about how few of the readers here are actually from Earth. To people on Crusoe, Earth is nothing more than a fantasy. Especially the Earth of the past. Horror stories only work when set against a familiar background. That's how we give the supernatural events a realistic foundation."

"But that doesn't make any sense on Crusoe. There's not a place on this planet that is familiar to us. Most people here came from elsewhere, and even within the cities, the people and cultures are different. Where people have managed to establish local cultures and traditions, they haven't lasted long. To the people of Bansarti or Akuti, how is Port Amman any different from twentieth-century Germany? Everywhere we go is unfamiliar, and will be for our entire lives."

"I didn't realize this before, but you have a nice voice," she said sincerely.

"Huh?"

"It's like George Sanders's voice, a comforting bass."

The manager's red face grew redder.

They had arrived at the top of the hill. She could see the pale white faces of the inmates of Building Five through its windows. Like most of Crusoe, Building Five crawled with all sorts of people from all sorts of planets, and yet the inhabitants of that building shared an uncanny resemblance. They had all adopted the same facial expressions and mannerisms, as if participating in a mass game. From time to time, at no one's direction, they would sing unknown, complex choral harmonies. Hogarth was one of the few places on Crusoe where this was not met with disapproving stares. In many places now, choral singing was feared and hated.

Forty-Two walked along the narrow path between Buildings Four and Five, which rose like huge walls on either side. She crossed the square and climbed all the way to the north edge of the hill where Buildings Eleven, Twelve, and Thirteen stood in a line. The manager panted with each step as if exhausted by the ascent.

Unlike the other ten buildings, these three on the north

side were unlocked. The people living in them had fewer symptoms, weren't of interest to the manager, or were just using the island as a hideaway.

Building Twelve, where Forty-Two lived, was the most luxurious building in the Hogarth Bethlehemian Sanatorium. It had been the home of number One Hundred Thirty-Seven, the billionaire from Monday who had fled to Hogarth after nearly being caught in a mass lynching of Bethlehemians. The building's splendor had faded gradually in the four years since he had jumped to his death, but it remained the most comfortable place on the island.

Forty-Two's residence was a small room on the left side of the fourth floor of the building. The room faced northwest and glowed golden each evening as light from the setting sun shone through the window. She closed the curtains as soon as she entered and tossed the sheaf of papers onto the bed. The manager stood in the hallway and watched her, an idiotic expression on his face.

What on earth does that guy want from me, Forty-Two thought to herself. Is he hoping I'll go on a date with him? Will I have to sleep with him? The latter was not up for consideration. She knew how the people of planet Bertieu copulated and what their reproductive organs looked like. No matter how much control he had over her life, she would not willingly submit to that sort of ordeal.

"I'll be going then," the manager said finally, disappointment in his voice as he gave up waiting to be invited in. "Must get back to work. Fifty new patients came in this afternoon." He stood with his heels touching, bowed lightly to say goodbye, and left.

Forty-Two waited for the tapping of his heels on the

wooden floor of the corridor to fade before closing her door. She untied the ribbon from the sheaf of papers on the bed and read over her draft once more, then opened a wooden cabinet on the other side of the room. Inside the cabinet sat over twelve thousand sheets of paper in four stacks. The five thousand or so sheets of paper crowding the left side were filled on both sides with writing in pen and stylus, and the other seven thousand sheets were blank. She put her draft on top of the leftmost pile and closed the drawer.

The pile of paper and the stylus necklace were, aside from the room and number, the only things she had inherited from Old Paisel. He had written five and a half historical novels totaling around four thousand pages in his seven and a half years living here. After Old Paisel passed away and Forty-Two came to occupy the room; she had spent a month reading his stories before setting directly to work finishing his last novel.

Forty-Two did not stop writing after completing Paisel's sixth novel. She merely changed genres and length. Mostly she wrote short pieces, and she didn't confine herself to writing fiction. She penned essays on Eleanor Powell and jokes about bathroom culture in the old Roman empire when she wasn't busy writing pornographic short stories set on Calancia. Her pornographic output was considerable. She wrote about the sexual behavior of every single human subspecies documented in the library cube.

She didn't write for other people. Had someone said they were going to burn all of her papers, she wouldn't have batted an eye. To her, it was the act of writing itself that was important. Taking knowledge from the library cubes and reconstructing it as her own, through sentences she wrote herself. This was how she created herself and differentiated herself from the outside world.

The sun went down. The sky through her window looked as unreal as the matte painting of a Hollywood artist. The scattered masses of phosphorescing clouds were obviously the work of Guinesses. Rothbart Center researchers had flown up to the clouds several times to gather samples, but they hadn't yet been able to figure out why the clouds existed. All they knew was that the clouds had been gradually increasing since the appearance of the new Olivier on Saturday.

Once her room had grown completely dark, she left and went down to the cafeteria on the first floor. All the other residents of Building Twelve had already come down and were picking up their tins and bottles. She held a tray and stood in line behind Two-Hundred-Fourteen, who was fussing about a fantasy soccer match. She selected a soup made from a yellow vegetable, probably a descendent of spinach, B241 protein cubes, rumored to be the closest thing in taste to human flesh, and black coffee made by Sydney's company.

When she finished picking her food, she took her tray and found a place to sit down at the cafeteria tables. The protein cubes were merely bland, as expected. The soup was alright. The coffee was disappointing. It seemed Spack wasn't doing his job.

The cafeteria door opened and One-Hundred-Forty came in. A dirty brown cardigan and fur in colored patches like that of a milk cow covered her body. She led three newcomers inside. They had been assigned numbers 2134, 2135, and 2136. All new numbers. Hogarth's population really was increasing.

One-Hundred-Forty concluded her noisy introduction and the three newcomers dispersed around the cafeteria. There were the sounds of a tray rattling, a tin hitting the floor, and utensils clanging together. Forty-Two ignored them and concentrated on the unpleasant taste of the protein cubes and soup mixing in her mouth.

She heard the clomping of feet and a shadow appeared in front of her. One-Hundred-Forty had led one of the new patients up to her. She could see the number plate 2134 affixed with glue to the chest of the patient's jacket. She gave a half-hearted greeting and returned her attention to what remained of her soup, but One-Hundred-Forty grabbed her shoulder and shook her. Forty-Two raised her head, irritated, and 2134's face came into view.

The gray face of Fred Astaire was grinning down awkwardly at her.

"What did I say? You two are a set!" One-Hundred-Forty chortled.

2

"What are you doing here?" Forty-Two whispered.

"I've got business here," the doctor said, "but I should be asking you the same question. I thought you were somewhere on Thursday planning a massacre."

"I'm not Sydney anymore. They separated those memories from my identity when I arrived at the Wednesday branch of the Rothbart Center. They turned me into an amnesia patient with the memories of a wacko, and I've been living in that condition for eleven years now."

"Then, what are you now?"

"Beats me. And what would it matter if I knew?"

"But at least you don't seem to be interested in massacring anyone anymore."

"It's hard enough just taking care of my own body these

days." Forty-Two stood up with her tray, which now contained only empty tins and bottles. After placing it in the return window, she walked out of Building Twelve. The doctor put a biscuit tin in his pocket and followed her out.

"Do the hospital staff know you're not human?" The doctor asked carefully, after making certain no one could overhear them.

"No. When I got here, I made a kind of pact with the medical computer."

"But what about brain scans and such? This is a research facility."

"They're easy to fool. I'm not just an artificial intelligence, I'm a human brain simulation running on an AI. With a trick or two I can put the simulation into a state that scans as real. And anyway, Building Twelve patients aren't called out very often."

"You put on a convincing act of eating just now."

"It wasn't an act. I was really eating. The computer inside my skull thinks my entire body, not just my brain, is actually human. At mealtime, I actually feel hungry. And when I'm tired, I crave sweets. I even combust what I eat and gain a bit of energy from it, though it's horribly inefficient."

"So what have you been up to?"

"I spent a while at the research center, and a while in other places. And now I've been here at Hogarth for a while. Three days ago marked the end of my third year here."

"And how has that been?"

"You really want to know?"

"Yes. We've got plenty of time."

Forty-Two snorted. "When the Bethlehemian Liberation War on Saturday ended, I was taken to the research center on

Wednesday. I think they wanted to learn more about Sydney from me. But Sydney wasn't Sydney because he was smarter or knew more than others. And besides, my memories were limited to the ones he had chosen. I had no more than about a quarter of his actual memories. Sydney had made me a single-use tool for one particular job, and I was of no use to the researchers. I think they debated whether to dissect me or just leave me as I was, and leaving me alone won out in the end. Later I heard that Bo had advocated for me before he left the research center."

"And then what happened?"

"The treatment to change my Sydney memories from first to third person threw my identity into confusion. Who was I? Was I human or machine? Was I Sydney, or someone else? If someone else, then who? That sort of thing. After pondering those questions for a year, I left the research center. I thought I was escaping, but seeing how no one came after me, I guess I was just allowed to leave.

"The first thing I did after leaving was look for others like me. I thought that if I had a quarter of Sydney's memories, then there must be others somewhere with the remaining three quarters. I searched Sydney's memories to trace the whereabouts of each of the Bellocian humanoid dolls imported to Crusoe, but it was a waste of time. The rest were all just sex dolls, not robots. In the end, you were right. Sydney hadn't been interested in preserving himself. My confidence and belief turned out to be just a fantasy.

"I was angry. Especially at Sydney. He had made me believe he had given me everything, when really I was no more than a disposable fork to him. That pissed me off. Because I was mad at Sydney, I was mad at everyone on Crusoe. If I had been handed another opportunity to trigger a massacre, I would have pressed the button without hesitation. But I was never given a second chance.

"Somewhere along the way, I began to feel an affinity with machines. Especially Linker machines. I traveled around Crusoe trying to meet with almost every Olivier and begging them to merge with me. But they weren't really interested in me. That, or I didn't measure up to their standards. Who knows. Most of the time the Coopers wouldn't let me near the Oliviers, and even when I did manage to approach, nothing happened. To them I was probably no different from all the other humans in the area.

"I started to hang out with those religious cultists who worship the Linker machines. You know the kind—the ones who think that merging is the path to eternal life or nirvana. If you try to get information about the Oliviers, you can't help but run into those cults. Besides, at that point I really wasn't any different from them. Aside from not being human.

"Thinking back now, I don't know why it sounded so plausible back then. What do we even know about merging? Who knows whether the self still exists after the merge. Maybe they only take the information they need and delete all the rest. Or maybe all they really need is the fat from our brains.

"The cultists were staying at Borodingrad in southern Thursday because they wanted to be near the new Olivier that had appeared on Saturday. It was a perilous situation. The Bethlehemian Resistance had just landed on the continent and was pushing up from the south. The Crimson Jihad, pressed by the Church Mafia, was coming down from the north. Ever since the Death March, everyone has been in a killing mood. At that time, the city alliance was on the verge of collapse. Then there were the Bethlehem worshippers and adventurers who showed up to try and build a new spaceport... But even with all that, I think we were really enjoying the excitement at the time, because we weren't terribly attached to the world anyway.

"It was four years ago that I first realized something strange was happening. One by one, people started to disappear. At first, I didn't think anything of it. People left now and then because things were so perilous, and others died in Crimson Jihad raids. It wasn't unusual for a few people to be missing at dinner each evening. Anyway, out of the original twelve hundred believers who had settled at Borodingrad, we were eventually reduced to about four hundred. The rest had gone down to Saturday or given up and gone home.

"Yet as people continued to disappear one by one, it became clear that the recent disappearances were all close friends of a guy named Akili, who was one of the most fanatical believers. There was something suspicious about how quietly they were all disappearing. I grew curious and tailed Akili. And that's how I saw what I saw."

"What?"

"I saw Akili stab his roommate to death, then dig out the roommate's left eye with his knife and eat it." Forty-Two shivered as if she could actually raise her body temperature that way.

"At the time I didn't know why Akili had gone crazy. But after returning to my dorm undetected, I studied the others. The situation looked bad. About one in ten had the same expression as Akili and they were stealing glances at their friends or lovers with a mixture of determination and bewitchment on their faces. With each passing day I noticed new disappearances and more people with that particular expression. I thought it must be some disease. Some disease that they could get but I couldn't was spreading through the dorm."

"The Word Worm?"

"Yes. At the time I didn't even know there was such a thing. It was several months before the assassination of Carlos Del Rio. The Word Worm had already evolved to carrier stage by then. Anyway, it had already dropped the unstable textual basis and now just served to strengthen conviction. You know what happens when something like that falls into the heads of religious fanatics? Their doctrine gets scrambled. Imagine a vampire, zombie, and werewolf in the same room, all biting each other. It was a spectacle, but not one you'd want to see.

"The Word Worm spreading in Borodingrad only had two Words attached to it: "Kill" and "Eat." These were added on top of all the beliefs already controlling Borodingrad and acted as a kind of catalyst. When the new beliefs carried on the worms conflicted with existing beliefs, people could more or less get by just by faithfully following the "Kill" and "Eat" commands. It didn't really matter how they understood those words. Most people just understood them in their most primitive meaning. The order wasn't particularly important either."

"I heard that the Church Mafia planted a worm with a self-extermination text to kill the Crimson Jihad. It made them kill and eat each other."

"That sounds like something they'd do. I don't know if it's true though.

"It hasn't been proven, but it makes sense. The second place where the Word Worm spread was six hundred kilometers away from Saint-Colombe. For an artificial parasite that spreads through drinking water to suddenly reappear that far away without any infections in between... Clearly it had been repurposed as a religious weapon after failing in its original mission to strengthen belief. Well, it was partially successful. Sixty percent of the Crimson Jihad on Thursday were killed and eaten by their comrades."

"And half the Church Mafia on Thursday too."

"That's what you get for playing with an uncontrollable microbe. It was ridiculous for them to ever believe that the worm could somehow distinguish between Crimson Jihad and Church Mafia."

"Even if it had been able to differentiate, that wouldn't have helped, at least not in Borodingrad. People who escaped from Borodingrad described the place as turning into hell, but at the time it was strangely tranquil. Sure, it was full of people-eating ghosts and corpses were piled up in the streets. Like I said, the chaos of the initial infection was terrible. Yet, the religious conflict that had been part of the city when we first arrived gradually disappeared as the contagion spread. Perhaps due to the worm's influence, the people seemed unable to feel fear or disgust toward the situation. They calmly killed, were killed, ate, and were eaten. That's why it was common for people who couldn't stand the fear to purposely drink polluted water and infect themselves. And that's also why the infection spread through Borodingrad so quickly. Everyone believed in some variety of nirvana or transcendence, and the Word Worm appeared as something that could help them along that path.

"Were I a real person, I might have drank some worm

egg-laden water myself. But I'm not. Even had I wanted to go crazy like the others, I couldn't have. All I could do was be careful that I didn't get stabbed in the back by someone I knew, and look for a way to escape.

"That's when I met Hasha.

"Hasha belonged to a group of Bethlehemian worshippers. But she wasn't a fanatic like the others. She was a scientist. According to Hasha, the Bethlehemian Resistance is quite a rare phenomenon. There are many planets populated with only Bethlehemians, yet as far as Hasha knew, never before had Bethlehemians who shared a planet with other races and cultures tried to form a political force, much less succeeded.

"Hasha wasn't interested in all Bethlehemians. Ordinary people don't really differentiate between Bethlehemians and normal mental patients. To them, Bethlehemians are just people who've had their brains changed in unusual ways by Linker evolution. But the ones whom Bethlehemian worshippers follow are unusual among Bethlehemians in that they act as if they had achieved nirvana. Hasha was interested in this type of Bethlehemian: ones who have a certain pattern to their thinking and action that we simply can't comprehend. While the meaning of the pattern is beyond comprehension, the thinking and actions are maintained precisely because they seem to miraculously protect the people involved. If I remember correctly, your engineer was of a similar type, wasn't she?

"Hasha had been obsessed with the Bethlehemian question since before she was trapped on Crusoe. She was drawn to the existence of a mysterious pattern of human consciousness that lay beyond the ordinary spectrum, and thought that by following the Bethlehemians she might be able to understand it. That was what had given her the courage to leave the safety of her home planet and travel the universe.

"Hasha changed me. Until her, I had been lazy. I had just wanted to abdicate responsibility and dump my own existence on someone else's shoulders. But then I saw Hasha walk into Lofoten Square wearing her red pressure suit and backpack and singing 'Always Look on the Bright Side of Life' in her quavering voice, not minding that the square had been dyed dark red by the blood flowing from the ghouls' mouths as they ate the internal organs of their friends and lovers, and that's when I knew I had to do something. I didn't know what, though. Hasha had to tell me.

"Hasha planned to go down to Saturday. She would meet the Bethlehemians there and create a language to connect them, us, and the Grandinians on a psychological continuum. That's how I understood it anyway. Hasha's concept was based on English, but because it had changed with the psychology of the Grandinians, it wasn't easy for me to grasp. Even the basic concept of language itself may have been completely different to them. Hasha said I would understand it better if I changed the artificial intelligence behind my simulation, but we didn't have the appropriate tools for that, and it would have been quite risky, so we had to abandon the idea.

"Hasha told me about the planet Grandin. It started out as a sanatorium for autistics. Hasha told me how it turned into a world of high-functioning autistics, the sanatorium's doctors and nurses among them, how their psychological identity formed over the century during which the Linker Universe merged, and how they regulated their internal diversity and designed the Grandin planet to match.

"Hasha also talked about other planets that she had either

visited directly or learned about from the cube. She spoke of how diverse human psychology had become over the course of Linker evolution and how wonderful that diversity had made the descendants of humanity as they spread through the Linker Universe. To Hasha, the Bethlehemians spreading across the Milky Way were humanity's true pioneers. And leading that settlement process were certain individuals who had arrived at what Hasha called the Omega level.

"She didn't mean the concept theorized by Pierre Teilhard de Chardin. Grandinian scientists didn't believe in a limit or end point to evolution. Such a concept made as little sense in the Linker Universe as it did in the Darwinian one. To Grandinian scientists, Omega signified not the end of evolution but the front line of human psychological diversity. Omega was not a particular point; it was a frontier that was continuously pushed forward as all sorts of new Omegas arose further beyond. The boringly named planet Williams that had been Hasha's ultimate destination was one place where a group of such Omegas lived. She had been only twenty-eight light years away from it when bad luck dropped her on Crusoe.

"Hasha believed that a group of Omegas had led the Bethlehemian Liberation War. To Hasha this was merely a scientific hypothesis, not a messianic belief. She had carefully studied the Liberation War and confirmed that gaps in our understanding existed at each critical juncture. Grandinian scientists had built a considerable database of information about Bethlehemians, and Hasha assembled indirect evidence that Omegas could fill those gaps in understanding. To confirm this hypothesis, Hasha had to go down to Saturday. And she would have gotten there had the Bethlehemian worshippers not mistaken her for a saint and imprisoned her along the way.

"I decided to help Hasha. Thinking back now, I actually hadn't given much serious thought to the merging problem before that point. My memories from Sydney would have allowed me to find my own way down to Saturday, had I really wanted to go. But I suppose I liked the chaos of Borodingrad and had wanted to settle down there instead. It wasn't until the city turned into the ghouls' paradise and Hasha appeared and wanted my help that I found I didn't need to stay there any longer.

"Once I made up my mind, I didn't hesitate. I hacked into the Rothbart Center's address book and found the contact information of key figures in the Resistance Army who had received help from Sydney during the Liberation War. Most of them declared themselves to be normal people and had left Saturday as soon as the Liberation War ended. Fortunately, I was able to contact someone who lived on the south coast of Thursday and continued to work on the front lines of the Bethlehemian Liberation. You've probably heard of him: Amal Hasan Murcas."

"What? Bernburg still lives there?"

"He's probably dead by now. He was severely ill when I contacted him. He had come down with brain flu and lost control of the left side of his body. But he helped us buy a boat and a permit to pass through territory occupied by the Bethlehemian Liberation Front and get to Saturday.

"As we departed on the boat, Murcas left us with a grave warning: 'Don't expect to see the Saturday of a few years ago. It's entirely different now. The Bethlehemian comrades who fought alongside me back then have also entirely changed. I still go from time to time but I no longer know how or to what end the people there are living. All I can say is that I'm proud I contributed to making that world.'"

"How cliche."

"Exactly, it was like something right out of a movie or novel. The brave adventurer sets out for the Olivier at the south pole and suddenly encounters an eccentric old man who says, 'There's something here that you don't understand....'

"But what else could he have said? The Bethlehemian Liberation War was the only thing of value he had done in his whole life. He had founded a country. How can you expect him to believe that as soon as the war was over it would become a playground for the insane? Even if he had believed it, he'd still have said the same thing."

"Why is it that Linker machines like the south pole so much?"

"Supposedly, on the Linker homeworld, the south pole was originally the north pole. That's why people say they're the product of a civilization where hemispheres rotate like hands of a clock. But I think there's some other reason. I don't think Linker machines have that strong a sense of culture. Hasha had a theory of her own, but she couldn't properly explain it. Well, that or I couldn't properly understand her explanation.

"The journey to Saturday took us three days. If our motor hadn't broken along the way we could have made it in two. But Hasha and I both were completely new to boats and understood them only in theory. It was a miracle that we made it to Saturday without any disasters.

"At first glance, Normandy Beta didn't seem to have changed much. The area around the harbor remained thick with the sea thorn branches, and the shabby village nearby bustled with people just as before. The only thing that had changed was that the Bethlehemians, still wearing army uniforms, had supplanted the merchants. Everyone was busy preparing for war with Thursday.

"To me they didn't seem particularly different from us, though it wasn't really the right environment to observe a difference. No matter how different their thinking may have been from ours, there's still only one way to walk on two legs, fly a plane, or shoot a rifle.

"While undergoing an inspection, I ran into a Bethlehemian officer whom I remembered from before. He recalled with amusement one bit of trouble I had instigated, and harbored no grudge against me. To the contrary, he thought it might have been easier for them had I succeeded. That some of his brethren might have died as a result of the trouble didn't even cross his mind.

"His name was Durstan. Unlike the other Bethlehemians who lived through the Liberation War, he hadn't belonged to the German or Soviet armies. He'd come to Saturday to liberate his comrades. He spoke and acted so naturally that he didn't seem the least bit Bethlehemian. He told us a group of people like him occupied the entire north pole continent of his home planet of Fingal. The difference between his people and normal people was emotion. His kind didn't experience negative emotions like anger and sadness, and felt happiness only weakly. Instead, their motivations were created by the combination of two conflicting emotions they called 'Ayuteri' and 'Jin.' The result seemed not so different from us. They ultimately acted in ways similar to us, it was just the interior experience forming the basis of those actions that was completely different from ours.

"Durstan told me how Saturday had changed during my absence. Most of the Bethlehemians now lived together at Normandy Alpha and Beta, and a group of high-functioning Bethlehemians plus a small number of normal people held all the power. They were the ones starting the war now. The rest of the people, who couldn't live normal lives in the ordinary environment of Crusoe, gathered together and built villages here and there with people like themselves.

"Hasha asked Dustan about Omegas. At first, he didn't understand what she meant. I had to explain a bit in my own words before he nodded his head in seeming comprehension. 'Sounds like you're talking about Lieutenant General Yefremov and his group. Those guys are freaky even by our standards. We encounter all sorts of freaks here, and you'd think we'd get used to it, but those guys are really something else. Being Bethlehemian just means your brain biology is different to the point of having different opinions and perspectives. It can seem unpleasant or confusing to you normals, but it isn't incomprehensible. But Yefremov and those guys are completely different. They're so different I can't even explain it. Anyway, recently they've created something like a religion. They're living together in the old German headquarters now, where the new Olivier was born. I've heard that lots of weird stuff has been happening there recently.'

"'Weird how?' I asked.

"'So weird that it's impossible to explain in words. We all want to create a new spaceport, right? But they're blocking us from above. Occasionally spaceport pioneers manage to fly through their defensive perimeter, but they're always caught, imprisoned, and sent back out. Having heard the stories they tell, I don't want to go there either. There's something extremely wrong happening there,' Durstan said.

"With his help we found a vehicle in the black market warehouse that was more or less usable: a former smuggler's Schwimmwagen that had been modified with huge wide tires for Saturday's muddy terrain. We filled it up with all of the biofuel we had brought with us on the boat and set out for the German headquarters in search of Lieutenant General Yefremov and his group.

"Once we put Normandy Beta behind us, all we could see were ruins. Destroyed buildings, sets that had originally been built as ruins, downed Horlas, destroyed tanks, and burnt, mutilated, frozen, decayed corpses. It wasn't that the people of Borodingrad hadn't known how to get to Saturday. It was that they'd known what awaited them if they went, and had preferred to stay in Borodingrad instead, even as they continued to talk about Saturday.

"Hasha looked calmer than she had in Borodingrad. Linker machines weren't as scary as the insane residents of Borodingrad. It even seemed like Hasha knew something we didn't about the Linker machines. Although there was a clearly faster way, she was set on taking a counterclockwise spiral to get there. Later I investigated whether there was some meaning in the direction we took, but I found nothing. It's possible it held no meaning at all. It may have just been luck that we didn't run into any Waynes along the way and arrived at the Olivier without trouble.

"What bothered me was something else. For maximum travel efficiency, I thought I should treat my body as much as possible as a machine. By eating and sleeping less, and ignoring the environment around me. But it didn't go as I expected. I remained hungry and sleepy, and my body rhythms were a mess under the midnight sun. My mind stubbornly recognized only my imagined body of flesh and blood, even though that body didn't exist. I tried everything I could to free my mind from such thinking, but ultimately I had to give up. Ridiculous, isn't it? I was the machine with an artificial intelligence, but really Hasha was the one who thought and acted like a machine.

"I don't know much about what Saturday was like before. Sydney had gone there twice, and I remembered his first trip clearly. But he had boarded an Horla immediately upon arrival at Normandy Beta and flown to the resistance base. So he hadn't had time to observe the continent closely. Although Saturday was my home, in a sense, I had always been treated like a criminal and never allowed to go outside.

"However, I couldn't help but realize that something was strangely different now. The strangest thing was the sky. Two streams of fluorescent clouds drew a huge spiral outward from the south pole. Here and there, black plant stalks stuck out of the mud and melting snow. From time to time, these sprayed the air with a scent like air freshener. These stalks become more artificial-looking the closer we came to the German headquarters. At first, they looked like Japanese yews carefully trimmed for a French garden, but later they morphed into looking almost like buildings or machines, and blended in naturally with the Guinness structures around them.

"Every once in a while, huge bird-like contraptions skimmed over our heads. They were Horlas painted with camouflage to resemble German armored vehicles on the Eastern front, but instead of the tilted Hakenkreuz of the Nazis, their wings were marked by the perpendicular swastika that had been used by Buddhist groups on Earth. They flew around like frolicking children, frequently hurtling straight upward and disappearing into the clouds like rockets.

"Finally we reached what used to be the German headquarters. The German Headquarters of Sydney's memories was long gone. Its tanks and wombs were gone, too. Most of the roof was missing and what remained of the building was covered in what looked like layers of black netting.

"The Olivier's house was a bright white tower that rose like a stone phallus from the center of the former headquarters site. Objects like small Adjanis flitted around the tower. On closer inspection, these turned out to be not Adjanis but Horlas—the same Horlas we had run into on our way there. It was creepy. It wasn't impossible, but something about it was wrong.

"It took a little while for me to realize why I felt that way. The scene before our eyes was a too-plausible fiction. The Horlas circling the Olivier's tower were obviously mimicking Adjanis. What does that remind you of? Right, a cargo cult. It looked like something inside the tower was casting spells with its fake Adjanis to lure in flying creatures. If so, was the thing inside that looked like an Olivier tower really an Olivier? And where were Lieutenant General Yefremov and his group right now?

"We waited for a bit inside our Schwimmwagen, hoping someone would notice us and come out to greet us or warn us away. It didn't matter whether that someone was Yefremov's people, Coopers, or Waynes.

"But nothing happened.

"After hesitating for a while, we chose a door and entered

the ruin. The inside was covered with the same black netting material as the outside. It felt elastic to the touch like rubber. I remembered that on Sydney's home planet of Glendale, Guinesses made a material like this to cover objects that Waynes had plundered.

"The interior of the ruin was a purposeful labyrinth of twisted, winding corridors and rooms with multiple doors. But Hasha had an extremely precise sense of direction and didn't seem worried. While I, a cutting edge robot with plenty of extra capacity beyond what I was using to simulate a human brain, floundered along in confusion, Hasha strode confidently inward.

"As we walked, I felt the sky grow darker. At first, I thought it must be clouds. But that wasn't it. I could see glittering stars appearing one after another through the loose netting that covered the building in place of the destroyed roof. The closer we approached the Olivier, the darker the sky grew. When we finally arrived at the white door connected to the tower, the sky was black as a winter night.

"We went in. It was pitch dark. Hasha turned on the flashlight on her cell, but it barely illuminated even the space around us. I screamed. My voice did not echo. I stepped back along the way we had come, but the door and wall we had come through were long gone. All we could sense was the floor, and even that we weren't entirely sure about.

"Gradually I realized that we weren't the only people in the building. At first, I couldn't see anyone. Yet, bit by bit, at the edges of my vision, I began to sense someone emitting a white light. Every time I turned my head to check, one more ghost appeared at the very edges of my vision. Suddenly, I realized that we were surrounded by strangers.

"They frightened me. First, because they didn't seem to occupy any space. They were clearly in front of my eyes, but if I stuck out my hand to touch them, it was as if my hand brushed passed at an odd angle and missed them. As if they were two-dimensional, although they appeared to be three. Second, I couldn't discern their faces. I seemed able to see their eyes, noses, mouths, skin color, and various other features clearly, but I couldn't assemble these bits of information together into faces.

"They spoke. I couldn't tell who was speaking, but there was only one voice. The words were all English and seemed to be arranged according to some grammar, but I couldn't understand what they meant. The voice seemed slightly angry, but that might just have been me. I couldn't know whether they were really angry.

"Hasha was just as frightened as me. Her fear was more obvious, because she didn't know how to hide her emotions. She hadn't come this far due to a lack of fear. The opposite, actually. It was just that, to Hasha, 'normals' and Saturday's 'Bethelehemians' were both equally incomprehensible objects of fear. She would have confronted the fanatics in Borodingrad had it been within her power.

"Hasha opened her mouth first. She cried out in a loud, parched voice, 'Can you understand me?'

"We heard a clatter spread out like a wave. It seemed at first, like the sound of laughter. However, real laughter would not have sounded so emotionless and mechanical.

"Hasha didn't give up. She kept trying, in different ways, to talk with them. One by one she tried out Bethlehemian languages that used English vocabulary in different ways. As she did, the people slowly gathered around her, and she gradually raised her voice.

"I stayed where I was. I couldn't see what was happening around Hasha. But that was Hasha's business. It wasn't something for me to interfere with. I thought about other things. I thought about the irrationality that surrounded us. Why was this new frontier of human psychology, witnessed by so few in the Milky Way, so familiar? Why did I feel like I had seen these strange things before?

"A thought occurred to me. Many people had written stories about unknown realms that the Linker machines didn't want to show us. To stir a sense of wonder in us, these authors most often distorted space-time. The second most common technique was to introduce the existence of some intelligence that thought or acted in a way that was beyond the capacity of human language to describe. And it wasn't only authors; braggarts used these methods too. Don't you understand? The extreme, meaningless unfamiliarity that I felt was itself a cliche.

"From that point onward, I felt like we were standing in front of the Wonderful Wizard of Oz. I felt that something was hiding behind that artificial strangeness and toying with us. That what I saw was at most just an illusion of an explanation. I also understood why I couldn't discern the ghost faces right in front of me. What I until then had believed my eyes were seeing amounted to nothing more than the sentence, 'several ghosts are standing in front of me.' The sentence told me that the ghosts were there, but no matter how many adjectives I added to it, I would never be able to clearly see what they looked like.

"Once I arrived at that point in my thoughts, I couldn't stand it anymore. I began to wave my hands at the ghosts, skip, and sing: 'We're off to see the Wizard, the Wonderful Wizard of Oz!'

"In that instant, light returned. I sprinted around the Olivier tower like a madwoman. The spiral stairs leading up to the top were attached to the wall, and the interior was completely empty. Summer sunlight came through the windows. Hasha and the ghosts were nowhere to be seen. It had all been fake. Even Hasha, who had been at my side until just moments ago! Clearly at some point I and Hasha had begun to see different illusions and had reacted differently. Had Hasha also seen hallucinations? Or had Hasha seen reality while only I was stuck in hallucination?

"A scraping sound came from somewhere on the southwest stairs. I thought I glimpsed a small, yellow hand that looked like Hasha's close the door and disappear. I ran that way. But on the other side of the door was just another spiral staircase almost identical to the one on the outside. I ran up it.

"I arrived at the top floor to find four Coopers shaped like faceless quadrupedal animals guarding the Olivier in the center of the floor. Through the broken windows on all four sides, I could see the Horlas flying around imitating Adjanis. Looking down below, I saw Guinnesses working in the ruins, behind walls that had previously hidden them from me.

"But I didn't see Hasha anywhere.

"I spent ten days combing through the Olivier tower and the ruins of the German headquarters. I mapped the labyrinth. I named all the terrestrial creatures around the tower. I investigated all the holes through which Hasha and Yefremov's group could have disappeared. My brain warned me I could not keep going without food or sleep, but I ignored it. In the end, my computer turned me off. Maybe it got mad at me for continuing my games beyond the point where I could keep up.

"I woke up rebooted five days later, hungry and suffering a migraine. That and a heavy sense of despair pressed down on me. Hasha wasn't there. Yefremov's group wasn't there. Whether they had died or jumped to another dimension, they were all gone. Only I, a stupid, slow-witted machine, was left behind.

"I drove the Swimmwagen back to Normandy Beta. I passed two Bethlehemian villages along the way, but learned nothing from them. They looked like mental hospitals. Not a single person was sufficiently mentally intact to tell me what had happened to Lieutenant General Yefremov and his group. They told me all sorts of fantastic stories, but they were nothing more than stories.

"At Normandy, I boarded a Free Ship Alliance vessel to Isola Bella. I couldn't think of any other place that was nearby and safe. Sydney's idiot son was still playing Star Trek games in the house he had inherited, apparently. He had even formed a special team at the company to push a new Klingon Bloodwine product. It was nothing I wanted to get involved with. At first, I thought it was a good idea. It's good to reflect your interests in your work, right? And there are tons of Trekkies on this planet.

"I rented a room near the sea, shut myself in, and spend several days submerged in thought. I thought about Hasha, Yefremov, Bethlehemians, Oliviers, and Adjanis, and tried to figure out how they were all connected.

"Then I was struck by another thought. It hadn't only been me and Hasha there in the tower. Someone else, someone with a rational psyche, had been there too. My computer, I mean, the thing that holds my human psyche. I'm no more than a robot dreaming human dreams. But my computer is different. While I was being tricked by the hallucination, the computer was observing what really happened inside the tower.

"So I began looking for ways to contact it. I gathered all the information I could find on the computers of planet Bellocio. I tried all the hypothesized ways of communicating with my 'outer psyche.' There were side effects; I did all sorts of crazy things. Then Isola Bella's militia mistook me for a Bethlehemian and sent me here.

"Oh, I think I know what you're going to say. But you'd better not make some joke about me doing theological research or whatever. No matter how guilty I may be, it's not so bad that I have to tolerate such jokes.

"Now it's your turn. How's the world out there? What have you been doing all these years? Why did you come here?"

3

The doctor stood up silently and gazed at Forty-Two's gray eyes. The sound of waves coming in from the other side of Building Twelve and the voices of the inmates of Building Five singing a chorus combined to form an awkward sort of background music. The phosphorescing clouds and the moon, which seemed especially large, illuminated them like stage lighting.

How could the world seem so fake?

Unable to bear it, he began to whistle "The Way You Look Tonight" and walked past Forty-Two. Forty-Two, made anxious by his lack of answer, followed. They chose a dirt path at random and walked aimlessly, not knowing where they were headed.

What should he say? The doctor was, for the first time in his life, at a loss for words. He didn't want to talk about the mass slaughter he had witnessed at Tritonia Beach during the Death March. Nor did he want to talk about how the people of Monte Grande had been incinerated by Coopers in retaliation for attacking an Olivier. He didn't want to talk about how Bayan Purple had died in the Ilia sea war, or the laziness that had gotten Jezebel caught up in that war to begin with. He didn't want to talk about the confused fight that ensued when the Church Mafia fanatics from Saint-Colombe, having lost their grammatical subjects to the Worm, boarded the deck of the Jezebel. He didn't want to talk about the fact that over the last decade he had gotten sick and tired of the world, his temper had worsened, and he had grown old and no longer saw the world as a playground.

"Well?" Forty-Two stepped in front of him and blocked his path.

The doctor stopped whistling and gazed into the space between the tree branches to avoid her eyes. Annoyed, she tapped him on his chest. He gave up and pulled a small paper book from his pocket, sneaking a glance at his wristwatch as he did so. Forty-Two grabbed the book from him and read the title, then returned it to him with a confused expression on her face. "The Mystery of Edwin Drood. I know Dickens too. So what?"

"Read the ending again."

Forty-Two re-read the final page. An ambiguous gray wrinkle appeared between her eyebrows. "Is this some sort of Maria Wutz-style joke?" She asked.

"No. It's real. At least we think it is. Although these days, we doubt whether 'real' has any meaning."

"They still don't know who the criminal is though."

"Of course. It's only about two thousand words longer than the version we know. Even so, it is Dickens's work. In that world, he lived that much longer. There are little differences here and there throughout the work, but nothing major."

"Where did you get it?"

"On an island called Leventon. It's the first mate's hometown. Her uncle bound it and hid it in his library, and her sister found it there much later. There were plenty of other interesting books, too. Have you heard of the version of The Magic Flute in which Sarastro plays the villain?

"We found traces of spaceships from parallel universes similar to ours on Leventon and in the Monsophiad Jungle. A spaceship called Maria Theresia was sent from the United Austro-Prussian Empire in year 2245 of the Western calendar. The ship threaded its way through layers of parallel universe to land here fifty thousand years ago. Linker evolution occurred on this planet for a brief period following the ship's arrival, then ceased.

"The ship is long gone. We've only found traces of it, but even so, we know quite a lot. On its journey, the ship encountered and merged with an alien intelligence. And that alien intelligence is quite similar to the species we call the Linker machines, yet different. Think of Linker machines without the differentiation into terrestrial and flying types. They've been buried for tens of thousands of years and only recently became active again."

They were now walking on top of the hill in front of Building Twelve. Jagged trees stuck up through spaces between the piles of crumbled stones on the beach, giving it an untidy and precarious look.

"Think about it. Until now, the known universe has been entirely Linker territory. And now, on this planet, there's another species growing and preparing to make themselves known, a species that can stand up to the Linkers. Even more surprising, they seem capable of some kind of tenuous connection with us. They merged with that ship built on Earth in 2245. In their universe, humanity managed to build spaceships equivalent to Garbos before coming under Linker attack. Consider what their relationship to humans must have been. What if we could meet humans from that universe? Or if some of them are already here?"

"So what? What does that all have to do with your coming here?"

"I came because Maria Theresia's Olivier is here."

He kicked a stone that had caught his foot. The stone started a small avalanche as it rolled down the hill to the beach.

"You must know about Rrose Sélavy because of that trick Sydney had Bayan Purple play on it. Sydney used Rrose Sélavy as a disposable tool to fire a missile at the McKinsey Bloc slaughterhouse.

"Our captain, who stole into Rrose Sélavy at the time, told me a strange story about it. A small Olivier had hidden itself inside Rrose Sélavy and controlled its neural network. We didn't know what to make of it at the time. At first, we thought it might have been part of some plot by Sydney or Bayan Purple. But it turned out that neither of them knew anything about it. Anyway, we weren't sure it was really all that strange. Sure, Oliviers did not often parasite off boats, but it wasn't impossible. Like catching a hard-core vegetarian sneaking bites of a hamburger.

"The rest of us tried to forget it, but the captain couldn't, because of his history with Rrose Sélavy. For the first few years after he escaped from the ship, he tried to forget about it entirely, but after the mutiny he grew obsessed once again. He had an old friend aboard who contacted him weekly and informed him of what was going on, though he didn't tell us this. He carefully combed over captains' logs copied from the ship, looking for information about how the Olivier made it on board, to no avail. Stranger still was that after the mutiny, the Olivier could no longer be found. The mutineers and the informant all scoured the ship, but the room where the captain had seen the Olivier was empty and they couldn't find any trace of it. So they didn't believe the captain's story.

"Things seemed to go well on Rrose Sélavy at first. They selected a new command and changed the operational style. They gave up their city status, greatly reduced the crew, and changed their business from war to chemical manufacturing with ocean resources and trading. Everyone worked hard, and they turned a profit in their first year.

"It was the following year that the boat began to turn strange. At first, the crew experienced a vague disruption of their senses. Their own rooms and the corridors they always walked down felt unfamiliar. The ship started to feel like it was always off-balance. The crew complained of inexplicable dizziness, headaches, and of feeling like someone was watching them behind their backs.

"At first, people thought it was a side effect of the chemicals coming out of the factory. But the situation changed when one meticulous crewmember protested that his room had actually shrunk by two centimeters. Once he'd opened that can of worms, similar complaints came from all directions. According to the blueprints in the main computer, however, everything was just as it always had been. Was this evidence that they had all gone crazy? Or did it mean that there was an elaborate plot involving the forging of fake blueprints in the computer?

"They started carrying around tape measures, homemade cameras, and paper notebooks to carefully record changes in the ship. Rooms shrunk and expanded, corridors slowly changed shape and direction. Here and there, new rooms appeared, and previously fine rooms disappeared. Yet, these changes were not visible from their pictures and the measurements in their notebooks. The numbers they clearly remembered having written down were different from the ones they later read back. They then tried to memorize the measurements, but that didn't work well either.

"Despite what the blueprints and notebooks said, the ship gradually changed. One third of the chemical factory started making something else, and unidentifiable tubes grew in the ship's vents. They heard heavy creatures moving behind the walls. Rrose Sélavy was changing from a Kitty-Hawk class aircraft carrier into a huge metal monster.

"They began to seriously reconsider what the captain had said. Obviously something hiding in Rrose Sélavy was causing the ship to change. They couldn't be certain it was an Olivier, though, because Oliviers usually didn't work this way.

"The first thing they did was shut off all power in the ship. As predicted, the ship continued just as before. They tried and failed to figure out the energy source that kept their equipment running. Everyone who approached the energy source disappeared, and soon after their disappearance, the remaining crew members' memories of them vanished as well. Even though the remaining crew knew that their numbers were shrinking one by one, they couldn't remember keep track of who was disappearing.

"They were scared. They tried to go to Christina, where they had received citizenship after the mutiny, to ask for help. But the ship was now moving of its own accord. They couldn't contact the outside world, and the ship had already converted the escape craft to some other purpose.

"Several tried to escape using primitive methods. Someone made a raft out of waterproof canvas. Another made a hot air balloon. Some of them even made a flyer. No one knows how they met their end. But it is clear that all attempts failed. Because, although the traces of their work remained, the people themselves disappeared from memory. Out of desperation, people broke pipes in the hallways and threw bombs into the factory, to no effect. The ship continued to move and people continued to disappear.

"Rrose Sélavy quietly turned away from the course it had been charting along the equator and began to head north. Of the nearly one thousand crew members who had been aboard the ship following the mutiny, only about sixty were left. They gathered on the bridge, where they slept and ate together, and only went to the bathroom in groups of three or more. They couldn't recall a single death since the mutiny. All they felt was the fear of oblivion.

"Their situation was unsustainable. The bridge they were gathered on soon began to change. It was already strange that the bridge had lasted as long as it did. Rrose Sélavy had long ago eliminated everything that did not fit into the seamlessly streamlined, bilaterally symmetric body that it desired. The flat top was long gone, and the Horlas, submarines, escape capsules, and missiles had all melted naturally into the body. The bridge, too, was now preparing to dissolve. The windows disappeared, as did everything else with straight lines, and everything to the right side of the bridge was pushed into the middle of the ship's stern.

"That was when the captain's informant rekindled the fires of rebellion that had flared briefly several months earlier. He was an engineer named Ulixes, and one of the very few people who had selflessly taken the captain's side during the captain's stint on Rrose Sélavy. He wasn't someone to jump out and confront danger head-on, but nor was he a coward who would always hide in the back.

"Fighting memory loss, Ulixes investigated the monster now controlling Rrose Sélavy. He concluded that the current circumstances, now that Rrose Sélavy had transformed into a metal sea monster, were entirely different from when it still looked like an aircraft carrier. The flexibility the ship had maintained during its transformation was now gone. Rrose Sélavy's brain, like that of other similarly-shaped life forms, was probably located toward the front of its body.

"Ulixes gathered about twenty of the crew. They prepared weapons and advanced off the bridge to do battle. They moved slowly along corridors that now curved softly through the ship like arteries or intestines. The ship had been their home for years, but was now a totally unfamiliar labyrinth. Ironically, though, they had quite an excellent new map. They hadn't been able to connect to the main computer for several months, but when they finally did, the blueprint they downloaded had been updated to reflect the changes. Of course, they didn't know the extent to which the map was telling the truth. For starters, the 'brain'-like thing that was their destination did not appear on the map.

"What was their goal? Get rid of the Olivier and regain control of the ship? How many of them would have believed that was even possible? I think most of them volunteered just to see the face of their jailer before they died. Or to at least try to properly resist before it was all over. They had sacrificed so much to seize the ship, they couldn't just stand by and let it be taken over.

"Their trip was a nightmare. And I don't mean that as the usual cliche. It was really like dreaming a scary, unpleasant dream with their eyes open. Danger lurked on all sides. People continued to disappear, yet they couldn't remember who and how. They had no idea what was attacking them, and they gradually lost track of why they were where they were. The reason for their actions had long disappeared, and although from time to time they briefly regained their senses, it was never long before they fell back into confusion. In the meantime, all they could do was swing their guns around, fire, and continue to advance.

"Ulixes and his team continued like that for nearly three days during which they managed to advance less than three hundred meters. They must have experienced three or four books' worth of adventures over that time, but afterward Ulixes couldn't properly remember any of it. When he finally arrived at a spherical room at the ship's bow, he was alone. He couldn't remember even a single one of his companions. That was evidence of what must have happened to the people who had remained on the bridge. Ulixes was the only intact human left on Rrose Sélavy.

"He stood up and went into the spherical room. The room was the size of an old study. Its walls and floors were covered with a complex mosaic pattern that gave the illusion of bookshelves everywhere. Several aggressive machines like Waynes rolled this way and that along the floor, the insides of their open skulls empty. From the bookshelves on all sides, small beings with four eyes stuffed into their roughly baseball-sized spherical heads stared at him. He stood there gazing dumbly at them for moments until he remembered what was happening. These harmless little amphibian-like creatures were the enemy that he and his companions had been fighting against for the last several months.

"He no longer felt any fear. Exhaustion and curiosity were all he had left. He lay down in the middle of the room and watched the little machines move busily around. Some of them wielded little tools, some watched little blue shapes appear and disappear like ghosts from various places in the room, some slowly approached him. Throughout this, the room gradually contracted and expanded.

"The amphibian creatures approaching Ulixes showed neither malice nor curiosity. They just stared at him with the four dots that were their eyes. They were all empty-handed and he could see no weapons. He picked one up like a stuffed animal and none of the others reacted. Losing interest, he put the machine back down and stood up.

"Something strange caught his eye. Right in front of him stood a cylindrical metal object, stuck there like an abandoned piece of junk. It was about one meter both in height and diameter. Although quite different in size from the Olivier the captain had seen, Ulixes couldn't miss the revolving pinwheel sticking out of the top.

"Ulixes slowly approached the object. The amphibians pretended not to notice, and no Coopers could be seen in the immediate vicinity. He grabbed the object. Nothing happened. He pulled the object out and saw that in the space it had occupied were several metal accessories that looked like Cooper limbs.

"Now certain that the cylindrical object was the Olivier, he dragged it into the middle of the room. Strangely, the amphibians remained silent and apparently unconcerned. Ulixes carefully wiped the Olivier with his sleeve and embraced it. The Olivier continued to do nothing but coldly spin its pinwheel, yet Ulixes felt that the machine was telling him something.

"Ulixes spent the next two days preparing to escape. He walked around the vicinity of the spherical room gathering metal scraps and parts, and cobbled them together with glue and screws into a capsule-shaped boat. While doing this, he left the room to map the interior of Rrose Sélavy, and finally he found a way out of the ship. The amphibians ignored him and remained engrossed in their own work.

"As soon as his boat was complete, he loaded the Olivier on it and dragged it down the hall toward the exit. Two of the amphibians followed him but didn't interfere. They just stared at him and the Olivier with their four expressionless eyes. At the hallway exit, he climbed inside the capsule, closed the lid, and thrust his bodyweight forward. The boat slid forward and tumbled out of Rrose Sélavy. Finally, he could see the new shape of Rrose Sélavy. It was a huge metal sperm whale, with the toilet picture still hanging off the bow. Metallic creaks sounded as the whale swam across the surface of the sea and then disappeared below.

"For six days Ulixes followed the currents of the north sea. When a fishing vessel named Leia found him, they said that all the fat had melted off his shoulders and he was suffering from dehydration and hallucinations, but he still clung tightly to the Olivier. No one suspected that the metal can he dragged around with him was an Olivier.

"Leia dropped him off at the city of Toule on Sunday. People thought he might be a Bethlehemian due to his slightly unusual attitude and speech, but since Northerners had no prejudices toward people like him, he had little trouble finding a fisherman's house who would take him in. While he convalesced there, he wrote out his experiences on Rrose Sélavy with paper and pencil. He wrote it in a substitution cipher he created on the spot and as soon as his record was complete, he hid it in a corner of his room.

"Once he had regained his health and saved up some money from helping the fisherman, he took the Olivier and boarded a boat named the Pallida Mors. A retired military vessel converted to cargo ship, it carried fourteen passengers, twenty-one crew members, and twenty tons of canned fish produced on Sunday. Three days after they departed for Tuesday, the Pallida Mors reported to the Free Ship Alliance that an unknown contagion had infected the entire ship. A medical flyer was dispatched for the ship, but by the time it arrived, the ship had disappeared.

"A similar incident occurred several months later on a passenger ship named Galicia that had departed from Claudel on Monday. One day after leaving harbor, it complained of a contagion and of equipment malfunction. It had disappeared without a trace by the time the Alliance's flyer arrived. This time, the disappearance involved more than a few people, and the Alliance was forced to pay attention. A search party was dispatched and a warning sent to all ships of the Free Alliance. Despite this, ships continued to disappear.

"Not until the disappearance of the Mina Murray, the fifth ship, were we able to connect the serial disappearances to Ulixes. One of the captain's friends had discovered Ulixes wandering the streets of Juno on Thursday, pushing a cart carrying a barrel with a pinwheel on top. When she tried to talk to him, Ulixes's eyes moved uneasily and he spoke gibberish. The only words she could understand were, 'Still, I'm a Cooper now...' Before she could ask him what he was talking about, he ran down to the harbor and boarded the Mina Murray. And three days later, the boat disappeared.

"The instant we heard the news, we connected Ulixes to the disappearances of Pallida Mors and Rrose Sélavy. We found the fisherman's house in Toule, and that's when we read the last report he had written with an intact mind.

"Then everything started to make sense. Ulixes really believed that the amphibian machines had left him alone because he had become a Cooper and was defending the Olivier. And he really had carried out his duty as Cooper. He had carried the Olivier around and let it infect other ships so they too could turn into sea monsters, just like Rrose Sélavy.

"The metal cylinder Ulixes now dragged around with him acted somewhat differently from the Oliviers we knew. We knew Oliviers as the central figures and philosopher kings of the terrestrial Linkers. But Ulixes's Olivier seemed to be servant, nanny, or catalyst to the amphibian creatures. However, all of the differences and similarities only served as evidence of the hypothesis that Ulixes's Olivier was part of the Maria Teresia. Although similar to the terrestrial species we knew, these were different beings that now strutted around Crusoe. They were the Bethlehemians of Linker machines.

"Ships continued to disappear regularly even after the Mina Murray, and at least fourteen more of these disappearances were definitely caused by Ulixes's Olivier. Yet, eyewitness accounts of Ulixes and the Olivier ran dry three years ago after the Pasadena disappeared. Ships continued to disappear, but mostly for ordinary reasons: this world is gradually becoming a more savage place.

"However, we didn't give up on finding Ulixes and the Olivier. The main reason was that we had a kind of religious faith in Oliviers. An Olivier was an Olivier no matter how much it might mutate. Not one of us believed that an Olivier could fail or die. Especially after we learned about what happened at the first mate's hometown 50,000 years ago.

"Finally, we tried to track the Pasadena, the last ship to disappear. The fact that it had belonged to the Church Mafia stumped us at first. It didn't seem to matter. In a stroke of luck, though, we managed to ascertain that the Church Mafia leader, Manus of Melville, had ordered his minions to capture Ulixes and the 'foul machine' at any cost. We also learned that a few survivors from the Pasadena had been rescued by the Church Mafia's aircraft carrier, which had been waiting nearby.

"With the help of those clues, we began to unravel the mystery. We were even able to confirm that Manus of Melville had met the Olivier. His murder a week later was due to suspicions that he had been infected and started behaving like a Cooper just like Ulixes. The Osteen group, who—in alliance with Manus—had ousted the Schiller group, planned to destroy the Olivier. But before they could, they were robbed of Ulixes and the Olivier.

"It wasn't hard to figure out who had robbed them. It was the powers supporting Larkin City on Rothbart. When Bo and Sydney's team figured this out, they tried to steal Ulixes and the Olivier themselves, and amidst the ensuing chaos, Ulixes and the Olivier disappeared once again. At first, we thought it must be the Crimson Jihad, but they don't have the strength to pull off anything like that these days, and besides, there were plenty of other suspects. Other city governments had started to realize what was going on.

"It was the captain who figured out that the Olivier is on this island. While others were tracking the Olivier, the captain thought backward. He tried to figure out how the Olivier had gotten on Rrose Sélavy to begin with. He checked how many times Rrose Sélavy had gone near Leventon Island and matched up those dates to sort out suspects. It had approached the island five times and docked three times. And the ship's doctor had been on the disembarkment list for each docking. He was a man named Kleinzach from Bertieu. And once we tracked him down, everything fell into place."

"Kleinzach? Our manager?"

"I'll never understand why people torture themselves with their own names. Why Kleinzach, of all names?"

"And you came here to get the Olivier."

The doctor frowned. "No. I didn't. The situation's too high-profile for us to get involved. The information has already spread all over Crusoe. We're not the only ones with brains. Bo knows. Larkin City knows. The Schiller and Osteen factions of the Church Mafia know. The Crimson Jihad knows. Every faction of the Rothbart Center knows. The Linker machines probably know too. They've all gathered around here and are just waiting for the signal to attack. If our information is correct, the war will start within an hour. By the end of tomorrow, there won't be any trace left of Hogarth Island. Why get caught in the middle? Where's the glory in that?"

"If you didn't come here to join in the plunder, then why did you come?"

"To save people."

Forty-Two clucked. "The captain's idea?"

"Jezebel's idea. We voted: it was unanimous. Why are you looking at me like that? You think it doesn't fit my image? I'm a doctor. Someone who saves lives. And what I know is that there are over two thousand crazy people living on this island."

4

Forty-Two did not follow the doctor into Building Twelve. Instead she walked along the beach path to the hospital building on the west side. Lights were still on here and there on the first floor of the hospital and in the employee apartments next door.

She hid behind the bronze statue of Saint Sebastian that stood crookedly in front of the entrance and stole a look through the windows. Two doctors on duty were drinking coffee. A guard in a black uniform passed in front of them pushing a cart with a toolbox on top. She heard faint sounds of music.

No one seemed to have any idea that a catastrophe was about to befall them.

What did she really know about the manager? She knew that he had briefly stayed at the Rothbart Center. But everyone had some connection to the Center these days. She realized now that the ship he had sometimes talked about voyaging on could have been Rrose Sélavy. But mostly he just talked about his home solar system Bertieu. He was proud of his ancestors for having made their own old-fashioned spaceship, instead of riding Adjanis, and having conquered a neighboring planet with it. Of course that was the extent of their adventures. The lightspeed barrier prevented them from going any farther.

How had the makers of the Maria Teresia broken that barrier? Had they done it themselves? Had they stolen the knowledge from their world's Linker machines? Or were they themselves the source of the knowledge, and they had created the Linker machines? If by one-in-a-million chance, the latter were true, then we now were living off of the children of their children.

We. She shook her head. Since when had it become we? I'm not human. At most I'm a badly drawn caricature of a human.

Forty-Two stepped backward. She had forty or fifty minutes until Jezebel and the other ships of the Free Ship Alliance landed. Maybe the captain and first mate had come with the doctor and were already here. She guessed the engineer had come to Hogarth before the others. There was no other way. They needed at least one high-functioning Bethlehemian to control and mobilize the patients out of the closed wards in time. And that was at a very minimum. Bethlehemians couldn't all be treated the same way, as one big bunch. Unless the engineer was some kind of super-Bethlehemian.

She knew about Jezebel's engineer through Sydney's memories. Sydney had collected information on everyone that he made use of. He certainly wouldn't have overlooked a remarkable being like the engineer. He knew how that freak, who the first mate called Cleïs, had been discovered on the beach of New Malta City on Wednesday, and he knew how Cleïs had managed to escape on her own from the Bethlehemian sanatorium where she had been confined for twelve years, and how she had then been coaxed by the first mate into joining Jezebel's crew as engineer. Only about half the eyewitness reports of the strange things that happened in the course of Cleïs's escape were credible. Forty-Two had once talked with Hasha about the engineer, but she couldn't remember the details. Her damn memory. She got angry at the programmed oblivion. Her outer consciousness ought to clearly remember everything.

A chorus sounded from far away. The patients of Building Five were singing. Unlike before, the song paused at specific times and the tones were random. A Webern lullaby. Isn't that what the Jezebel's crew had called one of the engineer's song patterns? Since when had the people here sung in that pattern? Had the engineer already infiltrated Building Five?

Forty-Two's whole body itched. Something big was about to happen and a huge truth about to be revealed. She needed to shut herself in a corner and keep her mouth closed to avoid getting in the way. For a time I was Sydney! For a while I held Crusoe in my grip!

She recalled Bo. His face bore a quiet resemblance to that of a young Paul Robeson, if one could ignore his sharp chin and the third eye stuck in the middle of his forehead. She had known him while she'd been working on the other Bellocian dolls at the research center. The final time they'd met, he had said this to her:

"We're all Sydney. I have a bit of Sydney in me just like you. Like you, I've inherited his unfinished work and am following his path. Dr. Flagg is Sydney as well, to an extent. The other research groups here who are hostile to me are also Sydney. Without Sydney, none of us would have been able to come this far."

She had replied, "But that's meaningless. How is what you're saying different from the Church Mafia's vague claim that all work is the work of God?"

"Sydney never claimed that all the work he left behind represented his intentions. Sydney didn't leave behind intention, he left behind ambition and momentum. Sydney never wanted us to follow his orders. He hoped we would follow his legacy by continuing to break unknown new ground."

But was that really the case? She didn't know. She was only one part of Sydney. She was a more intolerant, cold, and cruel Sydney. Or had been, at least. Following the procedure to separate her identity, she wasn't even that anymore.

Bo probably hadn't been certain either. Perhaps he had grown even more obsessed with the notion because he couldn't know for sure. It had been an unfortunate time for Bo. All the experiments in which he had placed his hopes ended in failure. And war had erupted again on his second homeland of Thursday following the southward advance of the Crimson Jihad. He became steadily more political. When she had last heard about him, he'd been gathering Sydney's mercenaries to fight on Thursday.

She heard a low whistle from above. She looked up at the sky and could see nothing aside from the fluorescing night clouds. Yet, as the whistling sound repeated, the atmosphere of the island shifted uneasily and stars twinkled like Christmas tree lights through gaps in the clouds. She clenched her teeth. Those were signs of a cloaking shield.

She didn't have to wait long. Less than a minute later, she heard the sounds of small, heavy metal objects landing on the ground all around her. Soon after, they extended their spider legs, lifted their spherical bodies, and crawled out of their small craters. The five who had dropped to the ground in front of her gathered in single-file and began to advance toward the hospital building. In just that moment, another whistle sounded from the sky. This time, the things were much larger and longer than the last ones. Screaming silver Horlas crisscrossed the sky above the island, no longer bothering to try and hide themselves with their cloaks.

The attack had begun.

5

Common sense told Forty-Two that she should run immediately to Building Twelve. She should run to her room, gather her things, and go downstairs to meet the doctor in the cafeteria and follow his instructions. Yet, she ran instead to Building Five, as if it were the most natural thing in the world. She didn't know why. As she ran, she felt that the Bellocio robot creators would be quietly proud of her. This sort of improvised irrationality was proof of how perfectly human she acted.

In front of Building Five she ran into one of the spiders that had just climbed out of its crater. The spider extended its eight legs and strode toward the hospital without any concern for things like her. She remembered the brand name of the spiders and the planet they came from. The Clarimonde Army of Euryanthe. Twenty years ago, Sydney had used them to attack the Church Mafia fanatics of Leopold the Second. Now they were Bo's army.

Building Five resonated with the din of the Webern lullaby. She rang the bell again and again, but no one came out. She ran over to the side of the building and stuck her nose up against a window. A masked guard stood screaming in the first floor hallway with his hands over his ears. She beat and shook the bars across the window, but he didn't hear her. He fell to the ground, and almost in the same instant the building lost power.

The sky and ground of Hogarth were blanketed with every kind of noise. Flyers dropped soldiers and robots here and there across the island. Most of these ran toward the hospital as soon as they landed, but some set off bombs in the square, dug holes to shelter in, and shot at each other. Sometimes soldiers rendered transparent by cloaking shields collided into each other and screamed as they sprinted around.

Forty-Two grabbed a shock pistol from one mercenary whose corpse still writhed on the ground in nervous convulsions and ran back to the main entrance of Building Five. She aimed and fired twice at the metal door. The shots tore it from the doorway and knocked it to the floor. The pistol felt familiar to her. She vaguely recalled Sydney's three years serving in the Glendale militia. But now was not the time to worry about someone else's past.

The inside of Building Five was dark and cool. If not for the sounds of singing that rang from all sides, she would have thought the building was empty. However, when she turned on the light on the shock pistol, she saw a living tableau of people standing and sitting in postures of repose against the walls of the corridor and on the stairs. They all stared ahead vacantly as if blind. Not a single eyebrow twitched as she walked forward.

"A few minutes ago I made myself a bet," a familiar voice said from above her head.

Forty-Two looked up. The manager grinned tiredly at her over the second floor railing.

"I asked myself where you would go when the attack started. Building Five? The hospital? I knew you wouldn't enter Building Twelve, because Sydney isn't that sort of person. Sydney would want to see the fruits of his labors with his own eyes. And I won the bet. Building Five was most plausible after all. You always did side with humans over machines, and that didn't change even when you transplanted your consciousness into a machine."

"You knew," Forty-Two spoke.

"You're more oblivious than I thought. A side effect of becoming a robot? Not once did it occur to you that I kidnapped and brought you here? You really did not know that these last three years have been my revenge? Yes, revenge. Do you have any idea how badly the wonderful Mr. Sydney screwed up my great plans when he used Rrose Sélavy to deliver a strike to the McKinsey Bloc harbor? Do you have any idea how much time and energy I had spent on those plans?"

Forty-Two believed what the manager said, but his attitude did not inspire any pity. It may have been because he kept stealing glances at her legs while he talked, and his George Sanders-like voice had a certain sad and languid quality that didn't match the content of his words.

"Did you really think you could control the Olivier?"

"Control? Why would I want to control it? You think I'm a cartoon villain? You think I want to conquer the world with it? My Olivier has nothing to do with that stuff. Few of the people setting up outside right now have any idea what it is they're looking for." The manager shrugged then, as if he didn't want to get caught up in any more complex emotions related to her, and disappeared down the second floor corridor.

Forty-Two began to climb the stairs in pursuit, but someone grabbed her wrist. A thin, cold, translucent brown hand. She looked back. It was the engineer. She had only ever seen the engineer in person once, on Saturday, but she couldn't forget the engineer's demonic face. It was expressionless, like the faces of other Bethlehemians, but Forty-Two could sense a will inhabiting that face that set it apart from the others. As she saw the engineer, the Webern lullaby that had been floating through the corridor like background music died down and the building grew quiet.

And in that instant she heard a scream from the second floor.

Forty-Two started up the stairs again, and this time the engineer did not stop her. When she arrived at the second floor, she ran into the manager crawling along the floor toward her. Dark red blood oozed from his chest and wet the wood floor. A large-framed man wearing a robe followed behind the manager carrying a transparent knife that still dripped with blood. Ulixes. The unnaturally thick shoulders and half-crazed face were unmistakable. The manager opened his mouth to try and speak, but Ulixes abruptly pushed the manager's head against the ground and stuck the knife into his back.

The engineer, who had followed Forty-Two, now grabbed her wrist again and shook. She left the manager's corpse and Ulixes and went back downstairs. Now the Bethlehemians of

Building Five were singing something like a Gregorian chant and moving outside. Forty-Two was swept along with the others and in moments had exited the building.

Outside was chaos. Corpses rolled around in all directions, bombs exploded all over, and all sorts of flyers flew around in the sky, their cloaking shields now off. However, most of the attacks were concentrated on the hospital. The building was already half destroyed, and a huge hole that looked twice the size of the hospital itself had been bored in front of the square leading to it.

The sky grew bright as midday. A huge orange cloud rose and expanded like a balloon. Four or five seconds later the shockwave hit the island and noise and warm air swept over them.

"Hello, Ms. Rogers!" Someone yelled from behind her as the sound of the explosion receded. It was the cat-faced first mate. She smiled brightly as she pointed the barrel of her laser rifle skyward.

"That was a kamikaze fighter jet from the Church Mafia's aircraft carrier Victoria. Bo managed to shoot it down with his Horla. Two more are on their way, but he'll take care of them before they reach the island. How have you been? I only just now heard from the doctor that you were here!"

"It hasn't been great. What do we do now?"

"The people in the northern buildings have already been evacuated by the doctor and his Free Ship Alliance friends. We need to gather the rest of the people and go join them in the harbor."

In the sky, the wings of a flyer drew a spiral as the flyer fell and just barely skimmed past Forty-Two's head. The flyer's wings beat against the ground of the square as it continued forward and finally collided with the wall of Building Four. The black mark of the Crimson Jihad engraved on the wings still flickered from the cloaking shield.

"That one came from the Victoria." The first mate shouted. "I never thought I'd see the Church Mafia and Crimson Jihad join hands. Has Armageddon arrived?"

"They share a fear and loathing of the 'foul machines.' I don't know how though. The two groups sure don't seem any different to me." Forty-Two said. "Oh, and Ulixes killed the manager."

"I see. Ulixes is still here? He is? Okay, well we'll just leave him be. He has his own plans, and it's nothing we should be getting involved in. Coopers do their thing, and we do ours."

Once they had gathered all the Bethlehemians from the locked buildings, they began to run toward the western harbor. As they ran, the first mate told Forty-Two what Jezebel thought the manager had been planning. As Forty-Two had guessed, he was a believer in scientific Bethlehemians. He had believed that he could communicate with the Maria Teresia Olivier through the many Bethlehemians he had carefully gathered, and through this form a new allied force capable of standing up to the Linker Universe. This hypothesis also explained his indifference to the Olivier. The Olivier was no more than a catalyst in his theory; the Bethlehemians under the Olivier's influence were the truly important part.

"His theory was no more credible than homeopathy." The first mate said. "But, we can't simply ignore it, because my older sister and I experienced something similar on Leventon where we grew up. Somewhere there must be a brain type that can communicate perfectly with the Maria Teresia Olivier. If such a person exists, they are certainly a Bethlehemian. We just don't know whether the manager gathered the right kind of brains together. Wait..."

The first mate inclined her head to one side to listen to a message in her earpiece. Her mouth formed an odd smile.

"The Victoria sank. It looks like the Waynes did it. They say the projectiles that sank it were launched from Monte Grande."

"Wasn't the Olivier there meditating?"

"It stopped meditating two years ago. We still can't use it as a spaceport, though. Huge changes have taken place on Crusoe in the time since the cities cut their networks and isolated themselves for fear of Bethlehemian infection. The frightened idiots don't even know it. Wait a second...we need to hurry. Five more missiles are on their way here from Monte Grande. This time they're aimed directly at the island."

The harbor was in tumult. The rumor about the incoming Monte Grande missiles must have already spread around, because soldiers were running about in confusion. The first mate met the doctor, who had arrived before them, and the two together shot them a path to the docks. Four boats were moored in front of them, and two other boats, already filled with passengers from the northern buildings, were preparing to leave. The Jezebel was the smallest and most damaged of the boats there. Its mast was snapped in half, half the forward deck was melted, and the wheelhouse was missing a corner as if a huge spoon had carved a chunk of soft cheese from it. The only thing that looked intact was the portrait of Betty Davis still exhibiting her perfect beauty under the reinforced coating on the bow. Forty-Two wondered what they had been through. Hadn't Jezebel been a boat for the lazy?

Under the engineer's direction, the Bethlehemians

streamed in perfect order, almost as if they had rehearsed it, onto Jezebel and the boat next to it. Forty-Two recognized the captain as the little teddy bear pounded across Jezebel's deck and yelled into a loudspeaker. He looked as happy as the first mate. She understood the manifesto he was shouting with his whole body: What we're doing is actually meaningful. You thieves don't understand anything.

"You made it! I was worried that you might do something stupid." The doctor yelled, waving his hand as soon as Forty-Two boarded Jezebel.

"I didn't think you knew enough about me to make such assumptions." She shot back.

The doctor laughed loudly and lightly tapped out a dance step.

Jezebel and the other boats barely managed to finish loading passengers and push away from the docks before silver streaks appeared in the sky. Five missiles, as they had been warned. All the flyers swarming around the island like bees flinched at the sight and retreated back out over the ocean. All the soldiers who had been searching the hospital now ran back toward the beach. Only the spiders were left searching the ruined buildings. To Forty-Two, the scene was picturesque, like one of the splendid disaster scenes depicted in Technicolor widescreen in old Hollywood movies. Her impression was probably enhanced by the background music spontaneously provided by the Bethlehemians.

That's when the engineer had a seizure.

At first, no one realized it was a seizure. Most people who didn't know the engineer had no idea what was normal for her. The people who did know her never imagined that something unusual would happen to her body and mind or that she would fall into a defenseless state.

Everyone was caught off guard when the engineer fell to the deck of Jezebel and began convulsing uncontrollably. It was only when she grabbed the first mate's ankle with her shaking hand that the first mate noticed something was wrong, sat down next to the engineer, and stroked her head.

The engineer's seizure also affected the Bethlehemians around her. The Bethlehemians aboard Jezebel pointed toward the island and screamed. Forty-Two turned her gaze in the direction they pointed.

A golden object almost the size of the hospital building was rising slowly from the center of the island. At this distance, it was difficult to determine the exact spot, but it looked almost certain that it was coming from the whole in the square in front of the hospital. As it rose, the buildings around it collapsed one by one and the spiders flew outward. The object was pointed sharply at one end to form the shape of a sleek water droplet unencumbered by any protuberances. Once it had finished emerging from the hole, it began slowly flying toward the sea.

Later the first mate related the experience to the others aboard Jezebel:

"The physical space around me dissolved as Cleïs's seizure increased in severity. Everyone else disappeared, leaving only Cleïs and I. The outside world dried up like a waterfall in a drought, and what had been hidden behind it was exposed.

"In that instant, I fell into the past. The past I had experienced on Leventon Island, the past of the useless Russian melancholy we had fallen into. Only then did I understand the emotions we had felt at the time. It was homesickness. Not for home as a particular physical place, but for home as one's most natural and comfortable state of being. Maria Teresia had been transmitting that feeling to us, and we had been interpreting it in our own ways to make sense of our experience.

"The spaceship that rose up from Hogarth was the Maria Teresia. It wasn't the wreckage of a ship that had been buried for fifty thousand years. It was a new spaceship, remade from the inherited consciousness of the Maria Teresia, born underground while Kleinzach's Olivier was hiding below the hospital. As it flew toward us, it played the familiar tune of homesickness, and for reasons I did not understand Cleïs was unable to bear the shock of the song. Neither could the other Bethlehemians who were influenced by Cleïs's experience.

"Cleïs continued holding me as she fought to overcome the seizure. First my ankle, then my shin, then as she staggered upright, my shoulder and arm. Finally she clung tightly to my body and pressed her mouth to my ear. Her convulsions were gradually lessening. It was almost as if something I couldn't perceive passed through her body and into mine, then again passed out of my body and disappeared.

"When Cleïs had stabilized, she removed her body from mine, and that was when something else appeared. Until that point, the sensations floating around me had been vague abstractions. But after that, it was different.

"It was like a kind of slideshow. An interstellar void. Smoke belching from a reddish marsh. A jet stream screaming into a black hole. The wreckage of a supernova. A potato-shaped asteroid covered with clusters of yellow net-shaped lifeforms. A gas giant with a huge tail. All obviously places the spaceship had been on its way here. The spaceship's consciousness was now preparing for the journey back to them.

"Momentary flashes of intuition came and went through my brain before I could completely understand them. The dreams and images the ship had given me conveyed something more than just the ship's destination. Something as important as the journey itself. But what? Was it connected to Cleïs's seizure? Had Cleïs seen more than me?"

Forty-Two didn't know. The only people who had shared the experience were her, the first mate, Cleïs, and several of the other Bethlehemians who had been on the deck of Jezebel and cried out.

Unlike the first mate, Forty-Two had taken in everything happening around her without interpreting it. The water droplet-shaped spaceship had appeared out of the hospital square, headed toward the sea, and disappeared underwater. The water had briefly turned golden, but soon darkened again. Just before the golden light disappeared, the five missiles sent by the Waynes struck Hogarth and turned it into a sea of fire. The shockwave shook the boat and almost flung her overboard. Had the doctor not snatched her collar and pulled her back into the boat just in time, she really would have fallen into the ocean.

The ocean seethed with people who had jumped in to escape the fire, and military operations turned into rescue operations. Now, people pulled up everyone and anyone they could find onto the ships, not just friends but also those who had until moments ago been their enemies. Jezebel and the other ships belonging to the Free Ship Alliance also began to rescue soldiers who had fallen into the water. Fortunately there were no more attacks. They didn't know how much the Linker machines knew about the situation on Hogarth, but it seemed the machines considered that last attack sufficient.

Forty-Two could not suppress a smile while she labored to carry buckets of the cook's vegetable soup up onto the deck. She had just seen the Linker machines fail. Instead of bringing down the spaceship, the missiles had merely turned the already useless hole into the ruin of an already useless hole. The missiles had killed and injured many people, but that didn't make them any less of a failure. The Linkers were no better than humans after all.

Was this the first Linker failure she had witnessed? She couldn't be sure. What was it she and Hasha had witnessed on Saturday? The Olivier there had flown Horlas disguised as Adjanis and had tried to learn something from merging Bethlehemians—hadn't that been a pitiful failure? Had the people from Earth just mistaken all sorts of Linker stupidity for respectable behavior merely because they wrapped it all in a cloak of mysticism?

Perhaps it wasn't just a failure. Perhaps it was an ultimate limitation of the Linkers. Despite having once had the power to exert physical control over the entire Milky Way galaxy, they were no different now than they had been four hundred or three thousand years ago. Something was inhibiting their development. They knew this and were trying to free themselves of it. Maybe the mysterious-looking meditative state they fell into was in fact a desperate attempt to free themselves of whatever inhibited them.

She thought about the future. Maria Teresia was still on Crusoe. As were the sea monsters. They would perfect themselves in order to fly out into the universe once more. What role would they play between humans and Linkers? What stories would they create? This was the beginning of a new future, a future filled with possibilities. The road off the planet remained closed, but Crusoe's future was open.

Perhaps she could find a place for herself in it.

The boat shook with a rattle. Jezebel was out in the open ocean now. She could guess their destination. Green Haven, the only city in the vicinity that would accept the Bethlehemians and open its hospitals to the wounded soldiers. Sydney had visited there once twenty years ago to sign the contract for a new store in his cafe chain. She wondered if the beach in front of the hotel still had white sand.

Forty-Two walked up the stairs to the deck with one heavy bucket of soup in each hand. From behind she heard someone humming "Let's Face the Music and Dance." She knew who it was without turning her head. Irritated, she ignored him and strode forward toward the bow where the hungry refugees waited. The doctor grumbled and followed her.

NOTES FROM THE AUTHOR

1

In 2005, I wrote a short story with the bland title “Invaders from Outer Space”[1] about Von Neumann machines coming to Earth. In it, the invading machines couldn’t care less about humans; they only want to use Earth as a base from which they can reproduce and prepare further expeditions through space. In 2008, when I was approached to write a novel, I returned to this idea of Von Neumann machines and combined it with other ideas that had been floating around my head. I have long been interested in writing stories based on discredited scientific theories, and creating a world in which Lamarck’s inheritance theory turned out to be true was an idea I’d been considering for a while. What if I were to create a narrative that would combine Lamarckism with Von Neumann machines? As I thought through this confluence of ideas that would later become the Linker Universe, I recalled what Isaac Asimov termed “Clement’s Paradox”: the strange fact that despite the vastness of the universe, alien races encountered in SF somehow tend to be no more than a few hundred years ahead of humans in terms of technological

---

[1] 외계에서온침입자. Published in the Daesan Literature Webzine. The story can be read online here (Korean only): http://daesan.or.kr/webzine/sub.html?uid=1313&ho=14.

development. Combining Lamarckism with Von Neumann machines would allow me to fill the universe with countless Star Trek-like planets and species without falling afoul of Clement's Paradox. Such ideas formed the basis of *Jezebel* and the planet it explores, Crusoe.

My initial plan for the Linker Universe novel included eight stories. "The Bloody Battle of Broccoli Plain" was meant to set the stage, followed by stories set on other planets in the Linker Universe. As I wrote it, however, *Jezebel* turned into a longer and more cohesive story than I had initially planned. In the end, I published *Jezebel* as a stand-alone novel. "The Bloody Battle of Broccoli Plain" became the title story of a separate short story collection that also included "Sea of Fog," the only other Linker Universe story I've published to date. I wrote another novella several years ago set in the Linker Universe, but circumstances have delayed its publication.

While I do enjoy worldbuilding, I try to avoid spending too much time in a single world (a lesson I learned from reading Asimov's later works). I'd rather write a variety of stories set on a variety of worlds. Kaya Press worried that readers of this translated volume might have difficulty following the Linker Universe world, but I don't think there's any particular need for this afterword, especially since "The Bloody Battle of Broccoli Plain" and "Sea of Fog" have both been included alongside *Jezebel*. Besides, aren't readers of genre fiction already used to jumping headfirst into new and unfamiliar worlds? Roaming unguided through new territory is, after all, the fun of speculative fiction.

2

I once read an online posting complaining that Connie Willis draws too heavily from old Hollywood movies in her fiction. If I remember correctly, this complaint was a reaction to her short story "At the Rialto." Well, whoever wrote that critique is going to find reading *Jezebel* unbearable. Despite not being written in English, and being set on an unfamiliar planet hundreds of years into the future, *Jezebel* refers to old Hollywood movies—RKO horror and musicals in particular—on every page.

The logic behind this is simple. If civilization has managed to spread throughout the galaxy, despite the fact that communication and travel remain unreliable, wouldn't it require a stable shared language? It isn't unreasonable to imagine that old Hollywood movies might serve as textbooks for such a culture, or that transatlantic-accented English might become the standard language. It's certainly plausible to me, a non-English speaker. Katharine Hepburn's English is easier for me to understand than Jennifer Lawrence's.

There are personal reasons for this, of course. As a child, many of the books and movies I read and watched were dubbed, subtitled, or translated from English. In the twentieth century, particularly in the 1970s and 80s, Koreans rarely watched Korean movies. It's true that today we've become voracious consumers of our own homegrown movies and TV dramas, but only ones that have been produced recently. Even now, the number of people who watch Korean movies from that era are few and far between; many consider them to be a sign of bad taste. The movies they have in mind are often crude creations, full of sex scenes that are almost indistinguishable from rape. Of course, there's much more to twentieth-century Korean cinema than that, but for many who came of age during those decades, Korean cinema may as well not have existed.[2]

For a fan of SF and mysteries such as myself, Korean fiction seemed just as barren a landscape. While mystery novels did exist in Korea—the publication of hardboiled fiction can be attributed almost entirely to the influence of prolific author Kim Seongjong[3]—readers from that era have judged such novels as spending too much time stripping women naked and not enough time describing mysteries or crimes. Needless to say, such books weren't suitable for young readers.

As for SF, well, Korean SF was practically nonexistent back then, and foreign SF was rarely, if ever, translated. Reading SF was simply something adults never did, and the few foreign SF novels that made it into Korean were not widely publicized. I do remember seeing a translation of *Flowers for Algernon* advertised in a women's magazine in the 1980s, but this was probably because the novel didn't look like SF. My SF reading was limited as a result, primarily to juvenile abridgements first produced in Japan and later retranslated into Korean. The only other SF works that existed for young readers in Korean tended to be adaptations, not original works. I first encountered Heinlein's *Have Space Suit–Will Travel* through an adaptation that recast its protagonist as Korean. I didn't even realize the book was an adaptation until the hero began conversing with an ancient Roman in Latin he had learned in school.

These days, the situation has flipped. Last year, I read more native Korean SF than English-language SF —a situation I

---

[2] Those of you who like cult cinema should check out the movie *Suddenly at Midnight* (깊은밤 갑자기, 1981). You may find there's more to 1980s Korean cinema than you thought.

[3] Director Park Chan-wook thinks that the movie *The Last Witness* (최후의증인, 1980), which is based on Kim Seongjong's novel of the same title, is a masterpiece.

would never have imagined possible. For my afterword to the 2012 Korean publication of *Jezebel*, I wrote:

> The foreign environments created by the translationese pervading these Korean editions of foreign fiction feel entirely natural to me. The ability to see through crude translations to imagine the whole, perfect novel beneath is a crucial part of the skill of reading. Whenever I read Korean-language fiction, I still feel an awkward embarrassment, as if viewing the naked bodies of strangers.

At the time, that was exactly how I felt. But, you say, it's only been a decade since you wrote that. Well, yes. Ten years in Korea is more than enough time for everything to change. Koreans today watch 1990s news clips on YouTube and wonder why people talked so strangely back then. Asking a Korean to read a newspaper from 100 years ago is like asking an American high school student to read Beowulf in Old English.

All of this to say, the setting of *Jezebel* is in a sense autobiographical. When in 2008 I imagined people on an alien planet recreating our world based on what I had seen in Hollywood movies, I did so because of the experiences detailed above. I still think the setting of *Jezebel* remains relevant today. One of the most popular genres of internet fiction in Korea these days is romantic fantasy, aka ro-pan, and most ro-pan stories are set in fictional Western countries. Twenty-first century Koreans also love musicals (despite the legend that Koreans once decided *The Sound of Music* was too long and so brought to theaters an edited version that cut out all the songs), and many new Korean musicals are, like the ro-pan genre itself, set in a Western past.[4] Lea Salonga playing Éponine in *Les Misérables* is just colorblind casting. But there's something truly different about Koreans playing the Brönte Sisters in a Korean-language script. Terming this cultural appropriation would be an oversimplification. We could talk forever about the relationship between Korean pop culture and the idea of cultural appropriation (we Koreans are unashamed to borrow anything and everything from Bollywood to Native American culture). But that's a completely different issue from the question of how we interpret and adapt Western culture on the whole. For *Jezebel*, I decided that instead of creating fake Westerners, it would be more fun to create non-Western, non-white characters who consciously mimic Westerners, the Westerners of Hollywood in particular.

Linguistic and cultural differences play a crucial role here. Korean is nearly as far removed from English as Klingon. Maybe even more so. While Klingon grammar is very different from that of English, its vocabulary is actually just a translation of anglophone concepts.[5] The mindset of Korean speakers is obviously different from that of Western-language speakers, and consequently, when Western culture is imagined from a distance—that is, in a context that is

---

[4] Those curious for a taste of this should watch a clip of the musical *Red Book* (레드북) on YouTube. Some clips include English subtitles.

[5] "Bloodwine," for example, is a very English word. I've always found it strange that English, unlike many other languages, doesn't have a single everyday word dedicated to alcoholic beverages. Korean has the word "sul" for that purpose, but there's no exact equivalent in English—it has been translated into the multipurpose word "drink" in "Memoir of a Joseon Bride." Klingon, on the other hand, does have a word equivalent to sul: "Hlq." Unfortunately, English speakers see the word appearing in the compound "Iw Hlq" (Bloodwine) and equate it to "wine," and this association has obscured the meaning of "Hlq." Furthermore, Korean translators of Klingon—who sometimes don't necessarily actually know Klingon—then end up transliterating the English "Bloodwine" instead of going the more accurate route of translating the Klingon meaning directly into "pisul" in Korean.

independent from that culture—the results can be truly strange. Fans of Japanese anime will likely recognize this difference-induced weirdness from their own experiences watching translated (or back-translated) anime.

Korean, like Japanese (which experts believe belongs to a different language family, despite its many apparent similarities to Korean), employs a complex linguistic system to indicate respect. Japanese influence during the colonial era (1910-1945) exacerbated existing sexist linguistic practices in Korean, including those manifesting in translations. You see, to render a foreign language text into fluent Korean, translators must choose which speech levels and honorifics they think would best fit each situation. Those translating works into modern Korean often depict women as speaking honorifically up to men and men speaking down to women. As a result, what was originally a conversation between equals in an English novel becomes a conversation between two people whose genders confer markedly different social statuses. Translators have made such choices frequently enough that this sort of sexism is actually more prevalent in translations than in Korean life. The reader, however, mistakes the extra authoritarianism and sexism contained in these translations as no more than "old-fashioned Western language." Fortunately, in Korean at least, translators are attempting to correct this.[6]

I said earlier that the Korean language is changing quickly (these days, primarily due to English); now I must add that even relative to Korean as a whole, the language used in

---

[6] Open Books, a Korean publisher specializing in foreign literature, has announced that it will revise its back catalogue of translations to remove as many instances of sexist language as possible. Open Books published the Korean translation of Sarah Waters's *Fingersmith*, and you can therefore thank it for Park Chan-wook's *The Handmaiden*.

translations is changing with particular rapidity.

In my own stories, I never set out to exaggerate such differences. But I don't try to hide them either. So it's only to be expected that my stories might feel a bit weird.

3

Let me end with a few notes about the non-Linker stories.

"The Rabbit Hole" alludes to the French poem "L'École des Beaux-Arts" by Jacques Prévert in its description of the mother appearing "like an origami flower that magically blossoms in water." I was first introduced to this poem as a child in its Korean translation. Min Hee-sik, the translator, explained the poem's "la grande fleur japonaise" as "a crumpled round paper ball that blooms into the shape of a flower when immersed in water." I don't know what French readers today picture when they read the poem.

"Under the Sphinx" is based on a true story: in the early days of IMDb, a prankster put up a fake transnational Asian movie titled *Indian Cult Fetish* that stayed up for quite a while. I came across it due to the Korean actors in its cast list, notably Choi Min-sik. That said, the Hollywood history in the short story is not entirely true to reality. For example, my *Under the Sphinx* movie is longer than Hollywood B movies of the time, and it basically disregards the Hays Code entirely. When I wrote the story, I imagined a parallel universe in which the reality of *Singin' in the Rain* was truth rather than fiction, and I seem to have thought it best to tweak Hollywood history.

I wrote "Through the Mirror" during a period when I was obsessed with Shaw Brothers melodramas and musicals. Although people outside Hong Kong remember that era for its martial arts cinema, I think we shouldn't be so quick to forget everything else the Shaw Brothers produced.

The fictional city of Uicheon that appears in "Pentagon" is a cosmopolitan metropolis situated on the border of (undivided) Korea, China, and Russia. I've used this city in a number of stories.

The original title of "Memoir of a Joseon Bride" is "Gu-bu-jeon". These three syllables, whose various possible meanings are disambiguated by the addition of Chinese characters in the original publication, individually mean father-in-law, daughter-in-law, and war. Though almost never appearing together, the combination of the first two syllables differs only by a single vowel from "gobu," a common pairing that often appears as part of the set phrase "gobu galdung," meaning conflict between the mother and daughter-in-law—a favorite topic of Korean dramas.

TRANSLATOR'S AFTERWORD

by Adrian Thieret

The story of Djuna's fiction begins with the blossoming of Korean internet culture in the 1990s. The popularity of Hollywood movies and the internet-enabled fandom that grew up around them in that period inspired a culture of fan fiction written by and for those who share a taste for specific types and genres of media and enjoy reimagining their favorite characters and tropes in new and unfamiliar settings. Djuna's work arose from this culture and continues to participate in it long after having stepped out into the world of print (Djuna's first compilation of short stories, *Proxy War*, was published in 1997). The numerous implicit and explicit references to Western culture in these stories, primarily but not limited to early mid-twentieth-century cinema and feminist literature, hint at these origins as they imply an author and a readership who share a particular cultural background. Readers already familiar with the Hollywood cinema of the first half of the twentieth century, for example, will recognize here the writings of a fellow aficionado. Readers familiar with English women's literature will likewise appreciate the nods to important texts.

Yet, one need not apprehend all the direct and indirect references to appreciate these stories. In many ways, when read outside of the subculture from which they sprang, these stories actually feel more at home in the English language than in Korean. One reason is that the characters and settings for many of Djuna's stories are not Korean. Sometimes they are Western, but often they are of no particular nationality. Sometimes they are not human. Reading the stories in Korean, one is at first struck, and possibly disconcerted, by the foreignness of the style and content, the latter particularly exemplified by the transliterated names and foreign references, which are far more ambiguous than in English. Read in English, those issues fade into the background, and the estrangement effect arises primarily from the fantastic settings and events within the narratives themselves. Regardless, whether one reads them as "Korean" fiction, as speculative fiction, or as feminist fiction, the stories offer plenty of enjoyment and food for thought independent of their influences and the generic and cultural traditions in which they are situated.

Categorizing these stories is a bit of a problem. In a bookstore, you might find this book on the science fiction shelves. Yet, while many of Djuna's stories have been published as "science fiction," to think of Djuna as a "science fiction writer" would not do justice to the breadth of themes and styles on display in this anthology and elsewhere. The works individually and collectively are more aptly considered "genre fiction," as they skip playfully between popular genres such as science fiction, horror, and mystery—the author is clearly well versed in these traditions—and occasionally venture into realist territory as well. Even the stories that solidly fall into the science fiction genre fit within the branch of that genre more concerned with social relations in the here and now than with science, technology, and the future. The broader category of "speculative fiction" is, for all it loses in specificity, less likely to mislead and disappoint.

Djuna's writing style is unconventional and rewards careful reading. More than anything else, these stories do not provide the full, often repetitive explanations that a reader might take for granted in much 21st-century American genre fiction. Instead, the stories provide ambiguity and openings for the reader themselves to fill logical gaps and exercise their own imagination in interpreting the text. I will provide two brief examples here, one highlighting purposeful ambiguity and one highlighting narrative voice. First, take this passage from chapter 11 of "The Bloody Battle of Broccoli Plain":

> For the first time in a week, he leaves the bus.
> Realizing that the weather has grown colder, it
> occurs to him that it has been autumn until now.

Here we have a way of saying "autumn was turning to winter," but rather than just stating that, the sentence instead highlights Cheongsu's character and subjective experience. Cheongsu in his disturbed mental state has failed to notice the season, and it is only the change of season that leads him to finally notice it. The change of seasons itself isn't particularly relevant aside from its symbolic use to emphasize his changing circumstances, and would feel out of place but for the fact that presented in this particular way, it adds to our understanding of his character. One could speculate further: for example, perhaps Cheongsu and other Linker travelers have encountered so many different environments that they no longer assume a new planet has seasons comparable to Earth's, and it is only with the colder weather that Cheongsu finally notices that this place has seasons. There may be other interpretive options as well—the point is that space is left here for the reader to fill with their own imagination.

Second, after something has been specified once, the text may not repeat the detail, even after paragraphs and pages have passed by and the detail may have faded from the reader's memory. A quick example from "Under the Sphinx" will suffice to show this trademark of Djuna's writing. When discussing a photocopy of the fictional tale "Legend of the Golden Crow," the narrator says, in a line that forms its own paragraph: "What intrigued me most, however, was the condition of the copy."

Here as in many other places throughout these stories, my editor asked me to add a bit of explanation to the line—in this instance "... in my uncle's office" or something to similar effect—to remind readers of which copy we're talking about. Strictly speaking, in this case as in most cases, there is really no need for such a reminder, because there is only one photocopy and no ambiguity. Yet, this sort of unnecessary, reader-oriented repetition is a widespread convention in fiction writing, hence the request to add it here. Djuna's fiction, however, does not share in this vice. To the extent that repetition appears in these stories, it is driven by a different logic: the narrator takes priority over the reader's needs. Constructing a believable narrator and putting us in that person's mind is paramount, and it is precisely because the narrator is not the reader that the reader may at times find themselves forced

to pause and think to discover exactly what the narrator is talking about (Notice how many of these stories directly address their readers? How the stories propel themselves by anticipating the questions of an imagined audience?). As in all good fiction, we are asked to imagine a mind other than our own. In this example, the narrator has introduced the copy, digressed for a single paragraph, and then picked right back up where she left off: hardly a demand on the reader's memory at all (there are other instances in these stories where the reader is expected to remember further back). This chapter of "Under the Sphinx" is in its entirety a good example of how Djuna's narrators work: relating their stories as details come to mind, and pausing, backtracking, and digressing according to their own trains of thought rather than presenting a neatly organized linear narrative.

While keeping in mind the particular needs of the Anglophone readers, I have attempted to preserve these features of Djuna's style as much as possible in translation. Certain aspects of a situation are left unexplained or in apparent contradiction, paragraphs break in places that might seem unusual, narrators make logical leaps that are obvious to them but perhaps not to the hurried reader. Readers of this volume will do well to pay close attention, especially to the parts that seem a bit weird. The writing style is inseparable from the meaning of the stories.

THE STORIES

"The Rabbit Hole" is translated from its publication in Djuna's 2006 collection Proxy War, and "Through the Mirror" is translated from Dragon's Teeth (2007). In distinct, surreal settings, these stories examine how social roles shape our lives and how we think of ourselves. From these two stories, readers new to Djuna's work will begin to sense the widespread genre influences and playfulness to be found throughout this compilation.

"Memoir of a Joseon Bride" was originally published in the magazine *Mysteria* (2015, no.4). This translation is based on the version published in Djuna's 2019 fiction compilation *Gubujeon*, for which it is the title story. Djuna wrote the story in an idiosyncratic style guided by the fictional pretense that the narrator was writing her memoir in 1940s English, and I have attempted to realize that premise in my translation. Of all the stories in this volume, "Memoir" is the one that would benefit most from some knowledge of Korean history in order to understand the story's satire of Joseon dynasty literati culture and the narrator's decision to turn against her in-laws. Joseon slavery, for instance—in the mid-Joseon dynasty, a third or more of the population was slaves. The number of slaves dropped slightly in the 18th century and sharply in the early 19th, but rich yangban households such as the one in the story continued to own slaves and employ them alongside non-slave labor until slavery was fully abolished in 1894—and it is for this reason that the word "jong", which can refer to both slave and non-slave servants, is translated here as "slave". The narrator's father-in-law would doubtless have been able to explain away the obvious contradiction between the Confucian ideal of meritocracy and the Joseon reality of hereditary class status.

"Under the Sphinx" and "Pentagon" are collected together in Djuna's 2000 compilation *Duty-Free Zone*; I translated from the 2013 edition of that book. "Under the Sphinx" describes internet fan culture in the 1990s, before broadband and cell phones took over our lives. Two decades later, the story's questions about what is real in the age of internet fakery are more relevant than ever.

"Pentagon," on the other hand, reflects the cyberpunk-era interest in the separation of mind from body that today persists in works such as Netflix's 2018 resurrection of the early 2000s fiction series *Altered Carbon*, and in the form of countless "artificial intelligence" movies, not to mention the more recent misattributions of human properties such as intelligence and intention to computer programs. The narrative of modern disenchantment notwithstanding, all too many people still unconsciously believe in souls: that mind and body are somehow independent, or that consciousness can somehow be separated from the physical. "Pentagon" plays with and rejects this fantasy. Dr. Zaminov's astute comments toward the middle of the story (today we are so accustomed to the conventional distinction between "hardware" and "software" that people often forget it is artificial rather than natural) hint that the author likes playing around with mixtures of scientific and fantastic premises, as in the Linker Universe stories. Aside from that, however, the questions raised in "Pentagon" about identity and moral culpability remain important in the real world when dealing with, for example, cases of brain injury leading to memory loss or personality changes.

The Linker Universe stories have been translated from the revised editions published by Neobooks in 2022. "The Bloody Battle of Broccoli Plain" and "Sea of Fog" were first published in Djuna's short story collection *The Bloody Battle of Broccoli Plain* in 2011, and Jezebel was originally published in 2012. "Broccoli" introduces the Linker Universe and is best read before the others. "Sea of Fog" and *Jezebel* can be read independently of one another. While I agree with the author's assertion that speculative fiction needs no explanation to be enjoyed, I nonetheless urge readers to visit the author's afterword: it will increase your appreciation of all the stories in this volume, not just the Linker Universe tales.

One of the outstanding features of Djuna's fiction, both the stories collected here and the rest of Djuna's oeuvre, is its gentle subjugation of political convictions to narrative concerns. Djuna is known for, among other things, opposition to the misogyny, religious orthodoxy, and homophobia that permeate mainstream Korean society, and these positions are immediately obvious in the stories collected here. Djuna's fiction often takes women and children as its protagonists and depicts them favorably. Men, on the other hand, are usually portrayed in a more negative light, as incompetent or evil and responsible for the problems of the world, which is on the whole not a very nice place. Yet, despite holding to a distinct and not unpopular viewpoint, Djuna's stories do not fall into the abyss of moral grandstanding, nor do they aspire to be political treatises. Rather, the stories in this volume recognize the complexity of human reality, and to the extent they manifest certain strongly held political convictions, these convictions never override the act of storytelling. I hope you have enjoyed reading them as much as I enjoyed translating them.

ABOUT THE AUTHOR

Film critic and speculative fiction writer DJUNA, who first appeared as an online presence in the early 1990s, has steadfastly refused to confirm any personal details regarding their age, gender, or legal name, or even whether they are one person or multiple. Djuna is widely considered one of the most prolific and important writers in South Korean science fiction. They have published numerous short story collections, novels, essays, and uncollected stories.

❁ ❁ ❁

ABOUT THE CONTRIBUTORS

KYU HYUN KIM is a professor in the History Department specializing in early modern and modern Japanese history, colonial modernity in East Asia, modern Korean history, Japanese popular culture, and Japanese and Korean cinema at the University of California, Davis.

ADRIAN THIERET teaches in History and Asian Studies at the University of Manitoba. He holds a PhD in Chinese from Stanford University and translates from Chinese and Korean.